A Shared Voice

A Shared Voice

A Tapestry of Tales

edited by

Tom Mack
and
Andrew Geyer

LAMAR UNIVERSITY press

ISBN: 978-0-9852552-0-6
Library of Congress Control Number: 2013942228
Manufactured in the United States of America

Front Cover Painting: Eric Beverly
Front Cover Design: Michael Sanchez

The stories in this book are works of fiction. Any resemblance of characters in these stories to persons living or dead is purely coincidental.

Lamar University Press
Beaumont, Texas

Acknowledgments

Carolina Tales

Seven of the twelve Carolina tales are original to this anthology; the other five appeared earlier in print:

Elizabeth Cox's "Saved" was published in *Bargains in the Real World* (Random House, 2001; copyright of the author).

Bret Lott's "Propriety" was included in his collection *How to Get Home* (John F. Blair, 1996; copyright of the author).

Jill McCorkle's "Starlings" is from *Creatures of Habit*, copyright 2001 by Jill McCorkle and reprinted by permission of Algonquin Books of Chapel Hill. All rights reserved.

Michael Parker's "Hidden Meanings, Treatment of Time, Supreme Irony, and Life Experiences in the Song 'Ain't Gonna Bump No More No Big Fat Woman'" appeared in *Don't Make Me Stop Now*, copyright 2007 by Michael Parker and reprinted by permission of Algonquin Books of Chapel Hill. All rights reserved.

Ron Rash's "Hard Times" was the first tale (pp. 3-18) in his prize-winning collection *Burning Bright*, copyright 2010 by Ron Rash and reprinted by permission of HarperCollins publishers.

Texas Tales

Nine of the twelve Texas tales are original to this anthology; the other three appeared earlier in print:

Oscar Casares's "Mr. Z" is from *Brownsville* by Oscar Casares. Copyright 2003 by Oscar Casares. By permission of Little, Brown and Company. All rights reserved.

Robert Flynn's "The Trouble with Eve" was published in *Slouching Toward Zion and More Lies* (University of North Texas Press, 2004; copyright of the author).

Stephen Graham Jones's "State" originally appeared in *Quarterly West*.

CONTENTS

Introduction

Why, one might ask, have the editors of this volume decided to compile an anthology of short fiction solely by writers from the Carolinas and Texas? The answer is multifold.

First, there is the evidence of history. Since the nineteenth century, there have been significant ties between the Carolinas and Texas. In fact, it can be argued that Texas might not have become an independent entity without the help of some of Carolina's native sons.

Consider Saluda County, South Carolina. Today's visitor to the small storefront museum in the town of Saluda might at first be perplexed by the presence of a diorama depicting the final moments of the heroic defense of the Alamo in 1836. During this thirteen-day siege, a Mexican army of approximately 1500 soldiers led by President General Antonio Lopez de Santa Anna overwhelmed a fortified mission complex garrisoned by approximately 200 Texians [that was the term used to identify the residents of what was shortly to become the Republic of Texas] led at first by James Bowie but eventually by William B. Travis.

Travis was from Saluda County, South Carolina, and so was James Butler Bonham, another Alamo defender, most famous for the fact that he could have escaped the massacre—he had been sent from the fortress to request reinforcements from another garrison—but he chose to return to fight by the side of his second cousin and face almost certain death.

Despite their terrible defeat, it was Travis's open letter "to the people of Texas and all Americans in the world" that served as a rallying cry for the Texas Revolution: "I call on you in the name of liberty, of patriotism, and everything dear to the American character to come to our aid . . . . Victory or death."

All told, at least fourteen of the doomed defenders of the Alamo were from either South or North Carolina. How did so many Carolinians find themselves in such a position? To some extent—and this is certainly true of Travis in particular—they were part of the larger westward migration of Southern slaveholders before the War Between the States.

In the 1840s and 50s, the sons of planter families in the seaboard South looked to the West for greater economic opportunity; and Texas, especially after it became a Republic in 1836 and was subsequently annexed by the United States in 1845, became a particularly popular destination. In her 1991 study entitled "The Disposition to Emigrate," Jane Turner Censer estimates that a quarter of planter families in North Carolina migrated westward during the antebellum period. In fact, she refers to the West as a "safety valve for seaboard planters with numerous progeny."

The migration, however, was not always in one direction. Texas transplant Lucy Petway Holcombe, whose father moved the family from Tennessee to East Texas in 1850, found herself back East after she married Francis Wilkinson Pickens, scion of an old Carolina family and one of the wealthiest planters in the state. When Pickens became the Governor of South Carolina at the outbreak of the War Between the States, Lucy threw herself into support of the Confederate cause, reputedly selling the jewels that she had acquired as gifts from the Czar during her husband's tenure as our country's ambassador to Russia from 1858-1860 to finance a regiment to be named the Holcombe Legion. Dubbed by some "the Queen of the Confederacy," Lucy Holcombe Pickens, Texan-turned-Carolinian, is the only woman whose image is featured on Confederate currency.

In short, exceptionally strong were the antebellum ties between Texas and the Carolinas, which served as the "bookend states of the Old Confederacy." Furthermore, one can argue that many of those connections persist right up to our own time, as is evidenced in the "blue state" and "red state" dichotomy that journalist Tim Russert first outlined in order to make sense of the 2000 Presidential election. The red states of the Deep South are still bracketed by Texas in the west and the Carolinas in the east.

While acknowledging the fact that these color-coded distinctions are perhaps an over-simplification of a much more complex political reality, the Southern red states, on the whole, tend to share certain essential characteristics. Their populations are more rural, more conservative

2

regarding social issues, and more likely to cultivate an image of rugged independence, particularly in resistance to federal attempts toward national homogenization.

Cultural Links

Because of their shared history, both Texas and the Carolinas—the latter was chartered as one entity in 1665 and not divided into North and South Carolina until seventy years later—share a similar cultural context, and this shared culture is reflected in the tales collected in this anthology.

Elizabeth Cox's "Saved," James Hoggard's "Rev. Richards's Confession," and Jerry Bradley's "The Great Derangement," for example, share the trappings of evangelical Christianity, a mainstay of traditional Bible Belt culture. Josie Wire, the protagonist in "Saved," dreams of growing up and becoming a missionary, an occupation for which she "trains" by attempting in her after-school hours to share the Gospel—she and her girlfriend give away their weekly allowance to the poor and try their hand at converting an anonymous stranger whose initial acquaintance they make through an unsolicited phone call to a local tavern. The Reverend Richards incorporates aspects of a short story that his brother has asked him to read—a paraphrase of Ron Rash's "Hard Times"—into a largely self-serving lament regarding the falling off of his ungrateful congregation. Economic geographer Cliff Ambres imagines that he can see in a slice of ham the face of Jesus, an image of consolation in his time of personal displacement.

Stronger perhaps than the role that church membership plays in Southern culture is the centrality of the family in all its permutations. Consider the struggles of Daniel, the first-person narrator of George Singleton's "Thank You," as he tries to find his place among his wife Ellette's zany relatives—and perhaps win the trophy for "Relative of the Year" at the next family reunion—by attending her cousin Tony's speech rehabilitation showcase. A similar exploration of familial identity occurs in Randall Kenan's "Ezekiel Saw the Wheel," wherein the main character arrives at a belated recognition of and respect for her daughter's relationship with her female partner.

In the name of family or friendship, many of the characters in these stories perform seemingly selfless acts. The fourteen-year-old sharecropper-turned-gas station attendant David in Phillip Gardner's "Brother"

3

endures a beating in defense of his employer's wife and then helps that very same boss hide the evidence of a crime. In "State" by Stephen Graham Jones, the first-person narrator makes his best friend Borde think that he has been betrayed in order to stop him from making a life-changing mistake.

Some of these deeds, done at times in consideration of others, are also ironically indicative of a sense of self-defined frontier justice, which has its roots in the Southern code duello. In his volume entitled *The Code of Honor or Rules of Government of Principals and Seconds in Dueling* (1838), former South Carolina Governor John Lyde Wilson codified much of what had been in the antebellum South common practice regarding how a gentleman demands satisfaction for a perceived insult to his personal dignity. Many Carolinians, especially after the War Between the States, took this self-selected practice of redressing personal wrongs with them to the frontier West. It is not surprising, therefore, that we see traces of this popular penchant to take the law into one's own hands in some of the tales from both the Carolinas and Texas.

Some examples of this mindset are instantly recognizable, as in the imminent shootout indicated at the end of Clay Reynolds's "Gethsemane," but others offer modern variations on the age-old formula. Tech's rather sloppy "duel" in "Two Birds with One Stone" by Deno Trakas—he is surprised by a homeowner in the act of burglarizing his residence—is predicated upon the classic rule of posting a public notice to degrade a scoundrel. In this case, Tech perpetrates the burglary to precipitate the homeowner's making a donation to a homeless shelter, all with the goal of forcing what he considers to be a complacent member of the middle class into helping others less fortunate.

Other acts of frontier justice, each connected with the preservation of personal or family honor, include Diego's providing extra fireworks to customers in retribution for his employer's defaming his father in Oscar Casares's "Mr. Z" and David's frantic drive with Bill toward the air base in pursuit of Rico in Phillip Gardner's "Brother."

The Southerner's obsession with honor and the Western hero's emphasis on self-command can take many forms in these tales. Partially from a festering resentment over the fact that her mother, out of economic necessity, tended to the children of others at the expense of her own child, the seventy-six-year-old Mary in Jill McCorkle's "Starlings" clings fiercely to an entrenched sense of self-determination. The hardscrabble Dee Price, as depicted by Jim Sanderson in "Pissed Away" and Elise Blackwell in "Before Texas," marshals her inner resources so that she not only survives rape but also eventually carves out her own place in a subterranean milieu customarily dominated by males.

Not all of the tales in this anthology, however, take the reader to dark places where violence—particularly gun violence—is a fact of life. Fully a third of these stories are marked by humor, a peculiar brand of Southern humor whose practitioners poke fun at themselves and their compatriots by exaggerating essential truths of the human condition. In this category falls Michael Parker's "Hidden Meanings," the author's delightful replication of one student's largely off-topic response to a class assignment, a monologue that stands as both a testament to misinterpretation and a comically poignant undergraduate plea for understanding. Equally multi-layered is its companion piece, Dave Kuhne's "Ending Comments," which purports to provide lengthy instructor feedback on that same student's paper—"there are some grammar and spelling issues, but we can get 'passed' that for now and talk about those problems 'ladder.'" In each of these pieces, the narrator reveals more than she realizes, and in so doing, the desperate student and the exasperated teacher reach common ground.

Equally funny and disarming are George Singleton's "Thank You" and Terry Dalrymple's "Nasty Things," whose shared character Felicia Winstock looks to group counseling initially for companionship, especially the company of non-threatening males, and ends up herself in need of psychotherapy. There are also, in Robert Flynn's "The Trouble with Eve," the hormonal but clueless Young Carter who is discovering the downside of plucking "forbidden fruit," and in Marianne Gingher's "Young and True," the far more "knowing" female narrator named True whose rite of passage takes her in a direction opposite from Flynn's character in that she reclaims her girlhood at the story's end.

Finally, it can be argued that the tradition of Southern literature—in which works by writers from both Texas and the Carolinas play a major role—is rooted in a sense of place, a connectedness to the physical environment that does not necessarily inform the vision of authors from other regions of the country.

In focusing solely on how well each tale replicates the geographical features of a particular region, for example, readers cannot help but respond to the Texas-based works that successfully evoke the arid, often rugged landscape of the western part of the state. Anyone familiar with the topography of West Texas would recognize the "hump of stony ground in the endless, undulating prairie" that forms the principal setting of Clay Reynolds's "Gethsemane" or the "dust-clay dirt of the home-site" in Laura Rebecca Payne's "So Much Carrion in the Night," temporarily invaded by the almost miraculous, certainly incongruous fecundity of "trumpet vines" in June and the migrating vultures that "seem to float in the atmosphere, barely moving—black majestic wings dipping precarious yet powerful."

In contrast, readers familiar with rural Carolina would respond to the lush greenery fondly remembered by the main character in Jill McCorkle's "Starlings" as she casts her mind back to a time when her house bordered "flat tobacco fields" and a "strip of woods that kept that old snake-infested river shady and cool." Palpably moist is also the atmosphere of the Carolina Low Country so admirably captured in Bret Lott's "Propriety." In that tale's principal scene, the main character crosses the Cooper River on his way to a Charleston worksite and views from his car "to the south, out beyond the flat rock of Fort Sumter settled in the middle of the harbor" a "gray smudge of open sea, the horizon gone, lost to the wet air."

Literary Correspondences

In the final analysis, however, all of these tales are linked by more than physical and cultural environment. They are also bound together by some of the basic elements of literature. These twenty-four paired short stories—twelve from Texas and twelve from the Carolinas—have been carefully crafted to interconnect. To begin, six Texas writers and six writers from the Carolinas contributed one story each. The stories from the Texas writers are set in Texas; or, as in the case of Jerry Bradley's "The Great Derangement," feature displaced Texans; and the Carolina writers' stories are set in SC/NC. Then six other writers from the Carolinas wrote fictional "replies" to the Texas stories, and vice-versa. The primary focus, as indicated by the title of the anthology, is on place and voice; but major thematic links between the paired stories include violence, religion, family relationships, the rule of law, race relations, courtship and romance, coming of age, and loss. In addition to the connections between the paired stories, these twenty-four tales also interlink across pairs with many of the same connecting characteristics as the fictional pieces in a short story cycle by a single author. As a result, *A Shared Voice* is part anthology, part story cycle.

Examples of anthologies include *New Stories from the South* and *Best American Short Stories*. According to *Merriam-Webster*, an anthology is "a collection of selected literary pieces or passages or works of art or music." Interestingly, its Latin root, *anthologia*, derives from the Greek term for gathering flowers. The basis for selecting the works in an anthology (as with the flowers that make up a bouquet) can be virtually anything; generally, however, beyond a single linkage like setting—or a double linkage like setting and form—the pieces that make up an anthology are not connected in significant or purposeful ways. This is definitely not the case with the tales in *A Shared Voice*. It is the many interlinkings across pairs that give *A Shared Voice* the character of a story cycle.

Examples of story cycles include Ernest Hemingway's *In Our Time* and Sandra Cisneros's *Woman Hollering Creek*. A short story cycle, broadly defined, is a collection of interconnected fictional narratives by a single author that are linked by shared characteristics. Because of the wide variation in form among short story cycles, a precise definition of the genre is probably impossible. But in *The Contemporary American Short Story Cycle: The Ethnic Resonance of Genre* (2001), James Nagel states that "a story cycle is generally less unified than a novel, but has much greater coherence and thematic integrity than a collection of unrelated stories." For instance, there is usually much less importance placed on a single, developed protagonist in short story cycles than in novels; while in collections of unrelated stories, there is no single protagonist. And in her seminal work on unified story collections *The Short Story Cycle: A Genre Companion and Reference Guide* (1989), Susan Garland Mann lays out a series of unifying strategies that differentiate the short story cycle from the novel and the unrelated story collection forms: setting, repeated and developed characters, plot or chronological order, themes or ideas, myth, imagery, and point of view. All of the paired tales in *A Shared Voice* are connected by at least four of these unifying strategies; in addition, all of the twenty-four narratives across the collection are linked by at least three of them.

First and most important is setting. The characters in stories, like their nonfictional counterparts in the real world, are products of heredity and environment. The South and the Southwest, arguably the two most "storied" regions in the history of American fiction, have given birth to and shaped the lives of every protagonist in this book and virtually every major character. The state of Texas combines elements of both the South and the Southwest. The flora and fauna of the eastern half of the state are essentially Southern; however, the western half of the state is South-western in character. Along with the physical characteristics of place—the rivers and towering pines of the South; the arid plains, mesquites, and junipers of the Southwest—the previously discussed ties of history and culture that bind the two regions intertwine in these twenty-four tales to give breath to the "shared voice" referred to in the title. Whether they are digging a grave on the West Texas frontier in Clay Reynolds's "Geth-semane" or stalking an egg thief in a North Carolina henhouse in Ron Rash's "Hard Times," there is a spare and beautiful harmony in the speech of the characters and the language with which the characters themselves are drawn—a music that could not be made anywhere else.

Repeated and developed characters link many of the paired tales in *A Shared Voice*. For example, in "Two Birds with One Stone," Deno Trakas takes up the lives of the two main characters in Stephen Graham Jones's "State" and gives an unexpected and gratifying resolution to the conflict between these two best-friends-turned-enemies. And in "Getaway," Betty Wiesepape connects the grieving protagonist of Bret Lott's "Propriety" with an aging and lonely Texas lady—and in so doing, helps both of those wounded people heal. While specific characters from within the paired tales do not repeat across the stories in the collection, one cannot help but see patterns emerge in the kinds of characters that these twenty-four writers bring to life on the page. Aging men and women bravely face the end of their days in Jan Epton Seale's "To Reap, To Thresh" and Jill McCorkle's "Starlings." Adolescent women endure brutal coming-of-age experiences in Elise Blackwell's "Before Texas" and Laura Rebecca Payne's "So Much Carrion in the Night." Indeed, all twenty-four of these tales focus on gritty people facing difficult situations with determination and pluck, regardless of whether they ultimately triumph or are defeated.

Intricately intertwined with character is the linking device of plot or chronological order, a key tool for connecting stories both within pairs and across the collection in *A Shared Voice*. Many of the authors who wrote responses to anchor tales chose plot and/or chronological order as their primary connector. Response stories in the collection take the form of both prequels and sequels. In "Nasty Things," for example, Terry Dalrymple tells the life story of Felicia, who is the love interest of George Singleton's protagonist Daniel in "Thank You." Dalrymple's prequel ends in the middle of Singleton's tale—a hilarious response to a laugh-out-loud funny anchor—in essence, filling in backstory and setting up the meeting at the Speak Up Center while at the same time fleshing out a supporting character into the protagonist of a strong new narrative. An example of a sequel is Dave Kuhne's "Ending Comments," written in response to Michael Parker's "Hidden Meanings." Parker's tale takes the form of a student's essay—an essay that goes hilariously off-topic and winds up saying more about the student and her estimation of the professor's class than about the song that is supposed to be the subject. Kuhne's response is the professor's reply, complete with explanations for various issues raised by the student, and an assessment of the student's work.

Perhaps more importantly for the collection as a whole, chronological order is the main basis for the arrangement of the stories in *A Shared Voice*. The tales in each of the two sections have been arranged chronologically by the time in which the anchor tales take place. In the first half of the book, anchor tales by Texas writers move forward through time from the frontier to the present day. In the second half of the book, anchor tales by Carolina writers start in the present day and move backward in time to the Great Depression. This arc of "history" lends a narrative quality to *A Shared Voice*, especially with regard to the shared cultural elements of the two regions.

As has already been discussed, themes and/or ideas are a major unifying element both within pairs and across the collection. Some response stories use theme as the major linking device to connect with their anchors. One such example is Cecile Goding's "Miz Mabel," written as a response to Oscar Casares's "Mr. Z." Casares's coming-of-age story chronicles the first work experience of Diego, a young Latino who lives in Texas's Rio Grande Valley. Diego feels a responsibility to live up to his father's expectations with regard to a job well done and manages to fulfill those expectations despite the less-than-savory moral character of his first boss. In "Miz Mabel," young Abby comes of age through the experience of her own first job, working as a waitress at the title character's restaurant on the Carolina coastal plain. Despite Miz Mabel's questionable moral qualities and her personal prejudices, Abby manages to acquit herself admirably and successfully complete her first bout with the joys and disappointments of gainful employment. But across the entire collection, recurring themes of violence, religion, family relationships, the rule of law, race relations, courtship and romance, coming of age, and loss help to connect all of the narratives and the lives of the characters who inhabit them.

A shared mythos of rugged individualism runs the course of the collection. The protagonists and supporting characters who people these narratives are not looking for handouts. Indeed, seldom do they willingly accept help in any form. In Clay Reynolds's "Gethsemane," rather than wait for assistance from a distant marshal, Gregory Allen rides from the grave he has just helped dig to deal personally with the murderer who gunned down the man soon to be interred. In Ron Rash's "Hard Times," the proud Hartley—whose family is going hungry during the Great Depression—returns the gift of meat that Jacob, the protagonist of the story, has left on the Hartley family's porch in the night. And when Jacob's wife, Edna, implies that Hartley's dog is stealing eggs from her henhouse, Hartley slits the dog's throat on the spot. The message? Better dead than dependent.

An abundance of shared imagery fills the pages of *A Shared Voice*. Sometimes those images take on a symbolic weight that entire tales are organized around, as in Jill McCorkle's anchor tale "Starlings" and Laura Rebecca Payne's response "So Much Carrion in the Night." Other times, a bird is just a bird. But the repetition of these images across stories adds a rich resonance to the collection. Firearms, knives, farm animals, the flora and fauna of the South and Southwest, lonely roads, the implements of manual labor, gravestones, the sign of the cross, the various parts of the human body bared in passion or in violence or in a combination of the two—all of these and a multitude of others engage the senses of the reader while binding the twenty-four disparate parts of the collection into a new and unique interconnected whole.

Aside from the fact that all of the stories in *A Shared Voice* are written in either first or third person, there is no clear pattern to the use of point of view. Thirteen of the tales employ a third-person perspective, while eleven employ a first-person perspective. With five of the paired stories, the responses are written using the same perspective as the anchor tale. This is the case with "Miz Mabel" and "Mr. Z."; "Ezekiel Saw the Wheel" and "To Reap, To Thresh"; "Two Birds with One Stone" and "State"; "Ending Comments" and "Hidden Meanings"; and "So Much

Carrion in the Night" and "Starlings." With the other seven pairs, the responses are written using a different perspective from the anchor tales. The collection as a whole begins in third person and ends in first.

Indeed, although much time has been spent in this introduction discussing the common elements among the pieces that make up the collection, it would be remiss not to talk about the incredible diversity that exists in them as well. Over the course of the great American experiment, perhaps no quality has been more representative than variety. The short story genre is no different. One of the few artistic inventions that American culture can truly claim, the short fictional narrative has appeared in a myriad of shapes and sizes and forms since Washington Irving first published "Rip Van Winkle" and "The Legend of Sleepy Hollow" in his groundbreaking cycle of tales and sketches entitled *The Sketchbook of Geoffrey Crayon*. The stories in *A Shared Voice* exemplify that variety. Dramatic monologues, fictions that take the form of essays and professors' responses, tall tales in the tradition of Twain, frame stories a la Irving, stream of consciousness narratives, all of these and more are present in this collection—and the quality of the writing is breathtaking.

Tom Mack and Andrew Geyer
University of South Carolina Aiken
2013

Gethsemane
Clay Reynolds

The grinding crunch of the iron-clad wheels of a well-used wagon accentuated the brittleness of air so hot and still, it seemed it would shatter from a harsh look. The noise of the rattling vehicle also silenced the buzzing grasshoppers and cicadas infesting the buffalo grass, scrub cedar, and summer-cooked mesquite that lined the nearly invisible trail.

A single mule—the survivor of a matched pair brought out from Missouri two years before—alone bore the burden of the buckboard and the men who rode in it, one driving, one in the bed half squatting, half kneeling next to a coffined third. For a certainty, he was dead weight.

The sun was directly overhead, and the sky had shifted from a cloudless, translucent morning blue to stark white. It seemed like an anvil on which the yellow orb hammered, banging silently but almost rhythmically and mercilessly down on the seared, barren hilltop below.

It wasn't much of a hilltop. More of a rude, naked hump of stony ground in the endless, undulating prairie. Surrounding the rocky rise and the sparse stand of hackberries and burr oaks that struggled to define its edges were ragged billows of golden sward, taller than a horse's withers in places, worn to wind-torn tatters in others. In some spots large circles, centuries old, had been tramped down and wallowed out by buffalo now long gone. Even their bones were gone, ground up for fertilizer and used, unscrupulously, to extend the yield of flour and corn mills for consumption in Eastern city tenements. Visible from the apex of the rise were a slight dozen half-finished adobe brick and clapboard-fronted buildings. These marked the nearby townsite, shimmering in the heat waves, tentatively clinging to the earth by shallow roots. Huddled around them, tents and canvas-covered frames signaled the hope of additional structures in progress. There was a saddler's shop and a cooper's, a saloon and whorehouse, a land office, a barbershop, a mercantile, a livery, one

13

ambitious two-story structure that functioned as hotel and café, and a ramshackle depot of sorts that also claimed to house a telegraph and freight office. If an eye came close enough, it would discern that beyond the hamlet's uneven edges, dugouts were gouged from the graveled hummocks that occasionally rolled up from the grass, most marked by rusty stovepipes and fronted by a leather-hinged door made from the remnant shards of a wagon or other scrap lumber. Then there was the railroad's water-tower, the only well-made edifice in sight.

That morning, unusually, there was no wind, not even a breeze to ripple the sun-bleached canvas of the tents or stir the yellow dust that had formed in the ruts plowed through what passed for a main street whenever it rained. Gopher boards and grossly warped planks haphazardly stretched from one doorway to another. Many had sunk deep into the mud during the last deluge and were now ossified into the bone-dry, crusty earth. The tiny community was quiet, with no sign of life, no one going about in the morning heat. A whistlestop. That's what they called it. The railroad hadn't named it, yet. The locals dubbed it Happentance. None thought the name would stick.

Driving the mule mostly by applying an occasional desultory slap to its rump was a derbied man named Jenkins. A miller by trade, he had, for want of a stone or any grain to grind with it, become a cooper, a wheelwright, a joiner or a stone mason in response to demand and necessity. He was a large man, ham-handed and barrel-chested. His cheeks were perpetually red above a dark beard that gave him a childish look complemented by bright blue eyes. He was known to have a sweet disposition, to be a man who, though loquacious, was of some tact, gentle in his handling of delicate things and reputed to be good with animals. He was, he claimed, a widower with no progeny. The mule and wagon were his.

Riding in the bed was Swindell, a journalist from Chicago, he said, who was running a small printing operation that had ambitions to be a weekly broadside out of a dugout on the town's outskirts. He wore a dented homburg over a bald skull ringed by a fringe of curly black hair, black serge suit, honed slick at the creases, and a white shirt with a thick burgundy cravat, a faux ruby as his pin. His collar and cuffs were stained but clean, and his waistcoat was wine red and accentuated by a brass watch chain anchored by a Masonic emblem. It was his perpetual costume. The steel Ingersoll on the other end of the braided greenish metal was perpetually slow, although he wound it frequently. Flanking a hawkish nose were small, nervous black eyes, and his cheeks betrayed the pockmarks of a childhood disease. He proudly wore a narrow but uncommonly full mustache, waxed and pointed on the ends. It concealed an improperly repaired cleft pallet. He, too, was apparently a bachelor; although, unlike Jenkins, he provided the town's brothel with regular custom and was inclined to recite poetry when drunk.

The third man in the wagon was dead. That was principally what was known about him.

Their destination was an open spot on the top of the small knoll. There, the grassy vegetation inexplicably gave way to a limestone crown, resembling the wrinkled pate of a giant buried deep in the mound. In the center of the bare ellipse stood two other men, both leaning on tools and panting in the heat as they contemplated the hole they had scraped out of the gravel. They watched the approach of the buckboard with outward indifference.

Clevinger, one of the men, was a barber and sometimes dentist. He was gaunt, thin and wiry, consumptive, and therefore given to sudden fits of violent coughing. But he was strong and would work hard, his large hands and gnarled knuckles extending to blunt fingers, several missing nails from mishaps with mishandled tools, mute testimony to his familiarity with physical labor in spite of his tonsorial trade. His hazel eyes were perpetually damp and were deep set beneath a shelf of forehead that was itself shaded by the brim of an ancient floppy felt hat. He wore no beard, and his teeth were brown from decay. His chest seemed concave beneath his overalls' bib, and he perpetually stooped, as if about to reach for something near his shoe tops. He was reticent, normally, kept to himself, an unusual trait for his profession. He had a wife and two children, he claimed, in Tennessee.

The other was named Allen. He had been there only a month and had announced no particular trade. A tall, well-proportioned man with longish brown hair worn under a soft workman's cap, he seemed to be reluctantly leaving middle age. He wore loose denim trousers, gray linen shirt, and high-laced boots. His hands were calloused but slender, graceful in a way, and his thick auburn beard was salted with premature gray, a feature that made his pale green eyes stand out when he was excited or angry. He perpetually chewed plug tobacco and spat where he pleased. He imbibed infrequently, but on occasion he drank straight rye, steadily and deliberately. His speech betrayed a deep Southern root and some

15

schooling, but he was regarded as more fractious than friendly. He revealed little about himself unless pressed. No one pressed him much.

Jenkins drew the wagon up parallel to the heap of rocky yellow and red dirt Allen and Clevinger had piled next to the grave. He set the brake and looked down. Allen spat a glob of brown juice onto the mound.

"Done a good job," Jenkins said.

Allen spat again. Clevinger shrugged.

"I'll second that," Swindell said. "A good job." He produced a silk handkerchief from his coat pocket, removed his homburg, and wiped his head. "In this heat, I'd say it was splendid."

For a moment, all of them stared at the hole. Two feet wide, it resembled a narrow trench with sharp sides that dove into the crusty ground for the traditional six feet.

"Don't get no easier as you go down," Clevinger said. "Bust open the top rock, you'd think it'd soften up. Don't." He lifted his shovel and pointed down to the side of the hole. "Gets harder as you go along." He addressed them as if explaining his point to simpletons, then stared at them, listened for a moment to the insects' songs that had quickened in the interval. "Could of used some help," he concluded.

"Had to make the box," Jenkins said. "You know that."

"What about you?" Allen asked, staring at Swindell. "You make a box, too?" Swindell didn't respond, but looked up at the sky, blinking into the sun.

"Take some water," Jenkins said. He pulled up a wooden canteen from the seat next to him, tossed it over by them. "Hotter'n hell out here." Clevinger picked it up, drank deeply.

"Damndest thing I've ever seen," Allen said, and he spat again. He planted the shovel he'd been leaning on in the mound, moved off to a small clump of huisache and turned his back to them. They all watched him for a moment until they realized what he was doing. Then they turned away, covered their sheepishness by finding something interesting in the near distance to occupy their attention.

Swindell stood up in the wagon bed and peered toward the townsite. "Must be more than a mile out here," he said. "Didn't realize it was that far."

"It's two," Allen said, hunching his shoulders as he finished, then buttoning up. "I know two miles when I walk it."

"Well, why not put him somewhere else?" Swindell asked. "I mean, nobody said we had to come out here."

"Here's where that other'un's buried," Jenkins said. He pointed off to a spot about thirty yards away. "We done agreed this would be the place for the whole town when the need come." He glanced around. "For any of us." Swindell and Clevinger looked at him sharply. "When the need come," he repeated.

"Don't know why the need had to come when it was so goddamn hot," Allen said as he walked back. He glanced at the other grave. "Who was that one?"

"Cowboy," Jenkins said. "Redskins got him right here. Kilt and scalped him." He opened his arms to indicate the bare mound. "Right here. His pards found him, planted him on the spot."

"Think they'd of found softer ground," Clevinger said.

"Think they'd have found colder weather," Allen said, as he moved over to the other grave.

Jenkins and Swindell climbed down and followed him, and Clevinger matched his shovel with Allen's and trailed after them. They gathered around the spot. It had been poorly marked with white stones that had, they surmised, initially outlined the grave. Now only a half dozen remained, although who or what might have removed the others was a mystery. A large yellow rock was at one end: a headstone. Jenkins reached up to remove his hat, then noticed no one else was doing so, so he dropped his hand.

"Have a name?" Clevinger asked.

"Who?"

"The cowboy?"

"Epson, I think," Jenkins said.

"No," Swindell said. "Not Epson. Epstein, maybe."

"Euless," Jenkins said. "Remember, now. It was Euless." He reached up and ran his hand over his mouth. "From Savannah, I heard tell." He shut his eyes tight. "No, that's not right," he said, thinking hard. "Charleston." He brightened slightly, looked around. "Heard tell he was half nigger."

"No," Swindell said. "That's wrong. I know that's wrong."

"How would you know anything about it?" Allen asked in a low voice.

"Indians don't scalp niggers," he said. He used his handkerchief to wipe his brow again. "Least, they weren't supposed to."

17

"Maybe they just half scalped him," Jenkins said, then laughed dryly. No one joined him.

"He was just a boy," Swindell said. "That much I'm sure of."

"I don't think you're sure of shit," Allen said, and spat conspicuously close to Swindell's shoe.

For a moment they stood staring at the flattened area. The ground was so smooth, so solid, it was impossible to believe it had ever been excavated. Swindell pulled out a tailor-made, lit it with a lucifer. For a second, the odor of sulfur struck their nostrils. The tobacco smoke gathered about them in the breathless atmosphere.

"Goddamned shame to be buried out here with no name," Allen said. He spat on the yellow rock. "Think they'd have carved his name in the goddamn rock." He looked at them. "Least they could have done was tell somebody his name."

"Wasn't nobody to tell," Jenkins said. "Wasn't nobody in this part of Texas back then. That was near ten year ago. Maybe longer." He glanced down. "I only heard about it. Wasn't here, my own self."

"Hell of a notion," Clevenger added. "Die out here. Scared, alone. Nobody around but heathen savages. Wonder what goes through a man's head, thing like that?"

"It was Savannah," Swindell said suddenly. "I'm sure of it. And it was Euless. Sure of that, too."

"You wasn't here. How'd you know?" Clevenger asked, seriously. He glanced at Allen, then back at Swindell. "He's right. You don't know shit."

"No name. No date. No nothing," Allen said, disgusted. He swiveled his head to look at the buckboard. "And here we are, about to do the same goddamn thing again." He turned and walked away. "It's not right," he said. "Nothing about this is right."

"That man has a name," Swindell protested, following. "I have that letter." He pulled a notebook from his pocket, thumbed it open. "Jerome Willoughby the Third," he read.

"You don't know that was his name," Allen said. The others were now following him to the buckboard. "That was just a name on a letter he had."

"Well," Swindell stopped and looked at the notebook, then walked on. "If it's not—"

"That letter might not even have been his," Allen said. "Might belong to a friend or something." He turned quickly, faced Swindell who nearly ran into him. His eyes were large, greener than cedar, rimmed red from sweat salt. His jaw bulged with tobacco. "Might have found it. Might have stolen it. Might be he was supposed to take it to somebody." He balled his fists. "You don't know jack shit, Swindell." Allen spat. "You're worthless as a cartload of dog turds." He spun around and dropped the tailgate on the wagon. "Tit on a boar hog," he added.

Swindell stood gaping at him, then at the others, who had stopped suddenly, watching. He swung his head back toward Allen. "What's the matter with you? Why'd you say such a thing to me?" Allen glared at him, then spat again and turned his back on him once more. Swindell stepped forward, flung down his cigarette. "You ought to apologize to me." Allen didn't reply. "I mean it. I demand an apology."

"I don't like you," Allen said sharply. "I don't like anything about you. That's all the apology you're getting from me."

Swindell stood as tall as he could, which still made him inches shorter than Allen. "What did I ever do—"

"Don't push it," Allen said. "Just leave it where it is." For a moment, they stood staring at each other, the heat rising around them from the stony ground. "It's too goddamn hot out here for this," Allen said.

Swindell nodded. Then, as if by mutual consent, they relaxed, but neither stepped away.

The others waited a beat, then came up beside them, and they looked at the coffin. Jenkins had no pine, so he used cypress he appropriated from a shipment of lumber the railroad had dropped off to use to build a warehouse and tool barn. They'd all agreed to the theft. It was that or no coffin at all. Jenkins had made it solid, bracketed it with iron straps. It looked heavy.

"Well, whoever he was," Swindell said, stung but holding his own. "He needs to be buried." The others didn't look at him. "He was a human man and we need to bury him."

"He needs to be buried quick," Clevinger said. "He's not apt to get any less ripe in this heat."

"Should have done this two days ago," Allen said.

"We've been all over this," Swindell said. "He said not to. Fact is he said to leave him where he lay."

"So you said he said," Allen grumbled. "He never said shit to me."

"Well, that's what he said to me," Swindell insisted. He checked his notebook again. "He was very clear about it. 'Leave him where he lies,' he said."

"Well, he's not paying me any wages to take orders," Allen said. "And I'll be goddamned if I'm going to walk around a rotting carcass for the rest of my days."

"It ain't Christian," Clevinger said. "Let a man lay there like that."

"Wonder why he shot him?" Jenkins asked. It wasn't a new question. They'd been asking it for three days, mostly in whispers behind closed doors. But they embraced the problem once again and stood and considered it in silence, then Jenkins added a coda: "Wonder why he didn't want us to bury him?"

"Who knows with a man like that?" Swindell said. "He shot him. That's all we know for sure."

"He didn't just shoot him," Jenkins said. "He shot the hell out of him. Murdered him. That's what he done." They all looked at him, then slumped. He'd repeated the story forty times. They all knew it by heart. They also knew that he wouldn't be stopped from telling it again. "It was murder," he affirmed. "I seen it. And nobody done nothing about it."

"What did you do?" Allen asked.

Jenkins ignored him. He took off his derby, slapped his leg with it. "You all seen it," he went on, then glanced at Swindell. "All but you." He stepped back a half-step and spoke to them all. "And none of you done nothing." He glared at them. "Not just me. None of you." He put his hat back on his head. "That man," he nodded at the coffin. "He just got off that train and walked down toward the store, and before he got there, that galloot," he nodded toward the town shimmering in the distance, "rode up and got off his horse and shot him." He shook his head. "Four times. Right through the liver." He put his hands on his hips in a posture of satisfaction. "It was murder."

"Wasn't murder," Clevinger recited, as if he was playing out a well-rehearsed part. Like the story, the argument had grown vintage over the past two days. Word for word. "He had a pocket pistol. Had it out. I seen it."

"Never did," Clevinger insisted, picking up his cue. "I'd of seen that. I was right there."

"I didn't find it," Swindell said in his turn. "I was first to go to the body. Didn't find it."

"That was an hour later, wasn't it?" Allen asked, narrowing his eyes in a squint toward Swindell. "Or maybe two? You wanted to wait to make sure he was dead, I suppose."

"I didn't see you running up to him," Swindell shot back. "You were there—just as they were," he added. Allen spat, looked away. Swindell waved his hands toward the other two. "Nobody went to the body till I got there."

"They had words," Jenkins said, ignoring them. "I seen them. They had words."

"Quiet words," Clevinger confirmed with a nod. "Nobody heard what they said. They just talked a minute, and then that old boy shot the hell out of him." He held up fingers. "Four times." He looked in the direction of the town. "Should of wired the marshal over to Wichita Falls." They all started. This was something new.

"And what makes you think he'd give a drizzling shit?" Allen asked. "You think he'd come on the howl in this heat?" He looked up into the empty sky. "Hell, he might get around to it when the weather cools."

"I wired him," Swindell said softly, looking behind him.

"You never!" Jenkins said.

Swindell snapped his face around. "I did! I sent him a telegram straight away."

"And?"

"No reply," Swindell admitted, looking down at his shoes. "Three days. No reply."

Allen chuckled, spat, shook his head.

"We need us a sheriff or something," Jenkins said.

"Who?" Clevinger asked, as if startled into sudden wakefulness, then he blinked at them when he realized he had their attention. "Hell," he swore in the manner of a man unused to swearing, "they's only a few dozen of us lives here. One's a cripple, four's niggers, and four others is women."

"Whores," Jenkins corrected.

"They're still women," Swindell said. Allen chuckled again, and Swindell gave him a hard look.

Clevinger continued, "Them two farmers come in last month don't even speak English. Wouldn't truck with this."

"Have better sense," Allen muttered.

"Well, one of us—" Jenkins started, but then he looked around, stopped. "We need a sheriff or something," he repeated quietly. None of the others would meet his eye, so he looked toward the town. "He's still

21

there. At Lola's."

"Sleeps past noon," Clevinger said, nervously. "Won't like what we done." For a moment, they were all silent. Swindell checked his Ingersoll, put it back.

"Somebody needs to do something," Jenkins insisted. "We can't have this kind of thing."

"Damndest thing I ever seen," Allen said. He spat onto the side of the coffin.

"Don't you have any respect?" Swindell demanded. "That's a man's final bed."

"That's just a box," Allen said. "I don't know who the man is, and I don't know why that other man killed him. And I don't much care." He looked down toward the town, bunched his shoulders, then relaxed them. "But we're going to bury him, and that's a fact."

"It's the Christian thing to do," Jenkins said.

"Man's still down there," Clevinger repeated, nodding toward Swindell's watch. "He'll be out and about directly. Won't be happy."

"His happiness ain't my concern," Allen said. He reached for a rope that was looped around the coffin and dragged the box toward him. It was heavy and didn't want to move. "Give me a hand," he said to Swindell. "Be of some goddamn use to somebody."

Swindell took a hold on the rope, and together, he and Allen drew the coffin out of the bed more than half way, then they strung another rope underneath it. Jenkins and Clevinger did the same to the head end of the box, and on a count of three, the four of them lifted it, carried it over the loose rock toward the gravesite. Allen swore with every stumbling step, Jenkins and Clevinger muttered oaths. Swindell huffed with the exertion. When they set it down next to the grave, Swindell mopped his brow again, went to pick up the canteen, and drank hard from it.

"Goddamn box is twice as heavy as he is," Allen said, panting slightly.

"Water round here tastes funny," Swindell said, spitting out a mouthful. "Like it's got rock in it."

"Gyp," Allen said. "Gyp water. You want sweet water, you got to find a spring." He took the canteen from Swindell, shook it to hear it slosh, and gave him a narrow look. "You wasn't too picky to take most of it," he said, and he finished it off.

"I got another one," Jenkins said, moving up to the buckboard's

22

driver's seat. From beneath it, he removed another, smaller wooden vessel, then he stared at it, abashed. "I put brandy in it," he said, remembering.

"Why'd you do a thing like that?" Clevinger asked, annoyed. "I've took the pledge."

"I didn't." Allen took the canteen from Jenkins, uncorked it, and drank deeply.

Jenkins gaped at him. "I thought . . . well, I thought that after we was done, we might . . ." He trailed off, took the canteen back from Allen, shook it. There was some left. "I mean. Since we didn't have no service or nothing," he muttered.

"Thought you knew some Scripture," Clevinger said. "You said your daddy was a deacon."

"He was," Jenkins said. He looked at the coffin. "I tried to think." He shook his head, embarrassed. "Memory fails."

"One of these days soon," Swindell said. "We'll have a preacher." He looked toward the town. "A proper preacher and a church." He took off his hat, wiped it out again. "A sheriff and a preacher."

"That's just what we need," Allen growled and spat on his palms. He bent down and picked up the rope. "Let's get this over with," he said. "Grab ahold."

Awkwardly, the four of them lifted the coffin with the ropes. Allen and Clevinger stepped over the grave so they could lower the box into the hole, but Clevinger abruptly stopped. A spasm of coughing racked him, he bent over, dropping his rope that instantly slithered into the grave beneath the coffin. Swindell stumbled backward, pulled on his end and drew the entire length out. He stood helpless, the limp cord in his hand. The head of the coffin had angled down into the hole, jamming itself crookedly into the narrow opening. The foot of the box was still on the rim, but the other rope was wedged against the coffin's corner and the stone-hard sides.

"Goddamnit," Allen swore.

"Sorry," Clevinger gasped. Then he coughed again, more violently. "Can't help it," he wheezed.

"God damn it to hell and back," Allen stared at the coffin. "Would it have broken your heart to put some goddamn hand-holds on it?"

"Done the best I could on short notice," Jenkins said. "Sides, it was heavy enough already."

Clevinger suffered another spasm, bent to his knees, and held a dirty bandana over his mouth. When he removed it, it was black with blood. "Sorry," he choked out, stumbling uncertainly to his feet. "Can't help it."

"You'll be the next one we bury up here," Allen said. "You sorry son of a bitch." He removed the wad and flung it aside. "Do something for us," he said, stepping away and cutting another plug. "Wait till goddamn winter to die." He stuffed the tobacco in his mouth, worked it for a few moments, then dropped to his knees and tried to lift the box. Jenkins grabbed at the end, but they could get no purchase on the smooth wood. The bottom of the box was below the rim of the grave, and it was jammed in too tight against the rocky side. The rope beneath the foot end was only looped, there was nothing to pull against. All four scraped and pawed at the box, sweat pouring off them, stinging their eyes. They tried to lift it with the remaining line, but it wouldn't budge. Finally, they all stumbled back a few feet, breathing hard.

"What now?" Swindell asked, gasping. No one answered. They just stood in the searing heat, hands on their knees, and panted, watching sweat fall from their noses.

The buzzing of insects continued to rise from the grass around them. Allen looked up. A pair of turkey vultures circled high overhead, riding thermals. The sun was a yellow blister on the opaque sky. "Goddamn it," he whispered. He looked down. "I know one thing," he said. "I've spent about as much sweat as I plan to on this sorry business."

"Meaning what?" Swindell asked.

"Meaning I ain't going to dig out that hole any wider. You want that, you take off your coat and get after it." He spat a fresh glob of juice onto the coffin lid. "Might do you some good."

"Well, can't we just lift it out?"

"You seen that we can't," Jenkins said. He glanced at the mule. "Maybe with old Donny. I could rig up a tripod of some kind," he said. "An A-frame, you see? Block and tackle . . ." He removed his hat, wiped a sleeve across his forehead. "Damn it," he said.

"Maybe open it up," Swindell offered. "Take him out. Lighten the load."

"That ain't right," Clevinger said.

"Damn it," Jenkins said.

The flat thump of a gunshot, muffled and distant, reached their ears, transfixing them. It was followed by a yell, an inarticulate bellow rippling across the sky, loud even at that distance. Then another shot followed. They turned and looked through the heat waves toward the town.

"He's out and about," Clevinger said. He looked around, panicked. "He'll be up here directly."

"No," Allen said. "He won't." He pulled his flat cap down over his forehead. "He'll wait."

"What for?" Clevinger asked. His eyes darted fearfully, face to face.

"Because he knows we're up here—or that we're someplace," Jenkins said. "And he knows what we're about. He's right. He'll wait."

"I don't know how you can be so damn sure of that," Clevinger said, incensed. "Why would he just wait?"

"Why not?" Allen asked, lifting his eyes to the horizon and surveying the world from the tiny hilltop. "Where would we go?"

"You think he shot somebody else?" Jenkins asked. In answer, a third shot reported over the grass. For a long moment, the four stood staring at one another, sweat pouring off of them, breaths shortened.

"Somebody . . ." Swindell started, then took off his hat, but he didn't wipe it out this time. He looked inside it, as if seeking something he'd put there for safe-keeping. "Somebody's got to do something," he finished in a soft voice.

"How about you?" Allen asked, a sneer complementing the question. Swindell put his hat back on his head, looked away. "That's about what I thought," Allen said and spat.

There was another shot, then another, and then two more. Regular, paced. The reports didn't echo, since there were no formations to catch and resonate the noise. They came over the still, heated air like flat thumps, reminding all of them of heartbeats.

Clevinger stepped out a few feet. "I'm not ashamed to say it," he said. "I'm scared of that man." He turned to look at the trio behind him and held out the bloody handkerchief. "I mean, shit . . . I'm goddamn dying. You might say I got nothing to lose. But . . . well, that don't stop up no holes. I got a family."

"And that makes you special?" Allen asked, sneering slightly.

Clevinger wiped his mouth with the gory rag and looked from face to face. "I'm still scared," he said. "I'm not afraid to say it. We need a damn sheriff to take care of this." His eyes filled with tears. "I got a family. I'm sorry, but I'm just not the man for this," he said in a choking voice. "I'm just not."

25

Jenkins stepped to him. "None of us are." He looked at Swindell for support. "Are we?" Swindell looked away, stared off into the empty, superheated distance. "Somebody's got to do something," Jenkins said, looking at Allen. "Else, we're all dead men."

For a moment they all stood looking into one another's faces, and in spite of the heat, the sweat dripping from them, they felt cold. Something dark and icy had at once opened inside all of them, something hollow, bottomless. It seemed to steal their very breath and amplified the pulsing that coursed through them like a rising dirge.

"Goddamnit," Allen said at last. He stalked over to a juniper bush where his coat lay wadded up. "I swore I was done with this." He picked the bundle up, hefted it, looked at the trio, who had not moved. "I swore I'd never do this again." He spat. "I swore that to God on High." He looked at the bundle. "Sometimes," he said as if speaking to it, "sometimes you just can't . . . Sometimes . . . I swore I'd never do this again," he repeated, shaking his head.

"Do what?" Swindell said. "You can't—"

"Get that goddamn coffin buried," Allen ordered, starting to walk away.

"You're leaving?" Swindell asked, imperiously.

Allen took a gunbelt from the bundled coat. A large, brown-handled revolver was in the holster. "Goddamnit," he said and spat. "Goddamn it to hell and back." He dropped the coat, buckled on the rig. The pistol was cross-strapped. The other three gaped. None had ever worn a gun that way or seen many men who did so. "What are you looking at?" Allen asked. "Get that man buried."

"What're you gonna do?" Clevinger asked in a small voice.

"Something," Allen said. "The only thing." As they stood watching in silence, not moving, he went over and unhitched the mule from the wagon. He took a stuttering hop, slung a leg over. The three stared, silent. "I ain't walking it," he said. "Two miles is too far." He jerked the mule's mane and turned him toward town, then stopped and looked back at them.

"Swindell," he said. "Get that man buried, then dig another hole. Make it bigger."

"What for?" Jenkins asked, after a beat. He looked at the town. Another series of shots resounded and another yell reached their ears. This time, it was high-pitched, maybe a woman's voice. Even from the

26

distance, they could hear terror in it. "Who for?"

"Name's Allen." He rolled his shoulders, as if to work out a kink. "Gregory Allen. Write that down, Swindell," he said. "Case you need it." He spat. "Don't you dare bury me under a goddamn blank rock." He kicked the mule and moved him on down the grassy trail toward the town.

The three stood silent, watching him go. Each man's thoughts raced, collided with themselves, swirled and tore at their insides, then lay quiet. For a few seconds, they couldn't move. The insects' humming buzz seemed to grow to a crescendo in their ears. Their mouths were gritty, dust-dry. They couldn't swallow. They couldn't meet each other's eyes. "One of us should go with him," Clevinger said, at last.

Swindell turned and picked up a shovel. "Yeah, one of us should," he said. He pushed the blade into the ground next to the grave, scraped off a top layer. He stopped, removed his coat and lay it over the wagon. "You gonna help me do this, or not?"

"One of us ought to go with him," Jenkins said, as if he hadn't heard the previous remark. He grabbed a pick and wheeled it into the groove Swindell had cut. It fairly bounced back, leaving no discernable mark. "One of us should," he repeated, then struck the ground again.

Clevenger looked at them, watched them working. "Yeah," he said. "One of us should." He pulled a shovel off the wagon, and went to work.

Brother
Phillip Gardner

When I was nine years old, my mother woke me and Jim in the middle of the night. Jim was sixteen. Our tiny room was winter dark and hard cold. Her voice filled it up. "Help me get him out of the wagon," she said.

Outside, our mule blew vanishing white puffs. At the rear of the wagon, my father, a tall, thin man, lay on his back upon the gray wooden planks, the span of his arms open as if to welcome us. Mama, Jim, and I stood in the silence of the black winter night, the aching cold from the frozen clay biting through my bare feet, cuffing my ankles. Mama turned, gathered the quilt to her throat, and walked toward the house. "At least the mule knows his way home," she said. Jim hoisted Father's shoulders and I clasped his muddy brogans. "Leave him by the bed, on the floor," Mama said. "That's what he gets."

We didn't know he wasn't drunk, that instead he'd suffered a stroke, or that my mute father would spend the next three years staring at the ceiling, shrinking, dying.

* * *

As I dressed for his funeral, the Japanese assaulted Pearl Harbor. At twelve years old, I was growing too fast for the clothes Mama made me, not fast enough for what Jim had outgrown. My shoes didn't fit. While machine-gun blasts of Zeros, the Japanese fighter planes, tore through the flesh of sailors and civilians and their bombs penetrated the steel decks of American war ships, Mama pinned up the sleeves of my dress shirt, a threadbare hand-me-down from Jim.

I remember nothing of the church service or of the tears I may have cried, or should have if I didn't. At the graveside, we all sang "Will the

Circle Be Unbroken." Afterwards, Jim stood apart from everyone, his back to us. Staring out across the barren cotton fields, he smoked alone. Mama's eyes were fixed on me, her face lean, austere. Neighbors, kin, and Mrs. Wills clustered around her speaking in somber, muted whispers; but I could see that she'd had a bate of well-intended store-bought grief instruction. She called to Jim, then me. Mr. Wills offered to drive us from the cemetery. She refused. In silence, we walked the two miles home, Jim, Mama, and me. Both my heels flamed with blisters.

The house was brittle cold, and I fetched firewood. Inside, Jim hunched over the radio. Ernest Tubb was his favorite singer, "Walking the Floor Over You" his favorite song. But this December seventh was a day without music.

Jim was soon drafted and fought in the Pacific where the Japanese burrowed in caves and bunkers. He carried a flamethrower.

Two years after Jim left, the war came to us. This was early March, 1943. That Saturday morning, Mama sent me to inspect the progress of Mr. Wills's tobacco beds. Mr. Wills owned the farm we sharecropped. He sometimes drank. A bad tobacco crop meant debt for Wills. It meant the end of us. The early morning sky was crimson, the sun a giant red smear. Weeks earlier, I'd burned a strip of land to purify the ground and make ash to enrich the seed bed soil. Now I carefully folded back the thin white linen that protected the tender plants from frost.

I looked up. From the river bottom echoed a low consumptive rumble. The ground beneath me trembled. Against the fiery sky a convoy of earthmovers slowly ascended from the dark horizon like a caravan of prehistoric beasts. For more than an hour I stood upon the quivering earth and watched their slow progress.

Over the weeks and months that followed, an ominous grey cloud appeared above the three thousand acres that would become Seymour Johnson Air Base. We paused from plowing, planting, and hoeing, looked up at the gathering storm of dust and smoke, sopped our sweaty brows, and then turned back to our labor. Before we finished topping and suckering in July, the facility was operational.

In most ways, the air base was a world apart from ours, living as we did within the confines of the farmland we did not own. We had a cow, pigs, and chickens. Mama made all we wore but shoes. Without money for extras, we had little reason to go into Goldsboro, where we'd be reminded of our conditions and subject to want, and where the recent arrivals, faceless young men in crisp blue uniforms, paraded about the hotel, honkytonks, and movie theater. We rarely saw them. But their presence bore down upon us. Their flight maneuvers turned our days into lightning, our nights into thunder. We lived beneath a roaring hive of giant piston-pounding steel bees. For a time the cow stopped giving milk, and the hens quit laying as they should. We were robbed of good sleep, our dreams splintered. Our tempers became tender to the touch. It seemed that a huge bite had been taken from the world we knew and that in its place there festered a black asphalt scab.

Late the next winter, the P-47 Thunderbolts arrived and with them a different kind of airman, replacement pilots in training, young, arrogant city boys with last names you couldn't pronounce and dispositions that attracted blowflies.

Hoeing cotton that spring, we'd hear them come shrieking toward us just above the tree line. "Don't you look up," Mama said, pressing the blade of her hoe deep into the black soil, holding it there. "Don't you give them the satisfaction." But sometimes I did look. They'd slash in so low you could see the eight .50 caliber machine guns, four on each wing. If the sun was right, you'd catch a glimpse of their ravenous smiling faces when they spotted the stooped white sharecroppers and black field hands. They were practicing strafing the enemy. We were their practice enemy.

The following winter, Jim's letters stopped arriving.

There was little work for Mr. Wills, and in January the side meat ran out. Mama and I ate sweet potatoes and dried butterbeans. Bill Patterson, a drinking buddy of Wills, ran a crossroads country store before the war. But with the base came a fluster of traffic, enough for him to bury a fuel tank. He needed a boy to pump gas, and we needed the five dollars a week. Bill gave me a job. I manned the pumps, cleaned windshields, and quickly worked my way up to oil changes. I washed the cars of the newly moneyed town merchants.

Gasoline was rationed, of course, and at that time reduced even more. All pleasure driving was outlawed, and the speed limit was set at thirty-five. But laws and limits meant nothing to the Thunderbolt cadets. Or to Bill. Inside the station, he sold bootleg whiskey. His place was the nearest one to the back gate of the base, and carloads of airmen headed to or from Morehead City or Wrightsville Beach stopped for gas and liquor, and hopefully to catch a glimpse of Jen.

31

* * *

Bill had a wife and then he didn't. Then he had Jen, his new wife, who was half his age, seventeen, only three years older than me. Bill's new wife was one way when Bill was around and another way when he wasn't. She rarely spoke in Bill's presence, assuming a stately school teacher manner, chin up, shoulders back, hands clasped before her as if she were awaiting the class's complete attention. Jen was reliable and responsible. She kept the books balanced and the coffee fresh and could read Bill's moods. She baked him pies and knew the game of baseball. She provided Bill a timely formal kiss when a kiss was in order.

But when Bill was away, she was more of a girl. While we loaded the drink boxes with Coke Colas, Pepsis, orange and grape drinks, she described to me the latest gossip surrounding Ava Gardner, who had grown up only twenty miles from us and whose folks still lived near Brogden. In wide-eyed excitement Jen whispered the lurid details of Miss Gardner's most recent and tempestuous sins. When I feigned disbelief, she'd raise one finger as a place holder then dash off to their apartment at the back of the station. Her limbs were long, her hips still narrow. In motion, other girls of similar shape and design were gangly and clumsy; but Jen's movements were harmonious and graceful, her arms and wrists and fingers gliding as if under water. She'd return smiling victoriously and brandishing a movie magazine, from which she recited Ava's scandals in low, breathy whispers of collusion. I watched her lips form the words. She had the face of a girl, narrow and long. But the flush lips of a woman, large and plump, always a little swollen. Thick brown hair danced upon her animated shoulders, and her index finger moved in and out of the ringlet she wound round it as she read to me. When she looked up from her magazine, her titillated eyes were as black and soft as a doe's.

Most evenings Bill drove me home after closing time, which varied depending upon pay days and liquor traffic. But on Thursday nights, when Bill made midnight trips to his bootlegger, a man named Lancaster who lived near Saulston and made whiskey in one of his tobacco barns, I'd lie awake on a cot in the dark storage room. The station and the apartment had running water, and I'd listen to Jen bathing on the other side of the cinderblock wall that separated us. Eyes closed, I listened. When Bill returned, I'd help unload the whiskey.

* * *

At home, I'd begun sleeping in Jim's bed. I don't know why.

Mama woke me. "Bill's come for you," she said.

"But it's Sunday," I said.

"There's a warm biscuit on the stove."

My room was cold, and I dressed quickly. From the kitchen window, I saw Bill's black Ford, its chugging exhaust puffing smoke signals into the frigid morning air. Mama stood at the sink, her apron knotted in her hands, eyeing me as I ate the biscuit. "You be partic'lar," Mama said. "You best be partic'lar."

Bill didn't look at me, didn't speak, just shifted into gear. As we lurched forward, I heard a clanging and turned to see a shovel in the back.

I tried to read him. His body was thick, his sinuous arms muscled, his fingers blunt as pork sausages. He hadn't shaved, and flecks of white beard shone in the bright morning sunlight. Dark half-moons sagged below his severe blue eyes as we jolted over the rutted dirt road. He had installed heavy truck springs at the rear of his car on account of the weight of the whiskey he hauled and the sharp eye of the Wayne County law. When his trunk was empty, the car rode with the jarring discomfort of an old tractor. "Do something about that shovel," Bill said. "Make it shut up." When we turned onto the smooth pavement of New Hope Road toward the Beston Stretch, I spoke.

"Where we goin'?"

"To the station. Then you and Jen are going to the movies," he said.

He backed the Ford to the side door that connected the station and their apartment. "You haul it out," he said. "I'll watch the road." He handed me the key to the storeroom. As I passed the open door to their apartment, I saw Jen sitting at the small kitchen table wearing only a loose housecoat. She was drinking coffee. Her hair was up in a towel. The gallon jugs of whiskey were packed inside motor oil boxes. I stacked the boxes on the two-wheel dolly and rolled them back to Bill, who filled the boot of the Ford. "One more load will do it," he said, his anxious eyes fixed upon the road that led into town. "I got help on the other end. You stay here with Jen. If you see the law, lock the doors and y'all climb down into the changing bay," he said. "Stay there until I get back." I watched as he drove away.

Jen called to me from the apartment. "You want a cup of coffee,

David? I made a whole pot."

From the doorway I saw her standing with her back to me, her long fingers kneading the towel that cocooned her hair. I'd never seen her sleek, bare shoulders. In one long smooth motion she pulled the towel away, allowing the dark wet hair to cascade to her shoulders. She turned and smiled. "Want some?" she asked, indicating the pot on the stove.

Looking away, I said, "I'd better get up front."

"If the law comes, they'll come from town, silly, right past this window." She smiled. "Sit. I'll tell you the latest Ava news. You know she's only three years older than me? Imagine."

"What's happening?" I asked.

"She's divorcing Mickey Rooney."

"I mean here."

She poured. Her naked legs were too long for the housecoat, her feet bare, her toenails bright red. "I don't know what's happening," she said over her shoulder. "I only know what I don't know."

"That's funny," I said. She handed me the steaming cup.

"That's Ava. She's something, ain't she? That's what she said to the magazine writer about her and Mickey. Or that's what the writer wrote that she said." We sat at the small table.

"So, what don't you know?" Above the pleasant aroma of coffee, I smelled the scent of Jen's shampoo.

"I don't know that the phone rang about five this morning. And I don't know that the man on the other end said Bill's bootlegger shot an airman during a poker game last night. I don't know that when that airman don't show up today that the law might come around. And if they do, I don't even know what I don't know." She smiled as she brought the cup to her lips and winked at me.

It was almost noon when Bill returned for the second load. In a matter of minutes, the Ford's trunk was again packed full. Jen sat up front, I in the backseat. Bill reached for his key, paused, then looked up into his mirror at me. "Go back inside and bring me a pair of coveralls," he said. "And my boots." On the way into Goldsboro, I held the shovel handle on my lap.

Bill parked on Center Street in front of the Paramount Theater. I checked the show times. "Don't start until two," I said at Bill's window. He opened his wallet and handed some folding money to Jen. "Get yourselves some hamburgers. Take a walk. See the picture." He turned to me. "When

34

the show's over, you come to the lobby. If I ain't parked where you can see me, y'all sit through the picture again, understand?" He turned back to Jen. He handed her more money. "If I ain't here by then, call a taxi." He said to me, "Open up the station. Everybody knows we open on Sunday night for the airmen returning to base. Tonight's no different. But if the law shows up, you don't know where I am. They want to look for liquor? You let 'em cause there ain't none. I'll call you." He looked at Jen. "You be safe." He looked at me. "Keep her out of this."

Jen waited at the candy counter while the usher drew fountain Coke Colas. A few people still in their church clothes dawdled about the lobby waiting for the show to begin. She handed me a foamy cup and tucked the box of popcorn under her slender arm.

"What do we say if somebody sees us together?" I asked.

"What are you talking about?" she asked. I felt my face redden. She stepped closer and spoke in a whisper. "We can sit in the back of the balcony with the colored people if you want. Might be just the two of us." She smiled. "Come on, you," she said, taking my arm. The theater was dark and quiet. We sat close to the screen and shared popcorn. Our shoulders sometimes touched. I closed my eyes. The scent of shampoo was in the air. My hands felt foreign to me.

The entertainment began with newsreel footage from Point Cruz, where the Japanese had dug in, and we watched as our boys heaved hand grenades to loosen up the embedded enemy. Streams of flaming petroleum incinerated their bunkers. Popeye and Mickey Mouse cartoons came next. Followed by coming attractions, then the feature, *So Proudly We Hail!* When the picture was done and its credits began to roll, I stood in the lobby. Bill's black Ford wasn't outside.

During the repeat of the newsreels, I studied the faces of the soldiers. The face of the man with the flamethrower was hidden from view.

"It got dark," Jen said when we stepped outside. The usher had called a taxi. I'd never been inside a taxi. We sat together in the dark backseat. My hands still felt foreign to me.

"I couldn't do what those women did," she said, speaking of the movie. "I could never be a nurse. The sight of blood makes me woozy."

"But you could be an actress and play one in a movie." I could say that only because the taxi was dark. "Like Ava."

She turned to face me, opened her arms, and looked down at her

35

slight bosom. "Ava?" she said. "Maybe Olive Oyl."

I unlocked the station, shut on the solitary light outside the door and hit the power switch for the gas pumps, then changed into my soiled work clothes. From seven until ten I pumped gas. Jen made change inside. The cars carried four or five airmen, and most often one would open his door and start inside. "He ain't here," I said. "Won't be back before closing." The cars drove away. I sat on the stoop beneath the hooded light, my mind adrift, and studied my shadow as I smoked. Fighter planes came in so low a hint of spent petroleum wafted upon the crisp breeze. Then all was quiet. The cold was like a heavy weight settling in for the night. After a time, I went inside. Jen sat reading a magazine at a small table where old men sometimes played checkers and young men poker.

"You got some paper, a pencil?" I asked. "I want to write a letter. To my brother."

She twisted her hair around her finger and slowly turned a page of the magazine. "Where is he?" she asked into the magazine.

"I don't know."

"What are you going to tell him about?"

"I don't know."

Not looking up from her reading, she raised her arm and pointed. "There's stationery in the nightstand beside the bed. In the drawer."

The bedcovers were in a heap. There, splayed upon the white sheet, were Jen's black silk panties. My fingers felt foreign to me. Jen called.

"David? David. There's a man here."

The man stood framed by the open doorway, head down, swaying slightly from side to side. The outside light above and behind cast his face in black shadow. He was a slight man, not much bigger than me.

"You want gas?" I asked.

"Walkin'," he said. He looked up at me. "Youse open for business, right?"

"He ain't here," I said. "Won't be back till after closing."

The man sauntered unsteadily into the room. He looked at Jen as if she'd suddenly materialized before him. "Jeeze, kid," he said. "She your girlfriend?"

"I said he ain't here."

"Ain't that a shame." He looked at Jen. Smiled.

"Ain't no liquor here neither," I said.

"You're wrong about that, kiddo." He reached inside his coat pocket.

Brought out a small silver-plated revolver. "Let's sit down. I'm tired and thirsty." He pointed the gun at me and spoke to Jen. "That means you, doll." As she rounded the counter and crossed to the small table, he performed a mocking little shuffle, his wolfish eyes cartoonlike. "Damn. Look at that mouth, kid. You can't buy lips like that in Jersey." Jen wouldn't look at the man. He affected a southern drawl. "Now don't y'all fret. I don't mean no harm. I'm just in need of a little hospitality, that's all. We're all friends here." He returned to his own voice. "You," he said to me, "bring the lady and me a bottle of that bootleg booze, the good stuff."

"Ain't got none, I told you."

A look of contemptuous surprise flashed across his face. "No booze? Well, well, well. Let me just see what we can do about that." He gently rested the pistol on the table, lifted a pint bottle from inside his jacket, then ceremoniously offered it to Jen. "Help yourself, darlin'." Jen wouldn't look at him. "Name's Rico," he said, offering his hand. Jen didn't take it. I eyed the pistol on the table. "And you and me, we're gonna be friends." He laid his hand over Jen's and spoke in a lyrical childlike voice: "Now. I. Said. Have. A. Drink. Of. That. Whiskey."

Jen unscrewed the cap and tilted the bottle up to her lips. When he reached to force the bottle higher, I went for the gun. His right elbow harpooned my left eye. Jen screamed. I floated upon the cold cement floor, feeling blood swell my cheek. When my vision cleared, I saw the pistol only inches from my face. "Sit," he said. He pushed the chair out with his foot. "That's a good boy."

He pointed at the bottle. Jen took a pull, her face contorting then retching. Looking over at me, he reached for the bottle and drank in three short jerky hits. He turned the pistol on me. "This one," he said to Jen, "he's a regular hero, ain't he? Yes, I do believe he is. Your little bumpkin in shining armor, he deserves something special, don't you think, sugar lips?" He looked at me and smiled like a circus clown, his yellow teeth spanning the width of his face. He pressed his hand to my shoulder. "Don't we all, brother, don't we all. History of war? Man goes off to fight, leaves his girl to cheat. The bitch. He comes home a regular hero. Comes back to get some of that candy he's been missing, been fightin' for. Ain't that right, sugar? Now this regular hero, the one here with the swollen up eye, he deserves something special. And what would that be?" He drank, this time slow and long. With mechanical deliberateness, he set the bottle before him and brought down his eyes upon Jen. "Unbutton that blouse for your hero lover."

Jen looked at me. Disbelief begat terror begat pleading.

"Now would be good," he said. The man sat at attention, pressing his rigid back against the wooden chair and slowly folded his arms across his chest, the pistol leveled at my eye. He looked from Jen to me, then back at Jen. "Well?" He drew in a deep labored breath, nodded in apparent disbelief, and slowly released the breath with a deep sigh. Then he slammed the pistol butt against my ear.

For a few seconds, I was out. He fisted my collar. "You're missing it, kid," he said, heaving me up into my chair. I sat head down, both palms on the table to steady myself, feeling that I might fall left or right. "Yummy, yummy," he said.

"David?" Jen said. I looked up at her. She had loosened the first button. Her fingers rested on the second one. "Look at me, David, like he ain't here. If you don't, I'll cry. Don't make me cry, David."

The clown-faced man drank as Jen opened her blouse. In a limp-wristed cranking motion he rotated the gun. "Now, get rid of that little white bra, sweetheart." Again, he laid his free hand on my shoulder. "What's hidden under those little white ice cream cones? You've never seen this before, have you, kiddo? But you want to, don't you? You do. I know you do. Me, too. I want to. You and me boy, we're gonna see what candy's on this stick."

Jen spoke in a whisper as the bra fell away. "I'm looking at you, David, only at you. I ain't giving him the satisfaction. You are all I see."

"Ahhh," the man said. "That's so sweet." He tilted his head to one side. Conducted his extended inspection. "Well, now. That's more like it. Ain't it, squirt? If them puppies are for sale, I'll take the ones with the brown nose." He turned to me. "Damn, hero. I always said everything over a mouthful is wasted. But one of them little things could put your eye out, don't you think?"

My fist caught him square in the mouth, and he fell straight back in his chair. He lay on his back, still in the chair. But he didn't let go the revolver. He pulled back its hammer and slowly rose to his feet. "You know the last words of a dead hero?" He ran the back of his hand over his bleeding lip and pressed his face close to mine. "I'll tell you what he says!" He held the gun in his right hand, punched my swollen eye with his left fist. I fell back but I did not fall. "I'll tell you what he says!" I went down with the second punch. My face was on fire. My arms and legs were not

38

my own. "Nothin'. That's what the dead hero says."

The sound of a car horn drifted in from the gas pumps. Then blew a second time. A blurred ghostly image of the man backed toward the door. "Don't you move," he said, waving the pistol at me. "Don't you fuckin' move. I ain't done with you." He shouted out the door, signaling to the driver to shove off. "Get outta here, you bum!" Somewhere a telephone rang. And rang again. Outside someone shouted a curse at the man. When the man glanced back at the driver, Jen made for the phone. The man pointed the gun at her. "You!" he shouted, then looked outside, then back at Jen.

"You bastard!" she screamed. She lifted the phone. The man jammed the pistol into his pocket and ran out into the night.

* * *

I sat on the stoop smoking. Sounds that entered my left ear seemed to come from under water. My eye was nearly swollen shut, but the bleeding from my mouth and nose had stopped. From way off, I saw headlights. Bill skidded into the station lot, flung open his door, and ran toward me. He didn't speak as he rushed past calling to her. Jen answered from their apartment. In less than a minute, he was back, something heavy and L-shaped in the brown paper bag he held.

"Here," he said, handing me the keys to the Ford. I was too young for a license, but I'd been driving Mr. Wills's truck for two years. When I opened the driver's side door, I saw the shovel, its face and handle stained with red river clay, the soiled coveralls and the muddy boots in the back. "Jen said he was on foot," Bill said.

"That's right," I said.

"You know where we're headed, don't you?" Bill said.

"Yes," I said. The man had only one place to go, the base, and there was only one road to get him there. Bill lit a cigarette. I watched the road but could feel his eyes moving over my battered face.

"You pull up beside him, slow, like you're offering him a ride. You understand? Till then, keep your speed at thirty-five. Look out for the law."

The road was dark. The night cold. The shovel in the back trembled like a divining rod. "You're gonna kill him, ain't you, Bill?"

"Yes. Yes, I most certainly am."

"Good," I said.

I was not angry, and I was not afraid. Instead I felt a great emptiness was about to be filled, that somehow what was to happen had been waiting for me all of my short life. For three years I'd stood alone at my father's bedside daring myself not to look away from his shrinking, fading figure, arms like the limbs of a sapling, fingers as thin as chicken's feet, eyes receding a little slower than the sockets that held them; I alone there looking upon him, grieving, my heart spilling over with repentance and terror, thinking of the sweating and crying at brush revivals, the wailing in foreign tongues, then seeing before me as I stood at his bedside his sheets erupt into the flames of hell, aching most for what I did not possess, a voice to pray to God to wash away my father's sins and my own, certain only that God looked down upon me there, alone at my father's side, God above waiting, waiting as I stood watching my father die. And all that was given to me, all that I had to take away with me was the hot blood of my father's pride, hard fierce pride. And now pride rushed in to fill that empty place inside of me.

"You need to say what you're going to do when this is over, David. When you get back to your mama's. I've got to know. And what you tell me is what you've got to do. You understand?" Bill looked at me. He wasn't talking to a boy now.

"I'm writin' a letter."

"I mean as soon as you get home."

"I'm writin' a letter to my brother."

"Where is he now?"

"I don't know."

"Are you going to tell him about everything?"

"Yes."

In the mirror, a speeding car closed in on us. "That the law?" I asked. Bill didn't answer. Seconds later, painfully bright, predatory headlights filled the inside of the Ford as the car lurched near our bumper then fell back as if readying to strike again. "Steady," Bill said. "If they ain't too drunk, they'll pass us." The driver laid heavy on his horn, producing a long sustained blast. In the mirror I saw the distorted face of a shouting passenger leaning outside his window. Then the bright lights shifted to the other lane. A chorus of slurred curses roared past. As the car rounded the curve ahead, it swung fully into the left lane and disappeared.

"We're close now," Bill said.

40

We crossed the Neuse River and began to climb. When we topped the hill, I saw the headlights of the speeding car in the distance. In the spread of those headlights stood the silhouette of a man on the side of the road, holding out his thumb. The red brake lights of the car flickered, then lit up. The car slid to a stop. The man leaned into the window of the passenger's side.

"Slow down," Bill said. "They ain't giving him a ride. They ain't got room. They're all drunk. They're just fuckin' with him. Slow way down. They're gonna leave him for us." Bill pulled the long-barreled pistol from the brown bag. "Go on, you bastards," he murmured. "Git." He looked over at me. "When I crank down the window, you look away. Understand? Don't look."

Ahead, the car's rear door swung open. "No," Bill whispered. The man climbed into the back seat.

"What do we do?" I said.

"Son of a bitch," Bill said. The car ahead threw gravel and burned rubber as it fishtailed onto the highway. "Damn it to hell," he said, slowly squeezing and releasing the handle of the pistol.

I thought, We could kill 'em all, Bill. Soak the car with gasoline and send them all to hell.

Bill set the gun on the seat beside him. "Ain't nothing to do. Pull over," he said. "I'll drive."

* * *

Our tenant house was dark. Bill shut off the headlights but left the engine idling.

"What are you going to tell your mama about that eye?" He touched his finger to my chin. I tilted away as he examined my face.

"Won't be the first time," I said.

He offered me a cigarette, and I took it. "I 'preciate what you done for Jen." He didn't know and I never told him. "What's he like, your brother?"

"I don't know."

"What you done for Jen—"

"I'll take that shovel, your boots, and them coveralls," I said. "They'll be under Wills's packhouse when you want them, when the law's done."

Bill pressed out his cigarette butt in the ashtray then looked away.

Slowly, he ran his thick fingers through his hair, then reached for the pack in his shirt pocket. He bowed his head against the window and spoke to the out yonder. "Don't even know his name."

"Jim."

"Where you going to mail it, that letter?"

"I ain't. I don't know where he is. I'll hold on to it till he gets home."

"Good." Bill turned and looked at me. "Maybe that will bring him good luck, give him a good reason to get back in one piece."

"Maybe."

Bill retrieved a bottle from under the front seat. He took a pull and offered it to me. I declined.

"If I ever see that guy again," I said, "I'll know him. We'll finish this."

"You won't see him again. He won't be back. What's done is done. Ain't no satisfaction comes for some things, David." He offered another cigarette. I declined. A light appeared in the kitchen. "What are you going to tell your brother?"

"That I love him and miss him."

"He'll need to hear that," Bill said.

"No more than I'll need to say it," I said.

The Trouble with Eve
Robert Flynn

America was in the third year of a world war. Young Carter was in his first year of confusion over girls. Everything they did was so . . . confusing. When a girl said he had long eyelashes, he rubbed them, not sure whether she meant a loose one was falling into his eye or that he was a sissy. He was sure that "You have nice hair" really meant "Why don't you wash it sometime?" and that "cutest freckles" really meant "Did all of them survive a washcloth?"

When girls looked at him, he couldn't meet their eyes, afraid of what his face would show. When they smiled at him, he gaped at their lips. Why were their mouths so . . . different? When they laughed, he fled. He also fled the presence of Clarissa for fear of what he would do. Fall on the ground and kiss her feet probably.

Clarissa Bowman. Girls had such pretty names. Clarissa. Bowman. He tasted the words with his mouth. Clarissa Bowman. He was given his mother's maiden name, Young. Young Carter. It made him want to cry. Why would anyone name a baby *Young*? It was bad enough being called *kid* when you were fourteen and the country was at war. New teachers called him *Carter Young* until he corrected them. Men said his name sounded like a law firm or a funeral parlor.

He had tried to get his friends to call him *Car*; or *Sandy*, because his hair was almost red; or *Rabbit*, because he had long legs and big teeth and when he got a G.I. haircut, his ears looked too big for his head. Even *Freckles* or *Red* was better than *Young*. He wished boys could change their names like girls when they got married. He would change his first name. It drove him to despair that *Young* would be carved on his gravestone. Maybe the war would last until he was old enough to serve and he could be a hero and pretend he was dead and pick a whole new

43

name.

Young Carter stood outside The Corner Drug looking at the wonders in the window—ointments, liniments, corn plasters, something called a *truss*, a rubber water bottle with a long hose attached—pondering what he had just heard in the Church of Christ Bible School. Young went to the Baptist Church with his parents. But all three churches in Chillicothe had summer Bible School and he went to all three, hoping Clarissa would attend one of them. Also, because his father said he didn't want Young to spend the summer following his mother around complaining about his name.

The Church of Christ preacher had taken the older boys into a separate room and told them that Eve had led Adam into sin and that they were to avoid Forbidden Fruit. Young had glanced at the other boys, but they solemnly stared at their feet. Afterwards he asked Harold what he thought. Harold was supposed to be smart although he went to the Church of Christ.

"Woman was the first to sin, the last to repent," Harold said.

"What is forbidden fruit?"

"You know," Harold said, pretending he knew and so should everyone else. Young waited. "Girls who wear red lipstick and stuff like that."

That was a question he was going to have to ask his mother, Young thought, catching Clarissa's reflection in the drug store window. Too late, she had already passed. He berated himself for worrying about forbidden fruit and missing a glimpse of Clarissa. Then he saw her reflection as she passed again, slower this time. He studied her as she passed, then turned to stare as she walked away. Only she didn't walk away. When she got past the window, she turned her head and caught him ogling her walking parts.

Young returned to his scrutiny of the corn plasters, pretending he hadn't seen her.

"Do you like me?" she asked.

He couldn't even look at her reflection. All the blood in his body crowded into his head so that he couldn't think. His tongue swelled to fill his mouth and his throat constricted. He locked his knees that threatened to swoon so he could kiss her toes. "Yes," he croaked, unable to swallow.

"What?"

"Yes," he tried again.

"Do you want to go out with me?"

44

The roots of his hair blazed. He nodded the head that was trying to contain the brain that skittered around inside. She waited for a verbal answer. "Okay." Still he could not look at her for fear that his eyes would bulge in open-mouth adoration.

"Do you have a car?"

Young's heart sank into his unusually crowded jeans. He had failed the test. "No," he admitted.

"Can you drive?" she asked doubtfully.

"I can drive," he said, pretending anger. He could drive, sort of, although neither his parents nor the law allowed it. Anyone could drive.

"My brother has a car we can use, but we'll need stamps."

He was pleased that she asked admirers to prove their patriotism before going out with them, but he wasn't sure how much patriotism she required. "I buy a fifty-cent war stamp every Friday, even when school is out," he said, hoping that counted. He had already accumulated enough stamps for two bonds. He hazarded a glimpse at her face.

"Gas ration stamps, silly," she said.

"Oh. I don't have a ration book."

"Your father does, doesn't he? Get some from him. Wait for me across the street at seven o'clock. Don't ring the doorbell. I'll pretend I'm visiting my girlfriend. When mother goes inside, we'll get my brother's car."

"Where's your brother?"

"He'll be at work. Be sure to bring the stamps. We'll have to push the car out of the drive so Mom doesn't hear it start."

Dating was a lot more complicated than he had imagined. And scarier. His father walked to work and home for dinner, and unless the weather was bad they walked to church. Because the bank sold war bonds, Dad said he had to be stricter about rationing than anyone else. Clarissa poked a finger into his chest. "Seven o'clock. Gas stamps. And money," she added leaving nothing to chance.

"How . . . what . . . where are we going?" he stammered.

"You're taking me to a dance in the McCarty barn, and it costs fifty cents to get in. Fifty cents each. And I'll have to have one Delaware Punch because I'll be thirsty and another to show my girlfriends that I am not a cheap date. And whatever you want for yourself. And some gas so my brother won't say anything. And don't forget to open the car door for me."

He tried to do the math with a brain that didn't want to compute but to lie down and gaze at the clouds in the strange world he had entered. A dollar to get in, at least four bits for gas, a dime for drinks, unless they charged more at the barn. Two dollars to be safe. "Maybe we should just—"

"I am not walking. I would be humiliated. What if my friends saw me? What if someone thought we were too young to drive? God, I would just die."

Hope that she would call the whole thing off and let him remain untroubled warred with the dream of unknown adventure. "What if your brother suspects something?" he asked.

"That's why we need the gas, silly. He won't say anything if there's gas in the tank. It's on empty now. There's a Humble station a couple of blocks away. I'll steer and you can push." She felt his thin arm. "I bet you're really strong."

"Yeah," agreed short-haired Samson.

She poked him in the chest again. "Seven o'clock. Stamps. Money. And don't be late."

She swished her way down the street, pretending not to notice that he gaped after her. A car stopped and the passenger door flew open. She pretended not to notice. "Hop in," he heard a male voice say. An older male voice. Maybe sixteen.

"I'm not going anywhere until I have a milk shake; it is so hot." She turned and looked at Young. "And then I'm going straight home," she said, blessing Young with a smile. She bent over, looked into the car, then turned to Young and nodded before getting in.

Young watched them drive away. Everything she did puzzled him. She was in his grade at school, but he doubted he would ever be that mysterious. He didn't even have secrets.

Where was he going to get two dollars? And gas stamps? He had 50¢ for a war stamp, a quarter for church, a dime left of his allowance.

"Harold!" he yelled at a boy passing on a bicycle. "Wait." Harold wore thick glasses, hadn't grown into his ears, and tried too hard to make friends. "Can you loan me some money?"

"I can let you have a dime," Harold said.

"I need fifteen cents." That and his money would get them in the dance. "Is that all you have?"

"It's all I have to loan."

Harold wasn't as eager for friends as Young had hoped. "How much will you give me for my funny book collection?"

"To look at or to keep?"

"To keep."

"What do you have?"

"Superman, Captain Marvel, True Comics"—his father made him buy those—"Katzenjammer Kids, Mighty Mouse, G-Men, Archie—"

"Fifty cents."

"I have to have a dollar. And a fifteen-cent loan."

Harold hitched up his glasses by wrinkling his nose. "Okay, but you have to give me everything you have."

"Scout's honor."

"No. I search your room and I ask your mother if she has any funny books I can borrow . . ."

"Okay."

". . . a week after you give me all you have. And she better not tell me to look in your room."

"Okay, okay." No wonder no one liked Harold, Young thought as he took the money from him. "I need the dollar by five o'clock."

"Seven," Harold said.

"Six," Young countered.

"We eat at six."

"Six thirty and a one-funny-book fine for every minute you're late." Two dollars. That would buy gas and get them into the dance. He still needed ration stamps.

He hoped to catch Dad in a good mood when he went to the bank, but Doris warned Young, "They can't get the books to balance." Young went in the office and sat down. He loved Dad but wished he were a soldier or maybe a policeman.

"In a minute," Dad said, punching numbers in an adding machine. Betty watched over his shoulder. "Okay, run those and see what you come up with." Dad handed Betty strips of paper and got his hat to walk home for dinner. "Did you buy a stamp?" Dad asked, and Young had to give fifty cents to Doris for the most unwilling, therefore patriotic, stamp he had ever bought.

How was he going to tell Clarissa he didn't have enough money to take her to the dance? Maybe Dad would give him an advance on his allowance. And gas stamps. When he asked for an advance, Young got the lecture he expected. "The reason your mother and I give you an allowance, for chores that you should do for free as a family member, is to teach you financial responsibility. And giving you an advance after you have squandered your allowance is not going to do that. And I don't expect you to spend the money we gave you for church on yourself. That would be stealing from God. Mom and I might never know; but God will, and so will you."

"Yes sir," he said. Young had expected to lose that round. "Dad, what are gas stamps?"

"Gas is rationed so that civilians don't waste it for frivolous reasons when it's needed to fight the war."

"How can I get some?"

"Don't be dumb, Young. You know how much that annoys me. You don't own a car."

"I need some stamps for a friend."

"Young Carter, if you sell any kind of ration stamps, you will be betraying your country. If you're that kind of boy, I don't want to know it."

"I won't sell them, I promise." He couldn't tell his father he needed them to take a girl to a dance. He was pretty sure his folks didn't approve of girls or dances.

"You're going to give them to some friend, and the two of you are going to drive around town wasting gas and looking for some mischief you can get into."

Young knew if he asked again, he would not be allowed to go out that night. They walked in silence. Mom knew almost everything and he preferred her answers, but he needed to get Dad's mind off gas stamps. "Dad, what is forbidden fruit?"

"Gas stamps," Dad said.

Young frowned. What did that have to do with red lipstick? His father turned to look at him. Young was almost as tall as his father, but he knew he would never feel that big. "If we forbid you to do something," Dad said, "like go to the picture show on Sunday, and it's something you really want to see, that's forbidden fruit. I guess anything that you want to do that you know you shouldn't do is forbidden fruit."

Young wanted to ask about girls and red lipstick and kissing, but he was pretty sure he knew the answer. "At Bible School the preacher said girls—"

"Don't start troubling yourself over girls. You have the rest of your life for that. If you need a dime for the picture show, get a hoe and edge

48

the driveway. You shouldn't expect to get paid for things like that. You should pitch in because you're part of the family."

He wasn't being given a choice of edging or not edging. He was given a choice of getting a dime for doing it or being told to do it. After dinner, when his father went back to the bank, he got a hoe and edged the driveway. When he finished, he went to his room to get his funny books together, even the one about Guadalcanal that was his favorite. He read them one last time waiting for supper.

Dad came home, told him he had done a good job edging, and gave him a dime. While his father bathed and his mother fixed supper, Young slipped into his parents' bedroom, a place as frightening to him and as unfamiliar as the preacher's private office. He pulled open the chest of drawers; and there in the first drawer were ration books, loose change, scattered keys, a pocketknife, several pencils, and a box of something that looked like rubbers but couldn't be because his folks wouldn't do anything like that.

He counted the change. Sixty-five cents. If he took it all, Dad was sure to notice; but it would guarantee no embarrassments at the dance even if Delaware Punch was a dime, and he would replace any money he had left over. He would repay God later. How many gas stamps would he need? He forgot to ask Dad. One for each tankful? He took two to be sure.

After supper he put on clean jeans and a t-shirt and took the comics out on the porch to wait for Harold. He didn't have a watch so every five or ten minutes he went in the house to check the clock until his mother told him to stay in or stay out.

He accused Harold of being late so that Harold would know that he couldn't get away with anything, but didn't argue because he was afraid he would be late. He ran all the way to Clarissa's street and walked fast down it in case she was waiting. When he reached the corner, he looked at her house but could see no one in a window or at the screen door. He walked slowly down the street this time, then waited longer on the corner.

Was he more conspicuous walking up and down the street or standing under a tree, pretending to watch the clouds? He stood under a tree. He had changed trees three times before Clarissa came outside and walked slowly across the street. He started toward her, but she walked past telling him, "Stay there." She knocked on a door, was greeted by a friend, waved to her mom, and went inside. Young wondered if he was supposed to knock on the door of the house she went in. Clarissa emerged from the side of a house three doors down and signaled to him to follow.

They walked to the corner, crossed the street, and walked around the block, back to the alley beside her house where the car was parked. He tried to open the car door for her, but she whispered, "Not now, silly." She helped him push the car out of the alley, then jumped in, quietly closed the door, and steered the car down the street. He lowered his shoulder into the back of the car and began the pilgrimage to Humble at least three blocks away. While pushing, he remembered that he didn't know how to dance. He wondered if he should have told her that.

He had pushed the car as far as he could, and Clarissa had gotten out to help when Mr. Parker from the church came by in his pickup and offered to push them. Clarissa moved to the passenger's side so he could steer. Getting behind the wheel made Young feel big; but he knew that Sunday in front of Young's folks, Mr. Parker would say something about him driving and ask who the girl was.

"You made me scuff my heels," Clarissa said. "I had to borrow them from Linda, and I don't like her, and now they're scuffed."

"Fill her up," he said at the gas station, trying to look contrite and big at the same time.

"You're supposed to let me tear them out of the book," the attendant said taking the stamps and bending down to look at Clarissa who had folded her arms across her chest and looked cross. A strand of wet hair was stuck to her forehead. He pumped gas for a while and came back to the window. "You don't have enough stamps to fill it. Do you have any B stamps?"

Young counted out the change for the gas. The car wouldn't start.

"Turn on the key," Clarissa said. "Choke it. Give it some gas. Now you've flooded it." He wondered if when she grew up, she was going to be a teacher.

After a lot of cranking he got the car started and lurched away, aware that Clarissa rolled her eyes. She waited too late to tell him where to turn and when she did, he hit the curb and killed the engine. "I thought you said you could drive," she said.

"I can," he said. But when he tried to restart the car, nothing happened. He stared at the useless starter on the floor of the car.

"Look under the hood and see what's wrong," she said, and had to show him how to open the hood. She shook her head as he stared at the innards of the car as mystified as if he were examining human innards to see why it wouldn't breathe. "It must be the battery," she said. "Take it to Humble and get it recharged. There's a wrench in the trunk."

He removed the battery from the car, surprised at how heavy it was, and started back to the station. He hoped recharging batteries wasn't expensive. "I'll go with you," she said. "I can't sit in the car like I've been jilted. I hope no one sees me walking."

Charging the battery took a while, and he had to pay for a Cream Soda Clarissa took out of the cooler. "Have you seen Betty since school was out?" he asked.

She flipped her wrist. "I don't want to talk about kid things."

What did grownups talk about? Religion probably; that's what his folks talked about. That and the war and the weather. He didn't know anything about weather so he began with the war. Clarissa hated war and war comics and war movies. So there.

That left religion although Young wasn't sure he should talk about religion while carrying stolen money. And he wasn't certain they hadn't stolen the car. "Where do you go to church?"

"I don't."

Young's jaw snapped. He had never known anyone who didn't go to church. "You believe in God, don't you?"

"I believe in Jesus, and I believe in Christ."

"Some people think they're the same," Young pointed out.

"I don't trouble myself with what other people think."

"You believe the Bible, don't you?"

"I believe an angel came to Jesus and told him to go look in a secret cave, and when he went there he found the Bible written on gold. I'd like to see a Bible written on gold. That would be worth a lot of money."

Young didn't know that story, but there were a lot of stories they didn't tell at the Baptist Church. He wondered if she knew about forbidden fruit. "Do you know the story of Adam and Eve?" She looked doubtful. "They were the first man and woman, and they lived in this garden until Eve ate—"

"She was in this wonderful place," Clarissa interrupted. "There was no boring war, no algebra, no mother telling her she couldn't wear red lipstick—"

"It was perfect," Young said. "They weren't troubled by anything."

"It had snakes so she had to leave. I can't stand snakes."

"I think they were driven out."

51

"Adam was thrown out because he ate fruit and threw the seeds on the ground. He trashed the place. Like my brother. Eve would have left anyway."

Everything she said confounded him, yet nothing seemed to trouble her. They were in the same class at school, but he doubted he would ever be that smart. "What do you think forbidden fruit is?" he asked.

"Oysters. Mother says I can't try them until I'm eighteen."

"How do you know you'll like them?"

"If they weren't good, they wouldn't be forbidden, silly." She opened a tiny purse, so small he hadn't noticed it before, and took out a tube and mirror. He watched open-mouthed as her pursed lips turned crimson. He had never seen anything so fascinating before, not even the bullet-riddled car that Bonnie and Clyde had been killed in that Dad had given him a nickel to see.

She turned and smiled at him, and he blushed and looked away. "Girls like to be looked at," she said.

He never knew that before. Every time he passed a group of girls, they turned and looked at him like he had bombed Pearl Harbor. He determined that Clarissa would not be a cheap date. He would buy her two, maybe three Cream Sodas, even if he had to go without. He carried the battery back to the car and hoped it started. If the battery had to be charged again, he wouldn't have enough money to buy her anything. The car started. He backed away from the curb and negotiated the turn, and when they got to the barn, Clarissa said, "Drop me off in front. I don't want to get these heels muddy."

After opening the door for her, he parked where he wouldn't have to drive between two cars close together or back up to turn around. When he paid so they could go inside the barn, she said, "Do you jitterbug?"

"Not exactly." She rolled her eyes, making sure he saw. "Get me a Nehi," she said, turning to smile at an older boy who took her hand and led her to the dance floor. She danced three dances with older boys before she returned, introducing Young Carter to an adult and manly passion that divided childhood from adolescence. He had never hated a female before.

He had drunk her Nehi and had to get her another. He returned to where she sat between two boys and she gasped, "Oh, my God." He looked down and saw that liquid from the battery had eaten holes in the front of his jeans and underpants. "Oh, my God," she wailed again. "How could

52

you do this to me?"

"It must be from the battery," he tried to explain. He had ruined his best jeans because of her brother's battery.

"Don't even think about asking me to dance," she declared, looking at the boys sitting beside her for confirmation of her horror.

"I . . . I think we better leave," he said.

"Leave? I can't leave now. I have hardly danced at all. What will my friends think? They'll think I'm leaving to go park with you."

He thought she put unnecessary emphasis on *you.* "What am I supposed to do?" he asked.

"Well, for one thing don't stand in front of me."

"I think I had better go home."

"Do not think of driving my brother's car; I will call the sheriff."

"How will I get home?"

"Call your parents."

Might as well tell him to call the Marines. "I guess I had better go," he said. "Could you . . . walk in front of me until I get outside?"

She heaved a sigh that would blow chalk off a blackboard. "If I ever live down this night . . ."

Once he was safe outside, she turned on him. "You have ruined my evening. Maybe my entire life. I hope I never see you again. Do not ask me to your church. And, sweetheart, don't ask me out again. I don't care how many gas stamps you have."

Young started for home knowing that tomorrow—maybe tonight— he would have a lot of questions to answer. Questions about stolen money and gas stamps and his ruined jeans. Questions he did not want to answer directly because his parents wouldn't understand the kind of world he had fallen into. He had never had secrets before. Now he didn't know how to keep them.

He longed for the day he would be an adult. When everything was simple. Right or wrong. Forbidden until you were eighteen or forbidden forever. Then he would know whether he wanted to see Clarissa again. And what he would do if she asked him for gas stamps.

She had called him *sweetheart.* And he would never forget the way she looked painting her lips. He wondered if he would steal stamps to kiss those lips. The thought sent him running for what he remembered as home.

The house was dark. His parents were asleep. He was alone with his thoughts. Clarissa. Clarissa Bowman. Sweetheart. He tried to make it sound sweet. Sweet heart.

Young and True
Marianne Gingher

It's the night of my mom's thirteenth wedding anniversary—except Mom's not completely married anymore. She and my dad split up about a year ago, divorce pending. And we've all pretty much adjusted; but given one bizarre circumstance—which I'll get to in a sec—it's not exactly the best of times, this unlucky, uncelebrated anniversary night: Mom and captive teenaged daughter slumped together on the den couch, watching re-runs on Nickelodeon. Zeroland in the fun department, you might say. So here comes the risqué circumstance: Mom's nine and a half months pregnant, I kid you not.

We're just *relaxing* you'd say, if you felt weirdly euphemistic, when suddenly Mom gasps and puts one hand on her blimpo self. "Wouldn't it just be the icing on the un-anniversary cake if the old un-wife here went into labor this very night? Because, guess what? Ouch!" She sits up straighter. "I think I feel an attack of irony coming on."

"You shouldn't iron in your condition."

"Shhh," she says, tilting her head as if she's listening for proof. "Nope. False alarm. Gas pains—I think."

But she's always talking as if she believes this baby is never going to materialize, because it shouldn't materialize, given her unwifely circumstances. She's almost got me believing that it won't come, too, got me believing to the dangerous point of relief when she says she felt a gas pain. She cocks an ear toward the great dune of baby as if hearing a contraction is believing one. "Well I am a little rusty. I haven't felt a contraction in about fourteen years," she says.

Yep, fourteen years, thirteenth anniversary. You can be an air brain in math and figure that one out. The old hippie had me out of wedlock, too. Then, on my first birthday, she and Dad got married—something to do with Dad's career taking off and income tax breaks for married couples.

And if you could see our family album after that, you'd swear that it had been painted by Norman Rockwell. Mom even stopped weaving feathers and beads into her braids. Dad chopped off his Fu Manchu. I'm girly-girled up like Little Bo Peep.

Mom nudges me off the sofa and colonizes its entire length. She's got that balmy look of que sera, sera. "What did I ever see in George Maharis?" she says to the TV. She's tuned into an ancient rerun of *Route 66* in which two buddies bum around the USA in a spiffy Corvette Stingray. Dad used to own an old Stingray. "When I was your age, I thought George Maharis hung the moon," Mom says. George is one of the stars of the show: the dark, taut, weasel-faced dreamboat hothead. His friendlier sidekick has freckles and a burr haircut. When things get tense, the sidekick's jaw merely corrugates with tension. But when George gets angry, he slams the Stingray's doors and peels a wheel when he floorboards the gas. "I just lived to watch *Route 66*," Mom says. "My friend Peggy Twitchell would come over to spend Friday night and we'd glue our faces to the TV. We'd kiss the screen when George came on. Do you think George is cute?"

"He reminds me of Dad," I say.

"But Dad's blonde."

"The personality. Wired."

"I've been attracted to that sort of man my whole life," Mom says. "What makes a woman that dumb?"

Poor Mom. She's wearing the ugliest dress in the universe. It's khaki and as big as a circus tent.

A wine commercial comes on. A man and a woman eating dinner on a castle balcony. There are violins, a ferocious sunset. The wine unspools from its bottle in slow motion like a gleaming purple rope, coiling into glasses. For a while, the man and the woman would rather kiss than drink. "Sheesh," Mom says. "Do people really act that way in public—anywhere? For very long? Even rich people with no worries? Pisses me off that you're supposed to think that such a life is possible. Even with wine."

"It's just a commercial," I say. We watch the man and woman holding hands, sipping their wine after finally disentangling themselves.

"I never even had a honeymoon like that."

"Why don't we play some Scrabble or cards, Mom?"

"I don't feel like it."

"You love Scrabble."

A Shared Voice

"It's too complicated," she says, frowning. "I can't play Scrabble and be pregnant at the same time. Shhh. George is back on." He's seated in the driver's seat of the Stingray with his arm around a pert brunette. She's fussing with her hair, tucking curls into the chiffon scarf so that her hairdo won't blow when George accelerates and they go rocketing along old Route 66.

"I'd better tell you something, sweetheart," the woman says to George. "I'm married."

"That does it," Mom says and makes a cross with her arms the way people do to fend off vampires. "Where's the remote?"

I find a baseball game on Channel 9 and pause to watch the pitcher's wind-up, the agile rotation of thigh and crickety kick of his leg.

"I didn't know you liked baseball."

"I like their butts in those tight uniforms," I say. "I could watch their butts all day."

She laughs, but now she's watching their butts, too. "I like men, honey," she says after a while. "In spite of my disappointments, I like men very much. I would never do a number on you concerning men." She reaches over and takes my hand. She gives me that tender, you poor little father-abandoned lamb look. "You've started biting your fingernails again, True."

Yep, my name's True, and don't rub it in because I live with it daily like some oppressive moral.

"Honey, where did you get those ratty old shorts? They are plumb piteous."

I grin and twang the sprung neck of the piteous t-shirt that matches the shorts. "Why, at the Goodwill store in Old Slobovia, of course."

"You're too pretty to walk around looking like a bum, honey. You've got to take more pride in the way you look. When I was your age, I wouldn't have been caught dead without fixing my hair and putting on lipstick. When did you last comb your hair?"

"Let's walk down to the Yum Yum Café and get ice cream," I suggest.

"The Yum Yum? Honey, I can't walk that far."

"Tell you what, Mom-o-rama" I say, "Let's jam you into the new baby stroller and wheel you down to the Yum Yum, take the stroller for a little test drive."

"I'd bust it," she says. We both laugh pretty hard imagining the

57

spindly little stroller collapsing, crushed flat beneath Mom's avalanche.

"God almighty," she says, "I feel like the hugest pregnant person alive." Then she burrows her gaze into me. "I know I'm ruining your life."

"Stop it."

"No, listen to me. I want you to stop hovering, honey, and get out of this damn incubator. Go call up Young or something."

"I'm busy."

"Call him, but comb your hair first," she pleads, and I don't blame her. The last time I saw myself in a mirror I had to admit I was starting to look like Huckleberry Finn.

Young Carter is the boyfriend I would probably have if I were desperate to have a boyfriend—which I'm not. Isn't a boyfriend at my age always a liability? All the time you put into something that isn't going to last. And a boyfriend at a sensitive time like this? Think I'd be so slimy, considering Mom's condition? No thanks, I'm saving my brain for science.

Young and I met in art class—he's a genuine artist, I just signed up for an elective—but we struck up a conversation because of our names. We have adjectives for names, *true* and *young*. Not many people do. I have a friend named Mimi Grumbles; but *grumbles* is a verb, and combined with Mimi, makes a complete (and, we think, funny) sentence. The names True and Young just float blithely along, unattached modifiers that seem to promise something cheerful. A young puppy or a wish come true. But Young and I are both scowlers. Young scowls because he's always concentrating on important thoughts about his art, and I scowl because I just do. Young was named after his father and his father was named after Grandpa Young and Grandpa Young says he hated his name, growing up. So why did he pass it on? He says circumstances often win out over ideals and hangups. But the legacy chain went like this: Grandpa Young hated his name and passed it on to his only son, Young Jr., and Young Jr. hated his name and passed it on to Young the Third who actually liked his name because he was an artist and saw its "metaphorical possibilities." That's really how he talks.

Young the Third, truth to tell, looks a little like George Maharis himself. He's got a sleek, brooding face that when I first met him made me suspect that he was either a poet or a punk. He's sixteen, lanky and tall with a flag of dark hair that he's always wiping out of his eyes. He has gray eyes with flashes of green glitter in them. He has a tattoo of an old-fashioned artist's palette on one shoulder blade—I forget which one

58

because I've only seen him bare-chested one time and that was because he'd taken off his shirt for some messy art thing, not me. We're just good pals, really, comfortable with one another, which does not include groping around, even though Young suggested it once as an experiment. "Just to test the systems, rev our little engines and see if they're in working order," he said.

"I think I'm going to be sick," I said.

He looked a little crestfallen (one of his favorite words, *crestfallen*) but he shut up.

He'd already called me on Mom's anniversary, right before supper, to ask if I'd help him replicate the installation photographed on a postcard he admired. It required driving his ancient Ford Galaxy through a pyramid he'd constructed of old television sets he'd harvested from the dump.

"Can't tonight," I said, "I have to babysit."

"She had it?" he shouted. "Why didn't you call me? Girl or boy? Damn, I hope it was a boy. You all need a guy around that place so you can brush up on your servility."

"No, she hasn't had the baby yet. She's never going to have it. This is the Twilight Zone."

"Oh, I get it," he said. "Wow, you're practicing babysitting. Avant garde!"

"Yep, I'm practicing babysitting," I said. "On Mom."

* * *

So I don't call Young the Third like Mom suggests. I leave her on the sofa reading a dogeared copy of Dr. Spock and mosey into her bedroom and sit on Desert Island—what Mom named her bed—and reach for the phone. Desert Island is piled high with life support supplies: a clutch of bananas (she's big into potassium); some svelte *Vogue* magazines for torture and inspiration; a book on Chinese baby massage techniques; a copy of Scott Peck's *The Road Less Travelled* she read back in college; a fresh, unopened package of Chocolate Pinwheel cookies, the only cookie we both adore. Slowly I punch in Dad and Holly's number, long-distance. When Holly answers, I don't say anything. "Hello? Who's calling, please?" Holly says in that aerobics teacher's voice of hers, a voice as neon elastic as Spandex. I start panting huskily into the mouthpiece. If Holly had ever had a baby, she'd recognize the rhythm as Lamaze. "Hello?" Then she says to Dad, "Roger, I think it's the pervert again." (We have an unlisted number, haha, so my prank's not traceable.) Dad mumbles something to her, probably asks her to give him the phone and he'll handle it, but she doesn't. "Look here, buddyrow, you think you can keep getting away with this, don't you? Well you can't, because—guess what—we've got your number!" Then she slams the phone down.

Buddyrow?

Holly's okay. I don't disapprove of Holly or anything so normal. I feel about as neutral towards Holly as I feel towards Mom's Dustbuster hanging on yonder hook overlooking our ruins. I forget about Holly the same way I forget about the Dustbuster, preferring to simply live around the mess. The mess being Dad's attraction to Holly in the first place and his ditching us about a year ago for her. About two months after he'd left, Holly—in a fit of temporary sanity—threw him out of her hot tub and he ended up slouching home to us just long enough—overnight—to do this hot lava rush on Mom whose heart—she'd sworn this—was supposedly a fireproof brick. Having Dad back illicitly—they were legally separated— immobilized her. It was a case of panic and ecstasy experienced simultaneously. She just wasn't fast enough and got incinerated in her tracks. And all that remained when the ashes cooled and Dad had oozed back to Holly was a tender baby seedling, growing beneath the rubble where the pillar of Mom once stood. So you want to try to tidy up Pompeii with a puny contraption like a Dustbuster? I think of what happened as a valuable history lesson—and who could ever clean up history?

* * *

"True, get the car," Mom calls from the sofa.

I'm about to say, 'But Mom, I've never gotten the car in my life. I don't drive; I don't even have a Learner's Permit and don't want one; I'm only fourteen and I hate internal combustion engines' (Dad's a professional race car driver, I forgot to mention that). But there is something about the aerodynamics of Mom's voice that makes me leap off Desert Island.

I jet into the living room and there she lies, stretched out on the sofa, grinning. "I do believe that Goliath here is on his way," Mom says. She looks fourteen herself, radiant, a fool for love.

"No more gas pains?"

"Get the car, True. It feels like I've swallowed the ocean at high tide."

"Not to throw a damper on anything, but you know I don't drive."

"Honey, anybody can drive."

"I'll drive," somebody calls through the screen door, and we both jump. The face on the other side of the screen looks vaguely George Maharis, but it's Young.

"Young!" I race across the room and unhook the screen. Just seeing him there, that gangly aw-shucks slouch of his, makes me weak with relief.

"Let's take my car," he suggests. I hear it idling at the curb.

"Not so fast," Mom says, and heaves herself upright. "We've got plenty of time. Been there, done that. Trust me." She waddles off to take a shower and we sit down to wait.

"Is this normal?" Young asks. I just give him my goony look.

She takes a long shower. We get to see the Braves win the game in the ninth inning; although sitting beside Young, the Braves seem like old men and I'm not watching their butts.

"I'm going to braid my hair this time," Mom calls cheerfully from the bedroom. "I didn't braid it when I had you, True, and after writhing on the delivery table for eighteen hours I gave myself dreadlocks."

We listen to her primp, the drawers of her dresser popping open and clunking shut. It's the sound of somebody being picky, primping for a date.

"You nervous?" Young asks me. "I mean, you've never been a sister before."

"I'm practically old enough to be its mother," I say.

"You most certainly are not!" Mom shouts. I forget about her radar ears.

"It was a figure of speech! Could you hurry it up? You're in labor for Pete's sake!"

"I can assure you that nobody named Pete has anything to do with my being in labor!"

We listen to her bam around some more. "Think I ought to go kill the engine?" Young asks.

"Maybe," I say. "Are you going to run out of gas?"

He shrugs.

"Is this the weirdest night or what?"

"I only wish I could figure out a way to conceptualize it," Young says. He's got that artsy, visionary look on his face. I hate when he gets that look. It's a look of exclusivity, of not needing anybody but himself— and subject matter. "I wish," he says, "that I could figure the perfect medium in which to render the peculiarities that have befallen you and your mother tonight."

Why can't I be attracted to a boy who talks plain? Plus, he smells a little bit like eggs.

"You smell like eggs," I say. "Is that egg yolk on your shirt?"

"It was Grandpa Young's idea. We staged an egg fight in his backyard and filmed it."

Grandpa Young is the oldest young person I know. He may even be the youngest, in spite of the fact that he was born in 1929. When he's not helping Young with some art installation, he likes to play video games. One time we got him to play Truth or Dare, and he chose truth and told us the story of the night he began to grow up. That night he'd lied to his father, stolen from his father, sold his soul to the devil in order to take the girl he thought he loved to a dance. It was during the Second World War. A lot was at stake. Who could afford the luxury of innocence? And yet, Grandpa Young had clung to it. He believed that innocence was sustainable. A renewable resource. Without it, there would be no surprise. Even though he went to bed betrayed by the girl, he remembered that she had called him *sweetheart* as she simultaneously insulted him. He'd chosen to believe the best and not the worst of her; believing the best and not the worst throughout his life had, in many peoples' minds, made him a fool.

"Would you rather be old and wise or young and foolish?" Grandpa Young asked me once.

"Old and wise," I told him. "It's a dirty job, but somebody in my family ought to try it."

"Oh dear," he said.

* * *

"So, because you wouldn't drive with me through the towering inferno of TV sets, Grandpa Young and I had the egg fight," Young the Third says.

"Well, I was busy here."

"I see that."

"Don't be pissed off."

"I'm not pissed off. But even if I was, would you care?"

"She'd care," Mom says, waddling forth. "And what do you mean that she wouldn't drive through the towering inferno of TV sets with you? What a wimp!"

Holy guacamoley, she's wearing a brand-new tomato-red tent, a price tag dangling from one sleeve. She's got on flip-flops, and she's painted her toenails gold.

"No big deal," Young says. "She's had more important things on her mind."

Mom's tossed a nightie and a toothbrush in a Food Lion sack. "Just a sec, I'm almost ready," she says. And then she starts kissing everything in the room: the sofa cushions, one by one; the TV set; her copy of *Doctor Spock*; the stupid Dustbuster. "Good-bye, good-bye," she coos. She kisses the lamps, the mantel, the curtains, the Oprah magazine lying on the coffee table. She salaams each of the four walls, then kisses them, too. "And stop giving me that Mom's-flipped-out look, True," she says. "I kissed everything goodbye on the night you were born, too."

She rides upfront in the Galaxy with Young and me. He's tuned in to some raging song on the radio about burning down shopping malls and how, in America, it's illegal to buy beer when you're eighteen, but you're permitted to go to war and vote for any fool who runs for office and Visa yourself into massive debt and marry too young and really ruin your life. She's nodding to the beat. Me, I'm just along for the ride, glad that somebody else is driving. See, I don't want to be the man of the house. I don't.

Just when I'm thanking my lucky stars that the hospital is so close that it would be impossible for Mom to have the baby en route and what a relief it is that Mom seems to be proceeding painlessly out of her Twilight Zone of denial into, well, some realm of anticipatory glee, Mom turns to Young, grinning. "You know something? I would simply love to drive through those television sets with you, Young Carter the Third."

Is Young really taking her seriously? "Sure, once you come home from the hospital, sure, that would be cool."

She drops her jaw and gawks at him. "Honey, I don't want to wait. I'm talking about now." Never for a minute, even under the direst of circumstances, think that you can control your parents.

"Not to be a nag, but aren't you in labor?" I yell.

"The contractions are still a whopping three minutes apart. Trust

63

me, we've got time to take a thrilling detour. You believe in thrill, don't you? I still do." She must detect hesitation and horror scrambling to claim the expressions on our faces. "And you call yourself an artist," she says to Young.

That does it. Against all laws of common sense, Young streaks past the hospital exit and heads for his studio.

In some dreamy state of recklessness, we drive to the weedy field behind the warehouse where Young has his studio and where the unlit pyre of trashed televisions—portables and ponderous cabinet models, gutted and blown out—rise in junky formation, a pop-culture Stonehenge, glittering in the moonlight. Young springs from the car—everything's happening too fast for second-guessing—and activates the floodlights. A sleepy audience of birds begins to twitter in the brush. Quickly he mounts his camera on a tripod; rigs the timer so that the demolition will be filmed; and without further ceremony, leaps into the Galaxy and revs the engine. We speed forward, the prow of the old Galaxy parting the televisions on either side like so much water. Banners of glitzy pink friction sparks unfurl on both sides of the car. By the time we brake to a halt, all of us are squealing like we've just won the lottery.

Mom doesn't say too much after that. She goes docile on us, or maybe as Young suggests later, what calms her down is the pleasure of surviving a risk that makes more art than sense. But who really knows about moms? There's always some highspeed nail-biting chase after something going on in the labyrinthine chambers of their hearts. "Not to worry," she says, resting her head on my shoulder, "but the hospital might make a good pit stop."

* * *

Our drive through the towering inferno of TVs ought to have been the climax of the evening; but nope, the inferno was merely our warm-up. We have a baby to bring into the world.

"Look," I'd said to Mom back at the dark field of televisions. "You don't have to prove anything to anybody. I already know how brave you are."

"Brave?" She'd laughed. "This is just something to do for fun, True. Don't make it into anything more than that."

But isn't it always this way with parents: that they are able to recycle your very own words to their advantage? Because in the labor room, as I stand beside her, gripping her hand, wiping her forehead with a cool washcloth, spooning her chips of ice, she's the one telling me how brave I've been and how strong and how proud of me she is, how proud. "Want to know why I never thought twice about having this baby? You," she says. "You're why."

"Brave?" I ask, "who me? Why this is just something to do for fun, Mom."

"Don't joke at a time like this," she says. "It's not dignified."

* * *

And when they settle my rosy little brother into her arms, and I see her face so seriously given over to love that it looks more like a bouquet than a face, I relax. She snugs the baby close and reaches for me, too. Such an unexpected windfall of tending hands.

"Would you like me to call in the child's father now?" asks a nurse, straightening Mom's gown.

"Father?" Mom and I both shout.

Standing in the doorway, decked out in a green smock and mask, stands Young, the opportunist.

"He's not the father," I say. "He's my . . . sweetheart." I say it loudly, boldly, first time I truly know it. And then I rush at him and kiss him smackdab on the surgeon's mask he's wearing. "It's a boy!"

"Yes." He nods, wrapping his arms around me. "And it's a girl again finally, too."

Mr. Z

Oscar Casares

The boy rode in the car with his father. It was late afternoon, and they were on their way to buy fireworks. The father had worked a full day and was tired, but he had promised to drive his son to the stands. This was the Fourth of July. They had made the short trip to the edge of town for as long as the boy could remember in his eleven years. He had two older sisters, but they had never enjoyed doing this with their father. When the boy was little, his father lit the fireworks on the sidewalk as the boy watched from the porch with his mother. He would let go of his mother's hand and clap at each small explosion as if he had forgotten the one that had gone off only a minute earlier. Now that he was older, he lit the fireworks with other boys from the neighborhood, and sometimes his father stood on the porch to watch.

The fireworks stands were just beyond the city limits sign for Brownsville, Texas. The long and narrow wooden structures were scattered along the dry edges of the highway like giant matches that had fallen from the sky. Behind the stands, the flat sorghum fields stretched for a couple of miles until they reached the Rio Grande. The father stopped next to a stand with a large sign that read MR. Z'S FIREWORKS. The owner of the business introduced himself to the father and they shook hands. "Juan Zamarripa, para servirle," the owner said. Then it was the boy's turn to shake hands. "Diego Morales, sir," he said. The owner was an old man, and he wore a red baseball cap with the words MR. Z'S FIREWORKS stenciled across the front. His long white sideburns reminded Diego of cotton strands glued to brown construction paper. On his right forearm the owner had a faded tattoo of an eagle. The two men spoke in Spanish while Diego picked out fireworks. A teenage boy who worked behind the counter helped him. After his father paid for the fireworks, the owner motioned for Diego to come closer.

"I think you forgot something," the old man said as he dropped an extra bottle rocket inside the bag.

"What do you say?" the father was quick to ask.

"Thank you," Diego said.

The old man nodded. "How old are you, son?"

"Eleven."

"Eleven?" the old man asked. "N'hombre, by the time I was your age I had a job and my own money. Are you good in math?"

"Yes, sir."

"Vamos a ver, let's say I buy three dollars and fifty cents' worth of fireworks and I give you a five-dollar bill. What's my change?"

"One dollar and fifty cents," Diego said.

"Hey, you're faster than some people I know," Mr. Z said and glanced at the boy behind the counter. "You should come work for me, son. I don't pay a lot, but you get all your fireworks for fifty percent off."

Diego looked up at his father.

"If you want the job, you can have it," his father said.

"Bueno, I have enough help right now," Mr. Z said. "But I'll call you before New Year's and let's see what we can do."

That night Diego popped his fireworks in the street with the other neighborhood boys, but he couldn't stop thinking about what had happened earlier that day. He thought of all the other jobs in the world he could have, and none of them were as great as working at a fireworks stand. His sisters didn't even have jobs yet. They were always asking for money to go out with their friends. And now he would be earning enough to buy his own fireworks. Who knew how much he could buy if they were only half price? He told his friends, and some of the older boys wanted to know if they needed more help at the stand. He told them he couldn't say, but he would let them know. The dark sky flashed before him in brilliant colors, and New Year's seemed as if it would take forever to get here.

The summer and autumn months passed slowly until Mr. Z phoned Diego the second week of December.

"Are you still interested, son?"

"Yes, sir."

"And you're willing to work hard?"

"Oh, yes, sir."

"That's good, because the boys I hired last summer were lazy. They started off okay, but they got lazy on me."

"I'll work hard. I'm not lazy."

"I didn't think you were. Your father doesn't look like a lazy man."

"No, sir."

"Bueno, we're opening next week, a few days before Christmas, and going all the way to New Year's. My boys come in at noon and work late. How does that sound to you?"

"It sounds good. All my friends, they wish they could work at your stand."

"That's good to hear, son," the old man said. "You stop by next Wednesday and I'll show you how we work at Mr. Z's. Tell your father I can give you a ride home when we close down."

Diego spent the next few days wishing that he could be at work already. It was a good thing he didn't have to share a room the way his sisters did. He wanted to be alone. He heard his parents talking the night before he started. His mother thought he was too young to be working until the stand closed, but his father said Diego had already promised the man he would work. His boy was not going to back out now. He wouldn't let her treat him like a baby. They were quiet after that. Diego fell asleep wondering how different his life would be if tomorrow ever came.

His father drove home at lunch the next day. He wanted to take his son to his first day of work. Diego had spent some time getting ready that morning. After he showered, he brushed his teeth and put on his favorite blue jeans. He used a few drops of his father's Tres Flores to comb his hair. When they heard the car horn, Diego's mother kissed him on the cheek and told him to be careful. He said okay and ran to the car where his father was waiting.

They cracked the windows open at the top to let in the cool air. The sky was ash gray, as it had been for the past week. On the way to the stands they passed the cafés along International Boulevard, the panadería and its glorious scent of fresh sweet bread, the restaurant that sold barbacoa on Sunday mornings, the service station where the father had worked as a young man.

"You need to pay attention to Mr. Zamarripa," his father said. "Don't be playing around with the other boys. I want you to be serious. ¿Me entiendes?"

"Yes, sir."

These were the only words they exchanged on the way to the stand, but Diego knew what his father meant. He wanted Diego to behave and not do anything to embarrass him in front of Mr. Z. The tone of his father's voice was serious. It was the same tone he used right before he got angry. Once, his father had told him to be careful with the orange soda he was drinking in the car; and then a minute later, when the soda spilled on the cloth seats, his father slapped him. His father had hit him a couple of other times, enough for Diego to know that tone of voice. When they arrived at the stand, his father stayed in the car and waved to Mr. Z. "Pay attention," he said.

Another boy was inside the stand with Mr. Z. His name was Ricky, and he had also been hired to work. Although they were about the same age, he was shorter and huskier than Diego. Ricky lived in the projects near Diego's house, but they had never met.

It was warmer inside the stand, and Diego put away the windbreaker his mother had made him wear. The old man handed each of the boys a red MR. Z'S FIREWORKS cap. They thanked him and put them on. Diego was too busy adjusting the size to notice that his cap was bent and the brim was worn down and dirty.

"Bueno, I'm going to tell you what we got here at Mr. Z's. Black Cats is the most popular firecracker there is." The old man showed them the black and red package. "You got no Black Cats, you got no New Year's. It's my all-time bestseller. Nobody beats El Gato Negro." He raised his hands as if they were claws. The boys backed up.

"These are the Black Snakes. You light the fuse and it starts smoking and a tiny snake comes out—these are good for the little kids. Sparklers, too. If a man comes in alone, he probably has kids at home. And, Diego, what do you offer him?"

"Black Snakes and sparklers."

"That's right, son. Now you're using what God gave you," the old man said and pointed to Diego's head. "Over here are the smoke bombs, another bestseller. Who doesn't like smoke bombs?"

The boys stared at the old man.

"Who?" he asked.

"Nobody?" Ricky said.

"Good answer," Mr. Z said. "The older kids go for bottle rockets, guaranteed. Roman candles are Roman candles. If you don't know what those are, you're in the wrong business. Silver Jets are new. They make a loud sound like a coffeepot when it's ready. Every pinche perro in the neighborhood barks when they hear it take off. It's for the big kids."

The boys listened to Mr. Z explain how to sell some of the less-popular fireworks, place the money in a tin box under the counter, and bag everything the customers bought. He covered the stand from one end to the other. Diego already knew all the fireworks because he'd been buying them for years, but he didn't want to tell the old man this and be disrespectful.

When Mr. Z finished, he left the boys in the stand and walked to his pale yellow truck. He had parked it a few yards beyond the stand, the front end pointed into the ditch. There was a camper on the bed that looked rustier than the ancient truck it was attached to. The old man sat in the driver's seat for a long stretch of time. He finally walked to the front of the stand to watch the boys help some customers. After the people drove away, he brought Diego and Ricky together.

"Diego, what's the matter? How come you don't smile more? Who wants to buy fireworks from somebody who's got a serious face?"

"I don't know."

"You need to smile, son. Right now you look like you're going to the restroom, making number two." The old man strained his face and pretended he was sitting on a toilet.

Ricky laughed. So did Diego, but then he remembered what his father had said and he tried to be serious again.

"Y tú, Ricky, what are you laughing at?" Mr. Z asked. "Didn't I tell you to sell the Black Snakes to the men who come in alone?"

"Yes, sir."

"¿Entonces? What happened with that last man with the red shirt?"

"I forgot."

"I *forgot*. You better not *forgot* next time."

The boys did better with the people who stopped by the rest of that afternoon. Mr. Z kept walking behind the customers and exaggerating his smile to make Diego remember what he had said. Ricky sold three packages of sparklers and Black Snakes.

Just after 4 p.m., Mr. Z said it was time for dinner. If they waited until five or six, there would be too many customers. He asked the boys what they wanted from Whataburger.

"I didn't bring enough money," Diego said.

"You don't need no money. I pay for all the meals my boys eat. You just tell me what you want."

Mr. Z brought back three cheeseburgers, fries, and drinks. They sat

71

on the tailgate of the truck and looked at the passing cars and trucks. The boys wouldn't get paid for another week, so the meal was a small reward. Diego liked working hard. His father worked hard as a mechanic, sometimes taking side jobs to bring in a little extra. On those weekends, two or three cars would be parked in the backyard, waiting to be repaired. Diego took another bite. He thought this had to be the best cheeseburger he ever tasted.

The stand closed at 10 p.m. Mr. Z counted the money while the boys swept the inside of the stand and locked the doors and windows. Ricky had ridden his ten-speed bike to work, but Mr. Z told him to put it in the back of the truck because he was giving them both a ride home.

The old man used his hand to sweep the crumpled newspapers, used bags of chicharrones, soda cans, and Mexican lottery tickets from the passenger's seat onto the floor. Diego sat in the middle and Ricky leaned against the door. A tiny hula girl was glued to the dashboard. The boys watched her grass skirt swish around each time the truck hit a bump in the road.

"You two remind me of my boys." The old man pulled out a black-and-white photo that was clipped to the sun visor. "Mira, aqui están, when they were still in the hospital."

He turned on the cab light to show them the photo of the twin babies. Their faces were scrunched together, and they were both crying.

"What do you think? Do they look like their old man?"

"Kind of," Ricky said.

"What do they look like now?" Diego handed back the photo and Mr. Z put it in his shirt pocket.

"You have to ask their mama that question. She left to Chicago when they were still babies." The old man was quiet for a while, looking at the truck's headlights on the road. "But if they're my boys, they're probably some handsome men now," he said and laughed a little.

They were at the Four Corners intersection when the old man opened the glove box. Some receipts fell out and he grabbed a quart of whiskey. The bottle had a picture of a fighting cock on the label. Mr. Z took a quick drink and handed the bottle to Diego.

"Andale, you got to drink to your first day of work. It was a good day, we made some good money," the old man said.

Diego winced as soon as he tasted the whiskey. He wanted to spit it out, but he drank it instead.

"You too, Ricky. Today you're working men, hombres trabajadores."

Diego was glad that the old man held on to the bottle for the rest of the ride.

His mother and father were waiting for him in the living room. His sisters came out of their room when they heard him walk in the door.

"How was your first day?" his father asked.

"Are you hungry, mi'jito?" his mother asked.

She reheated some tamales, and the family crowded around him at the kitchen table.

"So, Diego, are you going to lend us money now?" his oldest sister asked and laughed.

"You girls leave your brother alone—he's eating," his father said.

When Diego finished his meal, he told them about learning how to work inside the stand and eating cheeseburgers on the tailgate of the truck and selling fireworks to little kids and going to the restroom behind a mesquite and almost seeing a wreck between an 18-wheeler and a car that pulled out onto the highway too fast and cleaning the place after they closed. He told them everything, except the part about the ride home and the bottle with the rooster on it.

The next day Diego made it to work before Ricky. He took care of the few customers that came by early. Mr. Z kept looking at his watch and shaking his head. At one point, the old man wrote something in the little notepad that he used to record all the sales for the day.

Diego was rearranging the bottle rockets when Ricky finally showed up for work. His mother had driven him to the stand. Diego noticed she was a lot younger than most of his friends' moms. She wore large hoop earrings, and her dark hair was in a ponytail. She apologized to Mr. Z for Ricky being an hour late. Someone had stolen his bike. Ricky's eyes were swollen as though he had been crying.

"It won't happen again," she promised.

"No te preocupes por eso," Mr. Z assured her. "I'm sorry you had to bring Ricky all this way. I would've been happy to pick him up."

Mr. Z walked her to the car, and he stood talking to her for a couple of minutes until she drove away. He was smiling when he came back to the stand.

"Why didn't you tell me your mother was such a beautiful woman, eh, Ricky? And alone, without a man? I thought you and me were friends."

Ricky looked at the ground.

73

"N'hombre, if I didn't have a business to run, I might have taken the afternoon off." The old man laughed.

Diego tried to turn away, but the old man looked straight at him.

"That's a joke, son—laugh. I thought you were going to smile more."

Diego gave him a half smile, but Mr. Z only turned his back and walked to the truck. Ricky was quiet, and Diego felt bad for even trying to smile. He didn't understand why Mr. Z was talking about Ricky's mom. At school you didn't talk about anybody's mother or sister. There was a boy in class who wrote some bad words in the restroom about a girl named Letty, and her four brothers jumped him on the way home, near the canal by the church. The brothers took turns kicking him in the stomach and head.

Later in the afternoon, Mr. Z bought a family box of fried chicken and biscuits.

"Is your mother a good cook, Ricky?" the old man asked.

"I guess so."

"Nothing like a beautiful woman who can cook."

"My father barbecues in the backyard," Diego said. "My tío Lalo, he's my uncle who was in the navy, he comes over and they make chicken and fajitas, and sometimes they throw beer on the fire to make it . . ." He stopped when he saw the old man glare at him as if he had a piece of food hanging out of his mouth. He realized that Mr. Z didn't want to be interrupted. No one said anything. They ate the rest of the chicken and listened to the passing cars on the highway.

On the ride home, Mr. Z opened a new bottle of whiskey and turned the radio to a Tejano station. The old man knew the song and was swaying a little in his seat. Ricky looked out the window. Diego watched the hula girl's skirt. When they were in front of his apartment, Ricky swung the truck door open.

"Tell your mother good night for me, eh, Ricky?"

The boy just walked away. The old man drove to Diego's house.

"What do you think, Diego?" he said.

"About what, sir?"

"Is she a good-looking woman, or is a she good-looking woman?"

"I don't know, sir."

"That wasn't one of the choices, son."

They stopped in front of Diego's house.

"Thank you for the ride, Mr. Z."

The old man gunned the engine and took off.

The next day, Diego and his father drove by Ricky's apartment and gave him a ride to work. Mr. Z looked surprised to see both boys getting out of the car.

"Eh, Ricky, why didn't you tell me you needed a ride?" the old man said. "I would've stopped by your house."

"It's okay, Diego said his father could give me a ride."

"And who the hell is his father? You don't work for his father." The old man stared at the boys until they looked away.

Diego thought he was helping out by giving Ricky a ride to work. Now he felt sorry that he had somehow made things worse.

The boys restocked the displays. They placed everything in the same position it had been in the past two days, the bestsellers in the front and the less-popular fireworks on either side of them. An hour passed before the old man stood in front of the stand to watch the boys work. Ricky was helping Diego sell more fireworks to a man who had driven up alone.

"The best one for little kids are the Black Snakes," Ricky said. "They're safe because there's no popping, and that way there's no chance of getting hurt. All you do is light the fuse and a little snake comes out."

"Yeah, they come out like the rattlesnakes do on the King Ranch," Diego said. He thought it was a clever way to explain what they actually did.

The man added two packages of Black Snakes to the fireworks he was buying.

Mr. Z walked inside the stand after the customer left. "Diego, how come you told that man a lie?"

"What do you mean?"

"Rattlesnakes," the old man said. "There's no rattlesnakes on the King Ranch. I've hunted there, lots of times. I've never seen rattlesnakes."

"My father told me there was."

"Then your father lied. Your father told you some bullshit."

"He's never lied to me."

"You're calling me a liar?"

"No, sir."

"¿Entonces?"

"Nothing, sir."

"Bueno, you better watch what you say to people or you're going to turn out the same as your father, a bullshitter."

Diego didn't know what to say. He wanted to be angry with Mr. Z, but he also wondered if he should apologize for arguing with him about the snakes.

Mr. Z walked back to the truck. He stayed there for the rest of the afternoon. When he left to buy dinner, the boys stood in front of the fireworks stand and threw pebbles into the ditch.

"I bet there are rattlesnakes at the King Ranch," Ricky said.

"That's what my father says," Diego said.

"Don't listen to the old man. He's just mad because my mom didn't bring me."

"My father doesn't lie."

"I know. You don't have to tell me."

Mr. Z brought fried chicken again. The boys each grabbed a piece with a paper napkin. They looked out at the cars driving past them. The sun was burning on the horizon, and it would be dark soon.

"How's the chicken today, boys?"

"It's good," Diego said.

Ricky nodded.

"You know, people tell me that snake tastes like chicken," the old man said. "What do you think, Diego?"

"Maybe."

"What do you think your father would say about that?"

"I don't know."

"Really? I thought your tío would come over to the house and barbecue snakes."

"No, sir."

"Ahh, I think you forgot, Diego," the old man said. "Maybe I should ask your father myself. He probably has some good ways to barbecue a snake."

A family in a white van stopped next to the truck, and Diego put away his food to help them. He stayed in the stand for the rest of the night. They were busy that evening, and the old man didn't have time to say anything to him.

After work he made sure to sit next to the passenger door, where he wouldn't have to hear as much of Mr. Z talking. His father was watching the late news when Diego walked in and sat next to him on the sofa.

"How was it today, mi'jo?" his father asked.

"It was okay."

"Good. Are you paying attention to Mr. Zamarripa?"

"Yes, sir."

"Are you going to college so you can study to be a businessman?"

"Maybe," Diego said. "But I'm kind of getting tired of selling fireworks."

"You been working three days, Diego. You don't know what tired is."

"But we're not even getting paid until the last day."

"It's only one more week. Just be glad you have a job. ¿Me entiendes?" His father was serious now.

"Yes, sir."

They watched the weather report for a few minutes. His father wanted to see if there was going to be a cold front.

"Dad, remember last year when we drove by the King Ranch?"

His father nodded.

"And remember how you told me there were rattlesnakes all over the ranch?"

"Yeah."

"Have you seen them?"

"No, mi'jo, but I can imagine there are lots of them. Why?"

"Mr. Z goes hunting there and he's never seen one."

"Pues, maybe he's right. I'm not a hunter."

Diego had trouble sleeping that night. What his father had said about the rattlesnakes didn't sound like a lie; but it wasn't exactly the truth, either. He thought about how it might be possible to imagine something and for it to be true. Diego wished there were an easy way of telling his father what had happened. Explaining it to his mother wouldn't help. His father would find out, and he'd have to tell him everything, straight to his face. Diego pictured himself trying to say what Mr. Z had said, and he knew he couldn't embarrass his father that way. Even if he was only repeating the words, it was still an insult. He hated the old man for saying his father was a liar. And he hated the fact that he couldn't quit his job.

Diego's father dropped him and Ricky off at work. Mr. Z met the boys in front of the stand. They watched Diego's father wave as he drove away.

The old man was the first to wave back. "Come on, boys, say goodbye to the bullshitter."

The words stung Diego like a fresh scab being torn from his arm.

The rest of the day was filled with Mr. Z making jokes about Diego's father, about how he'd make a good politician, about how he could fool one of those lie-detector machines, about how he probably lied all the time, even to Diego's mother.

The old man left to buy dinner at the usual time. Diego told Ricky he was going to the restroom. Then he sat behind a mesquite and cried. He held the loose dirt in his hand, and it slipped through his fingers. There was nothing he wanted more than to be older and be able to talk back to the old man. He didn't know what he would say, but he wanted to hurt him. Maybe he could set the stand on fire and ruin his business. Diego could see himself going to jail for this, and he thought it would be worth it. If he were bigger, he would've fought him and knocked him to the ground. He'd hit the old man hard, maybe knock out a tooth. There would be tears in his eyes and blood dripping from his mouth. Diego would keep kicking him in the stomach until he begged him to stop. People passing by in cars would laugh. And he'd slap him with the back of his hand one more time, just to make sure the old man knew he had done wrong.

Mr. Z and Ricky were sitting on the tailgate. Diego wiped his eyes and runny nose on the inside of his shirt. He walked to the truck and started eating his cheeseburger. All the crying had left a funny taste in his mouth, and he wasn't that hungry. He was eating his french fries when two young boys came by on a bike, one of them sitting on the handlebars. Diego said he'd take care of them.

The boys were brothers, and their hair was cut the same way, in a straight line across their forehead. Diego brought out the sparklers and Black Snakes, but they weren't interested in little-kid fireworks. One brother wanted bottle rockets, and the other wanted Silver Jets.

"Bottle rockets are stupid," the younger one said.

"No, they're not," the older one said.

"I'm sick of bottle rockets."

"Stop being a llorón. Bottle rockets is all we got money for. The Silver Jets cost more."

"You're the llorón. You're the one that wants bottle rockets. Those are for stupid babies. Give me half the money."

They argued for several minutes, calling each other names. The younger one kicked dirt at his brother, which led to a shoving match the older one eventually won. In the end, they bought two packages of bottle rockets.

The boys were still arguing when Diego dropped four Silver Jets in their paper bag without them noticing. He did it as if it were the most natural thing in the world to do, as if he were standing in the middle of the street lighting the fuse to a long pack of Black Cats.

The brothers rode away with their fireworks, and Diego wished he could see their reaction when they found the Silver Jets. He felt himself kicking the old man in the gut.

Later Diego helped a man wearing a black cowboy hat with a tiny horseshoe pin stuck to the front of it. The man bought Roman candles, bottle rockets, Silver Jets, and Black Cats. Diego put them all inside a paper bag and then slipped in two more Roman candles. If the man noticed, he didn't say anything. Diego charged him only for the fireworks he had asked for. The man nodded and walked to his truck.

Diego gave away fireworks every chance he had. The packages of Black Snakes, smoke bombs, bottle rockets, Black Cats, and sparklers tumbled to the bottom of the paper bags for the rest of the night. It became a game for him, a challenge, the same way learning how to sell Black Snakes and sparklers had been a challenge. The trick was to figure out what kind of firework the customer really wanted and to stick it in the bag without anyone noticing. A heavyset lady with three kids almost caught him putting some extra smoke bombs in her bag.

"¿Y ésos, qué? Are you trying to trick me, make me buy more than I want?"

"No, ma'am, these are two for one."

"¿Estás seguro? Because I don't like tricks."

"Yes, ma'am, they're on special."

"Pues, entonces let me buy two more de esos smoke bombs."

He had started by giving away the fireworks only when he was alone in the stand, but with the evening rush he became more daring. With Ricky working next to him and Mr. Z at the other end of the counter with a customer, he dropped the fireworks in a bag and then smiled at the old man as if he'd just made the biggest sale of the night.

Mr. Z told more of his jokes on the ride home. The one he laughed at the most was about how Diego's father probably never went to confession because it would take too long. Ricky ignored the old man and stared straight ahead as if he were on a long bus ride. Diego sat next to the door. It was colder now, but he rolled down the window because he didn't want to hear the jokes. He wondered what would happen in a day or two when the old man did an inventory check. It was the first time he had thought about it all night. Each time he had added extra fireworks to a customer's bag, he felt he was somehow covering up the last time he had done it, so that in the end it wouldn't be dozens of fireworks that had been given away but only one or two packages that could easily be written off as a mistake. It became less of a bad thing the more he did it. Now he was getting nervous that one of his customers would come back to ask Mr. Z for free fireworks, telling him that one of his boys had been loading up bags the night before. He was afraid Ricky might get blamed, and then he would have to come forward and confess the whole thing. Given the choice, he would prefer to get fired and not have to confess. He didn't feel bad about what he had done, because the old man deserved everything, maybe more. In the distance, fireworks lit up the dark sky, and Diego imagined they were the Roman candles he'd given away. He smiled as he watched the bright lights.

When Diego opened the front door, he saw his father drinking a glass of water in the kitchen. He had hoped that his parents might already be asleep. He wanted to go to bed without having to talk about his day, but as soon as he walked in, his father asked him to sit at the table.

"How was work, mi'jo?"

Diego hesitated for a moment. He stared at the salt and pepper shakers on the table, trying to find an answer in the grains.

"It was good," he said. "I think I sold more fireworks than anybody."

"That's the kind of news I like to hear about my boy."

Diego smiled.

"Then you're going to keep working for Mr. Zamarripa?"

"Yes, sir."

"Qué bueno," his father said. "I knew everything would work out. Sometimes you just have to wait a little while for it to get better."

Miz Mabel
Cecile Goding

"Well, Abby?" said Mama. "Would you like to help out Miz Mabel in her new restaurant?"

Mabel McFerson was sitting right there with Abby's parents at the kitchen table, so what else could the girl say? "Yes, ma'am. I want to."

The girl was a little scared then, but more excited. A job might take her mind off her boredom and loneliness. Mae Alice Comb, the only other white girl anywhere near Abby's age within walking distance, was away at some rich girls' camp up in the mountains. And so was her horse, Pee Wee. Abby had planned to exercise Pee Wee while her friend was away, but Mae Alice had decided to take Pee Wee to camp with her.

Abby's father believed, and he said it aloud, that it was sweet of Miz Mabel to offer her the job. No matter that Miz Mabel could not pay her. "It's what's called work experience," he told Abby. "Nothing wrong with that." He was just about to leave for swing shift at the paper mill in the next county. By the time he got back home, Abby would have finished her first night of work experience, waiting on hungry travelers.

Miz Mabel said, "She'll have her tips, mind."

"I'm just glad her first job she won't be working for a stranger," Mama said.

"Well, Jo Ann said she'd watch my babies tonight." Miz Mabel pushed herself up from the table. "Said she would take them to choir practice with her, bless her heart. I better get them something to eat before."

From a recent church potluck, Abby recalled those children, stuck to Miz Mabel's old-lady dress. They were red-haired and pale as banana pudding. Mama, in a bright blue A-line shift she had sewn from a pattern, had squatted down to ask the children, eye-to-eye, what they wanted for dessert. Mama never wanted anyone to feel left out.

The whole congregation felt sorry for the way life had transpired for Miz Mabel. It was a shame she had to move to that old dogtrot house down the river road, with only a wood stove and no TV and those two little children. The congregation believed no white woman should have to live like that. Most believed that Burgess Comb had agreed to let Mabel run the 301 Motel Restaurant, one of several Comb properties, as an act of kindness.

A while back, Miz Mabel had been doing all right. She was known for her good country cooking and had her own restaurant, where Abby's family went once or twice for Sunday dinner. That restaurant was in a big empty house closer to town. The customers served themselves from pots kept warm on three kitchen stoves, then sat together on benches at long tables. They ate chicken 'n' dumplings and pole beans and biscuit, the same food people cooked in their own kitchens, but a little bit different. Miz Mabel liked to turn on a loud, hillbilly voice—to make up for her shortness, some believed. At around five feet tall, she would lift the tea pitcher high over her poufed-up hairdo, shouting "How y'all doing" to every person, young and old. She looked over her top-heavy breasts down at your plate, and if you had missed any "vittles," she would say, "Oh, Lordy, look at that empty spot," then run to bring that pot and give you some, whether you wanted some or not.

* * *

Abby's first day as a waitress began about half past four, when Miz Mabel returned to pick her up. Miz Mabel had to sit on an old phone book to see the road, pressing her pillowy breasts into the steering wheel. Abby wondered if it hurt. She was glad Mama was normal up top, as it was a good sign she would be normal, too.

The 301 Motel was a strip of rooms facing the highway that ran straight into town. Abby counted three cars parked at the motel, one in front of the room marked OFFICE. Grass and sourweed punched up through the asphalt lot in places, wherever there was the tiniest crack.

"Honey, I sure wish I could pay you a little bit," Miz Mabel said for the third time. "You can have your tips, mind."

"That's all right, Miz Mabel," said the girl. She wore her favorite white blouse and a blue skirt from last school year that stuck to her underwear in the hot car. She hoped she was dressed all right. The waitresses on TV wore uniforms with their names on plastic tags.

Abby thought Miz Mabel dressed like an old woman, in the kind of shirtwaist dresses grandmothers wore. She never wore Bermuda shorts like Mama's. Mrs. Comb, Mae Alice's mother, believed that Mabel would be attractive if she dressed normally and kept her mouth shut.

The restaurant sat at one end of the motel parking lot, close to the highway. It had been closed for months; but even when open, it was not a place where locals met for coffee or a grilled cheese sandwich, like the Station Grill in town. Abby did not know of anyone who had ever eaten there. Near its back door, a thin colored lady waited in a car with its door wide open. The colored lady threw down her cigarette and stood up, wiping her hands on her white apron. "Now Abby, this is Louise," Miz Mabel said. "She's going to help me out in the kitchen. Oh, she's been helping me out a good long time here and there; ain't that right, Louise? Abby's going to help me with the customers."

"Glad to meet you," Louise said, smiling at Abby. "That's real fine."

Abby followed the women inside, through a narrow kitchen, and into the dining area, Miz Mabel switching on lights as they went. The front of the room had large plate glass windows, so that customers could watch the highway as they ate. Miz Mabel turned on a window air conditioner, and the dining room rumbled and hummed. As Abby helped Louise open all the Venetian blinds, she counted fourteen tables, with four chairs at each table. The room was barely big enough. She pictured herself squeezing between the tables, trays of food held high, saying, "You're welcome" or "My pleasure" like waitresses everywhere. Miz Mabel asked her to turn the sign around on the front door, so it read OPEN, TUES-SUN, 5:00 P.M.—9:00 P.M., CLOSED MONDAY. Miz Mabel said she knew she should open for breakfast, that people would stop for a good breakfast; and maybe she would, down the road.

Her first day as a waitress, Abby learned how to operate the cash register on its pedestal near the kitchen door. She learned to separate the bills and the coins, placing each denomination in its proper place in the drawer. She learned how to set the tables with paper placemats and how to serve food. "Always serve to the customer's left," Miz Mabel said. She said to take away the dirty plates from the right side of each customer.

The restaurant fed three customers that evening. The first was a big, red-faced truck driver. His semi was parked in the motel parking lot. "Ask if they can put some fried onions on top that hamburger steak, honey," he said, handing the menu back to Abby. He gave her a sad smile. "I'm so tired I don't know if I want to spend another night in that truck or sleep at that motel."

"I'll be right back with your sweet tea, sir," she said.

In the narrow kitchen, Louise was chipping ice that had built up inside the freezer, while Miz Mabel stood at the sink, staring out the back window. A few rows of eating-corn grew right up to the asphalt, and farther back, an auto graveyard wallowed in kudzu. Tobacco fields filled in at right and left, their young plants a certain distance apart. From the sky, it would look as if a rectangle had been cut out just the size of the 301 Motel and its little restaurant. The thin gray line beside it would be the highway, with the crisscross tracks of the Seaboard Coastline Railroad its closest relative, everything else a tangle of greens and soil.

Abby told Miz Mabel what the man wanted for supper. "Louise, slice me one of those onions, please ma'am," Miz Mabel said, still staring out the window.

After Abby served the truck driver, a bald man and a pretty woman drove up. The woman had short, blonde hair and wore pedal pushers with a matching top that showed her midriff. Abby thought she looked like a model in a catalogue. "I've been waiting all day to say this," the woman said, as she sat down next to the plate glass window. "I'll have a tall gin and tonic. As soon as possible." She turned her eyes up, as if in church.

"Idiot," said the man. "Don't you recall what state we're still in?" He grinned at Abby, as if the two shared a joke on the woman.

"Jesus Christ, then, just bring me a Coke. Lots of ice."

"Yes, ma'am," said Abby. "I'll be right back with that Coke."

"Where y'all from?" asked the truck driver.

The bald man looked across the room at him but said nothing. He kept looking until the truck driver turned back to his plate.

About then, Miz Mabel came out to meet the three customers. "How y'all doing?" she called out, over the buzz of the air conditioner. "How you like my vittles?" Miz Mabel had on her play-acting voice. She sounded like Aunt Bee or Granny Clampett. No one else talked like that anymore, not in real life.

"You're too pretty to be a cook," said the truck driver, as he stood up to leave.

"Well, listen to him," said Miz Mabel, looking up at him, her hands on her hips. "I just love to cook, boy, that's what my good Lord in his

84

goodness made me for."

The blonde woman hid a smile with her napkin, while the bald man looked at Abby and rolled his eyes. She rolled her eyes back. Then she felt ashamed of herself for making fun of Miz Mabel, but mad at her, too, for talking like a redneck. Did the customers think she and Miz Mabel were related in some way?

After her customers left, Abby saw that the truck driver had left a quarter tip on his table, while the bald man had left her a dollar. She wished it had been the other way around. "You remind me of my baby sister," the truck driver had said. Abby watched him climb back into his cab and turn north toward Florence.

Miz Mabel took the cash out of the register at 8:30. She told Abby she should eat some supper. "I'll watch the front, honey," she said. "You can have anything on the menu. Just ask Louise to fix it for you."

Louise had already cleaned the sink and turned off the griddle. She was sitting on the back stoop smoking, swatting at some silent moths attracted by the kitchen light.

Abby went back to the dining room. "That's all right," she told her employer. "I'm not hungry tonight."

When Abby was dropped off, she saw a light from her parents' bedroom. Mama called out her open door. She was lying on the bed in her pink slip, reading a library book and smoking her last cigarette of the day.

"Yes, ma'am," Abby said from the threshold.

"How was it? Did you learn how to make change?"

Abby said it was fine, that she liked it, and that she could eat anything on the menu.

"Is the cooking like at Mabel's other place?"

"Some of it's like that." The girl was tired and wanted to get something to eat. She wanted to read her library book without waking up her brother, who shared a room with her. She wanted to tell Mae Alice all about being a waitress, but Mae Alice was far away.

One rainy day, right before Mae Alice and Pee Wee left for the mountains, the girls were playing in the Comb conservatory when Mae Alice's fashion doll Candy announced, in a squeaky little voice, "You know me and you won't be going to the same school anymore. You know that, right?" Mae Alice made Candy's long hair wag back and forth.

"Yeah, yeah, I know," Stormy, Abby's fashion doll, said back.

In the fall, Mae Alice would go to the new private school beyond the

Country Club out Pine Forest Road. Mr. and Mrs. Comb, and some other like-minded parents, had been raising money for years, ever since integration branched out from the capitol, filling up a few public schools and abandoning the others. This fall, Thurmond Baptist Academy was finally opening its doors to those who had the means and the complexion. Mae Alice had no choice, of course. There was nothing else to say about school. Abby tried to make her doll say something else, but Stormy's stupid pink face just smiled on and on as if nothing had happened.

"Tomorrow I'll show you how to make change," Mama was saying. "I'll show you how I do it."

* * *

Miz Mabel had for some reason lost her restaurant. A Christmas tree farm, its young pine and cedar trees hoping for rain, now covered the place where the old house had stood. Abby pictured families from Florence driving down to buy their Christmas trees, if the little trees survived that long.

Abby's family always received their Christmas tree from the Combs. No one said why. Was it because the Combs owned the house where Abby and her parents and her brother lived, along with many other houses and trees? Or because Abby was Mae Alice's best friend? Theodore and Mister, who both worked for the Combs, would scout the woods that lay between the two houses. Theodore would cut down two cedar trees—a regular-sized tree for Abby and a taller tree for Mae Alice. Then he would hitch up Mister to the trees and drag them out, Mister's wide hooves churning through the smilax and skunk cabbage and every other creeping thing that creepeth upon the earth.

On Christmas morning, after opening gifts with her family, Abby would run down the road to the Combs' place, where she would find them still at breakfast in the best dining room. Mrs. Comb, a tall freckle-faced woman who always told people she was "actually from Charleston" as if this were an amazing fact, always sat at the end of the table. Mr. Comb, at the other end, was always jumping up to take a phone call, even on Christmas morning. It was awful, Abby believed, the way Mrs. Comb made them wait and wait for Christmas to start, not only through breakfast, but even longer. "Wait for Janie and Theodore," she would say from the head of the table, as if they needed reminding.

It was understood, long before Mae Alice and her older brothers and sisters were born, that Janie and Theodore, who cooked the meals and did a host of other things for the family, were not to be left out of the festivities. How hard it was to sit there at the table, listening to the couple in the kitchen as they washed and talked and put away each dish and plate, while in the conservatory a mound of presents waited to be ripped apart. Finally, Janie and Theodore would appear. Theodore would cross, very slowly, to the big French doors, while Janie smiled from the dining room doorway. Only then could the children get up and push past Theodore to what awaited. There was always a present for Janie and Theodore, as well as one for Abby.

Over the next two weeks as a waitress, Abby made $9.25 in tips. One evening a dozen customers, miraculously, turned off the highway or walked over from the motel. Miz Mabel had to help wait on them, turning on her pure country charm. Most of the evenings were much slower. Miz Mabel would drive off "to check on the chillen," then return an hour or two later. Sometimes Abby saw her employer's car parked at the motel in front of the door marked OFFICE. Whoever worked there never came over to eat, though.

One evening there were no customers at all, and Abby read her library book in the dining room. Louise sat and smoked out back until Miz Mabel said she might as well go home. "Now, you take a chicken from the freezer, Louise," Abby overheard. "That's all I can pay you tonight." If Louise answered, Abby could not have said.

Locking up, Miz Mabel pressed a quarter into Abby's hand. When Abby thanked her, she said, "When school starts, you keep yourself to yourself, now."

By this time, Abby had learned that when Miz Mabel said something like that out of the blue, it was okay not to answer. Stuck in the front seat next to Miz Mabel, who squinted her eyes with suspicion at the other cars, Abby had heard all about "them." The old car would proceed in silence for a good while, past the soft green rows and impenetrable woods. "Trying to get in everywhere," Miz Mabel would say, sounding mad and scared at the same time, "and take everybody down." She would say, "never tell what they're thinking." She would say, "babies out of wedlock." She would say, "something for nothing."

"Now I'm not talking about the good ones," Miz Mabel said one night, as if Abby had raised the question. "Look at Louise."

Or George Washington Carver, Abby thought, the only colored name in the fourth grade history book. Or that man on *I, Spy*, the funny one.

Linda, Abby recalled. Linda had sat in the back of Abby's fourth grade classroom. She never said anything, and the teacher never called on her. How shy she was, compared to the teenagers who worked with Abby's brother at curing time, playing practical jokes on each other all night while they kept watch over the tobacco in the tall smoky barn, watching for that prized and perfect color.

Mama had said Abby should introduce herself to Linda. But before she could overcome her own shyness, Linda had disappeared, her desk sitting empty for the rest of the school year.

Miz Mabel kept going on and on, naming every good one she could think of, all down the highway. Abby's father said that the highway ran all the way from Baltimore, Maryland to Sarasota, Florida. Riding the school bus as little kids, Abby and Mae Alice had seen license plates from Canada, Florida, and everyplace in between. Lately, most of the cars were from either North or South Carolina. Her father said that the 301 Motel would close any day now, the same way his gas station had. He showed them on his state map how new highways had drunk up much of the north-south traffic, carrying the cars miles farther to the west. "It's Progress," he told them. "You can't blame Progress." Then he said, more to himself, "Even if you wanted to, you couldn't find it."

One evening, for the first time all summer, a colored customer drove up. Tall and weary, he stepped down from his truck cab and started for the front door. "Sorry, we are closed," Miz Mabel almost shouted, bustling out from behind the cash register. Abby looked up from the library book she had been reading all night, without a single hungry person to interrupt the mystery.

The man stopped in the open doorway, letting flies and heat into the empty dining room. "For real?" he asked, as he took off his cap. Then he smiled right down at little Miz Mabel, as if she must be joking. Abby knew Miz Mabel was serious, though. She had that same look when she squinted over the steering wheel of an evening, staring into what lay just beyond her sight.

Then Miz Mabel began talking fast. About how they had to clean up the dining room but if he wanted to go around back she thought Louise could fix him something to take with him, and the man said, "Okay, okay," and smiled even wider, backing out the door with his palms turned up like that funny spy on TV.

Miz Mabel said she was going over to the office to get some change. After she left, Louise appeared to tell Abby what the man had ordered. She handed Abby a five-dollar bill. Abby pushed the button that opened the cash register and counted out the change.

When Abby came back through the kitchen, Louise was sitting on the stoop. The man stood in the heat with his supper in a paper sack. Abby counted the change into his big palm, the way Mama had showed her. "Out of $5.00," she started. "4.25, 4.50, 5."

"Miss," he said, "I gave this lady here a ten." He smiled up at the setting sun, or something else above the girl's head. It was the kind of tight-lipped smile her father made when he was mad at some appliance he could not fix.

Louise squinted up at the man, then gave her own cheek a little slap. "My Lord, Abby, I don't think I even remember." To the man she said, "Where is my head?"

"Just a minute," Abby said. "I'll be right back." As she went through the narrow kitchen and back to the dining room, she could hear Louise telling the man how bad her memory was these days.

Miz Mabel had taught Abby to leave the customer's money on the counter until the proper change was given back, but the girl must have forgotten. Louise had given her a five, right? There were three fives and two tens in the drawer, set in their proper places. She removed one of the fives and went back to where the man waited. "I'm sorry about that," she said, handing him the bill. "Where is my head?"

"Thanks," he said, without looking at her. "Bye, ma'am," he said to Louise, and she waved her cigarette.

"He still could've tipped you," Louise said, after the man disappeared. "Oh, well."

At the usual closing time, Miz Mabel walked back from the Office and emptied the cash register into her purse as she did every night. "Time to go," she said. "Time to go."

Back home, Abby stood at the kitchen sink, trying to see into the tangled woods beyond the yard. Even in daylight, it was hard to walk straight through the woods to Mae Alice's kitchen door. You had to go under or over a multitude of thick vines and fallen trunks, always listening for copperheads. Easier to go by the road to the Combs' wrought-iron front gates, where the school bus had always stopped in the past.

Again, she tried to picture the five-dollar bill Louise had handed her, but she could not make it out. If she talked the whole thing over with Mama, would Mama ask her where Miz Mabel was at the time? The idea of a ten-year-old being left alone in a highway restaurant, with only Louise to protect her from robbers and such, would not sit well with Mama. Maybe she would make Abby quit the job. And the girl liked serving people, watching them walk in and be cooled by the window air conditioner. She liked pouring them ice water while they studied the plastic menus.

* * *

Sometime in early August, Miz Mabel announced that she had a new job, morning manager of an IHop off the interstate. She sat with Abby and her parents in their kitchen, telling them how Burgess Comb would close the 301 Motel restaurant, maybe forever. "And Mr. Comb's worked out with the Academy about the tuition," she said, jumping from the IHop to the Academy as if they were right next door to each other. "So my babies will be able to attend. And sure as the Lord's in heaven, he would do the same for ya'll."

"Well, I tell you," Daddy said, touching Miz Mabel's little shoulder. "I think Abby and her brother are all right where they are, Mabel." He kept a smile on, but later Abby would hear him tell Mama that he was not about to let anybody "work out" anything for him or his wife or his kids.

Mama said, "Oh, my, look at the time."

"Well, now you've got some experience," Daddy said, giving Abby a squeeze.

"Thank you, sir," she said. "My pleasure." She cleared the table, taking his plate from the right.

All told, the girl was not sorry to lose her summer job. Mae Alice would be home soon, and besides, Abby believed she had learned all she was going to learn from Miz Mabel. She had devised a few tricks of her own, too, like getting the drink orders right, in front of the right person. You imagined a rectangle, like a miniature table. Then you pictured a glass, a cup, a Coke bottle or whatever in the corners of your mind where they would stay in the corners of your mind just long enough for the people to get what they paid for and drive off.

To Reap, to Thresh
Jan Seale

Wesley wanted a combine on his tombstone, not necessarily one with the John Deere sign on it, nor green and yellow like the miniature his wife had found him and put on the shelf in the bathroom next to his Avon Noble Prince glass collie filled with after-shave.

"We got sheep. We got the Good Shepherd. We got angels. We even got wheat sheaves—that'd do." Roger at Allen Feed & Seed & Monument Works in town was trying to be helpful. Wesley knew that.

"We could put Ardith's name to one side of the shock, yours to the other, make a border of the sheaves, carve in the dates you were born, and ... I'd fix the other dates a little later." Roger was thin, had no teeth, and coughed and hitched up his pants simultaneously.

"I think not," Wesley said, "I do think not," and left through the side door.

"Clouds?" Roger called after him.

* * *

Ardith had sure been cool toward the idea of Wesley having his own headstone with a combine on it. Death to her was a double headstone, red granite, a border of morning glories, with her and Wesley's full names and dates, the names and birth dates of their four children, and BELOVED FAMILY right in the middle.

"You can have whatever you want on yours," Wesley said, staring at the dominoes as he shuffled slowly. It was April and they'd played themselves silly since the first of the year, especially now since he'd given up feeding cattle in the off season. He'd felt unsettled lately.

Ardith dotted the tally sheet over and over with the pencil stub. Finally, she took the corner of her apron and carefully wiped her eyes.

91

"Time to draw," Wesley said. They drew their seven dominoes across the white oil cloth and studied their luck.

Ardith sighed. "What if I was to say I wanted my very own tombstone with a sewing machine or a milk separator carved on it?"

Wesley looked up. "You could have that."

"Well I don't." She anchored a string of gray hair behind her ear. "I sure don't. Don't want to be reminded of any kind of work when I die."

Wesley laid down the double-five as the spinner. Ardith played her five-three. "To tell the truth, I don't give a hoot or a holler, one way or the other, except folks will think you're crazy."

"I'll be past caring," Wesley said.

"Not if you get it now."

"I don't want to wait." Wesley played the five-two and Ardith gave him a mark.

Wesley had thought off and on about death, mostly off, ever since he'd had his prostate whittled on and radiated five years ago. Doc said after that not to worry at all. Said, "You got a lot a company—men your age—in this thing. Most of them outlast it." So Wesley had kind of let it go, up until Earl pulled his stunt.

Wesley brushed his hands together lightly, and the callouses made a thin whisper. "Look what happened to Earl. Look what Priscilla had to do." He wanted her to think he was being considerate, but they both knew he wanted to be sure he had his combine.

Earl was the mechanic for all the farmers and ranchers around. He and Wesley had been friends for forty-some-odd years. One day last fall Wesley had gone over to get a tractor belt, and Earl stooped down to pull the belt out from under some junk and toppled over dead. The week after the funeral, Wesley bought the lots right next to Earl's and Priscilla's.

Ardith rearranged her dominoes. "But Earl's crescent wrench wasn't as hard to do as a combine. Priscilla said all they had to do was take a staff of life, cut the tail off, and fatten up the sides a little."

Wesley spread his hands out flat on either side of his dominoes and looked straight at Ardith. "Can you think of something that's meant more to us in this life than a good wheat harvest?"

Ardith found a new place on her apron and dabbed her eyes again. "You don't need me to answer that," she said. "Play!"

* * *

So Wesley got in his pickup and drove to Amarillo to order a tombstone with a nice big combine etched into it. On the road, it came to him how he could even humor Ardith a little with the design.

He had hardly gotten out of his mouth what he wanted when the salesman said, "Sure we got 'em," and disappeared into the back.

He returned with a die-cut pattern of a flower. "This here's a daffodil, but I can make a columbine out of it by adding some little horns on top. You won't know the difference." The man blushed and cleared his throat. "I mean, it's all the same." He rushed on. "They grow like crazy up in Colorado. Me and the wife saw them all over once on a trip up there."

Wesley took the picture he'd torn from *High Plains Harvest* out of his billfold and gave it to the man.

"Oh, that," the salesman said. He studied it a while. "Our cutter's going to sweat this one. And I'm afraid it'll cost you extra."

"No matter," Wesley said.

Then he picked out a red granite stone exactly like the one Ardith described—a red granite double. He made sure it had a border of morning glories and BELOVED FAMILY.

About a month afterward, on a Tuesday, the freight company in town rang them up to see when they could bring it out. It wasn't the sort of thing they would leave on a neighbor's doorstep.

In the late afternoon, Wesley told Ardith where he was headed and went to meet them at the gate down on the highway. Peaceful Dell Cemetery lay on John Jordan's section, and Wesley already had the gate open when the truck got there. He motioned them through—the load rattling over the cattle guard—and closing the gate, stepped around the prairie dog holes and cow chips to his pickup.

The cemetery was up the long hill, the dirt road slow-winding until it crested and revealed a hillside dotted with graves. If there was some place on this earth that a person could settle down and sleep forever, Peaceful Dell was it. Others might not think it beautiful, with its one lone bushy evergreen on the rise sitting lopsided from the constant southeast wind, and with no fence and no sign. So much the better. Wesley liked the way the dead looked to be just grazing there, happening to clump in that spot. It seemed that, anytime, they were free to move on.

He found his plot by pinpointing Earl's new tombstone, a white marble glittering in the late afternoon sun.

When they were positioning the stone, Wesley merely glanced at the

93

etching. It seemed too public, with the freight men around, to scrutinize it. When he'd led the men back to the highway, he returned and sat down in front of it. The combine was carved just as pretty as could be. They'd even put it in a little field, harvesting. He could feel the kernels popping, breaking up in his mouth to tell him it was time to climb on that thing, be ready to ride it day and night, if need be, to get the crop in.

On the stone the combine was turned at an angle so he could see even the pick-up reel—if he strained, maybe the tines—inside the header. He ran his hand over the surface, feeling the sharpness of the grooves. It dawned on him how funny the dump auger looked, poked out sideways.

"Looks like a devil's tail, eh Earl?" He chuckled and looked over at Earl's grave, studying with new eyes the crescent wrench cut into Earl's stone. For a moment he thought his combine was more elegant, certainly more detailed. And then, ashamed of himself, his mind tried to patch it up by telling him Earl's stone looked more balanced, what with the other date filled in. He noticed a mole had tunneled across Earl. Next time he came he'd bring mothballs to sprinkle around.

Wesley heard a car crunching up the hill and turned to see Ardith coming on in her maroon Pontiac. He got to his feet, stiff in the hips from sitting on the ground. His heart bounced a little, and he realized he seldom saw her at a distance anymore.

Her coming this way reminded him of when she and the kids had brought their supper to the field during harvest. Those times he'd climb down from the combine, and they'd eat from the tailgate of the pickup by Coleman lantern. Cornbread and cold fried chicken and pound cake washed down with a quart jar of iced tea. The kids hopping around in the rows pretending the big combine with its staring headlights was a Martian landing. Then it was back on that thing for the night.

Ardith pulled slowly to a stop and got out. Her door closed with a silly, clipped sound in the hush. He searched her face. She made her way to him, standing beside their lots, her apron furling sideways in the breeze.

"Are they done?" she asked.

She looked down at the stone and, after a moment, realizing he had bought a double one after all, she linked her arm in his. "Look at you!" she said shyly. "You do want to sleep on the same pillow with me."

So, that was it.

Squinting, she began to read the names of the children and their birthdates. When she finished, she sighed. "It's a miracle. They're all right."

"I made sure," Wesley said. He knew she saw her morning glories but that she would keep silent about them to save back a little of her pride.

She looked up. "Peaceful Dell. The sky always looks like a big clean Pyrex bowl up here," she said.

Wesley shaded his eyes and pointed. "I was just thinking, how if Jesus was to come and raise Earl up, the first thing he'd see was that clump of ash and elm where his schoolhouse used to be."

Ardith laughed. "For Pete's sake, that wouldn't be any heaven!" she said. "Wish him something else."

As if in answer, there arose the howl of a lone coyote. It came out of a windbreak to the southeast. Wesley cupped Ardith's shoulder in his hand, and she hooked a finger in one of his belt loops. They stilled themselves to listen.

The old coyote had let out only a few yi-yi-yi's when another coyote joined her, and then another, and another until there was a whole chorus singing and moaning, scattering the sound up and down the slopes, across the buffalo grass, into the little two-bit canyons.

"Pups," Wesley said. "Listen to 'em."

Finally, the tender yearning calls died away.

They turned slowly to go. "Sure not much grass on Earl's grave yet. Grass takes a while to catch on up here," Wesley said.

"Earl made a big lump," Ardith said.

Now the sun was running out in long lines, dividing the sky into wedges of pink and gold. Wesley pointed. "Looks like your peach pie," he said. They started toward the cars and Wesley looked back one more time at his combine. The operator's seat was still empty.

Ezekiel Saw the Wheel
Randall Kenan

Gloria Brown dreamt her daughter would die in a helicopter. Tamar was a master sergeant in the Army due to fly out for her third tour next Thursday. Tamar's birthday/going away party was later that very day. Tamar's father, Gloria's ex-husband and business partner, would be there. Gloria needed to stop by and pick up the cake—a giant, rectangular-shaped red velvet cake, Tamar's favorite. Gloria kept glancing at the clock on the wall. She needed to go soon.

The man had sat in silence for the last ten minutes. Perhaps longer. Gloria was not really sure. But this sort of awkward silence was part of her job. Had been since the beginning. People would be surprised how often exactly this sort of thing happened. News of the recently deceased— especially someone mighty close—sometimes conjured up something like paralysis, as if the mind had gone off-line, had shut down to reboot.

The man and his wife had been taking a long-postponed trip to the Outer Banks. The story was that she had kin there, though she had never met them, nor did they try to connect on this particular visit, and the couple had been on their way to Wilmington when she was stricken by a massive stroke at a Hardee's in Crosstown. The coroner had a "bug up my behind"—as he himself said one cold morning out back of the county offices, cigarette dangling from the corner of his mouth—about any corporate-run funeral homes, so he always contracted out to independents. Today he'd called Gloria and Ray, "Got an out-of-towner for y'all." What followed was paperwork, largely; a few phone calls; and an awkward conversation with a man who had not planned on driving home alone.

Gloria asked the man, who still sat in silence, "Is there someone I can call to come drive you back to Texas, sir?"

She could tell when it was about to happen, she could almost see it

97

happening, like watching the lights at the top of a tower switching off, going dim right before her eyes. One level at a time. Radio silence. For some reason these silences never bothered her. Her ex-husband once told her she was simply intuitive and a natural empath. At the time, Gloria had not a clue as to what he had meant.

Gloria wanted to call the cake-maker to make sure the big red cake would be ready. She felt certain it would be; but she had a tendency to worry about things of this nature, things over which she had some control. Things like a grieving widower, for some reason, perturbed her much less.

Indeed, she could tell he was not the sort of man who wanted someone to come and sit next to him, to hold his hand and say those things a mortuary professional was expected to say, practiced, road-tested proverbs and reassurances as eye-catching and non-threatening as fruit-baskets, delivered with highly convincing sincerity which, paradoxically, could not be faked.

Last night's dream had been in Technicolor, filled with swirling dust and lots of cussing. Big boys in big sand-colored boots. The sand-colored camouflage Gloria had come to hate seeing in airports. Anywhere. She dreamt a dream of blood. She dreamt a dream of helicopter blades going swoosh, swoosh and swoosh, and then stopping. Just like in the movies Gloria had watched about the troops in Iraq. *Black Hawk Down. Jar Head.* That TV series on Lifetime. She had gone in and out of periods of watching and reading lots of media about the war. Some weeks she tried to pretend, tried to imagine Tamar was coaching basketball at a small school, or teaching, until she got an email from her daughter, or did that talking through the computer (that never seemed to work right), or it was time to send off a care package. In truth, she spent little time not thinking about her oldest daughter being 7,437 miles away from home, more or less. Thereabouts.

The dream tasted like reality and had the weight of the evidence of things not seen and the substance of things yet to come, and Gloria wanted to talk to her pastor; but her new pastor—armed with his M.Div. from Union Seminary and his M.S.W. from Chapel Hill—would try to interpret the dream and talk about Alice Miller or some psychologist. Couldn't the man see she had been dealing with death and dreams for the last thirty years? She wasn't exactly a pullet. This sort of thing the pastor had done before. Gloria eventually stopped talking to him about her dreams. She knew when a dream was a dream and when a dream was more than a dream. This one felt like something more than a dream, and she knew there was not a thing she could do about it but pray. Tamar was getting on that plane. And Gloria was bound to see her off. Send her off. Cling to faith. See what the Lord had in store. Hope. Pray. Be humble. Believe.

Soon and very soon Gloria would finish up here with this gentleman, finish making the transfer arrangements with the funeral home in Texas, escort this gentleman out, lock up, and fetch the red velvet cake. There was still plenty of time.

She would arrive home and find her younger daughter, Eunice—so capable and reliable despite her seemingly silly and frivolous nature, her inexhaustible need to gossip, and her overweening need for attention. Eunice and her five children and her dour husband, who seemed only happy while watching basketball or football.

Gloria would find Lilith already in the kitchen, finishing up something delicious, something old, something new, showing off her almost supernatural skills, not so much a showing off as an offering of herself, her abundance, an ingratiation: 'I am doing this, putting forth this effort, so that you will like me, Mrs. Brown, and there is so much to like; if you do not like me, something must be wrong with you.'

Sometimes it took Gloria aback, startled her, when she considered how well she got along with—how much she actually liked and enjoyed—her older daughter Tamar's girlfriend—indeed thought of her as her own daughter, though in a guarded sense. Lord knows, in so many ways Lilith trumped either of her two girls as women . . . despite her affliction. But the Lord loved her just the same, the same as he loved Tamar. This lesson her new pastor was trying to teach her, had been teaching her, and what a blessing it was now to release the unease and vexation she had been harboring in her bosom, lo these many years. Since before Tamar played varsity basketball and all those loud whispers came from behind her back like coiled and poisonous vipers. But the Lord said you shall handle venomous snakes and yet live. Amen. This Gloria Brown had done. Many, many times.

Gloria sighed out loud.

She grimaced when she realized she had troubled the silence. How long had they been sitting here?

Gloria imagined Lilith sitting where this abject Texan now sat. Gloria allowed herself to wonder how Lilith would process Tamar's demise. With cold, icy, machine-like efficiency? Or with the light, butterfly warmth that seemed to accompany almost anything she did, surrounded by doves, rainbows, and unicorns? Or would she suddenly reveal the seams in her stitchwork, unravel, allow the tears and the snot to run, and jump aboard the grief train full of howls and woe, incoherent and feeling the growing void inside? Or would she be like the stoic Texan before Gloria, incapable of speech, downright cataleptic with fear? Gloria knew that fear.

She prayed, Lord, don't let my baby die over yonder. You are God, You send us signs and wonders, and Your will shall be done. Your ways are not our ways. Your ways are mysterious and awesome to behold. But You said, Lord, yes You did, that the prayers of a righteous man—a righteous woman—avail much. Let no harm befall my girl, dear Lord, our Father. Protect her as you have protected her, and I shall remain your servant.

The man was staring directly at Gloria, and for a moment she feared she had been praying in words and not just in her mind. As the stare continued unbroken, she knew it was something more, a recognition, something shared, something ineffable, very like the passing of an angel in the darkness of the night.

Listen.

Gloria Brown was very good at listening.

Pissed Away
Jim Sanderson

My father steps out the back door of the Cactus Lounge and into an early morning breeze. The sun is just coming up, and it lights a pumpjack. To somebody not from West Texas, the pumpjack looks like a giant mosquito sucking up blood from the earth. The line of orange the rising sun makes and the glitter from the new pumpjack almost make the morning pretty; but the cool, kind summer breeze, not a rough West Texas spring wind, blows tumbleweeds and trash against the pumpjack and a barbed wire fence farther away in the half-light.

My father squats, the way an old farmer would, looks down, and sees crumpled laundry at the bottom of the steps. Raising himself, he toes the laundry and hears a grumble and notices the laundry shifting. One of the drunk gamblers at Snake Popp's game must have come outside while it was still dark, maybe to piss, fallen, and then passed out. Best to let him lie, my father thinks, and squats back down on the step. His head hurts. His eyes still water from all the smoke inside the Cactus Lounge. He coughs up some goo from his burning throat and lungs. His clothes smell from the smoke. He has just closed up another one of Snake's invitation-only gambling nights. Amarillo Slim himself had spent the night in the Cactus Lounge, losing big and leaving well before sunrise. Snake had several tables set up and different games went on at each.

My father is Snake Popp's "assistant." My father is not tall, but he is a good two hundred and ten pounds. He is squat like a pulling guard or a bull dog. He is the type of guy that a troublemaker can look at and think he might be able to whip but wouldn't want to try. My father's face tells a troublemaker that he would have to pay for starting any shit. So Snake hires my father to keep peace.

All night, with Johnny Dexter, his partner, my father had watched over the card players. The pros stayed sober and concentrated on the cards. Amateurs faked laughing at their losings or went outside and cried about them. The lump of laundry at my father's feet was probably a crier. My father and Johnny Dexter watched them all. Somebody could have just lost control of his nerves. Somebody could have gotten pissed. So my father and Johnny just watched. At the end of the night, the way Snake Popp pushed his shoulders back, my father knew Snake Popp had won big.

Snake Popp is mostly a legitimate businessman. He is not nick-named Snake because he is as mean as a snake but because, when he was just kid, he was bitten by a rattler and lost a chunk of skin off his ankle. Snake grew up liking to show that scar to people. So he became *Snake*, and then he became fairly rich.

The door hits my father in the back. He looks up and sees Dee Price in the doorframe. Dee owns the building and the rights to the vending machines. Being a friend of Snake's, she arranged for the game after midnight closing. "Almost pretty, isn't it?" Dee asks and sits beside my father.

Her body is taut. She has lost a breast to cancer and likes to tell people about the operation. She even likes to show them her scar. Her hair is swept back from her face in wings, as is the fashion, so she is attractive. But a forked scar running down her forehead to her left cheek ruins her face. As with her mastectomy, she likes to tell people about that scar. A broken whiskey bottle gave it to her. My father looks at the bobbing pumpjack to avoid Dee because she wants him to work for her. "Long night," she says.

"It's what Snake pays me for."

"There's better money and shorter hours," Dee says. "If you want them."

My father looks at the trash lined up on the fences and watches a tumbleweed catch on the pumpjack and then roll away. Far off in a small pasture, a frisky young horse trots the length of the fence and then back again, just burning off his energy. "You're right. It is almost pretty."

The few clouds in the sky have pink undersides. A rooster crows. There is the smell of rain on the wind, though my father knows that it will not rain this Sunday. And it is as cool as it will be all day. He watches because this truly is as beautiful as it gets in West Odessa, the unincorporated, ill-planned community of trailers, cinderblock buildings, and small bars out west of Odessa. And in just a moment, as it happens in

West Texas, the sun pulls itself above the flat horizon, and suddenly, the morning is bright yellow light and hot.

It is 1984, the boom has busted, the locals have pissed away the money that they made. As the plaques in bars say: *An Oil Field Prayer: Please Lord, give us another boom, and I promise not to piss this one away.* But there is still gambling and bootlegging in dry counties and illegal girls from Mexico stripping in the Stampede Club, so Snake Popp is still making a living—even if people can't always pay him. So Snake Popp hires my father and Johnny Dexter. And Dee, recognizing a tough, intimidating man when she sees him, wants to hire my father too. "If you can tear yourself away from the view, Colton, Snake wants to see you."

As my father pushes himself up, Dee says, "You know with just a little more nerve, you could be making more money than what Snake pays you."

"I ain't gone to jail for what Snake has me do."

"Not yet," Dee says. "So are you making what you should for what you are risking?"

"I'm making do," my father says.

My father walks into the haze of cigarette and cigar smoke in the Cactus Lounge. Next to the bar, with his head on his folded arms and his snoring rattling the rickety bar and a glass, is Johnny Dexter, my father's partner. My father walks up to the barstool and lightly kicks it. Johnny doesn't budge. My father kicks it again. Johnny pulls his head up and shakes it. "Don't let Snake see you sleeping this soon after working," my father says. Johnny is much younger than my father. He is bigger but not as scary. He has a gentle look in his hangdog face and eyes. People might not think he will do what he threatens to do to them. They know my father would do what he threatens to do to them. But Johnny is quick, he tries hard, and he listens to my father.

The Cactus Lounge has an office, and my father enters it without knocking. He sits across from the card table that serves as a desk. Snake comes out of another door that connects to the bar. He slaps cologne on his face, trying to wake up. Snake's silver hair is combed straight back, making him look like that old country singer Porter Wagoner. Snake makes it a habit, even in these hot summer months, to never look hot. He makes his living with his big fancy bar, his bootlegging in dry counties, and his strip joint. But his passion is gambling. All his businesses and passions require that you bluff, but Snake wants no one to know when he is bluffing, including my father.

"Job well done," he says to my father. "Went real smooth tonight. 'Course there was some weeping and gnashing of teeth, but nobody just lost their shit."

"Dee's offered me another job," my father says.

"Now, Colton," Snake says. "I'm being as fair to you as I can. But this bust has busted more than the oil companies. Without roughnecks fucking around and throwing their money away, I ain't got the profits I used to."

"I got a family," my father says.

"That Mexican family you married into still eating up your money?"

"I got expenses."

"And just what you think you're going to do with your talents other than to work for me? You think that family of yours is going to help you climb up the social register? You think you going to join First Baptist and go to church?"

Snake, in his Polo shirt with the little horse figure where the pocket should be, combs his hair back up over his head, shakes his comb, and puts it back into his cotton slacks' back pocket. "Dee's talking shit. What can she offer you? Picking up and servicing vending machines? Throwing out drunks?"

"I think it's more along the lines of what I do now."

"And so there you go, you admit it. You got it pretty easy."

"I'm fixing to go home. Like you, I been up all night."

"Dee and I both got a problem with a deadbeat. Don Smiley owes me some money from our little games, and he owes Dee some rent. Neither one of us likes to call the police or the county. So we need you and Johnny to pay a visit."

"So I am working for Dee."

"See there, you get what you wish for," Snake says. "Dee and me go back." Snake smiles. He has worked on his suntan by sitting out at his pool two hours a day. He is lean from swimming in that pool. He has a thin silver moustache to match his silver hair. His slacks are white. His polo shirt is purple, and he looks as fresh as if he has just gotten up, showered, shaved, and dressed. "Listen, let's not get bitchy here. Why don't you let me buy you breakfast?"

"I got to get home."

"Got to or want to?"

"My family's going to be in church, and I'm supposed to watch my two boys."

"We can still get breakfast."

"Maybe Johnny'll go."

"This family business is twisting your stomach and your brain in knots. Relax a little." Snake pats my father's shoulder as he walks out the office door. A year before, my father and Johnny drove to El Paso and checked into a Holiday Inn. Then they went to a liquor store just outside of town and started carrying cases out of the store and into their car. It was payment for Snake. A month before, someone started saying nasty things to one of the strippers at the Stampede. Then he tried to follow her home. She didn't speak English, but she made Snake and my father understand. When that lonely man told my father and Johnny to fuck off, my father plowed straight into him, pinning him against the wall, and kneed him in the crotch. While Johnny pounded him, my father took off that man's thick belt and wrapped it over his knuckles, so his knuckles wouldn't get so battered. After pounding him with that belt, my father looked at his battered knuckles. It was a money belt with a zipper on its inside. So my father kept it and gave it to Snake.

My father steps into the Cactus Lounge and the slanting sunbeams filled with the dust falling down from the ceiling and the smoke wafting about. Snake comes out behind him and yells to Johnny, "Hey, Johnny boy, your partner don't want none, but you interested in breakfast?"

Johnny's face brightens up, and he looks at my father. "Boss is buying breakfast and you refuse?"

"Go on ahead. I got family to tend to," my father says. Johnny jumps off his barstool. Smiling, the new morning sun gleaming off his silver hair, Snake steers himself out of the Cactus Lounge, and Johnny Dexter, with one last look over his shoulder at my father, follows Snake into the sunshine.

My father steps through several sunbeams when Dee comes in from the back door. "That fella you saw outside got sober enough to stagger down the road. He can't remember where he left his car."

My father plants his elbows on the bar and worries.

"Maybe if you'd've studied harder in high school and gone to college, you'd be doing the books for Snake instead of busting heads," Dee tells him.

"I was never good with numbers," my father says.

"So you don't know what adds up to what," Dee says, and my father smiles. "You want a drink? I'm buying," Dee says.

"I got to go home," my father says.

"You know," Dee says, "I got a friend. Ol' Bill Sears. He sells old, beat-up cars to illegal Mexicans. He knows they're poor, knows they can't make the payments; but he sells to them, collects what he can for several months, takes a loss several months, then repos it. When he has a night off and needs cash, your partner, Johnny, rides shotgun for Bill's repo guys. Then Bill sells that car again, and again, and again. The oil bust has been good for Bill. I'm thinking of going into business with Bill Sears. Why not you?"

"Why you so interested in me?"

Dee pours herself a shot and sips it. "I don't like to see people sell themselves short."

Who knows why Dee wants to help my father. Maybe good, reliable people who provide the type of help my father does are hard to come by. So my father goes to breakfast with her, instead of Snake and Johnny, and listens to her schemes and scams.

* * *

My father lives with his family—and on and off with his in-laws—in a small house on Adams Street. The house is old and will probably soon just crumble, but it is cheap. My father knows that he wants a family. He knows that a family in place in a house is a part of what you are supposed to want, a part of social and economic advancement. But he hasn't prepared for a family, a house, or advancement.

He comes home to a nearly empty house. In the kitchen, his father-in-law, Raul, sits and listens to a throbbing Norteño song. It is about bleeding and broken hearts and the women who cause them. "We have TV," my father says.

"I like the radio better," Raul says.

"So they've already gone to church?" my father asks.

"Early mass," Raul says.

"And you?"

"I done fine my whole life without the church. It's for women anyway. Besides, I watch the boys now."

My father leaves my grandfather to his coffee and music, and walks down the hall to the last bedroom. He opens the door and steps in to see his sons. They are both in their pajamas and still sleepy because they have gotten up even earlier than on a school day. The older one watches some show about animals on TV. He looks up and smiles at his father. The younger one just keeps smearing deep blue across the coarse page of his coloring book and does not look up. "You boys, not going to say hello to your daddy?" my father asks.

And in unison, the boys say, "Hi, Daddy."

My father scoops up his younger son and then presses him up in the air until he almost touches the ceiling. This is me he picks up. I have lost amusement with the games that he plays with me and my brother. I see more of my grandfather and various uncles than I do of my father, and they play better games. So *father* to me is this shapeless term for the man who I know is responsible for the food, order, and money. Like food, order, and money, my father has a distant relation to me. I know that these things exist, that they are important, that they account for my life as it is. But I have no direct connection to any of them, only several old games, like the airplane ride under the ceiling. I stretch out my arms and hum as my father taught me.

My brother, Arnie, is interested only in his TV show. He has started school and has learned to read. I am waiting to start in another month or two and am both scared and anxious about being away from my house for the biggest portion of my conscious day.

What I don't know is that my father feels just like I do. He is not sure of his relation to me or the family. He knows that he should provide money, food, and order; and he tries to do that, but he can't really see the results of what he provides. My mother runs the house. And what she can't do, Raul usually does. My father doesn't know how to play with his kids. All he knows for sure is that they need more.

So we both know that we come from the same blood, that we are surrounded by the same people, that we both desire good for that group of people. But we aren't sure of much else. When my father puts me down, he knows that he does not know me or my brother.

My father leaves us and goes into his kitchen and pours himself another cup of coffee. He has already had breakfast and coffee with Dee, so though he is tired, he knows that he cannot go to sleep. He listens to my grandfather's sad songs that he cannot understand and stares into his cup. "A man's job is his job," my grandfather says. "So you don't got to worry when you come home."

"I've been offered another job," my father says. Raul twists in his seat and reaches up to turn down the volume of his radio. "There's some things about it that are . . . not quite right."

"You mean *legal*," my grandfather says. "I'm a Mexican. I know about these things. You got to figure out the risks. You got to figure what you got to lose."

"So you tell me. What have I got to lose?"

Raul reaches and turns the radio down lower. "What you mean?"

"I don't know nothing about this."

"What's *this*?"

"This family thing. All that goes on here."

"What's to know? Same as church. The women go. They take care of family. Your job is your job."

"But I don't know what goes on here."

"So don't."

"I got to live here."

"So live here, but don't think so much."

"So what if I was to go to jail, or get shot, or something?"

"My father swam across a river and pulled me after him. You takes your chances when you do what you got to."

Frustrated, my father stares into his coffee. His nerves dance and tingle because he wants to be in bed and well on his way to sleep. But he knows the coffee and his thinking will keep his brain sizzling. He walks through his house and looks at the crucifixes and paintings of the Virgin Mary, the brightly colored walls that Raul painted, the bare carpet. He opens the door and smiles again at his boys. He goes to his living room, turns on the TV, watches *Meet the Press* until the boring politicians and the political analysts cool his brain, and he goes to sleep.

His own snoring wakes him, and then he hears the hum of many voices speaking Spanish. He rises and goes into the kitchen to see children and in-laws coming into his house. The women busy themselves in his kitchen. His sons come running out, still in their pajamas, to play with their cousins. He has no idea of how many people fill his house. He has no idea if he even knows them all. Soon grease is popping, the smell of garlic fills the air, and the kitchen warms from heating the dishes that his in-laws have brought over.

My father goes into the backyard, and the in-laws and friends are there too. He does finally recognize my mother. She is small and petite—just over five feet. She can disappear into a crowd; yet when you pick her out within a crowd, you see her distinctly, and your eyes stick on her. Likewise, her eyes can hold you in place. My father smiles, and she gives the smile back to him. But behind her smile is a look that says she is happy with her family but disappointed with my father. He walks to her and kisses her forehead, and as he does, my father hazily wishes and waits.

* * *

After two years, I walked away from my courses at Odessa Community College. I was not yet twenty-one and bored. I didn't know what I wanted to do; mostly, I just didn't want to do anything. So I lived in a one-room apartment in South Odessa and smoked pot. My mother and my grandfather couldn't get too pissed off at me because, compared to my older brother, Arnie, who was in prison, I looked like the good son. My mother then came to me and said that she had a note directly from my father. I hadn't seen or spoken to my father for fifteen years; but like the voice of God, he was speaking to me through my mother via the U.S. Postal Service. My mother gave me a note with phone numbers on them. One had the name *Snake Popp* written above it in my mother's careful, looping script. The other had *Dee Price* written above it.

I called Snake Popp; and early on a spring afternoon, I walked out of the wild spring wind and into his new nightclub, the Midnight Rodeo, a cavernous, classy bar. The soles of my boots clicked as I crossed the wooden dance floor of his deserted bar to get to the office door. A bartender warily watched me. I knocked, and a voice told me to come in. I opened the door to silver-haired Snake sitting behind his desk. "So you're Colton's boy?"

I nodded and sat down in front of his desk when he motioned. He chewed gum in one side of his mouth. "This stuff is supposed to make you quit smoking," he said and chomped. He ran one hand through his silver hair. "Why do you suppose Colton sent you to me?"

"To get a job. I'm kind of down on my luck."

"You don't want the kind of jobs I got," he said.

"I don't think I got the right to be picky."

"I got nothing where you do something romantic like bartending."

109

"I need a job," I said.

Snake pushed himself up from his chair. His silver hair matched his silver slacks. He ran his hands through his hair again and left two indentations right at the top sides of his head. His mouth worked grinding the gum. "You been in many fights?"

"Few."

"Colton, Colton," Snake said and shook his head. With his head still hanging, he said, "Look, truth is, I just got nothing."

I nodded.

"No, truth is, I got nothing I want to give you. You catching my drift?"

I nodded again.

Snake sat back down in his chair and put his feet upon his desk. "Your father should have thought of that," he said.

"I think he did," I said.

"No, no. You run on and find someone else willing to give you what you shouldn't have. The old days are gone."

"I need a job," I said.

"Did your father say you should go see Dee Price?"

"Yes sir."

"Well then you go see her. I owe your father, but your father don't know Dee and me don't associate much anymore. Best of luck to you."

I went to the Cactus Lounge, where Dee had an office. She greeted me and said she had been expecting me.

"So you talked with my father?" I asked.

"Off and on. Mostly off. Nobody from the old days talks much to your father," she said. "So you need a job."

"How did you know?"

"I talk on and off to Snake Popp. What kind of work are you willing to do?"

"The kind that pays," I said.

I had better luck with Dee. She started me out cleaning, picking up, and hauling. Sometimes, on weekends, I rode shotgun on a repo truck. While some guy named Larry backed up the truck to a parked car and attached it, I'd sit in the cab with a shotgun. My instructions were to fire in the air if anybody tried to stop Larry. Only if I saw a gun pointed directly at Larry was I to aim and pull the trigger. Then Dee moved me up to collecting the coins from the vending machines. Since I was out late at night with bags of coins, she gave me a pistol and told me to be careful with it but not to take chances.

And when I had the time, I would sometimes drop into the Cactus Lounge and have a beer with her—even though, at first, I was shy of twenty-one. And sometimes, I went into one of the other bars she owned: the Silver Stallion, the Mustang, the Post, the Office. And when she felt like it, she told me about my father when she first met him. She told me about Johnny Dexter. Then she told me that I could never replace my father but I could become another Johnny Dexter.

After a year and half, just turned twenty-one and thus a legal adult, with a job, a car, and a gun, I felt good about myself. To my mother and grandfather, I was at least supporting myself. To Dee, as she often said, I had a future; but I was still kind of hazy about my future. On a cold day, with the chilly wind outside the Cactus Lounge but with some still finding its way into the bar and some still shaking the walls from the outside, I had just dropped off some deposits from coins and was sitting at a table, having a beer, reviewing my life—or what there was of it—when Dee walked out of the office with a short, mean-looking man. He had a scar across the bridge of his nose that almost matched Dee's scar. "Michael," Dee said. "This is your father."

Dee turned back to her office, and with the wind whistling through the walls and the frames of the windows, my father stepped toward me, his hands in his jacket, scaring me because I thought he might pull those hands out and beat the hell out of me. "Good to see you," he said. And then a smile cracked his face. "You changed," he said.

He sat down across from me. I saw myself. He was short and squat, just like me. But he was wide, and even with a jacket and fedora on, he looked like he was muscular. His face was not quite like mine: it was all angles, with scars, and baked to a dark brown. He was Anglo, yet he was darker than I was, and I was half Mexican. His lids seemed permanently draped over half his eyes. Under his eyes, his cheeks were puffy. He was a man who could do some damage to you. His face told you that he wouldn't mind damaging you.

"I got a rented Lincoln Continental outside. You want to take a drive around town while I reminisce?"

I just said, "Sure."

His face lit up as he drove around town and passed his old haunts. He told me about fights, about who he beat up, about close scrapes. He

111

told me about Snake: good enough man and tough as they come on the gambling table, but a real "pussy" in an actual fight, which was why he had hired my father and Johnny Dexter. We drove by the house on Adams Street that I barely remembered. Then we drove by the house where my mother and her new husband and my grandfather now lived. "Who you think bought that house for them?" he asked me.

I didn't have to answer.

Then we drove through the wind and the blowing trash and tumbleweeds and dust back to the Cactus Lounge. Some of the dust, wind, and trash followed us in, and my father sat at a table and put a pint bottle of bourbon on the table, and a young waitress brought us coke and ice. Dee was gone. So my father got to the point. "You see what I got. You seen that car outside. I own one just like it. In Dallas, I got a nicer house than your mama, and I live in it alone. You understand me, boy?"

"Yes," I lied.

My father slammed the table with his flat palm. "No, you don't. That was a set-up, testing your honesty. You don't know shit. Ain't no way I can be a father to you. Not now. I'm just this old guy with some money attached to him. But you looked at my face. Dee probably told you some things. I explained some things I done. And now I'm telling you, you stick with Dee, and you can have what I got."

"Yes sir, I'm working at it," I said.

"You ain't listening, Michael. You think you want what I got?"

"Yes."

"No."

"All right, no."

"That's right. I'm just this old guy with some money. So I will deposit money in an account for you to get your ass back in college and erase the bad mark you left there."

"But I got this."

"But you don't listen." He lifted his bottle and took a sip. "You seen that scar on Dee's face? She shown you that scar on her chest where they cut off a tit?" He didn't wait for me to answer, but the answer was that I hadn't seen her chest. "She likes to show off that surgery. Makes her think she's tough. Well, she is tough. And she'll make you tough. And tough can be useful to some people with money. And you can be living in a big house by yourself, driving a Lincoln Continental, and chewing on your own liver because you know all you got is nothing, is just the price somebody paid for you, and now they own your sorry ass. And there's your brother in prison eating his liver because he knows he made his life into total shit. And here you are flunking out of college and pissing away anything you got."

I was getting scared. "You ain't going to hit me, are you?"

My father started laughing. "No, beating you ain't going to do no good. You ain't listening. I'm telling you I'll pay for you to get your ass back in college and then out of it and make less money than me and end up with a shitty little house and some screaming kids of your own because you got a job only some college asshole can get. And that ain't the place where this job is leading."

"I don't get it," I admitted.

My father reached into his jacket and pulled out a check. He put it in front of me. "You get one of these a year for three years. You can piss it all away. Or you can invest it by giving yourself a glimpse of a different type of world than this and seeing if you like it better. Dee will be here awhile."

I couldn't believe the amount written on the check. "How did you get this kind of money?"

My father stuck his forefinger up under the brim of his hat and pushed up, so I could see his mangled face. "I had to kill a few people. I beat up some others. If the cops ever get me, I got enough information to plea bargain myself into a lighter sentence. You want to be me?" Then my father told me why he deserted me.

* * *

The Monday after the Sunday my father looked at his two boys and realized he had nothing to say to them, he and Johnny Dexter walk into Don Smiley's bar, which is mainly a shack where pot deals take place. This is their usual plan. My father is a compact, two-hundred-pound ramrod, and carries a gat in his jeans pocket. Johnny has his shirt tail out so that he covers the nine-millimeter pistol stuck in the back of his pants. First they talk, then my father rams. By this time, they usually have some earnest money. If not, Johnny waves the pistol. They have yet to actually use it.

Inside Smiley's bar, Johnny Dexter and my father stand on the customer side of the bar with Don Smiley in between them on the other side. Don has a trimmed beard and round glasses, like a professor. He knows who they are. "Fellas, look, this don't have to get ugly. I got the money. I really do. It's just tied up right now."

Don pulls two beers up and places them in front of Johnny and my father. "On the house," he says.

"Hell, I'd hope it's on the house," Johnny says, and my father drops his head, disappointed in Johnny's manner. My father is more businesslike than Johnny or Don.

"Look, I've been knowing Snake Popp for fifteen years now. You just go back and tell him I'm good for it. He'll tell you."

"Who you think sent us?" Johnny asks.

"What's in the cash register?" my father asks.

"That's for my family. That's how I make my living," Smiley says.

My father reaches across the bar, knocking his beer bottle over, grabs Don by his shirt front, and yanks him over the bar. As Don clears the bar, my father jerks up; but Don's shirt rips, and Don falls to the ground on my father's side of the bar. Quickly, Johnny kicks Don in the head and the side. "Fuck your *good for it*," Johnny says. "Snake wants you to say *now*."

My father bends over and grabs shreds of Don's shirt and jerks him back up. "Now is there any need for us to do this?" my father asks in a sincere voice.

"I say we kick the shit out of him," Johnny says.

"You got to show some earnest money," my father says. "That's just the way it works."

"I'll show you *earnest*," Don says. "Look behind you." Johnny jumps to one side, and my father slowly turns around to see Don's wife, Lula, holding a .38 pistol at her arm's length, pointed at his chest.

"You two get out of here," she says. While Lula keeps both arms straight and stiff with both hands wrapped around the butt and pokes the gun at my father's chest, Johnny slides one foot to the other to get around beside her. And when Don grabs a beer bottle and beans my father, spraying beer and glass across the bar, my father slides to the floor. Before my father hits the floor, Johnny has this nine-millimeter out; but before he can start shooting, Lula deliberately squeezes the trigger and sends a bullet into Johnny.

My father comes up with Lula in his arms. He clobbers her with one fist, then pulls the pistol away with his other hand. Lula is now on the ground and groaning like Johnny. Don advances toward Lula, and my father is not sure what Don intends. "You settle down," he says to Don; but Don, with a shattered beer bottle in his hand, keeps advancing. So my father shoots Don with Don's wife's revolver. Lula grabs his ankle, and my father feels a knife or razor blade cutting at the back of his calf, as though Lula is trying to sever an Achilles tendon. Not flinching, aiming carefully so as to not hit his own foot, my father shoots Lula.

My father squints through the blood and tastes it. It is running down his face from the crack on top of his head. Johnny has a strained look on his face that begs my father. My father knows his options. He can drag Johnny out, get him to Dee or Snake, and then hide out. That would work best if Lula and Don are dead; but he is not sure, and he does not feel like putting more bullets into them. He can call for an ambulance and just leave town, but he is not yet that desperate. Or he could call the police and plead self-defense. He looks at Johnny, who shakes his head and pleads with his eyes.

My father goes to Johnny, grabs him, and drags him out the door. My father gets the shoulder of his pullover shirt bloody when he stands Johnny up, pushes a shoulder into him, and then leans him up against the passenger side door of the car. He opens the door and stuffs groaning Johnny into the car.

He limps back into Don Smiley's bar. Neither husband nor wife move, and my father thinks that surely they are dead. He finds Johnny's gun and sticks it in his belt.

He finds the Smileys' gun and wipes all his prints off it with a bar towel. For good measure, not sure why, he pours a beer over it. Then with the same bar towel, he tries to sop up his and Johnny's blood. But mostly he just mixes the blood up, and that is okay too. Because that way, the ballistics experts—if Odessa has any—can't tell who killed who from what direction. The Smileys were both killed by their own gun, so he decides to leave it. He thinks some more, goes to the cash register, opens it, pulls out the money. The police, he hopes, will think that it is small-time robbery or that the couple just started shooting each other.

He gets another bar towel, wraps it around his calf, and notices the blood seeping into his shoes and the sting in his leg. He looks in the bar mirror and sees his blood-wet hair and the trail of dried blood down his forehead. He limps back out to the truck. He drives to Johnny's apartment, pulls screaming Johnny out of the car, opens the door, and pushes him into the apartment. "Bleed some," my father says. Johnny screams, my father grabs him, drags him back out to the truck, stuffs him in, and drives him to the hospital. My father stops the car and parks it just short of the Emergency Room. "Johnny, can you hear me?" Johnny screams. "You were fucking around with your gun, and it went off."

"But it ain't my gun shot me," Johnny screams.

"I'm hoping the bullet in you is all fragmented so they ain't going to be sure whose gun it came from. And listen, now you listen, Johnny Dexter. This is your truck. Hard as it was, much as it hurt, you drove yourself here. You got it? You ain't seen me." Then as much as it hurts, my father runs, and then he walks, and then he calls Snake.

By early afternoon, he sits in the Cactus Lounge with Snake and Dee. The stitches on his leg feel stiff; the ones on his head feel tight; he is light-headed from the pain pills; and he is afraid, as the nurse at the quick clinic told him, that he might have had a tendon damaged and needs to go to a hospital. Snake did not drive him to a hospital, but to the Cactus Lounge.

Snake Popp sits with his head in his hands and mutters, "Oh Christ, what we going to do? I can't think." He is so busy pushing his hands through his silver hair that he cannot take the cigarette out of his mouth and flick the ashes off.

"Nothing," Dee says. "You ought to be proud of Colton and Johnny. They did just as they should have. It's not going to be a clear case."

"So what is going to happen?" my father asks.

"They could shut me down," Snake says and rubs his head.

"They could piece together a bunch of things, and you could do some jail time," Dee says. "But it's clearly self-defense. All you've done is fail to report what happened."

"What if Johnny talks?" my father asks.

"Oh shit," Snake says.

"Then you'll definitely do some time," Dee says. "But if he knows what's good for him, he won't say nothing."

"Oh Jesus," Snake says.

Dee turns to him, her hard eyes focusing on him, "Snake, you ever figure you ought to get out of the gambling business?"

"I'm gone," Snake says. As my father and Dee think that he means he's giving up his gambling nights, Snake rises and walks to the door.

"Snake," Dee shouts after him. "You can play this one of several ways. We discussed the best way. We keep our stories straight."

"I got it," Snake grumbles.

They watch him go, and Dee turns her hard eyes to my father. "I been through this before. It's best if you just clear out and forget who you are for awhile."

"I can't just leave," my father says.

"I got a friend in Dallas could use a guy like you."

"I thought I could work for you?"

"You did real good today from your story. My friend could use a guy skilled in those areas."

My father can't think, so he drinks most of his bottle of beer. As long as he is in this blur, he figures he might as well plunge in. "I got a family," my father says.

"My friend pays very well for the skills he needs. He needs a man can come out on the winning side of a barroom gun fight."

My father reaches toward his ankle and feels the bandage, feels the slight moisture where the blood is soaking through, considers taking another Darvon. "But my family needs more from me than money."

Dee chuckles, "And just what is that? And what is it you figure you're giving them?"

My father tries to get his mind to see through the fog in his head, tries to get his mouth to make the right words, but nothing comes to him.

"You probably heard me say that, if you look at a whore real close, you can see she ain't got no soul. That's only part of the story. They aren't born without souls. Somewhere along the way, they lose them. I know. I used to run whores. I used to be a whore."

"I'm not a whore," my father says.

Dee doesn't even laugh. "I had people help me. I tried to repay them. So now, I'm helping you."

"I got two boys," my father says.

"So now make money. The sad fact is all you got left to give your family is money."

"God damn it, shut up," my father says.

"God damn it, listen," Dee says.

"I got a choice."

"Ain't no choice in something like this. You're beyond choice. You just got to have the smarts and the balls to recognize the obvious."

Still later, after a few hours of sleep in Dee's office, my father stumbles through his small house on Adams Street. He makes his way into the living room where he hears voices. Raul is in front of the TV in a recliner, sleeping. His snoring mixes with the chatter from the late night TV show.

My father makes his way down the hall to my mother's room, slowly opens their door so as not to wake her, looks at her sleeping, and looks at the side of the bed that should be his. For a long time, all that he and my mother have done in that bed is sleep.

He backs out of the bedroom and goes to one farther down the hall. He opens the door to look in. I am sleeping there in my bunk bed with my brother above me. We cannot know that our father is studying our faces because he will not know us beyond this night.

By early morning, before daybreak, my father watches spaced drops of rain splatter on his windshield. He sees FORT WORTH 45 on a green and white road sign in front of him. By the time people are heading off to work, he will be in Dallas with a name, a phone number, and an address that Dee gave him. He wishes he could be a better father.

* * *

With my father's money, I made some choices. I figured that part of my problem was Odessa, so I moved to San Angelo, got admitted probationally to Angelo State University, and got out with a degree in P.E. I found a wife and a job coaching middle school football and teaching history in Denver City, Texas. Denver City is dry, so I have to buy my beer in a New Mexico county; and when I drink my beer, I have to hide the bottles in an old bag and put them in the trash so that the Church of Christ superintendent doesn't know how much I drink. My wife and I have two girls. I take them all on shopping trips to Lubbock, on camping trips in Carlsbad, for long weekends in a Holiday Inn in Dallas or Fort Worth. So I think that I know my wife and girls better than my father knew his wife and boys. Sometimes, when we are in Denver City, we sit out in the backyard, each of us with a drink, look at the rolling land beyond our backyard, and wait or wish for something to happen.

I have just buried my father. I have no idea how Dee Price even knew what had become of me, but she called me and said that his casket was delivered by freight and dropped off at the bus company. My signature was the one they needed. I stood in the living room of my modest 1700-square-foot house in Denver City with my wife busy exercising out on the back porch and my girls playing in the air conditioning inside. I walked past my girls, who did not look up from their dolls and coloring books, and looked out the French doors at my wife practicing her yoga. I just figured that there ought to be more of something—even though I didn't know more of what.

My father had prepared well for his death. Along with the casket was a registered check for expenses, a funeral plot, and a handwritten will. My father spread his money out to everyone: me, my mother, Dee Price, Snake Popp, Raul, and my brother doing his second hitch in prison. Everyone was equal, except I got to be the manager, the coach, the quarterback for his death.

As per his request, we had no service, but gathered to watch as they lowered him into the ground. My mother didn't shed a tear. Raul, my grandfather, just shook his head. My mother hugged me, and Raul shook my hand. They had raised me; but somewhere along the way, after my father appeared again and talked to me, we lost each other. It was the same with my brother. He went to prison and couldn't stay out; I went to Denver City and my own family.

After the funeral, after refusing the offer to stay with my mother, I walked to my pickup truck and found Dee leaning against the door. "Why don't you come by the Cactus Lounge?"

"I got to get back home."

"You got to know how your father died. His will ain't completely executed yet."

So I walked through the sunbeams and dust at the Cactus Lounge, now under its fifth or sixth owner, but still housing Dee Price's office.

She sat at a table in front of the office door with a beer already waiting for me. She rose when I walked up, and smiled. Her smile seemed to make her face crack. The forked scar across her forehead and cheek now competed with the other cracks in her face. The West Texas heat and dryness cooked and baked most people, so we were all headed for looking leathery, especially a coach who squinted into the sun during the two hottest months of the year. Dee seemed to have gotten some extra baking. She was thin to begin with, but now she was extra skinny. Her eyes had a slightly yellowish tint. Though she tried not to be, she was scary. "Sit," she said. I sat behind a beer.

The door to her office opened, and Snake Popp stepped out. He stuck out his hand, and I shook it. Snake was about Dee's age. He was tanned but not wrinkled. He wore a starched Guyabara shirt and just as crisply starched cotton slacks and beige loafers with no socks on. He had a tiny silver earring that matched his silver hair. He sipped from a Bloody Mary in a clear glass.

Dee started, "Your father was an assassin, a hit man. He got hit."

Snake took over. "The casket was closed because he was a mess."

"But he gave it hell right to the very end," Dee said. "I suppose you kind of know why he left Odessa."

"Last I saw him, he gave me some clues."

"Johnny Dexter, his partner, wasn't so lucky. He had to get out of the business because that bullet lodged in his spine. So he ended up in a wheel chair." Dee grunted, "Course he is still alive." She looked at Snake. "He works for Snake."

"And does pretty good for himself, thank you kindly," Snake said.

"So you doing good?" Snake asked.

"Okay," I said. "I'm a coach."

"We know," Snake said. They both shifted in their chairs.

"Look, we figure we owe your father," Dee said. "So we wanted to help you."

"How much is that coaching job paying you?" Snake asked.

"Not enough," I said. By this time, the boom had kind of come back. It wasn't as wild as the last one; but wildcatters were drilling, and Odessa was busy. I had talked with my wife about deserting Denver City and coming back to the money that was flowing through Odessa. With the sunbeams and dust drifting in from the cracks, the Cactus Lounge turned sort of golden.

"I'm mostly retired now, but Dee might be able to use somebody."

"I got people like your dad and what Johnny Dexter used to be working for me. They do what you did. But I need someone with some smarts. Someone to kind of take over some of the day-to-day affairs."

I shifted in my seat.

Snake shifted in his seat, ran his hands up the side of his head to give his hair a pair of silver wings. "I'll leave you to it," he said to Dee. "I'm more settled now."

His shoes squished as he crossed the wooden floor, and he let in a flood of sunlight when he opened the door. When he closed it, my eyes adjusted on Dee. "So is this a real job you're offering me?"

"Yes."

"Would I need a gun like when I was repoing cars and emptying vending machines?"

"Not unless you want one." I stared over her shoulder and felt like I was back in Denver City in my backyard wishing. Dee started talking again. "If you look at a whore real close, you can see she ain't got no soul. That's only part of the story. They aren't born without souls. Somewhere along the way they lose them."

"I know."

Dee seemed to stare over my shoulder, but I looked at her eyes. "The point is, you can lose your soul doing most anything."

"Like working for you." I was sorry for being mean.

"Or being a coach in Denver City." Dee nodded her head to herself. "Look, you may not believe it, but I'm trying to do something good here."

"What about my father? Did he lose his soul?" Dee said nothing. "What about you?" I asked.

"I said you could tell with whores. I ain't a whore no more."

"Was my father?"

Dee looked around and saw no one. She pushed herself up, went behind the bar, and came back with two bottles of beer. "Let me tell you about your father." So she did through several more beers. But mostly the story was about her life and crimes and regrets.

That night, my wife and two girls and I went out to the backyard and waited for the sun to set. As are most sunsets in West Texas, it was beautiful, but it wasn't enough. I felt the itch that my father must have felt when he lived in Odessa. I felt very alone with my wife and daughters. But when the sun finally, fully set and I sat looking at the dark with the women in my life, I decided to keep wanting and wishing with them.

Before Texas
Elise Blackwell

Later in life, after she landed hard in West Texas, Dee started telling people that the scar on her face was carved by a jagged piece of broken whiskey bottle. "A fight," she'd say, "but I didn't get the worst of it. Not by a long shot." Over time she cultivated a set of details that stayed the same, more or less.

Because it's the kind of story people tell, she never knew whether people believed her or not. But given who she was, why shouldn't they? Only once had anyone followed with a question, and that's when a guy she was interviewing asked if the fight had been with a woman or a man. Unable to decide in the moment which would make the better answer, she'd just smiled and said, "A lady never tells."

Many would have made a joke out of that, given who she was. But Odessa's biggest oil boom had busted, and the guy needed the job stocking and collecting from her vending machines. He just smiled and said, "Good for you," and she hired him right there.

Dee wasn't from any part of Texas and hadn't even crossed the Mississippi River until she was twenty-five years old. Before she was twenty, she hadn't even been out of South Carolina except for a school hiking trip to Slippery Rock, North Carolina, and a half-family drive to a scrubby beach in north Florida that looked nothing like she thought a beach was supposed to look like but that maybe she liked better once she got over the gap between expectation and fact.

Between twenty and twenty-five were some long years in Atlanta where she finally got strong, but that seemed as long ago as the rest of it.

It was all before Texas, so it didn't really matter much. If she thought about it more these days, then that was just another side effect of growing old, no more desirable than the spots on the back of her hands, the etches that ruined the lines of her lips. The less there is ahead, the

123

more some people look in the rearview. It surprised her to find that she was one of that some, but we don't always know ourselves that well.

So from time to time, she redrew her scar with the tip of her pointer and remembered that there hadn't been a fight, that she'd been alone when she was cut. Alone when, but not alone before—when she hadn't put up a fight at all.

She'd gone that afternoon with an older boy from school—a boy she'd noticed but had never seemed to notice her. Same old story of a poor girl being impressed by everything she doesn't have: a nice house with a father who works and a mother who doesn't, plus the car, the club, and the friends who were just more of the same kind. Being young and being stupid—two things she wouldn't stay—she'd listened to his lines about her pretty hair and eyes, about how he didn't care what part of town she lived in, about how she was smart enough to go to college and he could help her.

But she wasn't all that young or all that stupid to think that help was all he wanted to give her that day he took her walking down along the Congaree, deeper and deeper into the pines and small hardwoods, a blanket rolled under his arm. And she was fine with that and didn't put up any pretense of saying no, knowing that for a girl like her playing hard to get was nothing but a way to not get got. No hesitation or hemming and hawing—just a near silent acquiescing to what was bound to happen sooner or later with this boy or some other. It was over fast and she lay on her back, listening to small rapids in the river, the whitewater foaming around rocks.

The boy rolled on his side and traced her hairline with one finger, kissed her temple. "My friend," he said. "We were hoping you could take care of him, too. He's been having a real hard time lately and all."

She kept her eyes closed as long as she could stand because she knew when she opened them, she'd see some other boy looking at her. She hoped it wasn't one from school, that it was no one she knew or would see again.

Later, in Odessa, when she touched the scar on her face, she asked herself why she'd said okay. Not *okay*, but she'd gone along, not stopped it. Maybe she'd been in shock, not knowing what she was agreeing to. Once in awhile she told herself she'd gone along with it because she wanted to, because that was the kind of tough thrill seeker she was, a hard ass from the get-go, a wild child from day one. She knew that was a self-protecting lie, though, and mostly she avoided it.

The right answer was more likely something about grief, grief at the realization that this was what he'd wanted from her—not to take her, but to share her—after she'd thought they could be at least something together. She thought that she might love him later if not sooner and that they'd make something out of it for awhile and that maybe before he left, he would help her climb out of her cramped life into one a little better.

Mostly she understood it was just her recognition of the inevitable: *Yes* was the only answer they would have taken. This was a form of self-acceptance, too: This is what I am in the world. This is how the world will see me. What had happened that afternoon by the river was a statement, not a question.

She liked this version of the answer best not only because it was truest but because it made truth out of what she did next, which was deal with the possible consequences, which was to cover her ass in case she had a baby whose father she could not name with more than half a chance of getting it right. They'd offered to walk her back; but she told them she preferred to make her own way, and they seemed happy enough to leave her behind. Once or twice she feared she was lost; but each time the panic stained her throat, she remembered the river was there. There was no way to get lost so long as she could hear the river and the river stayed where it should be.

Before she left the cover of the trees to trudge up the Gervais Street hill, she did three things. She ripped her dress hard. She punched her cheekbone with her fist, not hard at first but harder each time until she could feel the bruise that would bloom later. And she took a piece of broken glass, which she found resting clean on the pine straw, and made the scar she wore into Texas. This she started hard and went fast so there would be no chance to talk herself out of it. When her hand stopped, she felt the blood bead and two drops roll slowly around her eye, rivulets that ran dry at her neck. Then her cut started to bleed in earnest, and she knew she'd gone far enough.

At home she slipped by her father, who sat as he had since he'd been shocked on the job he could no longer do: trembling in his chair, soothing himself with slow sips of the cheapest beer carried by the grocery store where her mother worked.

When she heard her mother enter the house, she waited until her footsteps clicked in the kitchen before calling her into her room and telling her the story she had written in her mind, only half worried that she'd want to take her to the police station. "Were they colored?" her mother asked, and Dee shook her head, observing her mother's relief, and proceeded to describe physically the men that the two boys would be in ten years.

In the end, her mother did what Dee figured she would, which was to give Dee one of her father's beers, sew up her cut, and never mention any of it again. Sometimes her mother looked at her with disgust, as though what had really happened and not what Dee had told her was true. But that look was really nothing new.

The following summer Dee took a cleaning job at the country club by the artificial lakes just outside of downtown. Once in awhile she'd see the boy she didn't know, the second one, and it was all right. The first time, he gave a little nod. The next couple of times, he made eye contact long enough to acknowledge her but not long enough for anyone to notice or to make her feel bad about herself. Then he stopped noticing her at all, and she figured they'd both decided they'd never met and the thing had never happened.

And that was the end of it, except after about a month on the job, she saw the other boy: the first one, the one she blamed for the scar on her face. He was home from college and talking the late afternoon away with friends by the swimming pool, his voice cocktail loud, his gestures wide and happy. He turned to take another drink from a server's silver tray, and his eyes passed over her white uniform as she stood stock still, a dirty cloth hanging from her loose hand.

The thought came to her that she could walk right up to him, cock her fist, and punch him on the high edge of cheekbone just like she'd done to herself. She imagined him catching her hand, saying something like 'Whoa there, filly.' She saw his friends surprised but him taking it in stride, saying something to make them laugh about good help being hard to find. She felt her anger build with its impotence and imagined charging him into the pool, thinking how the heavily chlorinated water would ruin his nice clothes. Just as fast she saw how it would really be: him turning sideways, her momentum hurling her into the chemical water, her swimming to the other side, climbing out in a dripping uniform now transparent, ears mocked by laughter, knowing not to stop even to ask for her last pay.

So she'd turned away from him and gone back to her work, holding the job that she needed for two more years, until one day she met the man who took her to Atlanta and then left her there.

But all of that was before Texas, so it really didn't matter much.

State
Stephen Graham Jones

The first time I saw Slowpoke take somebody down in his particular fashion, it was the second-to-last weekend before our senior year got officially going. I was still in two-a-days, was still puking halfway through each one and cussing Borde, who should have been there with me. He'd got special permission to start in with the team the first day of class, though, because he was going to be roughnecking all summer with one of his uncles down towards Big Lake. As far as Coach knew, Borde—that's short for La Borde, my best friend since second grade—he was going to be on the rig until the very last Saturday before class, one day after our last two-a-day. What Coach had told him right before he left was not to get his thumbs pulled off, yeah? And then he'd mimed guiding a chain down into the hole.

Borde had turned around in the hall, kind of jogged backwards like he owned the world, and Fonzed his hands back at Coach, and then we'd exploded into summer.

This year, we were all returning, were going to make a run for Regionals, at least. Maybe all the way, if all the promises we'd made last November had been real.

Some of those promises included not drinking beer behind the Sonic and not driving our trucks through anybody's fields at night and not sneaking into the community pool afterhours, with the girls, and Coach hadn't been smiling when he laid all this down—but still, right?

You can always keep a promise later, I mean.

And, if Borde did manage to come back whole, a "man" now, if everything his dad wanted to happen on the rig happened, then his tight-end hands, yeah, they might just carry us to Regionals, where the college scouts watched, clipboards in hand.

It was the dream.

129

I didn't need the season to be good so much, had my grades to fall back on—but if Borde had to stay around Midland, he was one of those guys you could already see his life story: he'd bounce around from rig to rig, girl to girl, truck to truck, fight to fight, and then wake up one morning thirty-five years old, a warm beer in his hand, feeling cheated. He'd become his dad, I mean, and start glaring at his own son, a resentment building in them both that would poison each dinner, each game, each everything.

It wouldn't be a bad life, don't get me wrong. But I'd known Borde since we were nine, trying to save baby birds' lives with eyedroppers, and what I wanted for him was for that nine-year-old to grow up, as stupid as that sounds.

Not that I'd ever tell him this.

His girlfriend, though?

Yeah, maybe. In not so many words.

With Borde gone the summer through, he'd told me to watch out for her. I'd told him sure, *watch out*, quadruple quote marks, and he'd tackled me and I'd slung him around into the fence and then he was gone in his uncle's truck.

Lacy didn't need watching out for, though. She hadn't known Borde since elementary—hadn't moved here from Rankin until freshman year—but she'd seen something in him, I guess. That nine-year-old, maybe. And she still saw it. So, sure, she'd hit the pool at three in the morning with the rest of us, but she'd have a bikini on under her shirt, too. And anyway, she was Borde's. You'd have to be a walking suicide, right? The La Bordes were known throughout Midland County for taking crowbars and pipes to people in public places, then doing their thirty days in lock-up with a grin. Coach had kept Borde from this so far, but that was just because most of the cops wanted us to make it to Austin. That would all change once we graduated.

* * *

But, Slowpoke. Real name, Johnny Vasquez. He was a junior, just transferred over from Permian. Didn't play ball, just had SLOWPOKE airbrushed on the tailgate of his truck. And, we'd never known him before, but we knew the truck, had seen it cocked at the corner of the Odessa drag, all of us just staring as we eased past. He wasn't a football player, either. As near as I could pick up over the summer, the Vasquezes were the La Bordes of Odessa, pretty much. And, though we'd never say it out loud, never admit it, you never went to Odessa alone, at night. Even if your girl'd just dumped you and you were looking for a fight, somebody to take it out on, still—not Odessa. A friend of ours, Scott, he'd been trying to clamp a heater hose back onto his Trans-Am over there one night, on the way to pick up his cousin, and some Permian guys had pulled up, held him down against the hot intake manifold while they slammed his hood over and over.

Scott carries a gun under his seat now, yeah. And his dad does too. It's not going to end well. Coach has advised us to stay clear, if we can.

Yes, sir.

As for why Slowpoke had to leave Odessa, that's the mystery right there. And, none of us knowing, the reason he had to come here, to Midland, it gets worse and worse.

And, because Slowpoke didn't play football, that second-to-last weekend before school started, it was the closest I'd been to him.

The guy he was fighting was Manuel Garcia, who, because of his twin brothers Raymond and Ramone, was pretty much off limits, untouchable. And Manuel knew it too, had probably been brushing shoulders with Slowpoke every weekend for the last two months. But Raymond and Ramone had probably always been sitting back in their lowslung Impala, watching this situation.

This weekend, though, it was just Manuel.

And I don't have any idea what really started it, but I knew what it came down to: Slowpoke and Manuel looked too much like each other, had the same grown-out hair in back, wore the same clothes, walked the same way.

I was mostly there because I'd always kind of wanted to see what Manuel could do, having grown up with Raymond and Ramone, who maybe even the La Bordes would have thought twice about jumping.

Not much, it turned out.

Manuel was big, and strong from working on cars, and knew how to wrestle his brothers off, but Slowpoke took him apart. And it wasn't pretty, not even a little. Some fights, you watch because they're exciting—exciting because you're not in them, you're not there, getting pounded, don't have to deal with the consequences.

This wasn't like that.

Slowpoke drove Manuel back into the cinderblock fence, chocked his left elbow up under Manuel's chin, and slammed his fist into Manuel's side over and over. Not wild playground swings either, but all in one place, until, when Manuel coughed, it was red, frothy.

Slowpoke nodded, and, when Manuel kind of staggered forward, Slowpoke stepped aside, as if to let him fall.

It was all part of the dance, though.

When Manuel brushed past, broken in some important way inside, Slowpoke stepped in, his left boot standing halfway on Manuel's shoe, heel-on-toe.

Some girl in the crowd of us screamed then, knew somehow what was about to happen, but I didn't. Could just watch.

The reason Slowpoke was holding Manuel's foot in place like that, it was so the knee would really break when Slowpoke came down on it from the side.

Manuel folded, is going to be one of those old Mexican men with a wooden cane someday, and when Slowpoke looked up to us, to each one of us in turn, it felt like what he was asking was if we had any problems with this.

Nobody said anything.

* * *

That next morning, Borde knocked on my door. His dad had been right: "You, what, twenty-two now?" I asked, pushing his dumb ass off my porch.

Borde was brown with sun and thicker than he had been. More raw.

"I mean, not counting the brain," I added, and he tackled me and what we were saying was hey, hello, where you been.

In the garage I stole two of my dad's beers—he knew, let it slide—and we sat in the shade and I sketched out the new defensive coach for him, all the drills and sets he was bringing in from Monahans.

Borde nodded, sipped. Watched the street, like Midland was too small for him now. After living out in an eight-by-twelve orange doghouse in a pasture with five other guys for three months, yeah. But still. I'd shagged parts in an air-conditioned truck all summer, yeah? Scraped gaskets and listened to the radio in the downtime. I knew every song this town had to offer.

132

"What about that sophomore, Melissa?" Borde asked then, doing his hands in front of his chest to show, and I kind of tongued my lower lip out and shrugged, and by lunch we had no choice but to leave the house, just because we'd drunk all my dad's beer, might laugh too much through our noses if my mom offered us milk and cookies.

Out at Wallace's in Greenwood, we bought more beer—my dad's brand—then just kind of coasted around town, neither of us saying how good it was. How this last week, now, it was ours, so long as Borde could keep off Coach's radar. Or, even if he couldn't.

After we put the beer back, careful to make sure two were missing from the original count, we fell into our usual places in the street, spiraling the ball back and forth, going longer and longer, like a thousand Thanksgivings.

That night—because of something with his dad—Borde ate with us, and my mom announced to us all how I'd moped around all summer without my old running buddy.

"And what about Lacy?" my mom asked then, pouring us more tea.

Twenty minutes later we were gone, on the drag in the parts truck I still had the keys to. It was a mini, for the mileage, and had the stupid sticker on the door, but it had a tank I didn't have to pay to fill, too.

"She know you're back yet?" I asked, and, when Borde didn't answer right away, just looking into the milling bodies at the Western Auto, I understood: we were on a spy mission.

It had been nearly three months, after all.

We followed Lacy from the Sonic to the Whataburger three times, other cars and trucks screaming past, slowing down, shirts hanging out windows, beer spilling into defrosters, but the windows of our tiny little truck were up, and dark, the air conditioner on because this gas was free.

"Uh-oh," I finally said, at a light.

We were right behind them.

"She know this truck?" Borde asked.

Before I could shrug a maybe out, Christine Gentry's passenger door opened, Lacy spilled out, and Borde stepped down, right into the street, the light turning green and everything. And then they both just stood there, like waiting for the director to yell cut.

All the cars behind us were honking, of course, but Borde just smiled, that involuntary kind of smile, like he was caught, he was here, here I am, and then Lacy was shrieking across the distance between them, launching up onto him, and because Lacy's parents were moving one of their parents into a nursing home in San Angelo all week, that was the last time I saw him for four days.

The next morning at practice, I threw up again, but was able to make it off the field this time, so nobody would slip in it.

"Well?" Coach said to me when I was done.

I pulled my helmet back down, leaned back into it.

* * *

Friday, the call came in to the shop: the guys down at the Avis needed a D40 filter, stat. That was the way Gerald always said it: *stat*.

He tossed me the dusty filter and a case of belts they had on order and I was gone, the air conditioner on against the hundred and ten degrees Coach had even said was ridiculous. Not that getting lectured to in the locker room about grades and behavior and life after school was any less ridiculous, but still.

When I showed at Avis, though, Borde ambled up from the pit, tossed a broken wrench into the rag drum.

"You're not dehydrated?" I asked.

"Ask her," he said back, and shouldered into me, walked out into the sun.

Neither of us were saying anything about his dad. He'd called once, on Tuesday, but my mom had managed to answer all his questions with questions, her eyes asking me more questions across the kitchen. Now Lacy's parents were probably coming back, though, meaning Borde's camping trip in her bedroom was over. She was probably already checking all the trashcans and laundry piles for rubbers.

"Davy?" I asked, tilting my head down into the pit, and Borde chewed his cheek. Of course Davy. Our quarterback, learning the family business in case he tore his shoulder out some Friday night or tweaked his elbow slinging the ball sideways like Coach was always telling him not to.

Borde leaned over, spit into a grate, and wiped his mouth.

"She's different," he said. "Lacy. Somehow, I don't know."

"You just haven't seen her," I told him. "What?"

"Nothing. It's nothing. You were watching out for her, I know."

"And Melissa Stephens," I said, lifting one shoulder to punctuate it. "And Mandy Watson."

"She graduated, right?"

"Missy too," I added, having to smile to say it.

Borde looked to me, raised his eyebrows.

"Missy?"

"The one and only."

Borde nodded into the Avis, said, "Davy know?"

Missy was Davy's twin. We were a town of twins on every block. Something in the brown, brown water.

"Was it like, you know, was it like . . . " Borde had to lean in, whisper the next part: "Like you and Davy? You got a crush on him you need to tell me about, man?"

"Exactly," I said back, right up against Borde's ear, and he pushed me away, and, after hitting the tackle dummies all week—we'd started full pads, Monday—it gave me a gauge for how much muscle the rig had put on Borde. He'd always been bigger than me, even in second grade; but the few times we'd had to really fight each other, he'd always held back, I thought. In seventh grade in the cafeteria, everybody chanting in a circle around us, and that time in ninth, when Lacy was still the new girl.

Now, though, it would be one of those two-hit fights, and neither of them would be mine.

Not that I didn't push him back with everything I had, here.

It threw him a few steps back, right into the grille of a truck neither of us had seen ease up.

The trunk honked, just a short blast, and Borde turned around, his teeth set, hands balled, and then he smiled.

It was Coach.

He stepped down laboriously, like he was barefoot, and felt Borde's arms, looked at his head from each side then knocked on it with his middle knuckle.

"Shit," he said. "Was hoping you'd got some brains while you were gone."

Borde turned away, embarrassed, and while Coach's truck was getting serviced, he bought us barbecue sandwiches next door, and ate without talking, and then afterwards, using the sugar packets and the salt shakers, Coach laid out some of the new plays on the booth's table, and the way he would strike a Sweet 'n Low forward all at once, breaking through the line into open field, we could see it too, the whole season before us. How this was the year.

135

We were supposed to go out that night, our second-to-last night of summer, but Coach managed to mention Borde to Lacy's dad somehow, so we wound up over there for a napkin-in-your-lap dinner, Borde editing his roughneck stories on the fly, me playing some made-up card game with Lacy's little brother, their dog barking in the backyard, Lacy's Rotary Club dad shaking each of our hands when we left, looking us in the eye.

After that we just wound up at the pool with my dad's beer, but nobody even showed up, so we just sat there in the plastic chairs and listened to the pump and tossed our empties into the water, waited for them to sink.

* * *

The next night, Lacy sitting between us in the cramped parts truck—my dad still hadn't asked for the keys back, but hadn't really given me run of the truck either—we made the loop around the drag like everybody else, Borde a star now, especially with one of my white t-shirts on, so you could tell he'd worked in the sun all summer, not hid under hat brims and awnings like the rest of us.

Because the truck was a stick, I had to keep my hand down on Lacy's knee practically, but she was clamped onto Borde, and it's not like we hadn't done this a thousand-million times before.

We hit the Whataburger, stopped to shoot the bull at Western Auto, made the slow U around Sonic twice, looking for a slot, then wound up in a game of catch with a nerf football in the Furr's parking lot, Davy barking out plays, Borde rising up to snag that red and yellow ball out of the sky, me on the bench like always, my beer going warm in the floorboard.

"Missy?" Lacy asked me, then, from Borde's part of the seat.

I let my shoulders kind of chuckle up. Reached down for the beer I didn't want.

That fight me and Borde had had in ninth grade? Lacy hadn't not been a part of it, anyway, even if she hadn't been in the gym that afternoon.

"I told him you checked up on me every day," she said.

"Why?" I asked.

She shrugged, ashed out the window after checking to see if her dad was binoculared in on her, or maybe dressed up like a federal mail box.

"He say anything about me?" she asked.

136

"I know about that birth mark."

She hit me with the heel of her hand, flared her eyes out.

"Who would be the male equivalent of Missy anyway?" she asked, taking another long drag.

"Equivi-what?" I faked, watching Davy rainbow one up, a real Hail Mary, the kind Coach would crucify him for.

"I know, I know," she said, leaning forward, breathing smoke right into my face, looking past me where I was already looking: Davy.

I pushed her back and she grabbed my pushing hand, and we wrestled like that, my beer doing its usual spill thing, so we didn't even hear the deep growl of the Trans-Am when it pulled up, nosing into the parking lot that was a football field now.

Scott cocked his door open.

Borde looked to Davy about it and they just shrugged, but then somebody from the other group of cars said something.

"What?" Scott asked, standing up.

It was Slowpoke.

He wasn't in his truck, was riding with somebody else tonight.

He stood up and up from the hood he'd been leaned against.

"I was enjoying the game," he called across in his way, where the words were kind of clipped.

Scott just stared, stared some more, his face still scarred up from his own intake manifold, and my breath kind of caught: would Slowpoke have been one of the guys crashing that hood down on him that night? Was just being from Odessa enough to make that not matter?

Yes, and yes. And it doesn't matter either.

Scott sat back down into his captain's seat, kept his left foot out the door, and gunned his Trans-Am out a length farther. Chirped to a stop then just idled, his racing cam loping in place, that two-inch exhaust throaty.

Slowpoke shook his head like he couldn't believe this, and nodded to himself, stepped out onto the field as well.

"Hey, hey," Davy said then, always the quarterback, the ball back in his hands somehow.

He patted it against his other hand for attention, looking from Scott to Slowpoke, but this wasn't his game anymore.

"Just going to sit there, punk?" Slowpoke said across the field, his eyes boring through the Trans-Am's windshield. "I have to dragass all the way over there, you're not going to like it, I promise you that."

In response, Scott fired his big 455 up, buried his foot in it and dropped down into first, his other foot on those front disc brakes, so just smoke and sound welled up, like he wanted the cops here now, not later.

Slowpoke laughed, rubbed his mouth with the side of his wrist, and didn't step aside even a little. Just kept coming.

Finally Scott rose to meet him, Davy still calling something out, Borde just watching, trying to track this, almost missing the ball when Davy underhanded it over, like he was about to need both his hands, here.

But, because Davy was the quarterback, had been since elementary, none of his fights ever went all the way. Somebody always stepped in, between, wanted to save him.

It's what happened this time, too. Borde snagged the ball Davy had lobbed and hooked a hand on Davy just as Davy was about to step out, try to be the peacemaker.

Davy had been counting on that, of course.

By then Scott was to the sharp front of his still-idling Trans-Am, the parking lights on, and when Slowpoke still had maybe three steps to go, Scott's arm came up, the elbow never bending.

In his hand, that pistol from under his seat.

This time, Slowpoke did stop.

He looked around to all of us, so we could each see that Scott was asking for this. That it was out of Slowpoke's hands, now.

"This really the way you want it?" he said to Scott. "Baby can't take his medicine, that it?"

Scott's lips were writhing, his chest heaving, and he was crying too, some. I could even tell from back in the crowd where me and Lacy were, her left hand digging into my right wrist, leaving a line of blue half moons.

"Hey, hey!" Davy said then. But louder, deeper, with more authority.

And not Davy at all.

Borde.

Like this happened every day on the rig, he stepped in, palmed Scott's gun down like the legend he was already becoming, tossing it back to Davy without looking, Davy catching it with the flat parts of his hands, where there were no fingerprints.

Then Borde, with the football, pushed Scott back so he almost tripped over his car, and kept pushing him, got him all the way into the seat and reached in, dropping it into reverse. Or, trying.

Finally, Scott lit the asphalt up with his brakes and the engine growled lower, the transmission engaging, and Scott was still crying and trying to suck it in, and if I could write a check from Scott's dad to Borde, it would be for everything in the world.

When Scott backed up, the crowd kind of relaxed, looked to each other and nodded.

Except Slowpoke.

When Borde turned around, Slowpoke was right there in his face. Johnny Vasquez in the flesh.

"Whoah, whoah," Borde said, holding his hands up, sidestepping.

Slowpoke stepped with him, never breaking eye contact.

They were the same height, the same build. Same everything.

Borde narrowed his eyes, changed the football to his left hand.

"What?" he said.

"You," Slowpoke said.

"Me," Borde said back, smiling for the crowd, holding his arms out to the side, and Slowpoke slammed both his hands into Borde's chest.

It caught Borde unexpected, drove him back onto his ass, the ball tucked into his ribs like he'd had drilled into him.

"No," Lacy said, and I looked across to her, realized it could have been her who yelled that *No* out last weekend, for Manuel Garcia.

I creaked my head back over to Borde, the night coming at me in frames now, in pictures all stacked on top of each other, a stack I was never going to be able to climb, never going to be able to get over.

"No," I said too, and stepped forward, to the front edge of things.

Borde was the one shaking his head from side to side now. Smiling to himself.

Slowpoke just waiting for him to stand.

He did, coming to a three-point stance first to collect himself.

Lacy tried to fight past me but I held her, knew better.

Knew better for her, anyway.

But I'd known since the second grade.

"La Borde!" I called out, using his full name so he'd know this was serious.

Borde looked over, his jaw already set the way I'd seen it set before in the fourth quarter, when some defensive end had had him targeted all game.

I shook my head no, my most serious no, that he didn't want to do

139

this. That this was a mistake, and it was going to stay a mistake for the rest of his life.

Slowpoke was looking over at me too.

"Need to ask permission from your bitch?" he said to Borde, about me.

In reply, Borde tossed the football away. To nobody. To the ground.

What we needed here were cops, and dads, and coaches.

What we had was just us.

I broke from the ring of people, stepped in.

"Don't do this," I said again to Borde.

"Get back," he said to me, not breaking eye contact with Slowpoke.

Slowpoke smiled, limbered his shoulders up, did that thing with his neck that killers always do.

"Good," he said, his voice deep.

Borde nodded yes about this too, licked his lips to step in, and then, because I had to, I said it, just loud enough for him to hear: "You said she was different somehow, right?"

Every person in that parking lot looked to me. Every person in Midland, Texas.

I nodded, held my hands up, to count down: "Melissa, Mandy, Missy," I said, dropping a finger for each one. "But what comes before M, La Borde? They still teach that in remedial?"

Borde was just staring at me now, his hands fists.

"L," I spat out, smiling behind it to make it true.

Now Slowpoke looked from me to Borde, and back again.

"His woman?" he asked.

"He thought," I told him, "yeah," and stepped in, right up against Borde, chest to chest. "You were right about that birthmark, too."

Borde pushed me away, hard. Right into Slowpoke.

Slowpoke pushed me back into Borde, and Borde grabbed me by the shoulders, was going to slam his head into my nose, I knew—I'd seen him do it, seen the results, was ready—but then he guided me to the side, said, "I know what you're doing here."

The one fight of his my dad ever told me about, the part I never understood until now was how he said he never remembered the first punch, that he only really knew about it because he felt the shock in his hand, coming up his arm. But it's true. I know that now. You can kind of just wake up, find yourself already swinging, already committed, already

140

putting your whole entire life square against somebody else's jaw, and praying it'll be enough.

Borde fell back, to the side a bit, but caught himself on his fingertips. Stood again.

"Thanks," he said, looking around me to Slowpoke, "but my dance card's full tonight, I think."

And then Slowpoke planted his meaty hand on my shoulder, pushed me out of the way.

"Been hearing about you," he said to Borde.

"Likewise," Borde said, turning to the side to spit, keeping his eyes on Slowpoke, random hands clamping onto me, keeping my narrow ass out of this, for my own sake, but also because they were embarrassed for me, I think. That punch, it had been the most tender, obvious thing I'd ever tried.

"No!" I screamed anyway, still fighting, my own saliva a mist in front of me, and Slowpoke reached out slow like, just one hand, and pushed Borde in the shoulder.

"Oops," he said, and Borde did that movie thing, kind of dusted his shoulder where Slowpoke had smudged it, and then he breathed in deep to swing, to kick, to head-butt, to wrestle and bite and tear, to do whatever he needed to tonight, never mind tomorrow, or the rest of his life, which was when Lacy's voice split the night.

What she said at a volume I didn't even know she had in her was, "Three months!"

Borde looked over to her, then to me.

"Three months," she said again, lower. More real.

"Shit," Slowpoke said, and pushed Borde again, but Borde walked through it, his eyes narrow on Lacy.

"That's right," she said, stepping up beside me, "you were gone, what? Three months? Know how many times my mom had to go to San Angelo? Left me alone at the house? Want to take a guess?"

"No," Borde said.

"Fuck you, Derek La Borde," she said, then turned, took my face in both her hands, and kissed me long and deep, my mouth pushing her away at first but then not, then getting it. I brought my hands up to cup her head, pull her deeper into me, and, no lie, it was good. Lacy was Lacy, God.

"You wouldn't," Borde said when we were done. "This is—"

"Except that birthmark, man, it's not really shaped like a—" I started, never got to finish.

It was the night I lost two teeth, the night I still carry in three faded lines around my left eye, the night my best friend sat on my chest and pounded my face to pulp, his girlfriend hanging off his back, trying to take it all back. It was the night my mom could never understand, the night Coach just shook his head about all season, but it was also the night the Garcia Twins eased up alongside Johnny Vasquez in their primered black Impala, stepped out onto the asphalt as one person. And, sure, it was the last night Lacy and Borde were really together and good, and it was the last night for me and him as well; but when I see him now at the hardware store or at the games on Friday night, where the announcer still introduces him sometimes, the way Borde keeps his hand on his son's shoulder, trying to guide him here, or there—last Friday I saw Lacy watching him too, her second husband right beside her, still new to all this small town stuff, and she kind of smiled and pulled her lips into her mouth at the same time, nodded once across the stands to me, and I had to turn back to the game again, focus in on these seniors, my lips just like hers.

Two Birds with One Stone
Deno Trakas

Tech's apartment complex in Columbia didn't look like the home of a person who was ass out. A row of three-story buildings, gray clapboard with white trim, good looking in a pre-fab way. Summer flowers in the planters, pine trees, maples, and pink crape myrtles lining the road. I passed the front entrance, drove the length of the complex, and pulled into the parking lot in back. Sure enough, there it was, a pile of furniture beside the dumpster . . . and in the parking space closest to it, Tech, sitting in a rusty old Honda, reading a newspaper, half leaning out the window to catch the fading light. I passed him, he looked up, and I parked in one of the few empty spaces a row away. We got out of our cars at the same time.

He looked confused more than anything. Just stood there, dark against the pink sunset, propped against the car, taking his weight off one leg. He pulled a pack of cigarettes out of the pocket of his sleeveless camo shirt, shook one out and lit it.

We'd been best friends growing up in Texas, did everything together. Played baseball and football, went wandering when we were kids and cruising when we had wheels, blew up frogs with firecrackers and tried to save baby birds with eyedroppers, got drunk on beer we stole from his dad, got crushes on cute girls and gave each other hell about it. Typical stupid boy stuff. Until the summer before our senior year when I thought he stole my girl, he told me he stole my girl, even though he didn't, and he said it to protect me; but I didn't know, and I beat the shit out of him. We'd fought before, but never like that, never so one-sided, never with broken teeth and a concussion, and we were never close the rest of the year, had a mediocre season in football, didn't even make it to Regionals. But that's another story.

I got a football scholarship to Sam Houston State anyway, and he got an academic ride to Georgia Tech and sat the bench for a year as a walk-on. We gave each other new nicknames—he called me Sam or Sam Houston, and I called him Tech. But they weren't real nicknames, not the kind you get as a kid when someone calls you some random thing like *Deek* or *Boof* and it sticks because it's weird and mean but also cool . . . but they were all we had as we went our separate ways. I hadn't seen him much in twenty years, and not at all in five, not since my dad died, finally, the bastard. Tech came home for the funeral, surprised me, was the only one who could tell me he was glad the old man was dead. Also told me he was doing great, making good money, dating pretty women after his divorce . . . but he was over-bragging, all hat and no cattle. Now, as I walked toward him, he looked like he'd been rode hard—puffy and pale, his blonde hair and beard long and dirty—and he seemed to've shrunk down and spread out. I'd always been bigger than him, and I'd gained weight too; but I'd stayed in decent shape working in the oil fields, and, whatever his jobs'd been, they hadn't burned the fat. Feeling pity and shame, I didn't punch him in the shoulder or wrap him in a headlock the way we used to—I held out my hand and said, "Hey Tech."

After a second of hesitation, he shook it and said, "What the fuck, man . . . what are you doing here?"

"Came to help," I said.

"Help . . . help what?"

"Whatever you need. I ran into your ex—we sat in the Hog Pit, got drunk, and talked about you for a couple hours. You told her you were getting evicted and didn't have anywhere to go, so here I am. I have a rental car and a credit card—I figure we can use 'em to get you relocated."

He looked like he'd been whopped in the head with a fence post. "Melissa?"

"Yeah, Melissa. I was surprised you two'd stayed in touch."

"What, what all'd she tell you?"

"A lot. Everything. Stuff I didn't know, like about our fight, what that was all about, and I'm sorry. It's twenty years too late, but I'm sorry. There's no way I can make it up, but I'm here to help if I can."

"Man," he said in a whoosh like he'd been hit again, this time in the stomach, "what did, I mean, how'd you find me?"

"She gave me your address and I Googled it."

He shook his head and then responded to what I said three sentences ago, like he'd just caught up with it. "I didn't ask anybody for help or whatever . . . I mean, don't want your help, so go ahead home."

"Right, I figured you'd be a stubborn sonofabitch like always, but I'm here anyway."

"Sam Houston, hero, yeah . . . they ought to, you know, make a movie."

"Okay, be a smartass, but I'm still here. So, I guess it happened yesterday, the eviction—have you found another place?"

He ducked and scratched behind one ear. "No, not really, no . . . but I'm thinking . . . you know, one of those storage things." His voice was deeper than I remembered, more sand, less accent, and he talked slow, with some hesitation, made him sound scattered, even though he was the smartest person I knew when we were growing up, the one who took calculus and physics and five years of Spanish.

"Is this all of it?" I nodded to the pile by the dumpster.

"Um, yeah, except I've got my TV . . . clothes and so forth, in the car."

I wondered how he was planning to move the furniture, but I just said, "How 'bout we find you another apartment tomorrow and rent a U-Haul."

He flicked his cigarette to the ground and stepped on it. "Fuck that, man, no . . . I don't know." He looked around like he was trying to figure out where the noise was coming from.

"Where'd you sleep last night?"

"Put my mattress right across there, yeah." He pointed to the chairs and table.

"How'd that work?"

"Good, yeah, except for the bugs . . . like when we used to camp out, you know, behind your house . . . pretend we were cowboys . . . and I've got a gun."

"A gun?"

"Yeah." He pulled up one leg of his dirty cargo pants, reached into his boot, took out a handgun, held it by the barrel, and offered it to me. "SIG Sauer . . . one of the best, right? Bought it at a, you know, pawn-shop," he said proudly.

I had a couple of handguns of my own, also a rifle and shotgun—you gotta have guns in Texas—and wasn't impressed, but I let him put it in my palm. "Is it loaded?"

"Yeah . . . what good's an unloaded gun?"

I handed it back without comment. He stuck it in his boot, smiling like he'd won a round of Who's a Badass? I said, "Have you eaten? I can go get us some cheeseburgers or something."

He smiled for the second time. "Yeah, starving." He gave me directions to a Five Guys, then said, "I have to move my car because the fucking manager . . . he'll have it towed, you know . . . but, um, you can probably park here and so forth."

"No, I gotta find a hotel. I gotta call home, and sleep in an actual bed or my back'll give out on me."

He grinned, lopsided. "You sound, you know, like an old man, Sam."

"I feel like it. Don't you?"

"Me? I'm a spring chicken . . . or a summer chicken."

* * *

When I got back, he was sitting on the hood of his car, reclined against the windshield, smoking. "Wouldn't start."

"All right, let's eat." We set our greasy bags of food and six pack of Bud on his scarred kitchen table, sat in his two wooden chairs, and had a picnic by the dumpster as the lightning bugs glowed in the thick, warm air and the moon rose and reflected off the windshields. His neighbors came and went, giving us looks but not hassling us. We talked a little, did twenty years in ten minutes. He asked about Melissa, then Alexandra and the boys—he hadn't heard that we'd separated but didn't seem surprised. I didn't ask him too many questions, didn't want to embarrass him, and Melissa'd filled me in already. "So how'd that eviction thing work? Did you know they were coming?" I asked.

"No, not really . . . just showed up, you know, fucking manager, thinks he's CEO of the world or whatever . . . drives a Hummer, who drives a fucking Hummer? And, um, so a couple of young punks like college kids to do the moving, yeah, and a cop just with his arms crossed showed me some papers and so forth and started . . . but the boys, they gave me some of those, you know, trash bags and so forth." He pointed to the black plastic bags sticking out of the dumpster.

When he was mad, his voice rose and the hesitation sort of disappeared as his sentences jammed up. "No problem." I nodded to the bags. "We can pull 'em out tomorrow. Have you looked for another place?"

146

"Yeah, in the paper, you know, but nothing around here . . . cheaper."

"I guess you'll have to move to another part of town."

He shook his head fast. "Fuck that, man. I'm not moving to another part of town, no way, no—I've got my Krispy Kreme . . . and the library, you know, the branch, the Internet there, soup kitchen, my counselor, I can walk to them, my knee, you know, I need one of those replacements . . . you act like moving's easy . . . unless you can find me a house."

It was hard to listen to him. Soup kitchen? Krispy Kreme? "You're right," I said, "but you gotta find a place you can afford, so what are you gonna do?"

"I'll figure it out, you go ahead home, thanks for supper." He started to get up.

I held up my hands. "Hold on, Tech. I'm not going home 'til Thursday, and I'm gonna help whether you want me to or not."

He sat down and relaxed again, lit another cigarette, offered me one but I shook my head. He leaned back and looked at his smoke like a philosopher. "If I were in a house . . . man . . . I know a guy, just a guy I know, lives in a $400,000 house . . . got foreclosed, you know, Fannie or Freddie, but no, just stayed there . . . two years or whatever, without paying anything . . . I bet there're others."

"If that's true, it's not fair," I said.

"Yeah, no shit, man, rich boys have it rigged . . . and fucking Karl Rove running the country with the fucking Koch brothers . . . but the fucking governor wants to cut my disability and God Bless America the greatest country in the world."

His voice had risen again, and he was crumpling up all the papers and cans on the table. So this was what Melissa was talking about, the minor brain damage from repeated concussions on the football field—he got 'em all the time, but the coaches just held up some fingers for him to count and sent him back in—and the one I gave him. So now his temper fired up and his brain scattered and he couldn't hold a job. And Melissa, she said she hated to leave him, felt like shit, but she just couldn't do it any more. She also sketched out what she knew of his finances—he received a disability check of about $1000 a month, and his rent was $815. He lived on credit cards for a few years; but they maxed out, and credit agencies were after him. I tried changing the subject. "What do you want to do about your car?"

147

"Get it fixed."

"What's it need? Maybe I can do it."

He snorted. "Yeah, like me, needs everything, a fucking head gasket"—he pointed to his head—"and, um, valve job, and whatdoyou-callit, radiator . . . tires and belts and so forth . . . cigarette lighter doesn't work either." He smiled like a smart ass again.

If he was right, the car wasn't worth the price of a good pair of boots. "So?"

He lit another cigarette even though he still had one going, hanging on the edge of the table. "So what?"

"What about the car?"

"The car . . . I need to move it."

"We can have it towed—Goodwill'd pick it up, give you a tax deduction."

He laughed at me. "Man, you don't get it . . . I'm not like you, I don't live in a fancy house with, you know, a mortgage deduction and so forth . . . I don't even pay taxes . . . and I might need my car to sleep in, so—"

I interrupted him this time. "All right, I didn't think of that, but you don't know shit about me either. I don't live in a fancy house. And if Alexandra goes through with the divorce, I won't have any house."

He'd leaned forward to tell me off, but now he leaned back and grinned. "Hey, Sam, we can be homeless roommates, you know, a concept, yeah?"

"You wanna come back to Texas with me? We can leave all this right here, just walk away."

"Fuck you, man . . . and fuck Texas." He flicked his cigarette at me—I scooted back in my chair and it bounced off my chest, sprinkled me with sparks, but I brushed them off and didn't lunge across the table to slug him like I wanted to. I opened my hands, planted them on the sticky table, reminded myself that Tech needed me, I owed him . . .

"Let's just move your car."

"Yeah, okay, whatever," meaning sorry. "Tonight I can . . . leave it on the street and so forth, but permanent . . . some place around here but, you know, not near a business to report it, or a house or whatever . . . people see a car parked on the street for two days they, you know, think there's a bomb in it."

I nodded, seeing the issues—finding an apartment would solve them. "All right, let's push it out to the street."

148

"Where you gonna stay?"

"I think I saw a Holiday Inn out on the main road. I can look it up on my iPhone."

He raised his eyebrows and said, "Fancy."

* * *

I called home to talk to my boys: Luke, fifteen, and Matt, thirteen. When Alexandra kicked me out two months ago, they stayed with her, but I tried to go by and see them or take them out as often as I could when I wasn't drilling in the Permian or somewhere else. They seemed, I don't know, upset but mostly silent. I was pissed, really pissed at Alex, pretty sure she was cheating on me even though she denied it and I didn't have hard proof. I broke some things. Hit her. That's when she kicked me out. We didn't fight after that, didn't yell, didn't even speak except when I wanted to see the boys. But lately it'd gotten a little better, both of us sanding the edges. And she was happy for me to take the boys, even made me promise I'd be back by Friday because she had plans for the weekend. Right, *plans*. But I didn't ask.

She answered the phone and we talked for a minute—the boys were out playing baseball, it was still daylight there, they were fine, she'd tell them I called.

That night I dreamed I was in the backyard watching Matt play with a young mountain lion—it was almost full grown, bigger than Matt, who was about five. It wore a collar, and we had it tied with a rope to a tree. Matt threw a ball, and the mountain lion chased it, but the rope wasn't long enough and snapped it back and flipped it over. It tossed its head and growled, but Matt laughed and ran toward it, and I shouted . . . woke up.

I got up early, fidgety; but the hazy, heavy sunshine said it's gonna be hot, take it easy. I made coffee in my room and drove over to Tech's place a little after 8:00 a.m., right when the garbage truck arrived. I pulled up beside it, shouted at the driver to hold on, and shouted at Tech to get up, then explained to the driver why there was a guy sleeping on a mattress beside the dumpster. He shook his head like he'd seen it all, looked at his watch, and said, "If you wanna climb in there, I'll give you two minutes to throw them bags out with the rest of his stuff."

I looked to Tech, who was still groggy and just starting to roll off his mattress. "You want these guys to haul your bags away? Make your life

149

simpler."

"Fuck no, that's all my stuff, man, no."

"All right." I parked, climbed into the dumpster, and started lifting the heavier bags that seemed to be piled together up and over the side. The other garbage man, the Mexican who rode on the back bumper, helped Tech take them from me and set them down with the furniture. Finally I tossed over the last one, climbed out, and thanked the garbage men. They did their loud, grinding, metal-clanging thing, emptied the dumpster, waved, and left.

I wiped my dripping face with my t-shirt and wiped my boots on the grass. "I don't know how you live here, the humidity, like breathing through a wet sponge."

Tech was looking through his bags, but kind of offhand said, "Yeah, well, go to Heaven for the climate, but . . . go to Hell for the company."

When I got it, I said, "That's good. You come up with that?"

"Nah, I think it was . . . Twain, Mark Twain . . . or Oscar Wilde . . . everything funny, you know, those guys said it . . . or Jesus . . . he was funny . . . Love your enemies, yeah? Blessed are the poor . . . he was hilarious."

"Wha'd'ya say we go to the hotel and take showers? I smell like garbage."

Tech shook his head and said, "Don't want anyone to take my stuff . . . just, you know, drive down to the Krispy Kreme . . . wash up . . . bring back some donuts."

"What's up with you and Krispy Kreme?"

"It's my place, man, family room, office, kitchen . . . get my coffee and donuts there, you know, every day . . . they know me . . . like if I died, they'd be the only ones, yeah . . . so let's go, my treat."

"I thought you were broke," I said.

"Yeah, well, some of my neighbors, you know, left their cars unlocked." He nodded and opened his eyes wide to see if I got it. I just shook my head. "Also found some jumper cables . . . figured we might need 'em." I shook my head again.

Tech dug through his bags, found a donut coupon, $4.99 a dozen, and some paper and a pen. He made three signs: THIS IS NOT TRASH. THIS IS MY STUFF. DON'T STEAL IT.

The Krispy Kreme was a simple place with a fifties look and a red neon sign out front that said HOT NOW. The hyperactive, frazzled, middle-aged woman behind the counter, her nametag read *Flora*, smiled and said, "Hey Honey, who's your good lookin' friend?" Tech introduced us, proud both ways, and chatted with Flora while he pulled a handful of change out of his pocket and counted it. He also introduced me to two of the regulars, the South Carolina congressman who owned the place and a retired USC professor whose name was Thomas Jefferson.

The donuts were warm and delicious, and we ate two apiece on the way to the hotel, and I ate two more while Tech took a shower. When I got out of mine, he was lying on his back on the bed, propped up on pillows, wearing the same dirty pants and boots but a clean shirt he'd brought along, and his hair was combed back. He was watching TV and looking through my wallet. "What the hell?" I asked as I sat on the side of the bed to put on my boots.

"Just looking at your pictures . . . don't have one of Alesandra, no, but the boys . . . they're good looking, yeah . . . must take after her."

I held out my hand and he put the wallet in it. I didn't count the money, about $100, but it all seemed to be there. "Her name's Alexandra with an x, and right, she works out and colors her hair and still looks pretty good."

"You still love her . . . want to, you know, get back?"

I shook my head—I was doing that a lot. "Yes, no, maybe, I don't know. Everything's kind of falling apart. I want to think that if we got back together, it'd be like it used to be, but I don't trust her."

He nodded as if he understood. "Melissa left me because, you know, she couldn't handle my"—he made quotation marks with his fingers—"*disability.*"

"That's what she told me. She feels guilty about it."

"I don't blame her . . . she didn't sign up for this, you know, what I am." He lay there looking up at the ceiling, his hands, with his fingers interlaced, lying across his belly like a rope that's too short.

I didn't know what to say. "Let's go move your car and find you a place to live that's not a dumpster."

"Whatever."

On the way out we passed a maid's cart, and Tech grabbed a handful of miniature shampoo bottles, a handful of bars of soap, and a bath towel.

* * *

151

We found a parking place at a 24-hour Walmart not far from the hotel. "It has a McDonalds inside, Sam," he said. "What could be better? McDonalds and Walmart, the fucking American Dream."

We used the jumper cables to try to start the car, and when that didn't work, we used them to tie my car's rear end to his car's front, and with some bumper banging, I pulled and he steered his car to its new home.

But then he made me drop him off with his stuff—he flat refused to go by himself or to go with me to check out apartments. I almost gave up then; but hell, it wasn't that big a deal, so I drove around. Columbia and Midland were both middling cities, seemed about the same size except Midland was small in Texas and Columbia was big in South Carolina. Columbia had too many damn trees, made me claustrophobic.

I used my iPhone to locate the apartments, and after about three hours of driving, looking, and talking to managers, I headed back and reported to Tech. There were cheaper places, one near the university downtown, others on the north side, and some looked pretty good. He just shook his head. So I took my best shot, said there was an apartment about a mile away for $500. When he hesitated, I hit him again by saying, "Y'all eat barbecue in this part of the country?"

"Sure, yeah, but not, you know, brisket . . . usually pulled pork."

"Got any nearby?"

"Sure, yeah."

"Okay, my treat after we look at the place down the road."

* * *

The manager gave us a key, we let ourselves in, Tech walked through the family room, bedroom, bathroom, kitchen, and walked out without saying a word and was waiting for me at the car after I returned the key. "What's up with you?" I asked, frustrated and pissed.

"It's a fucking shoebox."

I unlocked our doors, got in, and slammed mine. "You're making me crazy," I said as I started the engine, turned up the AC, and burned rubber in the parking lot.

He didn't answer except to say, "Turn left up there, at the light." He just looked out his window at the houses in the neighborhood we passed through.

"You're not gonna find a two-bedroom around here that you can afford. There's another one-bedroom a couple of miles farther out—it might be bigger."

He shook his head again, but still didn't look at me. "Try walking a few miles . . . times two, you know, every day, with a bad knee."

"I'm sure there're buses."

Now he did look at me. "Man, you don't know shit about riding city buses."

"You're right, I don't. But what are you gonna do?"

"Let's just take it to the, you know, storage place."

"Listen you stubborn sonofabitch, I have to fly out tomorrow at noon. If we find something now, I can pay your deposit and first month, and help you move your car and your stuff. But then I'm gone and you're on your own."

He lit a cigarette, offered me one, and this time I took it. "Been on my own, a damn long time, Sam . . . yeah, you're trying to help and so forth . . . but, you know . . . pushing me to change my whole fucking world, in one day . . . whatever, I can't, need time to mull it."

I took a drag and liked the soft burn, cracked my window and blew it out. "So what are we gonna do?"

"I want to break into one of those houses."

"What?"

"Yeah, I saw one . . . with newspapers in the driveway, so, you know, people out of town." He pointed up ahead and said, "Turn right at the big intersection."

"Why? You wanna steal their stuff?"

"No, not really, no, I mean, yeah, I'd take money, whatever, lying around . . . and, you know, take a look at their stuff . . . but I don't want any TVs or shit like that . . . I'll have a plastic bag, you know . . . and a note you help me write it . . . something like 'I broke into your house because I'm homeless and have nothing and you have fucking everything, you know, but, um, I'm just taking things of value to you, you know, pictures and so forth . . . and if there's a laptop because you probably have like E*Trade . . . and I'm going to take it to a homeless shelter, see? and you get it back by, you know, writing a big check to the shelter, see what I'm saying? the shelter people don't know, but, um, I'll write a note, yeah, say someone'll come pick it up and so forth, and make a donation, but if, you know, I find out you didn't write a check, I'll be back.' See?"

153

I kept looking at him to see if he was messing with me and to process all the parts of his crazy-ass scheme. He was dead serious. "How would you get in?"

"Yeah, I don't know . . . maybe they'll leave a key under the mat, you know . . . maybe break a window and so forth . . . you have an alarm thing at your house?"

"No."

"You leave a key outside?"

"Yeah, in the storage shed."

"See? Can't be that hard."

"You're crazy, Tech. I kinda like the Robin Hood angle, but it's way too risky, and for what? Just so maybe some middle class family will make a donation to a homeless shelter and maybe you find a few dollars? I'm offering you more money than you'll find in one of those houses, I guarantee you."

"Yeah, don't want your money, Sam . . . your money, you know, has strings, guilt and so forth . . . but guerilla warfare, see? It's my new mission, and it'll be fun, because, you know, fun costs money . . . and I got nothing, except nothing to lose . . . all I ever do is . . . survive . . . but this'll kill two birds with one stone, yeah. Hey, this is it"—he pointed to a shack that flew a Confederate flag. "Big Moe's," he said. "Do the drive through . . . the guy's a fucking Klansman . . . but makes good barbecue."

I pulled into the line. "What if you get caught?"

"Yeah, whatever, spend a little time in jail and, you know, solves my housing problem."

"Have you ever been in jail?"

"Yeah, city jail, not so bad."

"Well, this wouldn't be like thirty days of lockup because you got in a fight with some redneck in some bar. When did you think this up?"

"Just now, driving around, you know, with my chauffeur."

"Well, I'm sure you know your chauffeur won't have anything to do with it."

"Yeah, I figured, but here's the deal, because, you know . . . if you drive me tonight and drop me off and, um, go park way down the street whatever . . . I do my thing and so forth, and if you hear an alarm or see cops or anything freaks you out, you just, you know, drive back to the hotel . . . go home . . . but see, if everything's cool, we'll take the bag to a homeless shelter, yeah . . . and if you help me, you know, because

154

tomorrow I let you move me and so forth, and you won't ever have to see me again."

Without considering all the angles of the deal, I said, "I don't want to not see you, Tech. We used to be best friends, and I thought maybe we could be friends again."

"Yeah, then help me . . . this is good, man, it'll be fun to be a team like we used to . . . and it's moral, yeah, I don't have morals, first thing to go, so this'll be, you know, a good deed . . . Sam, the good Samaritan, yeah?"

I shook my head, feeling sorry for him, but he had a point. His life seemed thin, empty; but this would give him something, not much, a little bit of mission and a little bit of fun. Still. "You have a weird notion of morality, Tech. And friendship. To be your friend I have to commit a crime—is that so we can be cellmates?"

"No, man, we can't be friends—you're a Republican, right, tell the truth."

"What the hell does that have to do with the price of beans?"

He shrugged his shoulders like, See?

"If I help," I said, "you promise you'll move tomorrow, or go back with me?"

"Yeah, want me to cut myself, mix our blood, you know, like when we were kids?"

"No, just promise."

"Promise." He punched me on the arm.

* * *

Just after 1:00 a.m. we pulled into a quiet, upper-middle-class suburb that had sidewalks and streetlights, neat lawns and flowerbeds. I stopped in front of a good-looking two-story white house, guarded by a fuzzy full moon and two big oak trees, with a closed two-car garage, two plastic-wrapped newspapers lying in the driveway, and a light shining behind curtains on the first floor. Except for the advice I gave Tech on the letters, I let him call the shots; it was his show, and he seemed to have a natural criminal mind. He dressed in dark clothes, with gloves and a pullover cap he found in one of his bags, and he took a pair of pliers, a screwdriver, and a couple of empty bags that he stuffed in his pants pockets.

I said, "I'll be parked in the place we picked out, and I'll wait an hour. But if I hear anything or see cops, I'm leaving."

"Yeah, okay, so if I end up in jail and, um, get to make a call, I won't call you."

"Damn right you'll call me. Do you know my cell number?"

"No." I repeated it four times, and he said he had it. "But if you don't hear from me, you know, just go ahead home and so forth."

"All right. Good luck. Be careful. If anything goes wrong, walk away."

"Don't worry, man." He punched me on the arm again, repeated my phone number, and got out.

* * *

I woke up sweating, with a mosquito buzzing in my ear—about seventy minutes had passed. I looked in the rearview mirror, no sign of Tech or anything else, and considered—to go or stay . . . or drive back to the house to see what was going on.

The house looked the same, no police car in front, so I turned around at the end of the block, came back, and parked at the curb. I walked up the driveway and sidewalk to the front door, stopped and listened, didn't hear anything and couldn't see anything through the curtains, so I walked around back. Didn't see or hear anything unusual there either—everything dark—but then I noticed a raised, broken window behind the azaleas, and as I walked up, I couldn't believe the scene inside. In a kitchen chair sat a balding middle-aged man dressed in a t-shirt and boxer shorts, with a dish towel stuffed in his mouth and masking tape wrapped around his mouth, eyes, and wrists that were bound behind the chair. Tech paced in front of him, talking, bleeding from the ear, and holding a golf club upside down, waving it around. Before I could signal or say anything, he swung the club like a baseball bat and smashed the grip against the guy's temple. The guy was knocked sideways but didn't topple over.

All my instincts said walk away, except one—Tech was in trouble. It looked like he was about to hit the guy again, so I said, "Stop!" He turned, saw me, but looked wild, out of control, so I climbed in the window and onto the kitchen table next to it, which still had some shards of glass on it, as well as Tech's gun. The guy heard me and tried to speak but only

156

managed a muffled mumble. I slid off the table and gestured toward the hall, gave Tech a push in that direction. When we got to the living room, I whispered, "What the hell are you doing?"

"Asshole came out of nowhere, you know, tried to kill me with this golf club, had to—" He cocked his head and rubbed his shoulder.

"Forget it. Did you get his stuff?"

"Yeah, some."

"Did you tell him about the homeless shelter?"

"Yeah, sure, I think, yeah."

"Then let's get outa here."

Back in the kitchen, the guy had nudged some of the masking tape off his mouth and halfway spit out his towel. His words were garbled, but I think he said, "I'm gonna track you fuckers down—"

Tech grabbed his gun from the table and stuck it in the guy's mouth, pushing the towel deeper into his throat. "Keep talking, asshole."

The guy gagged.

I wanted to grab Tech's arm and jerk it away; but I was afraid the gun might go off, so I held both my hands, palms out, in front of his face—*Stop*. He wouldn't look at me, his eyes were fixed like all the hatred in the world on the guy who was still gagging on the towel and gun. I motioned for Tech to pull the gun away; but he didn't budge and still wouldn't look at me, so I leaned right up to his ear and said, "Come on man, take the gun away." Nothing. I put my hand around the barrel of the gun and gently pulled. Finally, Tech let me guide it out. I looked around, found the masking tape on the counter, and started to wind it around the guy's mouth and head, to reinforce what was already there. But Tech stopped me and motioned to his gloves. I stripped the tape off, shoved it in my pocket, and handed the roll to him. He gave me the gun, wiped the roll of tape on his shirt, then wound it around the guy's mouth and head again and again until it was all used up. I pointed at the door. He shook his head, went to the kitchen, found another dishtowel, and wiped off the table and windowsill where I might've left fingerprints. Then he pointed at the full garbage bag by the table, and I picked it up. He snatched the golf club from the table and was about to whack the guy one more time, but I grabbed his arm and stopped him. He knocked the guy over, dropped the club, and we headed for the back door.

When he opened it, an alarm went off. Startled, we looked at each other and ran, Tech limping, around the house to the car, jumped in and took off as the next-door neighbor's house lights began to come on.

I thought I was pretty tough, but I was shaking as I tried to speed out of the neighborhood on the only road I knew. Tech squashed the bag between his legs to the floorboard and started to speak, "That asshole—" but I told him to shut up.

"Can I smoke?"

"No. Take off that damn hat, and those gloves, and wipe the blood off your face—is it yours or his?"

"Mine, I think, yeah, my ear . . . where you going?"

"As far away as I can." I rolled down my window so I could hear whatever might be coming, but it was quiet except for the fading alarm and the air rushing into the car as I ran stop signs and zipped past the dark houses.

"Come on man, we have to go to the shelter, you know, before the cops and so forth . . . what kind of asshole doesn't pick up his papers? We gotta go, I said I would—"

"That's why we can't. We gotta assume the police'll be there any minute, and they'll put out a call, or send a car to the shelter."

When he didn't argue, I asked, "What happened?"

"Couldn't find a key, you know . . . so, um, broke the window and crawled in, you know, like you, he came in cussing and swinging his fucking golf club at my head . . . if he'd caught me, but I ducked so, um, hit my shoulder, and ear—"

A car was coming our way, so I slowed down and stopped at the next intersection. We passed and nodded to each other. "Shit."

"Don't sweat it, man," Tech said.

"What else?"

He pressed his hand to his ear and looked at it—it was bloody, but not much. "Kicked him in the stomach . . . gave me time, you know, to pull out my gun . . . adjusted his attitude, yeah."

"Damn, Tech, that makes it armed robbery."

"Yeah, whatever . . . but he didn't have any fucking, you know, duct tape . . . had to use that other crap . . . and wouldn't shut up threatening me, you know, calling me *hippie, fag, pussy* . . . why I had to whack him."

I got to the main road and stopped at the stop sign. Looked around. Very little traffic. But. A police car with its blue lights flashing, siren off, was coming up the hill fast, right at us, and I froze, my heart stopped, I swear, I was sure he was going to jam up in front of us, jump out and pull his gun ... but he turned into the neighborhood before he got to us. I took a deep breath and pulled out in the opposite direction, toward the hotel. "That scared the shit out of me," I said. "Almost as bad as when you put your gun in that guy's mouth—I thought you were gonna splatter his brains all over me. I thought—" Tech interrupted me before I said the word *murder* or told him about the image that flashed in my head of us trying to dispose of a body and ...

"Yeah, kind of lost it there, for a minute, thanks for, you know."

"Was there anyone else in the house?"

"No, didn't see anyone, no, guy's an asshole, who could live with him?"

"What'd you take?"

"His wallet and, you know, computer like I said, photos and so forth." He opened the bag and reached in. "Here," he said, "a Dove bar from the freezer."

"I don't want it."

He started to unwrap it. "So, let's drop off the stuff, Sam, you know, then go celebrate."

"No."

"Yeah, I know this got fucked up and so forth, but we got away, man ... and I wiped your fingerprints, right?"

"That was good thinking." I wouldn't look at him, but I could tell he was pleased with himself and happy eating his Dove bar.

"So chill, man," he said.

"The neighbors could be describing us, the car, the tag number ... right now."

"Nah, it was dark; but if you think so, yeah, fuck it, leave me at my car ... you know, go home ... if I get caught, hey, won't say a word about you so don't sweat."

"Are you known around here? I mean if the police start asking questions at the homeless shelter and they describe you ... will everyone in town say, 'Oh yeah, that's Tech.'"

"No, no way, never stayed at a homeless shelter, and, um, nobody calls me Tech, no ... but the Krispy Kreme ... but why would cops go there? Come on, Sam, just, you know, look it up on your phone."

"I already did. The main shelter's for women, it's downtown; but I'm not going to any shelter—it's too risky. We'll have to find a dumpster somewhere."

"Yeah, forget it then, drop me off." He grabbed the handle of the door like he was going to jump out.

"Stop, Tech. You go to a shelter, you'll be in jail in an hour."

"You have, you know, a strange high opinion of cops," he said.

"I just don't want to go to prison and do hard time."

He was quiet for a minute, took out a cigarette but then put it back and said, "Yeah, hey, I got it, really, yeah, drop it at a, you know, post office, with a note saying deliver this to a shelter, and so forth."

We were coming up on the hotel, but I kept driving so I could think it over—a branch post office. I figured driving around with the bag was risky, dropping the bag anywhere would be risky, doing anything except getting the hell out of town would be risky; but we had to do something with it, and I didn't want to take it back to the hotel or leave it in the car, and we'd gone this far. "That might work."

I drove to the Walmart and found a spot that wasn't well lit and wasn't close to Tech's car. "Put the gloves back on," I said, "and get the paper out."

"What should I say?"

I checked my phone. "Write 'Deliver this bag of donations to The Haven on Taylor Street. Please.'"

While he was writing, I looked up the address of the Columbia post office and said, "The good news is there's a branch right on Garner's Ferry. The bad news is it's close to where we just came from."

Without looking up he said, "Yeah, good . . . they won't expect us to come back."

* * *

I drove past the post office—it was lit inside so people could check their boxes at any hour; but at 3:00 a.m., we didn't see anyone doing anything, and there weren't any cars in the small lot, so I turned around in a strip mall and came back. "I'll pull up—just open the door and leave the bag at the curb," I said. But when I stopped, Tech got out, lugged the bag inside, limping as usual, and left it in front of the mail slots with the note on top. Freaked me out again.

When he got back in the front seat, I took off and yelled, "Jesus Christ! Why'd you do that?"

He smiled, said, "Couldn't just, you know, leave it on the curb, man, might think it was trash, or, um, you know, all kinds of crazy homeless people out there might steal it." He looked at me and laughed, then laughed some more. He had a great laugh, always had, from deep in the belly. "Come on, Sam Houston . . . we did it, and, um, can't tell me you're not having fun." He punched me on the arm.

I pushed him and said, "Stop doing that. And you call this fun? Armed robbery? Almost shooting a guy? Almost getting caught?"

"Yeah, you know, adrenaline, it's good for you, right? What you need . . . fun to keep you young. Let's do it again, there's another house back—"

I looked at him thinking, Are you fucking crazy? But this time he was grinning, messing with me, and I might've even cracked a smile as I drove at the speed limit, pissed, but also relieved to be putting distance between us and the evidence.

"Yeah, see, you are having fun . . . I'm glad you came, Sam Houston, what a great day! I might even, you know, let you be my first Republican friend. You're not one of those, you know, Tea Baggers are you?"

"No."

"Okay then, I'll think about it."

"What an honor. Don't forget the deal, Tech—the apartment. Or else go back to Midland with me—that might be better now that you're on the run."

"Yeah, definitely, promise, mañana, man, I move, you leave, but tonight we're on the front lines, you know, the revolution, feels great, yeah?"

I did feel pretty good, breathing again, looser. Still. "You think your buddy's gonna forget all about this even though you cracked his skull?"

"He's an ignoranus, you know, stupid and an asshole, but, um, he'll be fine, hit him with the grip, you know, rubberized . . . he'll get a call from the shelter . . . be all happy to get his shit back and so forth, and, you know, be a better person."

"Or he'll hunt you down."

"Nah, back in Texas, maybe, yeah; but not here, no."

We'd made it back to the Walmart and I pulled in and parked because, well, I wasn't really thinking. Tech said, "Hey . . . our friend gave us about two hundred dollars . . . let's buy some beer and celebrate . . . we can, you know, sit in my Japanese car, drink German beer, eat French fries, and live the American Dream."

I laughed this time, couldn't help it.

161

"And duct tape," he added, "we'll get some duct tape too . . . that's the American dream too, yeah?"

I laughed again.

"Hey, you're laughing." He leaned his big body over the gear console and wrapped his arm around my head, rubbed it with his knuckles. "You're my hero, Sam Houston, and, you know, you can be my friend too, yeah."

Propriety
Bret Lott

Four months and two days after my wife has died, I wake up to the alarm clock on the nightstand, watch my hand move from beneath the sheets to snap it off, and for the first time since she has died, the silence after the alarm isn't deafening. I am in an empty house, the only sound around me the silence an empty house makes.

She died one cool April morning when she'd been walking to the post office from her own office, the same routine she'd gone through every day since starting her job. We moved here nine months and two weeks and three days ago, me transferred to a new office just opening up, a job that wasn't even a promotion. A lateral move, my boss had called it. He'd also told me I had no choice in this matter.

So it's my fault, actually, it happened.

What happened: She'd been walking along Broad toward King, then stepped off into the crosswalk, the light with her. When I think about it, which has been most of the last four months and two days, I see her glancing up at the light, then back to the wad of mail in her hand. She's sorting it already, putting the zip codes in order, one stack of envelopes for the 29401-29499 box, the other for everything out of state.

This, of course, is when I see the Trans-Am come through the light at an estimated fifty miles per hour, when I see the dead-drunk look on the seventeen-year-old machinist's mate's face as he sees too late the light is red, and that a woman is already halfway across the street.

I wasn't there. I was on the phone to Jeff Pinckney of Pinckney and Hutto, Engineers, talking to him about a renovation we had coming up in August.

Which is now, this month, this morning, the first morning I am to spend out of the office and on site, looking things over, making certain some of the problems I'd been discussing with Jeff on the phone the morning of April 20—the wiring, the plumbing, the framing behind the walls—would be taken care of properly.

And maybe this sense of propriety is what has finally fallen into me this morning, makes me feel as though Helen and her death are miles from me, our house only an empty shell. The machinist's mate was court-martialed; Helen's insurance company sent me a check within six weeks. These matters of her death were handled properly, as was her funeral: she had asked to be cremated, then have her ashes brought back home to be strewn into Lake Michigan above Traverse City, the place she spent her summers when she was a kid. I did things properly, got her brother to take me out on the water, then sifted through my fingers ash coarse and fine at once, and I watched that ash spread across the water. From behind me, I could hear her brother and his wife both crying, the engines on the boat shut off. And I could hear myself breathe, air into me and out, as I watched the water and the small chop the wind made, watched her disappear.

They'd offered to let me stay with them as long as I wanted; but after six days, every one of them spent inside their home, trees outside the front room window still the iron-gray of mid-spring in Michigan, I told them I had to get home. Home being, of course, a place we had lived only five months by that time.

But my job was there, our furniture, her clothes, and by the ninth day after she was killed, I found myself back in an alien place where the trees had never gone wholly gray, where days were already in the eighties. I found myself at my office desk, a cup of coffee in my hand, each time the phone rang me expecting it to be a policeman with the same bad news I'd been given already: Helen was dead.

* * *

This morning is different, different for the way the water feels to my touch as I turn on the faucet for the shower; different for the way the razor trails across my face; different for the bitter taste of the coffee I sip as I sit at the table, my vitamins in front of me—the small yellow multi-vitamin and the large, chalky Vitamin C Helen had taught me I needed to have every day because I don't eat enough fruit or vegetables.

This day is different, I know, because she is not here. On other mornings, my hand at the faucet, I could have seen Helen bent before the sink, air from the blow-dryer filling her hair, the razor on my skin. She could have been just behind me and to my right, trying to horn in on the mirror space to finish her eye makeup. At the kitchen table, I might have seen Helen across from me and sipping her own coffee, her own vitamins before her. But she is not here, is nowhere. Yesterday I would have felt her across from me, might have accidentally dropped two pieces of bread into the toaster. But not today.

Outside the sliding glass windows beyond the table, it is already August in South Carolina, the trees behind our backyard fence the heavy green of the heat and humidity in this foreign place. We bought the house new, and one of the projects I'd planned for late spring was putting in the yard, laying in sod. But the earth out there is hard-packed now, cracked with the little rain we've gotten so far this summer, the ground a barren pale yellow. Today will be near a hundred degrees, the humidity in the nineties. I bring my cup to my lips, sip and wince as the air conditioner clips on. It is only 6:45 a.m.

I sit at the empty table, the tie at my throat feeling tighter than it ever has, the space across from me even more empty now than it has been for the last 124 days, and I think perhaps this is the proper end of grief, the day I knew would come.

* * *

I have the tie off before I get to the car, the air outside a transparent wall of heat. By the time I am off the driveway, I am sweating, and the drive into town over the bridges seems to take an hour, the air conditioner in the car going full blast. Traffic stops entirely when I reach the crest of the first bridge, and from where I sit, I can see the humid haze of summer air in Charleston, the wharfs crowded with container ships, beneath me the Cooper River, minuscule sailboats already out. To the south, out beyond the flat rock of Fort Sumter settled in the middle of the harbor, is the gray smudge of open sea, the horizon gone, lost to the wet air.

Some nights since April, I've awakened to find myself sitting up in bed, Helen's name just uttered, the word fading into the darkness around me, and I've had to turn, run my hand across the sheets next to me to remember she is not there. Other nights I look in her dresser drawers for some piece of night clothing—a gown, a t-shirt she slept in—and then climb into bed, hold it close to my face and breathe in her smell as deeply

165

as I can, fall asleep to dream her more alive than she has ever been: her brunette hair, her deep brown eyes, her skin soft enough to startle me from sleep to find her gown knotted in my hands.

We had been married for eight years and two months and six days when she died. We had no children, this because of surgery to remove cysts the size of an orange on both of her ovaries three years into our marriage, and for a moment, as the pickup ahead of me inches forward and we move closer to town, I try to imagine what it would have been like had we had children. But the only thing that comes to me, the second span cleared now, cars all around me speeding down into the black slums one has to pass through before finding the wealthy brick and wrought iron south of Broad, is a certain kind of thankfulness, glad that the brand-new house behind me on the other side of the bridges is empty, the air conditioner there going nonstop to keep an empty house cool. There is only me left here to deal with things. Me, and her brother and his wife up in Michigan; and the lake comes to me again, the boat on the water.

* * *

Jeff Pinckney is at the site when I get there. It is a single house on one of the narrow streets only one car can squeeze through at a time, and I have to jam my car as close to his Wagoneer as possible in the short gravel driveway of the place.

The first time Jeff and I were out here, back in early April, we'd found the sill and bearing plates and plenty of floorboards on the right side of the house nearly eaten through by rain from a roof we figured had leaked for fifty years; the clapboards were beat to pieces, too, and we could only guess how bad the frame and wiring were behind the old pine panels lining the rooms.

Today the clapboards are gone, all except about a third of the back wall of the house; it is mostly only a frame of black wood, a dozen or so studs sistered in, new yellow wood nailed right into the old to help keep up the frame of the house. Some of the more significant support posts have been sawed in half, the bottom taken out and replaced with a new four-by-four, the old just too wrecked and dead to be of any use.

But nothing is any worse than what we had imagined on our first walk-through in April. Though I haven't been on site since before work had started, I know what has gone into the house so far: a wall out of line only needed to be winched into place, reattached to the trusses; the old sill and bearing plates needed to be torn out, replaced with new treated wood, eight-by-eights on the ground, four-by-sixes at the roofline.

Jeff is hunched over the blueprints spread out on a plywood table in what will one day be the kitchen. He looks up at me, still sitting in the car. He has on a pale yellow tie and a white oxford shirt, the sleeves rolled up, and he waves, starts toward me, passing through first one wall and then another with a mere twist of his body.

He could be a ghost, I think, a ghost passing through the walls of an ancient house that seems suddenly too easy to fix, its ills too easily identified, and I know only then I do not want to talk to him.

He is at the car now, and he smiles, knocks on the hood. "Glad you could make it!" he shouts, the thick air and the engine and the air conditioner all swallowing up his sound so that the words come to me almost too faint to hear.

I try to smile, wave, do something, but nothing comes.

Jeff puts his hands on his hips, tilts his head. "Hey, Dan, you all right?" he asks, and I shoot back, "No," shout the word louder than I've intended.

That is when I put the car in reverse, turn my head and place an arm along the top of the seat, and back out. I make for the maze of one-way streets this foreign town is filled with, then find my way back to Meeting and the bridges, behind me the man I'd been talking to the morning my wife had been killed and the wreck of a building that, by October, will be livable again, better than new, so quickly and easily healed.

The phone is ringing inside the house when I get to the door, and I know it is Jeff. It rings and rings, and I stand with my hand at the knob, ready to enter my empty and cool and near-new house, where the Sheet-rock walls are free of nicks, where the wood inside them is the same fresh pine as the new sisters in the old house downtown.

But when the phone finally stops ringing, I find my hand still at the knob, still waiting for whatever it is in me that will tell me to enter my house, where inside are only the things we'd owned ourselves: throughout the house, furniture we'd bought; beneath the bathroom sink, her lens cleaner and hairspray and bars of soap; in the cupboards, still cans of food her hands had taken from a plastic grocery bag and placed exactly where they sit right now. In the closet hang Helen's clothes, in the rooms her smell, but I know that if I enter the house there will be no more than that.

This morning has closed off whatever ghost of her has been here since a machinist's mate killed her on April 20, me on the phone to a man who passes through walls in a house a hundred years older than my own. If I go in the house, there will be no more of her than the dead things, inanimate objects of our lives together.

I turn from the door, stand with my hands at my sides, my shirt sweat through at the collar and under my arms. There is nothing I can do, neither enter my home nor leave it, my only company the supposed satisfaction of knowing that somewhere a seventeen-year-old lives in prison and that my bank account is bloated with cash calculated to be of equal value to the love of a wife.

On the front porch sit two lawn chairs, blue and white lattice with aluminum frames, and I sit in one.

"Helen," I say, and listen to the word just out of me, feel it disappear yet hang before me in the air, invisible but there all the same. "Helen," I say again, this time louder, and I see that today has only begun some new level of mourning, grief in me already settled like black wood behind new walls.

168

Getaway
Betty Wiesepape

Bertie Martin had not slept well. Voices from the street outside her house had kept her awake well past midnight, and when she finally managed to fall asleep, she'd been awakened by the sound of a truck door slamming. Although it was still dark, Bertie was fully dressed and seated in a straight-backed chair that she'd pushed from the kitchen to a window on the east side of her house. Knees together, black and white spectator pumps standing at attention on gold shag carpet, she took a drag off her cigarette, ground the stub into an ashtray balanced on the knees of her lime green trousers, and raised the Venetian blinds to peer out.

The sun wasn't up, but there was a rosy tint behind the Dallas sky-line. The gas station on the corner was still deserted. She could see the blinking red light on the coke machine that refused to give change; but even with her binoculars, she couldn't tell if the attendant had remembered to hang the key to the women's restroom on the hook behind the counter where it belonged.

Bertie had no idea what time it was because the alarm clock on her nightstand needed new batteries and the wall clock in the kitchen was set to Daylight Savings Time, although she'd recently turned the calendar on the door of her pantry to December. Bertie was not a fan of Daylight Savings because she could never remember when to turn the clock hands forward and when to turn them back. As she'd told her niece the last time Amy came to Dallas for a visit, people who wanted an extra hour of daylight should just get up an hour earlier.

Not that what time it was mattered all that much to Bertie after Amy took Bertie's car away. Now, even if she needed to be somewhere at a particular time—like at the beauty shop to get her hair colored—she had no way to get there unless she walked or called a taxicab.

"Taxis are expensive," she told Amy.

169

"Honestly, Aunt Bertie, if I didn't know better, I'd feel sorry for you. You can well afford to pay for a taxicab. And silver hair is more becoming on a woman your age."

"More becoming, my big toe. Have you ever seen a man turn his head to get a better look at a head of gray hair?"

The first thing Bertie was going to do when she got to Canada was make an appointment to get her hair colored. Mr. Sajak's assistant hadn't said exactly when Mr. Sajak's chauffeur would be coming for her, but Bertie had gone ahead and packed her suitcase and gotten her fur coat out of storage so she'd be ready. She'd only won $100 in the preliminary round of the Canadian International Sweepstakes, but winners in the preliminary round automatically qualified for the Super Sweepstakes Finals. And the grand prize in the final round was $100,000. All Bertie had to do was send in a $100 deposit for her hotel room and give Sajak's assistant the number of her checking account. Bertie had refused to give out that information the first time the man asked for it; but when he explained that the only way to avoid paying taxes was to let him make a direct deposit of her winnings, she'd not only given him the numbers but also made him read them back to make sure he wrote them down correctly.

Bertie refocused the lens of her binoculars. A man she'd not seen before was sitting on the front steps of the old Campbell house with what looked to be a roll of blueprints in his lap. He wasn't one of the street people who sometimes hung out on the front porches of vacant houses. His clothes were too clean, and his boots were too new. He needed a haircut, but otherwise he looked fairly decent. But why the blueprints?

* * *

Dan Adamson spread the blueprints on the porch and weighted the edges down with rocks that had once lined a flowerbed. He was aware he was being watched. Each time he looked up, he caught a glimpse of movement at the window of the house next door. He was almost certain it was the same person who wouldn't come to the front door yesterday afternoon. He'd discovered a leak in the water line that serviced both houses while making an initial inspection of the property. He'd knocked on the front door three different times, and each time he could hear a different television program playing in the background. Notifying

170

neighbors that their utility services were going to be disrupted wasn't his responsibility, but a friendly gesture in the early stages of a renovation project resulted in more pleasant working conditions later on.

Dan removed the plastic cup from his stainless steel thermos and filled it up with coffee. Then he sat for a moment with both hands cupping the plastic. The warmth felt almost as good as the coffee tasted. When he'd drained the cup, he placed it atop the thermos and let his fingers linger on the stainless steel cylinder that still bore Helen's fingerprints. He'd packed all of their other belongings into cardboard boxes and stored them in a rented storage facility before he left Charleston.

"It'll do you good to get away," Jeff Pinckney had said, the day he told Dan about the contract that Pinckney and Hutto, Engineers had signed with a developer in Dallas, Texas. The contract was for the renovation of a single family dwelling in what had once been a fine East Dallas neighborhood. If the work on the old Victorian structure met the developer's expectations, the company's contract would be extended.

"If that happens, we'll open an office in Dallas and make you the project manager," Jeff told him. "Take a few days to think it over and make sure you're ready to take on a job of this magnitude. I know how you hate the heat and humidity in South Carolina, and summers in Texas are even hotter."

"Yeah, but I hear it's a dry heat," Dan quipped and smiled at his weak attempt at humor.

"Good to see you smiling again, buddy," Jeff said, placing a hand on Dan's shoulder. "But think about it before you give me your answer."

There hadn't been much to think about. Dan hadn't even bothered to ask if he'd be working out of the developer's office or renting office space, or if he'd be getting a housing allowance and an increase in salary. Things that had once seemed so important—things like climate and salary and profit sharing—no longer mattered. All that mattered to Dan now was getting as far away as possible from Charleston, South Carolina and the memory of Helen's accident.

So Dan had gotten away. He'd taken up residence in a nondescript suite at a nondescript hotel located on the service road of North Central Expressway. There was nothing exceptional about the hotel or the North Texas landscape, nothing that reminded him of the life he'd shared with Helen. But the harder he tried to forget, the more he remembered—little things, like the jangle of Helen's keys when she unlocked the front door of their house and the smudge of pink lipstick on her front tooth when she came toward him, smiling as she took the Target sack from behind her back. She'd purchased the stainless steel thermos on the way home from her office the day she got the call from the case worker who was handling their application for adoption. "An early Father's Day present," she'd said, handing him the sack tied at the top with pink and blue ribbons. The sack was Helen's way of telling Dan that after five months, three weeks, and six days, their application to adopt had been approved.

* * *

It had been almost a week since Pat Sajak's assistant called to tell Bertie Martin she was a winner in the final round of the Super Sweepstakes Contest, and already she was beginning to have doubts about the trip to Canada. For years, every time a rerun of *Holiday Inn* came on her television set, Bertie had fantasized about spending the Christmas holiday holed up in an inn with a handsome man and surrounded by snow. But Bertie was older now, and her arthritis acted up something awful in cold weather. Nowadays, her daydreams went more in the direction of Acapulco, Mexico; Miami, Florida; or McAllen, Texas, places where temperatures rarely dipped below fifty degrees, where tropical fruits grew in abundance and flowers and strawberries had two growing seasons.

Bertie would already have paid down on a condo in McAllen if it weren't for some unfortunate business with her bank account. She hadn't understood everything the banker told her, but she knew there couldn't be a deficit in her checking account. She'd authorized automatic transfers from her savings whenever the balance in her checking account dipped below $200. "No," she'd told the banker before she hung up on him, "I have no idea when I'll be coming back from Canada. I'm still waiting to hear from Mr. Sajak. Yes, that's who I mean—Mr. Pat Wheel-of-Fortune Sajak."

Bertie hadn't said a word about the problem with her bank account when she talked to Amy. The less Amy knew about Bertie's business, the better Bertie liked it. But she had called the police. The female dispatcher who answered Bertie's 911 call sent a handsome young officer named Keith out to investigate. Bertie made Keith a cup of tea, and he sat at her kitchen table to write out his report. But the second time Bertie called 911, to report that a thief had somehow gotten into her house and stolen the wooden cylinder out of her toilet paper holder, a male dispatcher with a most unpleasant voice told Bertie there was a $500 fine for making crank 911 calls and hung up on her.

Bertie took the last cigarette from her package of Pall Mall Lights. Despite her dislike of cold weather, she couldn't go a whole day without smoking a cigarette. Just as soon as the mailman came, she'd put on her mink coat and walk to the Pak N Save on Greenville Avenue to purchase another carton of cigarettes. And as long as she was going, she might as well buy a couple of lottery tickets.

* * *

Dan had finally gotten a look at the old lady who lived next door when he was getting into his truck to go to lunch. She'd come wobbling down the sidewalk wearing a lime green pantsuit and shoes with heels at least three inches high. He'd stepped out of his truck to introduce himself, but the woman had walked right past him without so much as a glance. Dan had waited until she wobbled up the sidewalk and disappeared into her house before he started the motor. If he startled her and she fell and broke something, he'd be the one who had to summon an ambulance.

Dan closed his eyes to shut out the five-month-old memory. Once again he was standing in his office talking to Jeff Pinckney with a hand over one ear to shut out the sound of the siren, catching only a glimpse of the ambulance as it raced past the office window carrying his wife's lifeless body to the hospital.

When the flashback subsided, the underarms of Dan's shirt were drenched with sweat. He sat for a few minutes to regain his composure before he started the motor. He was pulling away from the curb when he saw the slip of yellow paper stuck beneath his windshield wiper. *Parking spaces on this side of the street are reserved for RESIDENTS only,* the note read. *Kindly find another place to park your vehicle or expect a citation.*

All through lunch, Dan fretted about the note. The woman at City Hall hadn't said a word about a parking permit; and if what the note said was true, not only did he need a parking permit, but the work crew that was due to arrive from South Carolina would need several. Perhaps the best course of action would be to return to Dallas City Hall and request an exemption.

Dan's mind was still preoccupied when he pulled out of the restaurant parking lot. Perhaps that's why he didn't see the diminutive figure standing on the curb until she stepped directly into the path of his truck. No cars were in the center lane when he swerved to avoid hitting her. His bumper only grazed the fur coat, but his truck careened out of control and hit the median.

Dan's hands were shaking by the time he regained control of his truck and brought it to a stop. And when he glanced into his rearview mirror and saw that the woman responsible for the near mishap was proceeding on across the street, oblivious to the havoc she had created, he was furious. He was even more upset when he recognized the lime green trousers beneath the full-length mink. Dan made a tire-squealing U-turn at the next turn-about.

* * *

Bertie Martin was walking down University Avenue, minding her business, when a maroon pick-up truck pulled up beside her, and the driver began shouting obscenities. There wasn't a man alive who could talk to Bertie in that tone of voice. He was screaming so loud and talking so fast that she couldn't understand most of the profanities, but she heard "God damn it," and she heard him when he told her to get into his truck before someone ran over her.

No way in hell was she getting into a vehicle with a man she'd never even met. She focused her eyes on the street ahead and kept right on walking, while the man in the pickup inched his vehicle along beside her. When an impatient driver started honking, the man in the pick-up took off down the street like a race car driver.

Bertie was so undone by the encounter that she turned the wrong way at the intersection of University Drive and Greenville Avenue and walked three blocks in the wrong direction. By the time she realized her mistake, the sun was directly overhead, and Bertie was roasting in the mink coat. Sweat was running down both sides of her face, and her spectator pumps were rubbing blisters on her heels. To make matters even worse, she was pretty sure that the man in the maroon pickup was stalking her. Overcome with exhaustion and too dizzy to continue, Bertie collapsed onto a bench at the next bus stop. That's when she realized that she'd been so intent on writing the note to put under the windshield wiper of the maroon truck that she'd forgotten to take her blood pressure medicine. That's why that the next time the man in the maroon truck circled the block, Bertie limped to the curb and motioned for him to pull over.

"Keep your hands to yourself," she told him when she was seated with her seat belt fastened. "If you try anything, I'll roll this window down and start screaming."

* * *

The old woman thought Dan was coming on to her! Despite his best efforts to contain his amusement, Dan burst out laughing. He could tell that the old lady wasn't amused. She was sitting as close to the passenger door as she could sit with her seat belt fastened, but Dan couldn't stop laughing.

"What's so funny, Mister?" Bertie asked when his laughter finally subsided.

"I'm sorry," he said, wiping tears from his cheeks and then wiping his hands on the leg of his trousers. "I haven't laughed like that in so long, and it felt so good, I couldn't stop." He extended his right hand to Bertie. "The name's Dan Adamson. I'm the architect who's overseeing the renovation of the house next door to yours. I've been following you to make sure you're all right and to apologize for the cursing."

"I know who you are. I recognized you when you tried to run over me, and I'll thank you to keep your nasty hands to yourself."

"Me?" Dan said, returning his hand to the steering wheel. "You're the one who was jaywalking."

"Now that you've got me in your truck, Dan Adamson," Bertie said, ignoring his accusing tone of voice, "where are you taking me?"

"I was on my way back to the Campbell house, when you stepped in front of my truck."

"I did nothing of the sort. You were exceeding the speed limit. But if you'll make a legal U-turn and drive six blocks to Pak N Save, I won't press charges."

* * *

175

Dan glanced at his watch. He'd been sitting in his truck in front of Republic Bank for over half an hour, waiting for Bertie to deposit her Social Security check. He couldn't imagine what was keeping her, but he wasn't about to honk his horn. She'd already given him a lecture about that when he picked her up from the bingo parlor last Friday.

"A lady never goes anywhere with a man who isn't gentleman enough to come up to the door for her," she'd told him again this morning, as he escorted her down the sidewalk and opened the door on the passenger side of his truck.

"Even if the man is doing the lady a favor?" Dan asked; but as usual, Bertie ignored him.

This was the fifth time in less than a week that she'd asked Dan to drive her somewhere. Because Dan didn't have a lot to do until the work crew arrived, and because Bertie agreed to let him park his truck in her driveway, he'd agreed to be her driver. But if she wasn't out of the bank in the next five minutes, he'd go inside and find out what was keeping her.

"Not yet," Dan said when his cellphone rang and the caller was Jeff Pinckney inquiring about Dan's request for a parking exemption. "I'm hoping to hear something by the end of the week. And believe me when I tell you that that can't happen soon enough for me. I'm beginning to feel like Bertie Martin's keeper." Jeff Pinckney chuckled. "Don't laugh, Jeff. When I picked her up at the bingo parlor on Friday, I heard her tell one of her bingo buddies that I was her date," Dan said, as Bertie Martin and a man in three-piece suit emerged from the revolving door of the bank. "Jeff, I've got to go. I'll call you right back."

The man who accompanied Bertie to Dan's truck was a bank officer. He needed to get in touch with Bertie's next of kin but was prevented by privacy laws from telling Dan why he needed this information. And Bertie, who was simultaneously threatening to sue the bank and "sic the police" on the bank officer, was refusing to give the bank officer her niece's contact information.

"I didn't know you had a niece," Dan said, as he guided his pickup truck onto North Central Expressway. "Why wouldn't you give the bank officer her telephone number?"

Bertie sat with her arms crossed over her chest, her eyes on the passing scenery, and refused to answer Dan's question until he guided his truck to a stop in her driveway.

"Going somewhere?" he asked when Bertie unlocked the front door and he saw the oversized suitcase sitting in the foyer. Once again Bertie ignored Dan's question and ordered him to take a seat in the living room while she went to the kitchen and made him a cup of tea for his trouble.

"It was no trouble," Dan called out from the living room, where every edge, shelf, and side table held some kind of collection. Among rose bowls, Belleek tea cups, Waterford vases, and Venetian glass ashtrays stood what looked to be cheap glass statues. Dan thought, at first, that the statues of birds and elephants and dolphins were made of molded glass; but when he picked one up, he discovered it was plastic. All twelve were made of plastic.

"I won those," Bertie told him, when she came into the room carrying a tea tray and saw Dan holding one of the elephants. "They're worth a lot of money. I have certificates of authenticity to prove it; but if you're interested in buying one, I'll make you a good deal." Bertie spread a cloth napkin in her lap. "I won't have room for them when I sell this house and move into the Senior Citizens Retirement Center in McAllen."

"Is that where your niece Amy lives?"

"Goodness no," Bertie said with a wave of her hand. "Amy lives in Fort Gibson, Florida."

"If you're interested in selling this place, the developer I'm working with might be interested in buying it."

"Well, the place will be available just as soon as I return from Canada."

"Canada? Why are you going to Canada this time of year?"

"Well, I'm not supposed to tell anybody." Bertie lowered her voice to a whisper. "Mr. Sajak doesn't want word to get out before the big news conference, but I'm the big Super Sweepstakes winner."

The more questions Dan asked about the contest, the more animated Bertie became, and the story that unfolded was so bizarre Dan couldn't be certain Bertie wasn't imagining it. She was convinced that Pat Sajak was going to show up at her front door and escort her to Canada. Dan could only imagine what these crooks would do to her once they got her out of the country.

"Are you certain about this, Bertie?"

"Wait right here." Bertie pushed herself up from the couch and disappeared into her bedroom. She reemerged with two paper sacks stuffed full of bulk mailings. She took envelope after envelope from the sacks and placed them on the coffee table until she found the one from Pat

Sajak.

Using the ruse that he could show Bertie how to retrieve messages from her answering machine, Dan located Amy Martin's address and telephone number. As soon as he could leave Bertie's house without arousing her suspicions, he returned to his truck and called the number.

* * *

Bertie was sound asleep when the alarm clock on her nightstand sounded. She lay in bed for a few minutes, wondering what day it was and why her suitcase was sitting in the middle of her bedroom instead of in the closet. Then she remembered it was Friday, the day she usually played bingo. But she wasn't going to play bingo today because Dan Adamson was driving her to Florida. But first, she had to unpack all the sweaters and pantsuits and thermal underwear that she'd packed when she thought she was going to Canada and hang them back in her closet.

And then she had to search for her bathing suit. She couldn't remember the last time she wore it or if perhaps she'd donated it to Goodwill. Maybe Dan would take her by North Park Mall to buy a new one. She'd definitely need a new bathing suit . . . and . . . and a new cover-up . . . and a new pair of sunglasses if she and Dan were going to spend the Christmas holiday at Amy's beach house on Sanibel Island.

* * *

Dan whistled as he loaded his suitcase and laptop and blueprints into the backseat of his truck. He was almost ready to go, and for the first time since Helen's accident, he was looking forward to something. All he had left to do was to check out of the Embassy Suites, leave a message about the parking exemption on Jeff Pinckney's answering machine, and wish him a Merry Christmas. Dan was on his way to Bertie's house when he braked for a red light at the intersection of Lover's Lane and Greenville Avenue, and the stainless steel thermos with Helen's fingerprints rolled out from beneath the passenger seat. He reached down and placed his fingertips on the traces left by hers and let the warmth of the smooth metal cylinder penetrate his skin.

Hidden Meanings, Treatment of Time, Supreme Irony, and Life Experiences in the Song "Ain't Gonna Bump No More No Big Fat Woman"
Michael Parker

In the song "Ain't Gonna Bump No More No Big Fat Woman" by Joe Tex, the speaker or the narrator of this song, a man previously injured before the song's opening chords by a large, aggressive-type woman in a disco-type bar, refuses to bump with the "big fat woman" of the title. In doing so he is merely exercising his right to an injury-free existence thus insuring him the ability to work and provide for him and his family if he has one, I don't know it doesn't ever say. In this paper I will prove there is a hidden meaning that everybody doesn't get in this popular Song, Saying, or Incident from Public Life. I will attempt to make it clear that we as people when we hear this song we automatically think "novelty" or we link it up together with other songs we perceive in our mind's eye to be just kind of one-hit wonders or comical lacking a serious point. It could put one in the mind of, to mention some songs from this same era, "Convoy" or "Disco Duck." What I will lay out for my audience is that taking this song in such a way as to focus only on it's comical side, which it is really funny nevertheless that is a serious error which ultimately will result in damage to the artist in this case Joe Tex also to the listener, that is you or whoever.

"About three nights ago/I was at a disco." (Tex, line 1.) Thus begins the song "Ain't Gonna Bump No More No Big Fat Woman" by the artist Joe Tex. The speaker has had some time in particular three full days to think about what has occurred to him in the incident in the disco-type establishment. One thing and this is my first big point is that time makes

179

you wiser. Whenever Jeremy and I first broke up I was so ignorant of the situation that had led to us breaking up but then a whole lot of days past and little by little I got a handle on it. The Speaker in "Ain't Gonna Bump No More No Big Fat Woman" has had some time now to go over in his mind's eye the events that occurred roughly three days prior to the song being sung. Would you not agree that he sees his life more clear? A lot of the Tellers in the stories you have made us read this semester they wait a while then tell their story thus knowing it by heart and being able to tell it better though with an "I" narrator you are always talking about some kind of "discrepancy" or "pocket of awareness" where the "I" acts like they know themselves but what the reader is supposed to get is they really don't. Well see I don't think you can basically say that about the narrator of "Ain't Gonna Bump No More . . . " because when our story begins he comes across as very clear-headed and in possession of the "facts" of this "case" so to speak on account of time having passed thus allowing him wisdom. So the first thing I'd like to point out is Treatment of Time.

There is a hidden meaning that everybody doesn't get in this particular Song, Saying, or Incident from Public Life. What everybody thinks whenever they hear this song is that this dude is being real ugly toward this woman because she is sort of a big woman. You are always talking about how the author or in this case the writer of the song is a construction of the culture. Say if he's of the white race or the male gender when he's writing he's putting in all these attitudes about say minority people or women without even knowing it, in particular ideals of femininity. Did I fully understand you to say that all white men author's basically want to sleep with the female characters they create? Well that just might be one area where you and me actually agree because it has been my experience based upon my previous relationships especially my last one with Jeremy that men are mostly just wanting to sleep with any woman that will let them. In the song "Ain't Gonna Bump No More No Big Fat Woman," let's say if you were to bring it in and play it in class and we were to then discuss it I am willing to bet that the first question you would ask, based on my perfect attendance is, What Attitudes Toward Women are Implied or Explicitly Expressed by the Speaker or Narrator of this Song? I can see it right now up on the board. That Lindsay girl who sits up under you practically, the one who talks more than you almost would jump right in with, "He doesn't like this woman because she is not the slender submissive ideal woman" on and on. One thing and I'll say this again come Evaluation time is you ought to get better at cutting people like Lindsay off. Why we have to listen to her go off on every man in every story we read or rap song you bring in (which, okay, we know you're "down" with Lauryn Hill or whoever but it seems like sometimes I could just sit out in the parking lot and listen to 102 JAMZ and not have to climb three flights of stairs and get the same thing) is beyond me seeing as how I work two jobs to pay for this course and I didn't see her name up under the instructor line in the course offerings plus why should I listen to her on the subject of men when it's clear she hates every last one of them? All I'm saying is she acts like she's taking up for the oppressed people when she goes around oppressing right and left and you just stand up there letting her go on. I'm about sick of her mouth. Somebody left the toilet running, I say to the girl who sits behind me whenever Lindsay gets cranked up on the subject of how awful men are.

Okay at this point you're wondering why I'm taking up for the speaker or narrator of "Ain't Gonna Bump No More" instead of the big fat woman seeing as how I'm 5'1" and weigh 149. That is if you even know who I am which I have my doubts based on the look on your face when you call the roll and the fact that you get me, Melanie Sudduth and Amanda Wheeler mixed up probably because we're A: always here, which you don't really seem to respect all that much, I mean it seems like you like somebody better if they show up late or half the time like that boy Sean, B: real quiet and C: kind of on the heavy side. To me that is what you call a supreme irony the fact that you and that Lindsay girl spend half the class talking about Ideals of Beauty and all and how shallow men are but then you tend to favor all the dudes and chicks in the class which could be considered "hot" or as they used to say in the seventies which is my favorite decade which is why I chose to analyze a song from that era, "so fine." So, supreme irony is employed.

As to why I'm going to go ahead and go on record taking up for the Speaker and not the Big Fat Woman. Well to me see he was just minding his own business and this woman would not leave him be. You can tell in the lines about how she was rarin' to go (Tex, line 4) that he has got some respect for her and he admires her skill on the dance floor. It's just that she throws her weight around, literally! To me it is her that is in the wrong. The fact that she is overweight or as the speaker says "Fat" don't have anything to do with it. She keeps at him and he tells her to go on and leave him alone, he's not getting down, "You done hurt my hip once."

(Tex, lines 25-27.) She would not leave him alone. What she ought to of done whenever he said no was just go off with somebody else. I learned this the hard way after the Passage of Time following Jeremy and my's breakup. See I sort of chased after him calling him all the time and he was seeing somebody else and my calling him up and letting him come over to my apartment and cooking him supper and sometimes even letting him stay the night. Well if I only knew then what I know now. Which is this was the worse thing I could of done. Big Fat Woman would not leave the Speaker in the song which might or might not be the Artist Joe Tex alone. Also who is to blame for her getting so big? Did somebody put a gun to her head and force her to eat milkshakes from CookOut? Jeremy whenever he left made a comment about the fact that I had definitely fell prey to the Freshman Fifteen or whatever. In high school whenever we started dating I was on the girl's softball team I weighed 110 pounds. We as people nowadays don't seem to want to take responsibility for our actions if you ask me which I guess you did by assigning this paper on the topic of Analyze a Hidden Meaning in a Song, Saying, or Incident from Public Life which that particular topic seems kind of broad to me. I didn't have any trouble deciding what to write on though because I am crazy about the song "Ain't Gonna Bump No More No Big Fat Woman" and it is true as my paper has set out to prove that people take it the wrong way and don't get its real meaning also it employs Treatment of Time and Supreme Irony.

One thing I would like to say about the assignment though is okay, you say you want to hear what we think and for us to put ourselves in our papers but then on my last paper you wrote all over it and said in your Ending Comments that my paper lacked clarity and focus and was sprawling and not cohesive or well organized. Well okay I had just worked a shift at the Coach House Restaurant and then right after that a shift at the Evergreen Nursing Home which this is my second job and I was up all night writing that paper on the "Tell-Tale Heart" which who's fault is that I can hear you saying right now. Your right. I ought to of gotten to it earlier but all that aside what I want to ask you is okay have you ever considered that clarity and focus is just like your way of seeing the world? Like to you A leads to B leads to C but I might like want to put F before B because I've had some Life Experiences different than yours one being having to work two jobs and go to school full time which maybe you yourself had to do but something tells me I doubt it. So all I'm saying is maybe you ought to reconsider when you start going off on clarity and logic and stuff that there are let's call them issues behind the way I write which on the one hand when we're analyzing say "Lady with the Tiny Dog" you are all over discussing the issues which led to the story being written in the way it is and on the other if it's me doing the writing you don't want to even acknowledge that stuff is influencing my Narrative Rhythm too. I mean I don't see the difference really. So that is my point about Life Experiences and Narrative Rhythm, etc.

The speaker in the song "Ain't Gonna Bump No More No Big Fat Woman" says no to the Big Fat Woman in part because the one time he did get up and bump with her she did a dip and nearly broke his hip. (Tex, line 5.) Dancing with this particular woman on account of her size and her aggressive behavior would clearly be considered Risky or even Hazardous to the speaker or narrator's health. Should he have gone ahead and done what you and Lindsay wanted him to do and got up there and danced with her because she was beautiful on the inside and he was wanting to thwart the trajectory of typical male response or whatever he could have ended up missing work, not being able to provide for his family if he has one it never really says, falling behind on his car payment, etc. All I'm saying is what is more important for him to act right and get up and dance with the Big Fat Woman even though she has prior to that moment almost broke his hip? Or should he ought to stay seated and be able to get up the next morning and go to work? I say the ladder one of these choices is the best one partially because my daddy has worked at Rencoe Mills for twenty-two years and has not missed a single day which to me that is saying something. I myself have not missed class one time and I can tell even though you put all that in the syllabus about showing up you basically think I'm sort of sad I bet. For doing what's right! You'd rather Sean come in all late and sweaty and plop down in front of you and roll his shirt up so you can gawk at his barbed wire tattoo which his daddy probably paid for and say back the same things you say only translated into his particular language which I don't hardly know what he's even talking about using those big words it's clear he don't even know what they mean. I mean, between him and Lindsay, my God. I loved it whenever he said, "It's like the ulcerous filament of her soul is being masticated from the inside out," talking about that crazy lady in the "Yellow Wallpaper" (which if you ask me her problem was she needed a shift emptying bedpans at the nursing home same as that selfish bitch what's her name, that little boy's mother in the "Rocking Horse Winner.") You'd rather Sean or Lindsay disrespect all your so-called rules and hand their mess in late so long as everything they say is something you already sort of said. What you want is for everybody to A: Look hot and B: agree with you. A good thing for you to think about is, let's say you were in a disco-type establishment and approached by a big fat man. Let's say this dude was getting down. Okay, you get up and dance with him once and he nearly breaks your hip, he bumps you on the floor. Would you get up there and dance with him again? My daddy would get home from work and sit in this one chair with this reading lamp switched on and shining in his lap even though I never saw him read a word but *The Trader* which was all advertisements for used boats and trucks and camper tops and tools. He went to work at six, got off at three, ate supper at five thirty. The rest of the night he sat in that chair drinking coffee with that lamplight in his lap. He would slap me and my sister Connie whenever he thought we were lying about something. If we didn't say anything how could we be lying so we stopped talking. He hardly ever said a word to me my whole life except, "Y'all mind your mama." Whenever I first met Jeremy in high school he'd call me up at night, we used to talk for hours on the phone. I never knew really how to talk to anyone like that. Everything that happened to me, it was interesting to Jeremy or at least he acted like it was. He would say, "What's up, girl?" and I would say, "nothing" or sometimes "nothing much" and I would hate myself for saying nothing and being nothing. But then he'd say, "Well what did you have for supper?" and I'd burst into tears because some boy asked me what did I have for supper. I would cry and cry. Then there'd be that awful thing you know when you're crying and the boy's like what is it what did I say and you don't know how to tell him he didn't do nothing wrong you just love his heart to bits and pieces just for calling you up on the telephone. Or you don't want to NOT let him know that nobody ever asked you such a silly thing as what did you eat for supper and neither can you come out and just straight tell him, I never got asked that before. Sometimes my life is like this song comes on the radio and I've forgot the words but then the chorus comes along and I only know the first like two words of every line. I'll come in midway, say around about "No More No Big Fat Woman." I only know half of what I know I guess. I went out in the sun and got burned bad and then the skin peeled off and can you blame me for not wanting to go outside anymore? She ought to go find her a big fat man. The only time my daddy'd get out of his chair nights was when a storm blew up out of the woods which he liked to watch from the screen porch. The rain smelled rusty like the screen. He'd let us come out there if we'd be quiet and let him enjoy his storm blowing up but if we said anything he'd yell at us. I could hate Jeremy for saying I'm just not attracted to you anymore but hating him's not going to bring me any of what you call clarity. Even when the stuff I was telling him was so boring, like, then I went by the QuikMart and got seven dollars worth of premium and a Diet Cheerwine he'd make like it was important. Sometimes though he wouldn't say anything and I'd be going on and on like you or Lindsay and I'd get nervous and say, "Hello?" and he'd say, "I'm here I'm just listening." My daddy would let us stay right through the thunder and even some lightning striking the trees in the woods behind the house. We couldn't speak or he'd make us go inside. I know, I know, maybe Jeremy got quiet because he was watching "South Park" or something. Still I never had anyone before or since say to me, I'm here I'm just listening.

I'm going to get another C minus over a D plus. You're going to write in your Ending Comments that this paper sprawls lacks cohesion is not well organized. Well that's alright because we both know that what you call clarity means a whole lot less than whether or not I think the speaker in the song "Ain't Gonna Bump No More No Big Fat Woman" ought to get up and dance with the woman who "done hurt my hip, she done knocked me down." (Tex, line 39.) I say, No he shouldn't. You say, Yes he should. In this Popular Song, Saying, or Incident from Public Life there is a Hidden Meaning that everybody doesn't get. Well, I get it and all I'm saying is you don't and even though I've spent however many pages explaining it to you you're never going to get it. If you get to feel sorry for me because I come to class every time and write down all the stupid stuff that Sean says and also for being a little on the heavy side I guess I get to feel sorry for you for acting like you truly understand a song like "Ain't Gonna Bump No More No Big Fat Woman" by the artist Joe Tex.

In my conclusion the speaker or the narrator of the song "Ain't Gonna Bump No More No Big Fat Woman," a man previously injured before the song's opening chords by a large aggressive type woman in a disco type bar refuses to bump with the fat woman of the title. In doing so he is merely exercising his right to an injury free existence. Treatment of Time, Supreme Irony and Life Experiences are delved into in my paper. There is a hidden meaning in this Song, Saying or Incident from Public Life. Looking only at the comical side is an error which will result in damage to the artist and also to the listener which is you or whoever.

Ending Comments Concerning "Ain't Gonna Bump No More With No Big Fat Woman"
Dave Kuhne

First, let me tell you that I do know who you are, that I don't confuse you with either Melanie or Amanda, and that I'm aware that you have never missed a class. But since you have never said a word in class, I'm pleased that you made the effort to find "your narrative rhythm" and that you have "put yourself" in the paper and "let me hear what you think" about the class as well as the famous Joe Tex song "Ain't Gonna Bump No More With No Big Fat Woman." However, after reading your paper on hidden meanings, treatment of time, supreme irony, and life experiences in the song, I have to agree with you when you write that you "only know half of what you know." Some of your points are not completely supported by the song's lyrics, but you have made a number of solid observations about the tune, observations that are clearly connected to the materials that we have discussed in class this semester. Most importantly, you have translated those critical observations into your own language, you have used your own terminology to describe the relevant points, and that use of voice is a step toward self-empowerment. You should never let yourself be "silenced" or "marginalized."

Your comments indicate to me that you have understood our discussions about Postmodernism, especially the point that Postmodernism resists the elitism imbedded in Modernism's focus on "high art." Your choice of a topic shows me that you embrace the Postmodern notion that artifacts of pop culture such as the famous Joe Tex song are just as important and meaningful as an elite work of art that might have been privileged by a Modern aesthetic. Of course, Tex wasn't the author of the lyrics (the tune was composed by Buddy Killen and Bennie Lee McGinty), but by performing the song, Tex gives the lyrics his imprimatur. You reinforce this understanding about the difference in Postmodernism and Modernism when, in the first paragraph of your report, you note that there are serious themes associated with pop lyrics, even the lyrics of so-called novelties such as "Ain't Gonna Bump" or "Convoy" or "Disco Duck." As my colleague, Professor Van Holstein-Smythe points out in her monograph, *Stepping up the Beat: A Literary Analysis of Popular Songs from the 1970s*, songs like "Convoy" reflect the anti-authority dissatisfaction of the working class while "Disco Duck" satirizes the silliness associated with the sexual materialism of the final years of that decade. And you are correct to focus on the gender issues associated with "Big Fat Woman." Like all art, Postmodern art reflects the culture in which it was created, and gender and class issues are always important cultural components. "Big Fat Woman" is an important work of art that reflects the values of a phallocentric culture.

Of course, Lindsay shares my opinion about men, how they so shamelessly stereotype, silence, and use women. I would think you would also agree that the lyrics are sexist, especially since you are, like me, how would one put it, a "woman of size." As you know from our class discussions, one of the most important principles of Postmodernism is that language determines reality, and Postmodernism has affected our very concept of size. The fact that I was once a few sizes smaller than I am now demonstrates perfectly the Postmodern point that reality is relative, especially when considered in terms of the treatment of time. Let me give you another example about how, through the passage of time, the meaning of "size" has been altered. When you visit a coffee shop, what would have been a "medium" coffee when I was an undergrad is now a "small," and what was a "medium" years ago is now a "large," and the new "large" is a "grande." You could go for a swim in a "grande." The point is that language does, in fact, determine reality. You might recall how in *White Noise* reality is changed when, in the almost-plane-crash scene, the "plane crash" is renamed a "crash landing," and that renaming reshapes reality for the passengers on the plane. Since the meaning of words can change due to the treatment of time, we have reached the point where nothing (no-thing) can mean anything (any-unnamed-thing).

But you seem not to fully comprehend the lyrics because you have read too much into the lines. Therefore, I can't completely accept your

Naturalistic argument that the singer of "Big Fat Woman" should avoid dancing with the "woman of size" in order to protect his ability to work. Nowhere in the song, as you yourself note, does the narrator or singer indicate that he has a family to support or a job to attend. We must be careful not to assume too much, not to read something into the lyrics, not to focus on something outside the frame of the narrative. But it is important to ask "What Attitudes Toward Women are Implied or Explicitly Expressed by the Speaker or Narrator of the Song?" In fact, the singer objects not only to the size of the woman but also to her determination to dance, her self-confidence, her sense of worth. You even note that the "woman of size" was aggressive, and you write that the woman "would not let him be." Remember that Tex sings "And this big fat woman, bumped me on the floor/She was rarin' to go, that chick was rarin' to go/ Man she did a dip, almost broke my hip" (lines 4-6). That the "woman of size" was "rarin' to go" illustrates her aggressiveness, her lack of submissiveness. And it's not just "Big Fat Woman" that reveals Tex's phallocentric attitude. As Van Holstein-Smythe points out, Joe Tex also recorded "You Better Hold on to What You Got," a song that promotes the ideal woman as one who will mind the children while he's at work (lines 13-14) and who will have his dinner ready when he comes home (lines 15-16). But although you seem to miss an important thematic implication in the song, you are correct to note that the lyrics of "Ain't Gonna Bump" are a product of social construction.

Class distinctions are yet another element of social construction worthy of our consideration, and, in your own way, you focus some of your comments on the class issue, especially when you point out that in both "Rocking Horse Winner" and "Yellow Wallpaper" the main women characters are privileged and have never had to work.

A lot of students think that their professors have never had to work a "real" job. Let me tell you, dealing with four classes of sub-literates every semester is "real," especially when most of the students would never take the class if it weren't required. I've even had some students tell me that this was the first class in which they were asked to read a book. But I've had more difficult jobs. All during undergraduate school (before the treatment of time shaped my size), I was a waitress at one of those places that make you wear the skimpy skirts and low cut blouses, and I had to put up with all those old guys staring at my boobs and patting my ass and I could never say a word about it if I wanted to get any good tips. So I

189

understand when you explain that your poor performance on "The Tell-Tale Heart" paper was the result of your demanding work schedule.

Professors are people, and I've had my "Jeremy" moments, only his name was Michael. Michael, he made such a fool of me. Michael, he's the one that finally turned me, made me give up on men and get my rainbow tattoo. It's a small one in a place you can't see. So you're wrong about Sean. I don't think he's "hot" (Lindsay, however, is another matter) and I don't admire that barbed wire tat on his shoulder. I can smell the cannabis on his breath when he starts to talk (I suspect that you can smell it, too) so I just stare at his tat so I can avoid listening to his polysyllabic blather: "ulcerous filament being masticated." Stoner diction. Maybe you're right. I should shut down some of the more talkative students, but I don't want to "silence" or "marginalize" anyone.

In my dealings with men, I've determined, as you have, that "men are mostly just wanting to sleep with any woman that will let them," and that includes "women of size." In fact, even the simplest of men, your Jeremy, for instance, have learned some lessons about how to deal with women, about how to trick us into satisfying their base needs. So I have to agree with you about men. Men mostly want us to spread our legs and shut up. That's why they demean us, silence us. And they've all read those stories in the magazines: "Want More Love? Do More Listening." They have learned to employ the rhetoric of silence, learned to use listening as a weapon.

Michael was like that; he used listening, used silence, as a rhetorical tool to shape me to his will. He would let me ramble on and on about my students or my most recent article on women and Victorian poetry or my developing admiration for Van Holstein-Symthe. Van, she's the one who eventually saved me. I think you would like Van. Like us, she's a "woman of size," and like us, she has had her "men troubles." Even when I married Michael, something in my gut told me it wasn't right. I was never like my girlfriends, you know, boy crazy, and I never really enjoyed "being with" Michael all that much. But all my friends were getting married, and without knowing it, I let the culture determine my orientation and my actions. I was silenced before I even knew I could speak. At least Michael and I didn't have kids. In the end, all he really cared about was sticking that silly little thing of his in me. I'm sure your experience with Jeremy was similar. A time may come when you just say, as I have, "Enough! No more men and their silly little things!"

And I find it interesting that you bring your family into the paper. This would usually signal a lack of unity, focus, and coherence; but now I see that you are simply illustrating another point about Postmodernism: the use of a shifting point of view and a blending of voices. You also emphasize an important principle of Postmodernism when you question the value of my sense of "clarity." Postmodernism challenges the conventional notion that there is one fixed reality and points out that there are multiple realities, that your reality is not my reality, and that logic should be questioned. You do a fine job of illustrating the point when you write "Like to you, A leads to B leads to C but I might put F before B." And, of course, a decentering of authority has always been associated with Postmodernism.

I'm sorry to learn that you suffered abuse from your father. I notice that he succeeded in silencing you; that explains why you are so quiet in class. My father hated thunderstorms because they would usually knock out the power during one of the beloved ball games he would watch on television. My mother never got much help from Dad. A day at work (he was a high school coach and social studies teacher, but he knew a lot more about sports than about people or society) would drain the life from him, and when he got home all he wanted to do was drink a Bud (he didn't have much taste in beer) and watch a game on the television. You never saw a man so much in love with sports. I often thought that if there were a sports spelling bee on TV, my father would watch it. But I can sort of understand how your father felt when the storms were coming. Sometimes, late at night, Van and I will sit on the patio of her townhouse and just listen and watch, alert as cats on a hunt, as the sky fires with lightning and the thunder rolls and rattles the windows and balls of ice crash from the clouds. We never say a word. What can one say, other than a prayer, in the face of such indifferent power? It's enough to turn one into a Naturalist.

And I know you can't wait to burn me in the evaluations. I'm used to some pretty savage comments. Here are a few of my favorites: "She wears black every day because it's your funeral." "Some drink from the fountain of knowledge; she only gargled." Then there was this one: "You'd be hawt if you were thin."

So, having been harshly evaluated myself, I don't feel too bad when I give tough grades. When I have to read, read, and reread all of those awful sentences and banal comments about some of the world's greatest writing, it makes me mad, and when I get mad, that's when I do my best grading. Besides, it's "Lady with a Dog," not "Lady with the Tiny Dog."

In conclusion, while I'm generally impressed with the content of your paper and with the creativity behind it, and I understand you have constructed a Postmodern response that blends genres, shifts points of view, challenges authority, and attempts to decenter the reader while providing an analysis of "Ain't Gonna Bump No More With No Big Fat Woman," there are still some problems with cohesion and organization. Also, there are some grammar and spelling issues, but we can get "passed" that for now and talk about those problems "ladder."

Final evaluation: C/C-

Thank You
George Singleton

Because I'd become bored with my own project collecting what living people hoped their last words would be—I'd signed a contract for a series divided into famous actors, politicians, and convicts serving life sentences—I agreed to attend my wife's cousin's Sunday afternoon recital at his speech therapist's office. This was some kind of cutting edge speech therapist who got grants from the National Institute of Health, the state's arts commission, and a generous donation from either Crest or Dentine, I forget which. Every Sunday afternoon a "reading" took place, wherein patients showed their "progress." My wife's cousin, a loser named Tony Timms, shot himself in the mouth and survived. He told everyone he hadn't attempted suicide, but his story changed too often. Sometimes it involved an accidental discharge while cleaning the barrel at the Happy Rancher motel out on Highway 301. Sometimes it occurred while he practiced his quick draw in front of a full-length mirror there. The pistol slipped, and the trigger depressed on one of those metal bottle openers screwed into the wall. No one in my wife's family ever questioned Cousin Tony's stories. In another scenario he aimed at a rat in Room 11, and the bullet ricocheted off the complimentary iron. Maybe I married into a family who thought it natural to clean guns, quick draw, or shoot rodents in motel rooms a mile from their own abodes, I don't know.

"It's only an hour, Daniel. Two hours at the most. You go in, some people talk, you tell them 'good job,' and then come home. It'll mean so much to Tony," my wife Ellette said. "You're always saying how you feel like an outsider at the reunions and whatnot. Maybe this'll make the aunts and uncles see you more like one of us. You know? They'll see you as a team player."

I had planned on sending out bulk emails to Hollywood agents, Congress, and convicts' Facebook pages in hopes of collecting enough responses to fill three 256-page collections. Already I had sent queries out via the United States Postal Service, but only a handful of people had responded. One guy convicted of murdering—get this—his wife's cousin wrote back and said he wanted his last word to be "you" and his penultimate word to be "fuck." He told me that I should've sent an SASE. I figured he must've spent some time in the prison library, what with his vocabulary.

To Ellette I said, "I'll start laughing. I'll try not to laugh. It'll be your job to pinch me."

Ellette's father was named Ell. His grandfather worked as a pipefitter. Somehow her zygote gathered all the good DNA in the entire family history. "Well, that's the thing," Ellette said. "I promised to go visit Lori on Sunday. She wants me to help her move some stuff into a mini-storage warehouse unit while Tony's doing his thing."

Most people might say, "How can you side with your own cousin's wife?" Most people might say, "Blood's thicker than water." Their last words, by the way, want to be "Take me, Jesus!" or "It's much more pleasant than I imagined," I'm betting. Not that I've ever comprehended genealogy and all of its nuances; but Lori was somehow a real cousin to my wife, too, just not in a way that broke incest taboo laws, which everyone brought up almost immediately at those brutal and endless reunions.

* * *

Because I know how people will react when I tell this entire story, I would like to point out that I hailed from a normal lower middle class family. I played second base on the high school baseball team, which gave me all kinds of reasons to explain to my high school girlfriends that I should play with their boobs. My little sister went on to become a schoolteacher. My father died early of a heart attack, my mother got remarried to an insurance agent, and then she died in a car crash after drinking too much after a State Farm Christmas party. I got a bachelor's degree, and then a master's—both from state schools, though the second one was in Delaware, which was a step above the one in South Carolina. I married Ellette between degrees, and then she went out and got a job back near her hometown. Me, I couldn't find anything, even with a master's. They wouldn't hire me on as an associate at Home Depot or Lowe's because I was overqualified, and they wouldn't take me on anywhere else because I didn't have credentials or experience. Ellette said, "I'd be happy—more than happy, and you'd be perfect—if you worked as a househusband. A stay-at-home daddy."

One of us is evidently sterile. We never went to a specialist. Who wants to be in a relationship wherein one person is always pointing an accusatory finger at the other? Well, maybe Abraham Lincoln, whose last words reportedly came out "It's not like I don't have a million things to do—this better be good."

Ellette's mother had Tupperware parties weekly, served draft beer, and gave out complimentary hat cleaner and lint remover brushes to whom she deemed the most proficient at replicating a burp top lid sound effect. Tony Timms's mother—Ellette's aunt—gave her children trophies for Christmas from Santa Claus, gold plastic bowlers atop faux marble bases with *You Better Watch Out* or *You Better Think Twice* or *You're My Favorite Spare* etched down at the bottom. She handed these things to her nieces and nephews, too, and when I first came to meet Ellette's parents, I had to stand there at the fireplace mantel staring at my wife-to-be's holiday spectaculars, the most impressive of which read *Most Likely to Secede*. I wanted to marry Ellette at that moment.

So my wife worked, I cleaned house and ran errands, and then came up with the *What People Hope They'll Say* series, though none had come out and a September deadline hovered. In my mind, I foresaw royalty money streaming in and—if I lived long enough and could somehow hire some research assistants—working on what famous politicians, actors, and prisoners really said at their death. Already I had one 3 X 5 notecard saved with what that guy out in California convicted of robbing twelve banks, kidnapping a couple Mormon missionaries, and forcing himself upon a mule said. A mule's sterile, too, and that's probably what kept that guy from receiving more than one life sentence. He said he hoped his last words would be "Look, I found the Golden Tablets," but right before he succumbed to one of those alimentary canal cancers—esophagus, stomach, colon—he said to either a nurse or prison guard, "I should've made more things with Popsicle sticks." Did he mean in grade school, so he wouldn't've turned to the life of a bank-robbing, Mormon-corrupting bestialitist? Did he mean there inside the prison craft class?

Anyway, even though I was stuck, in my mind I had things to do, so I told Ellette that hanging out with Cousin Tony Timms and his speech-impaired comrades seemed untimely, frivolous, and odd. I said, "What? I'll trade you. Why don't you go to Tony Timms's speech therapy recital, and I'll go help Lori move crap to her new mini-storage warehouse unit." I thought—but didn't say—how Lori would end up missing a payment and some kind of auction would take place where people would bid on her leopard skin thong panties and romance novels and tweezers collection.

Ellette shook her head. She said, "I'm not as strong as you are. I can't handle being around stutterers and harelips. I can't! And then you got goddamn Tony without a tongue because he had the bullet ricochet off the motel channel changer when he was playing along with *Gunsmoke*. How much can he say? What do you think his last words will be—'num-num-num'?"

What if Ellette underwent a massive heart attack right after saying this to me? "Num-num-num." Man. How could I have lived with a woman whose last words went like that?

* * *

The speech therapist, who went by Melinda Floyd-Hendricks and put *B.S., M.A., M.A.T., Ph.D., NBCT* after her name on the door, held her arms out when I walked into her Speak Up Center. She said, "Welcome, welcome," in a clipped perfect diction that reminded me of someone bouncing a ping pong ball with his paddle alone. She said, "We are here to witness miracles."

To be honest, I expected to confront only tongueless Tony and a couple of stroke victims, the occasional stutterer. But there might've been twenty of these people, all in their best clothes, fidgeting. Dr. Floyd-Hendricks dealt with what I'd expected, plus mouth cancer victims, cleft palate survivors, amnesiacs, and a couple of people with no linguistic problems who wanted to become TV newscasters.

Tony wore a tie. I said, "Are you going to a funeral later?" Understand that I'd not seen him since his "accident." I'd not seen him since he quick-drew and fired a shot that hit the shower rod, ricocheted off the metal towel holder, ricocheted back off the porcelain tub, hit the toilet plunger, then went into Tony's mouth. I hadn't seen dopey, useless Tony Timms since he had undergone two or three reconstructive surgeries. I said, "I'm Ellette's husband, Daniel. Hey."

He might've said "Hey" back, I don't know, it sounded like "Nay,

Nay-nay, nay-nay nay nay-nay nay?" which probably stood for "Hey, Daniel, what're you doing here?" He opened his mouth unnaturally wide, and his tongue-stub reminded me of a snapping turtle's little worm-like fish-attractor. Or a clitoris.

A woman I didn't know at the time—one of the readers—said to me, "Thank you. Thank you, thank you, thank you, thank you, thank you, thank you," in a way that didn't make her come off as speech deficient, but either nervous or simple-minded, though her voice came out soft, whispery, and buttery as orange sherbet.

I said, "No problem," but I had some mucus in my throat and I feared that it came out "Nay nay-nay," which about killed me because the last thing a childless househusband with no books yet out on the shelves wants to do is appear either heartless or flippant. I cleared my throat twice and said, "This should be a good day."

"Thank you, thank you, thank you," the woman said. I kind of wondered if she walked into the wrong recital, that maybe she belonged down at the end of this particular medical center strip mall where people afflicted with echolalia hung out on Sundays.

Tony came up to me. He pulled me by the arm, leaned in, and whispered in my ear, "Nay nay nay nay-nay nay nay-nay nay-nay nay nay nay, nay nay nay-nay nay nay-nay nay nay."

I shrugged. I felt pretty sure that he had said, "I know that Ellette is helping Lori move out now and that Lori is leaving our life." I said, "I'm here," probably because I'd read a book that dealt with the private lives of Sartre, Heidegger, and a couple of those other existentialists.

Dr. Melinda Floyd-Hendricks clapped her hands a couple times. She said, "Okay, everyone. You all who are my patients need to get yourselves to a station. How this works, visitors, is kind of like speed-dating." She went on to explain how there would be a buzzer or dinger. Listeners would start off with their loved ones, then move counterclockwise around the room while the speech-afflicted trudged onward either reading from their own autobiographies or from works of classic literature. I kind of quit listening to the doctor, but she said each of her patients would be reading either three or ten minutes—I didn't quite grasp that part.

Let me say now that the speech-afflicted tend to have unhygienic and/or simple friends for the most part. I don't want to make any broad generalizations, but outside of me—I'd put on deodorant and had all my teeth and had a master's degree like I said—everyone looked like they'd woken up in a refrigerator box. They looked as if a soup line might form spontaneously at any time.

"And . . . go!" the doctor said. I sat down across from my wife's suicidal cousin. He nodded at me, then cracked open *The Sound and the Fury*, of all books. For three minutes he said, "Nay nay nay, nay-nay nay nay-nay nay-nay nay-nay, nay nay nay nay nay-nay," and so on. Then the buzzer went off, I said, "Good job, Tony!" as enthusiastically as I could muster—I tried to remember what it felt like when the editor at my publishing house told me I had a win-win idea regarding *What People Hope They'll Say*. He might've said "Nguyen-Nguyen," seeing as he was Vietnamese, I don't know.

* * *

Tony read from *The Sound and the Fury*, a novel I had read in undergraduate school when I took an elective in Literature of fucking Sports and the dickhead professor thought the golf part of Faulkner counted, whereas all of us in attendance—mostly geology majors who played on the disastrous football team—thought we'd be partaking in works written by Arnold Palmer, Richard Petty, Joe Namath, Lou Alcindor, Jim Ryun, Cassius Clay, Bob Cousy, Don Meredith, Mickey Mantle, and Evonne Goolagong. Tony read his nay nays and then I moved to a woman with a cleft palate who said, pretty clearly, "Peter Piper picked a peck of pickled peppers," slowly and repeatedly.

I won't go through everyone. I won't go through what went through my mind when these people either read pieces of Shakespeare ("Na! Na na na?" for "Hark who goes there?") or Edgar Allan Poe (nay-naymore). "Nay nay, nay nay nay nay. Nay nay nay nay-nay"—Shakespeare again.

I made it through a one-armed man who thought it necessary to tell me all about his childhood on a berry farm, and how at the end of the day his daddy let him eat blackberries until the juice ran down his arm, how at night he ate barbecue sandwiches and the sauce ran down his arm, how he wasn't much in sports except for horseshoes and tetherball. I said, "I understood you perfectly" or "Wow" or "How about that?" to each patient, though in truth I couldn't understand half of them or had allowed my mind to wander, wondering exactly what Ellette was helping Lori move into a mini-storage warehouse unit. I hoped that there wouldn't be guns.

Then I switched to the "thank you" woman. Her name ended up

being Felicia. I sat down and said, "Why are you here?"

Again, in a voice as smooth and soft as perfect Irish whiskey served atop cotton balls, Felicia said, "Thank you. If you don't mind, I've been telling everyone about what happened to me, but not in order. So right now I'm going to tell you what happened when I was twenty-two. I'm in France during a study abroad semester."

I cannot describe this voice, even if I had a worn-out book of adjectives in my possession. I would bet that, somewhere in all the Hollywood archives, a movie depicting angels might come close to how Felicia sounded. I never took a chemistry class, but whatever's the lightest gas ever invented?—Felicia's voice lilted lighter. I expected dandelion spores to blow out of her throat, that's how soft and melodic she came off.

I said, "You do what you need to do." I thought, You never answered my question as to why you were here. How come you enunciate so perfectly? I thought, Are you the speech therapist's pet? Did you start working with Dr. Melinda Floyd-Hendricks at age twelve and have gotten this far? Does the doctor pay you money to appear in commercials that concern her miracle cures? Are you a ringer? At night do you fear people like no-tongue Tony Timms showing up at your abode wanting to kill you for being such a show off? I said, "I'm here to hear," because I'm unable to speak to women.

Felicia said, "They told me they'd teach me how to make crepes. I went with them voluntarily. We entered a building—this was on Rue de la Huchette—and took the stairs down below ground level. I guess someone hit me in the head from behind. I don't remember any pain, per se; but when I awoke, they had me tied to a chair. The chair was tied to a radiator. It could've been worse, I suppose. This was in May. *Printemps*, for Spring. So the radiator wasn't on. This one man—I thought he was American at first—kept saying to me, 'The reason why people are living longer is because old men aren't having as many heart attacks. They're not having heart attacks because they're not finding silver coins in their loose change as frequently as, say, 1965 through 1972. In the old days, an octogenarian would find an ancient Roosevelt dime in his pants pocket at the end of the day, and he'd yell out, "I found a silver dime!" and then he'd fall over dead. Finding silver coins helped control population organically,' he'd say. Somehow it was the fault of America. It was the fault of crepe-making-wishful American students like me. Now, I don't want to accuse my captors of being American—that seems to be the convenient thing to do—

199

but the leader kept using the term *y'all* and I don't believe that's a term taught in French, Algerian, or Tunisian school systems when undergoing the nuances of the English language. But it doesn't make sense for an American to kidnap an American overseas, either, does it? My best bet is it was a very smart French man who studied abroad in the South—maybe at Duke, or Middle Tennessee State—and he picked up some lingo and learned to speak without an accent. Do you know anything about dialect interference, Daniel?"

First I wondered how she knew my name and then realized we all had to shove one of those adhesive-backed HELLO, I'M stickers on our shirts. I didn't really inspect anyone else's, but expected theirs to read *X* or *A Homeless Friend of a Speech-Impaired Relative*. I said to Felicia, "No, that's not my area of expertise. I don't have an area of expertise, now that I think about it. Hey, what do you want your last words to be? If you could, now, pick your last words, what would they be?"

Was her shoulder-length straight hair blonde, red, or strawberry-blonde? Were her lips full naturally, or enhanced by Botox? What was the story with her long, perfectly sculpted legs?

Felicia said, "I knew it would come to this." I didn't know if she meant "Those will be my last words" or if she simply thought I would eventually ask such a question.

I said, "Well."

"Time's up. Move!" said Dr. Melinda Floyd-Hendricks, experimental speech therapist.

* * *

When I got home, I found Ellette sitting in our den with the channel changer in her hand. She was surrounded by an exercise bike, a sit-up station, some kind of contortionist-friendly machine that appeared to be part balance beam, part hammock. There were twenty-one cardboard boxes stacked up, the kind that'll hold medium-sized TV sets. Draped across the boxes were enough coats to warm an Inuit army. I said, "What's going on?"

Ellette peered through a disassembled elliptical trainer. "Hey, Danny," she said. "How'd everything go with Tony?"

Down the hallway I heard Lori clearing her throat. I looked toward our bedrooms, spread my arms out, and raised my eyebrows to Ellette. I said, "Tony can't talk."

"There are some daiquiris in the kitchen. Lori and I celebrated with daiquiris."

Celebrated what? I thought. I said, "I was saving that rum for when my book got finished. I'm about to add your last words in the final chapter." I didn't mean it, of course. I didn't even like rum, and only kept it around to remind me why I hated fraternity boys. The whole time standing there in front of my wife I actually thought, Don't start a fight only because Felicia's voice is on your mind. I thought, Who the hell's made daiquiris since Happy Hour circa 1979?

Ellette put her finger to her lips. She stood up and tiptoed through her cousin-in-law's belongings toward me. "They were all full. Every storage place is filled up, probably because of all the foreclosures. Either that or Tony knew what Lori was up to and went around paying off the owners to these places not to let Lori rent a spot."

I shook my head. "Unless the owners can all understand 'Nay nay nay-nay's nay-nay nay-nay nay, nay nay nay nay nay nay nay nay nay nay-nay' means 'My wife Lori's coming over here, and I don't want you to rent her a unit,' then I doubt that's what happened. I know what happened. You felt sorry for her and offered to keep this crap here so she could save money. You should've just told me. I would've been fine with it."

Lori came out, eyes puffy, drink in hand. Lori said, "I'm sorry about this, Daniel. You didn't tell Tony, did you? What did he say today?"

"I didn't tell him anything. I had to promise to go back, though. He read about these people in Mississippi. Not much success, so far. I had to promise to go back and listen to him again."

"You mentioned that already," Ellette said.

Why did I say this? What in the world made me lie about attending another recital? I said, "Let me go clear some space in my work room and we can stack things up in there."

My wife and Lori said, "Thank you, thank you."

"Y'all don't sound the same," I said.

* * *

Felicia didn't remember me on the next Sunday. Maybe because I shaved, didn't wear a hat, combed my hair, shined my only pair of dress shoes, and wore a coat and tie. I nodded to Tony when I came in. By this time he'd learned of his wife staying with us, of course, but he seemed to accept it. He didn't come over in the middle of the night and yell out, "Nay-naaayyy!" like Stanley Kowalski.

I said, "Hello, there, Tony. As you can tell, I'm here because I've chosen to be on your side in this situation."

He might've said, "You don't know how much I appreciate it," in his way. Peripherally I watched Felicia, seated at her station, nodding like a geisha and offering her thank-yous in a way that, if I closed my eyes, sounded like the whimper of a baby panda, or koala bear. Tony might've also said, "Now I want to kill and disembowel you."

Dr. Floyd-Hendricks welcomed all of us, et cetera, and Tony continued with his *Sound and the Fury*. I'll give him this—he seemed to comprehend and enjoy the Benjy section. He enunciated in his tongueless way while I—remembering a childhood filled with Musical Chairs—tried to figure out how to skip six seats ahead and face Felicia next. I looked over to see who sat in front of her first. It was a woman who appeared to be about thirty years old, wearing a beret, which meant she wasn't from this state. Was she Felicia's sister, or longtime partner? Was she a co-worker?

People started clapping and I realized the first readings were finished. I don't even think I said, "Good job, tongueless Tony," before jumping up and stealing the seat in front of Felicia. No one seemed perturbed by the disarray I caused. I said, "Hey, Felicia, how're you doing, I've been thinking about you all week, I hope your speech therapy lessons have been going well even though, if you ask me, you should've graduated long ago, I'm here with the tongueless guy whose wife moved all of her crap into my house and now occupies our guest bedroom, what can I say? Boy oh boy, I can tell you it's put a strain on the marriage."

Felicia sat with her legs slightly apart. She wore a skirt I'd seen in one of those upper middle class catalogs Ellette got in the mail. I made a point to make eye contact. Felicia said, "The bad thing was, it was my idea to go on the cruise. I'm sure that members of Eddie's family still think I had something to do with it, but I didn't push him over the deck somewhere between Miami and St. Thomas. Anyway, after the honeymoon I came back home and wrote a bunch of thank-you notes to everyone who'd given us wedding presents."

Thank-you notes, I thought. I interrupted Felicia by saying, "Are you fucking kidding me?"

"I don't want to backtrack any, but I've forgotten to tell anyone here about how back in junior high school the teacher wanted us to recreate a masterpiece for art class, so I glued a bunch of macaroni noodles into the Last Supper. My teacher told the guidance counselor, and the guidance counselor called my parents. My father beat me thirteen times with his belt. He kept saying, 'Do you think Jesus and His disciples were Italian?' I think I might've taken up a career as an artist if it hadn't been for this incident. There's no telling how many times he would have hit me had I told my entire story about the Last Supper."

Dr. Floyd-Hendricks blew a whistle—I think prematurely—I stood up, I sat back down. I said, "Do you know what David Hume's last words happened to be? Right before he died, he said, 'When I hear that a man is religious, I conclude that he is a rascal!' I wish he'd've met your father."

Felicia, rightly, said, "What are you talking about?" Like an idiot I started telling Felicia my story, which up until meeting her was useless. She smiled, but looking back on it I realize that her eyes said something like "You are the most boring person in this room."

The speech therapist blew her whistle right behind me—what happened to that buzzer, by the way?—and touched my shoulders, and moved me to the one-armed guy. He said to me, "I slid into second base and the umpire said I got tagged out!"

I didn't ask him anything about how he one-arm batted to get to first base.

I listened, I nodded, I tried to move backwards to Felicia but got beaten out by a woman who showed up in support of her stroke-victim aunt, and then I went out to the parking lot in order to wait for Felicia. Unless there was a back door I'd not noticed, she never came out.

* * *

I don't feel comfortable saying anything about how Ellette's and my marriage didn't seem secure, or how Lori might've contributed to the situation. It's not like I hated Lori there. She wasn't a bad person. I didn't mind veering through the stacked boxes that didn't fit in the room where I worked on the last words that people hoped to expel. It's not like I needed to make eye contact.

And then Tony Timms did show up the following Wednesday

afternoon. He showed up at 4 p.m., just as I quit writing down *Remember that Pancho Villa's last words were "Tell them I said something,"* and Ellette came back from her job working for the state. Tony said enough nay nay nays, and with the pointing involved toward me everyone inside my house—me included—knew that he meant, "Daniel here's in love with a woman named Felicia down at the speech therapy place."

"Felicia!" my wife screamed out.

I said, "What the fuck, man? Nay nay nay nay doesn't come out that I'm in love with a woman named Felicia."

"He said you were in love with a woman named Felicia, Danny. That's what he said! It's clear as day! So why don't you tell me about this woman?" Ellette said.

I looked at Tony standing there in my mini-storage warehouse house. I kind of shrugged and held my arms out and widened my eyes. I said, "You dumb fucker," because that was the first thing that came to mind. Politically correct people will always say, "You can't use *dumb* because it conjures the wrong thing," or whatever. Okay. Sorry. I should've said, "Shut up you non-thinking, wife-driving-away, no-tongue, suicide-failing, stupid son-of-a-bitch."

Tony reached into his front pocket, pulled a memo pad out, leaned against some kind of ab contraption I'd not even noticed, and wrote down, *We're doing recitals on Wednesdays, now, too*, and tapped it for me to read. Ellette had retreated to the kitchen, screaming about how she shouldn't've ever trusted me as a househusband.

Lori stood there flexing her trapezoids. She said to Tony, "I still love you."

He smiled. He said, "Nay nay nay, nay."

* * *

I left with Tony and Lori. I drove. Lori went on and on in the car about how nice Ellette and I had been, for Tony not to blame us, and how she'd been doing research on both manic depression and prosthetic tongues, and how the medical field neared a cure and/or perfection for both. In my mind—again, I'm laying out what happened and I'm not proud—I envisioned Ellette boxing up our belongings and getting herself ready to move everything into a mini-storage warehouse unit, or over to Tony and Lori's den if, indeed, all the nearby self-storage places remained filled. At the time, I didn't care. I saw it as being for the best. I fantasized about my going on the road to plug *What People Hope They'll Say* with Felicia, maybe getting her to do the readings I'd have set up at retirement villages and book stores and greeting card outlets.

"What're you going to read tonight?" I asked Tony as I turned into the speech therapist's parking lot.

He said, I'm sure, "*The Sound and the Fury.*"

Lori said, "That's so sweet. 'The Vows from Our Wedding.' That's what Tony said. I can still understand every word he says. I can!"

Tony didn't correct her.

In a way, it was a good thing for Lori to be there. She sat right in front of her husband. Felicia's beret-wearing supporter wasn't there, so I got to sit across from Felicia immediately. I said, "Hey, Felicia. This is just like a Baptist church, isn't it? Sundays and Wednesdays. You look beautiful tonight."

"Thank you, thank you," she said. "You are so kind, and I must thank you for your generosity."

"No, thank you," I said, like a fool. "Thank you, thank you, thank you. I hope I can get the chance to explain all of this later."

"Thank you."

I noticed for the first time that Felicia's eyes were a little cocked. Not as bad as a cow or dragonfly, but pointed outwards somewhat. I said, "Tell me more. Go ahead. So far you've gotten through the kidnapping, the honeymoon tragedy, and the pasta Jesus. I'm here. I'm all ears. I'm yours."

From a few chairs over I could hear Tony going through a litany of nay-nays, and I predicted he'd gotten to the point about when Caddy and Benjy met up with Charlie, and Charlie kept using a racial slur. Caddy smelled like trees, over and over, and so on.

Felicia said, "I'd rather be skiing than doing what I'm doing," which is supposedly Stan Laurel's last words to a nurse. She said, "Anyway, Jesus told me he wanted to wash my feet. I allowed him to do so."

Is said, "Hold on. Are you quoting someone?"

"No one ever talks about how He took me into a room and washed the rest of my body. This was a time before washcloths or moist towelettes, you see. He washed me with a eucalyptus leaf drenched in spring water. Oh, we had a wonderful time, both in Nazareth and the desert, and then in Spain." Felicia's lips turned upward in a smile. "I was there at the end. He said to me, 'Hey, Felicia, go back home,' and then he said, 'My God, my God, why have you forsaken me?' Or he said, 'It is finished.' Or he said, 'Father, into your hands I commit my spirit.' That's what's in the Bible, in Mark, Luke, and John. As I remember it, his actual words went something like 'I'm cold,' and then I tried to toss a shawl up his way, and then he said 'Thank you,' and then he expired. He wasn't speaking English, though, so it's difficult to translate."

I said, "Whoa, whoa, whoa." I turned to look for the speech therapist. She stood close to the far wall, her back turned to the patients, and she stared at a poster pinned up of a chimpanzee with its mouth wide open.

I turned back to Felicia and said, "Please stop talking."

"Thank you," she said. "I've been meaning to stop for more than two thousand years."

To my right, I heard Tony say clearly, "'I have come from Alabama: a fur piece,'" which ended up being from a whole other Faulkner novel.

I said to myself out loud, "I have misjudged my wife's people," and hoped that I didn't die. I didn't want those to be my last words. I said to Tony in particular, and everyone else in general—including Felicia—"I need to go now," which I could've lived with as my last words. It would make sense, really. Out of everyone I'd queried, no one imagined their last words as being "I need to go now." At this point everyone had only been witty, sarcastic, ironic, religious, or patriotic.

Tony said, "Nay-nay," which either meant "Okay" or "Goodbye" or "Fuck you."

Lori laughed and said, "Nay."

The speech therapist didn't react. Felicia said, "And then there was Julius Caesar."

"Please don't be insane and delusional, Felicia," I said. "Please, please, please."

I drove home thinking that nothing made sense. On the radio, a man said, "I prefer oak," so I turned the radio off so that it would be his last words. Was he talking about barrels for his bourbon? Was he talking about floors or cabinets or woodsmoke for barbecue? Did he look ahead to what he wished to own for a coffin?

I wondered if Ellette would believe my lies. Would she understand that my time with her cousin only made me love her more so? I wondered if, at the next family reunion, I would finally receive Relative of the Year, and I imagined my acceptance speech when I took that little golden trophy.

Nasty Things
Terry Dalrymple

The last time Felicia Winstock saw Daniel Alldon, she spoke of Jesus washing her feet. To understand why, you would probably have to understand how she had ended up in Dr. Melinda Floyd-Hendricks's Speak Up Center in South Carolina, originating, as she did, from Preston Hollow in Dallas, Texas. But that would require knowing about the harelip—staff at the speech therapy center he attended taught participants to refer to his malady as a *cleft lip*—she met at the Tell It To Me Slowly Center in Dallas. And even that would require knowing about her husband's death—or disappearance—at sea during their honeymoon cruise, a husband she met while attending a variety of group therapy gatherings—for dealing not just with speech impairment but with such matters as auditory impairment, visual impairment, alcoholism, drug addiction, parental dementia, spousal abuse, spousal death, pet death, unnatural relationships with pets, and so forth. But you'd have to know why she attended those gatherings, which would lead you back to what the high school quarterback attempted to do to her during her sophomore year in high school. But the trauma the high school quarterback created can only be understood in terms of her upbringing. Let's face it, we should simply begin at her birth.

Felicia Marie Winstock was born beautiful and intelligent and rich and perhaps a month or so earlier than her parents' wedding date might lead one to expect. Her father, William Carl Winstock, was tremendously wealthy, in large part thanks to his grandfather's and father's amassing of fortunes; although he, too, earned a stunning living as a family attorney for the financially elite in Dallas, Texas. Her mother, Ariel Constance Winstock nee Caruthers, was exceedingly lovely and bright but did not work because—well, because she did not have to. She was, however, quite generous with her time and her husband's money, not to mention her own small inherited fortune. She engaged in much volunteer work and most especially enjoyed her role as a patron—or, rather, matron—of the arts in Dallas, Texas.

Felicia grew up beautiful and smart with all of the advantages excessive wealth and elite social connections can provide. Still, she had a tender soul and treated everyone kindly, including those her mother said were beneath her. She did not always understand the things her mother said, one of which, when she was eight, being that boys liked to do nasty things to girls and that she should be ever-vigilant about not allowing those things to be done to her. At the time, they were in Neiman's shopping for a pretty dress that Felicia would wear to Brenda Joy Stillwater's birthday party. Boys would be in attendance as well.

"What things, Mother?" she wanted to know.

Ariel scrunched her face and shuddered. "Never mind," she said. She held a pale blue dress with lacy frills around the waist and along the hem up against Felicia. "You'll understand soon enough." She cocked her head one way and then the other and finally smiled and said, "This will be a lovely dress for the party."

But curious Felicia was not to be distracted so easily. "Does Daddy do nasty things to you?" she wanted to know.

Ariel clutched Felicia's hand and hurried them toward the counter. "Only once," she said in a hushed voice. "Only once."

What she said was true. The moment she knew that William had impregnated her, Ariel told him there would be no more of that. Despite the bleak sexual future her words forebode, he followed the guidelines of his stiffly conservative upbringing and married her immediately. After all, her family was far too wealthy to be bought off, and his parents rather liked the idea of his marrying that bright, lovely, wealthy Caruthers girl. They settled into a sprawling home in the Preston Hollow district. When necessary, he sought his physical pleasures elsewhere, behavior she tolerated so long as it was discreet and she could spend and donate his money at will.

William, however, was apparently rather boring in the physical activity department and over the years found fewer and fewer opportunities for elsewhere pleasure. His friends' wives lost interest; his female business associates lost interest; even the household help lost interest. And so he turned to Jesus. He took his great success in his law practice as a sign that Jesus loved him, and he threw himself into Christianity far more intensely than he had ever thrown himself into physical pleasures. He continued his very lucrative law practice; but at home he generally remained locked in his study, reading the Bible, praying, and weeping. Ariel and Felicia rarely saw him, and they ignored him when he did make rare appearances among them.

Felicia remembered her mother's warning. In her late pre-teen years when other girls spoke of some dreamy boy they wished would kiss them, she would shake her head and say, "He will do nasty things to you." As a result, the other girls began to shun her. To compensate for the frequent lack of company, Felicia began avidly reading everything from tomes of history to classic works of fiction and poetry to current events in two or three newspapers every day.

Being intelligent, she remembered everything she read, and in that way, eventually regained access to popularity. During lunch times at school, she would recount famous historical events in a way that charmed the other girls into thinking they were part of those august events. She retold fictions and epic poems in the same way, sometimes, for an especially emphatic effect, placing herself or one of the other girls in the various roles. Her knowledge of history and literature and current events and her ability to convey that knowledge so vividly eventually drew girls and boys alike to her, in large part because she was beautiful and interesting and animated; and, perhaps in larger part, because the knowledge she imparted in such a palatable way helped them pass the classes for which their busy social schedules left them little time to study.

In this way, Felicia became friends with the high school quarterback during her sophomore year. The boy was—and she recognized this—dumb as the proverbial box of rocks, but he was wealthy and handsome and made her feel things she had never felt before. Her soul went out to him— or, at least, that's how she explained to herself the sensations she felt when she looked at his handsome jaw line or his sleepy brown eyes, or when he said, "Wait, what?" She would scowl at first, but then he would say, "You're so hot, I got distracted. Tell me again about why that guy— what's his name?—met the devil in the woods." Then she would tell him again, looking intensely into his eyes, and she would feel things in places where she thought her mother might disapprove of having feelings. Thus, she thought of the reaction as her soul reaching out to the boy, something of which, since his family was wealthy, she felt sure her mother would not disapprove.

211

Once, when they'd had a study session after school, he offered to drive her home. She called her mother who, when she heard the boy's last name, said, "I'm sure that will be fine. Just don't let him dally."

Felicia knew the meaning of the word *dally*, although she wasn't entirely sure of its various specific implications in relation to boys. Thus, when the quarterback said he'd like to stop at a little park he loved, she said that would be fine because she loved little parks and thought they might see something interesting. He parked in an isolated area of the park and said, "Slide over here next to me. I want to show you something." She slid over next to him, feeling tingly and also pleased that this very stupid, handsome, rich young man appreciated nature enough to show her something fascinating. What he showed her was natural enough, she supposed, but it was not something she particularly wanted to see. Then what he tried to do was, she felt quite certain, one of the nasty things to which her mother had referred eight years earlier. She ejected herself from the car immediately. The boy apologized and said he would take her home. Fearing a second attempt, she declined his offer, opting to walk instead. On her very long walk home, she broke a heel on one of her very upscale shoes ordered from France. Her mother scolded her severely for the broken heel. Felicia accepted her mother's harsh words, apologized, and then explained that the quarterback had attempted to do nasty things to her.

Ariel shuddered and then said, "Never mind about the shoes. We'll get you some new ones. You're a good girl." She patted Felicia's shoulder, looked at her thoughtfully, and then nodded as if she had just made up her mind to say whatever was in it. "You should know, by the way, that if you drink alcohol you are more likely to allow a man to do those things." At her parents' social gatherings, Felicia had observed adults quite enjoying their alcoholic beverages, but it occurred to her now that she had never seen her mother drink anything stronger than carbonated water. Felicia nodded that she understood. They hugged, and they never spoke of the broken heel or the quarterback again.

Felicia made her way through high school and to college without further incident. She continued reading and telling spellbinding stories, still sometimes sprinkling her own appearance into some of them for dramatic effect. She still allowed boys into her audiences but devoutly avoided any hint of personal interest in them, despite the fact that some quite attracted her and made her tingle. After a time, then, boys lost interest and stopped listening to her stories. For some it meant lower grades in classes, but at least they spent their mixed-gender social interaction more fruitfully.

What the quarterback had attempted to do, coupled with her avid reading regimen, had instilled in her a solid general notion of what kinds of nasty things boys were capable—and quite eager and willing—to do to girls. The specifics as well as the nuances of the mechanics escaped her; but she remained certain, thanks to her mother's warning, that she did not want them done to her. Still, she found that reading about them, mostly via veiled references, often added interest and conflict to a tale— not to mention that it sometimes made her tingle in that pleasant way to which she had become accustomed. Sometimes, if the tingling were strong, her eyes did something funny that she couldn't quite identify. They didn't cross exactly, but they cocked in an odd sort of way, and she would have to stop reading until the sensation dissipated and her eyes could again focus on the page. Having become a master storyteller—or, rather, story re-teller—she decided to add such interest and conflict to her own presentations. The references, of course, never assumed the form of vivid description but were conveyed, rather, by implication, innuendo, and double entendre. They were a smashing hit with her female narratees, particularly when she cast herself as one of the characters.

Even so, gatherings to hear her stories grew smaller as other girls had more and more opportunities to attend frat parties and other similar celebrations. Felicia rarely received invitations, and she declined on those few occasions when she did. The parties, she knew, consisted of a high consumption of alcoholic beverages, and to hear other girls tell it, a significant amount of nasty behavior that she made every effort to distance herself from. After a time, she felt rather lonely in college.

Early in her sophomore year, a psychology professor required all students in his class to attend, as observers, a group counseling session of some sort. He randomly assigned a specific group to each student, and she was to visit a grief counseling group that met in the basement of an Episcopal church. A slender man with a shy smile whose shoulders slumped from the weight of his grief greeted her when she arrived. The session had not begun, he explained, but cookies and punch or coffee were available at the table behind him. Despite his droopy shoulders, she judged him rather handsome with his close-cropped dark hair and dark lashes above brilliantly blue eyes. He did not make her tingly; but she found him quite pleasant to look at, and thus, to visit with. His name was Eddie.

As more people gathered, they stood in a corner talking, and when she thought it appropriate she queried as to the source of his grief. "I was madly in love," he said, "with the kindest, gentlest, most beautiful woman in the universe." He paused to wipe a tear from his eye and then continued his tale. He worked as the Assistant Manager of Produce at an H.E.B. store in Richardson, and he had met her when she queried him about how to choose the best avocados. He placed his hand lightly on hers and showed her how to squeeze the fruit gently to determine its readiness. Some time after they became engaged, he was asked to attend a weekend ropes course the store manager had arranged for a select group of employees, and he felt he could not decline. While he learned to work with others at Laity Lodge near Leakey, his fiancée foolishly agreed to have dinner with a friend of her brother's visiting from Oklahoma. Later, riddled with guilt, she confessed to Eddie that they had a fabulous meal and three bottles of wine and then had participated in behavior unbecoming to a betrothed woman. She apologized and begged forgiveness. He told her he wasn't sure he could forgive her. Two days later, he decided he could; but before he got to tell her, she died in a fourteen-car pile-up on I-30, drunk and accompanied by her brother's friend from Oklahoma, whose pants were unzipped when the medics pulled his lifeless body from the car.

He wept at the end, and Felicia wept and hugged him. When he wiped his tears away, he said, "So, what about you?"

After the tragic story he had told, she felt she could hardly say she was a student at SMU majoring in—well, in truth she had no major—who had grown up with every advantage wealth afforded and had been traumatized only once by a near-miss with a quarterback. So she said, "My name is Mattie, and two years ago I went to New England to help keep house for my semi-invalid cousin Zeena. I fell madly in love with her husband, Ethan." She modernized the tale where necessary, conveniently omitted the ambiguous nature of Mattie's motivations, and significantly altered the ending so that she survived and poor Ethan was smashed to death against the infamous elm tree.

She wept at the end, and he wept and hugged her.

They sat together during the session, and when it ended, he hugged her again and said he looked forward to seeing her the following week. Of course, she did not return the following week.

However, her experience with Eddie impregnated her mind with a notion that she acted upon within two weeks. Eddie had been a kind, gentle man, and he had seemed so damaged and so vulnerable that she felt quite certain he had no desire to do nasty things to women. She reasoned that other such men might be found in other group counseling settings. And so, lonely as she was, she set about finding them. The large number of such gatherings in the metroplex quite surprised her. She avoided those designed to help rape victims and those aimed at rehabilitating sexual predators. But otherwise, she kept an open mind and visited a wide variety of sessions, generally two per week.

Sometimes the meetings were unproductive for her; but at least, she consoled herself, she was getting out for an evening and mingling with others. Other times were more successful, times when she would engage in fascinating conversations with women and men alike, conversations mostly about the nature of their particular problems—hers, of course, gleaned from the tomes of material she had read since junior high school.

In a support group for relatives of schizophrenics, she told of her older brother who believed dogs could talk and even write and who eventually determined that he was the king of Spain. In a support group for relatives of alcoholics, she told of her older brother who drank himself to death in Las Vegas. At others times, she relied on current events of the past few years, altering them just enough to avoid having some clever soul recognize her story.

She did, as she had expected, meet many men who were so otherwise distraught that they seemed to have little interest in the kinds of things men like to do to women. She even went out with one of them occasionally. There was, for example, one named Tom who maintained an unnatural affection for his cats. They went for coffee and had a lovely time until Felicia began sneezing so violently that she could not talk. Assuming—probably correctly—that she was allergic to cat hair, Tom became incensed and stormed out of the coffee shop, leaving her with the bill. Another one, Sidney, whose elderly mother suffered from dementia, took her for ice cream. He was proverbially tall, dark, and handsome, and he made her tingle in that pleasant way. As they visited across a small round table, the sensation became so strong that her eyes did that funny thing, cocking in an odd sort of way, and Sidney began to weep uncontrollably. "Not you," he said to Felicia between sobs. "Not you, too!"

He had to excuse himself but was at least gentlemanly enough to leave money for paying the bill.

At some point during her senior year, she began to think of Eddie, of his lovely dark hair and beautiful blue eyes; and though this had not happened when she met him, the memories made her tingle. She returned to the group of which he'd been a member, but a woman there who wore a beret and spoke with a thick French accent said he had been feeling better and did not attend regularly anymore. Felicia drove to Richardson, located the H.E.B. store to which he had referred, and found him misting crispy iceberg lettuce and fat heads of red cabbage. Delighted to see her, he accidentally misted her face when he reached to hug her in greeting. He did, indeed, look better. His shoulders no longer slumped, and his brilliant blue eyes almost sparkled, she thought. Despite her damp face—or, perhaps, because of it—she tingled.

They dated for a time, during which he never exhibited any desire to do anything nasty to her. When he proposed, she felt comfortable saying yes. Her parents, quite naturally, reacted negatively to the news that she would wed an assistant manager of produce. Discovering what a pleasant man Eddie was, however, her father thought he might help the young man secure a more lucrative position in the designer vegetable business. Then he made everyone bow their heads in prayer.

When she graduated with a degree in—well, no one was sure what her degree was in, including her—she moved back home and began planning her wedding—or, rather, listening to her mother plan her wedding. Ariel suggested the French Riviera for a honeymoon. Having been there several times with her mother, Felicia thought that was a fine idea. When she mentioned it to Eddie, he explained that he simply could not afford such a honeymoon and suggested Corpus Christi instead. She waved him off and observed casually that her parents would be happy to pay. But he remained steadfast, insisting that he would not accept charity. (Later, as they boarded the cruise ship, he also told her he would not accept her father's assistance in getting a job in the designer vegetable trade.) Being a tender soul, Felicia relented but suggested a Caribbean cruise as a compromise. Eddie balked, she pleaded, and he went home to calculate costs. She was pleased the next day when he said he could manage the cruise—though he still liked the idea of Corpus better.

The wedding was huge and elegant and beautiful, and the following morning Felicia and Eddie flew to Miami to board their cruise ship. On the third day of the cruise, Felicia reported Eddie missing.

How long had he been missing? the man she reported to wanted to know.

She said two days.

Why had she waited so long to report it? the man wondered.

She'd been seasick, she said, and had opted to stay in the room that first morning when Eddie went for breakfast. He said he might stop after eating to drop a few nickels in the slots. She claimed to have slept most of that day—except when she ran to the bathroom to vomit. When she awoke near dark, she assumed Eddie had been lucky at the slots, stayed all day, and then had gone to supper. When she awoke at 2 a.m., she assumed he had gone to the late-night comedy show. And when she awoke again at eight or so, she assumed he had, perhaps, sat on the deck watching the ocean go by until it was again time for breakfast. She felt better by five or so that afternoon and went looking for him. Not finding him, she finally reported him missing.

The man seemed suspicious, but he nodded and took notes and ordered a thorough search of the ship. No one found any trace of Eddie, although someone found ten or twelve nickels near the railing on the starboard side of the Lido deck. The Coast Guard was called and a helicopter search was conducted from Miami to St. Thomas. No sign of Eddie was found. He was declared lost at sea. Authorities questioned Felicia at length on several occasions but finally said she was free to go. After she signed a waiver agreeing not to sue the cruise line, she flew home at the line's expense and a couple of weeks later received a refund check for the cost of the cruise—minus a twenty percent handling fee. Her father said Jesus would punish them for stealing her—or, rather, Eddie's—money. Her mother, who had signed no waiver, wanted to sue. Felicia, however, begged her not to, observing that she did not want a drawn-out lawsuit that constantly reminded her of her terrible misfortune—not to mention Eddie's.

Despite her terrible misfortune, her mother insisted they have a heart-to-heart talk and asked if, during the two nights they spent together, Eddie had done nasty things to her.

"Certainly not," Felicia said.

"Well," Ariel said, "did he try?"

"Let's talk about something else, Mother. Did you know that Julia Tuttle was the mother of Miami?"

"But, Sweetheart—"

"Miami was named after a river, but the river was named after the Mayaimi Indians."

"I see," Ariel said, and despite Felicia's terrible misfortune, changed the subject to thank-you notes. She insisted that Felicia write thank-you notes to the several hundred folk who had given wedding gifts. Felicia stayed in her room for five days straight writing the notes. For five more days after that, all she said, no matter the occasions, was "Thank you." Her mother might say, "Sweetheart, you remember old Mr. Craghart, don't you? Do you know that a twenty-six-year-old bimbo agreed to marry him!" to which Felicia would reply, "Thank you." Or her mother might say, "Well, my goodness, the Darlings are moving to Los Angeles of all places!" to which Felicia would reply, "Thank you. Thank you, thank you, thank you."

Finally, Ariel pointed out this odd behavior to Felicia, to which Felicia responded, "Thank you." Then, blushing, she said, "I'm sorry. I'll try not to."

Now conscious of her odd speech behavior, she concentrated on saying something other than *thank you*. Still, her responses often weren't appropriate to the occasion. Her mother might say, "Shall I have Rosita prepare glazed lamb chops or chicken cordon bleu for dinner?" And Felicia might reply, "When I first met Mr. Lamb, I thought him quite handsome."

"What, Dear?" Ariel would query.

"But he was fast friends with Mr. Coleridge, you know, whom I could not abide. So egotistical, so morose at times, and really quite boring —not to mention that he pinched my bottom when no one was looking."

"Felicia, what are you talking about?"

"Dinner, Mother. I'm talking about dinner."

When Ariel would point out that she had not, in fact, been talking about dinner at all but rather about some awful man named Coleridge, Felicia would say, "Oh, I'm sorry. Thank you. Thank you. I believe I would prefer the chicken. Thank you."

And so forth.

Such occasions became so frequent that Ariel decided something must be done. Certain that no one in her family could ever suffer from psychological distress, she determined that Felicia simply had a little speech impediment. Having just made a rather large donation to Dr.

Albert Crane Farnsworth's Tell It to Me Slowly Center, she arranged for Felicia's enrollment in the clinic's Group Therapy for Overcoming Verbal Tics. Dr. Farnsworth, after reading *The Reluctant King: The Life and Reign of George VI, 1895-1952*, had made a sizable fortune in his first venture, the Farnsworth Enunciation Clinic for Elite Socialites. Recently, having read a cutting-edge article by Dr. Melinda Floyd-Hendricks in the *International Journal of Language and Communication Disorders*, he had opened the Tell It to Me Slowly Center in a remodeled building adjacent to his FECES clinic.

It was there that Felicia met the harelip—that is, the gentleman with the cleft lip—who spoke quite clearly except when he became overly excited about a subject. And he always became overly excited when he spoke of Dr. Melinda Floyd-Hendricks's Speak Up Center in South Carolina. His speech, he said, had been severely impeded by his cleft lip, and when he read in *Time* about the miracles that Dr. Melinda Floyd-Hendricks's Speak Up Center could work, he left Arlington and drove non-stop to get there. The center had, indeed, worked miracles for him, his impediment now surfacing only when he became excited and spoke too fast. Considering his speech significantly rehabilitated and feeling quite homesick, he returned to Arlington and enrolled at the Tell It to Me Slowly Center in hopes of learning to control his excited speech.

There, Felicia had made no progress but had, in fact, regressed a bit according to Dr. Farnsworth's reports—though of course he viewed her regression as a precursor to a huge and miraculous breakthrough she would soon experience. When she began at the center, she might say to someone, "When I first met Napoleon I thought him an odd little man, but he certainly knew a thing or two about how to treat a woman." Then she would pause, breathe deeply, concentrate intensely, and say, "No, what I meant to say is that it's very nice to meet you." Over time, however, the pauses did not work as well. She might say, "My relationship with Rodolphe was quite complicated, but we had such beautiful times together." Then, after the pause and the breathing and the concentration, she might say, "No, what I meant to say is that the most beautiful man I ever met was a very large dead man who washed up on the shores of a little village in South America where I lived for a time." And she seemed never to realize that she had not said, "Yes, it is quite a beautiful day," as she had intended.

Despite his cleft lip, Felicia found the man who spoke of the Speak

Up Center rather attractive, and she tingled a bit when they visited. His name was Rupert, and he worked at a Dodge service center in Arlington and spent every dime he saved on speech therapy. One day, after a lengthy description of the extravagant dinner parties Jean Des Esseintes gave before he retreated to a reclusive life in the country, she somehow managed to convey that Rupert was invited to dinner at her home—or, rather, her parents' home.

Ariel was not especially pleased to have a harelip auto mechanic dining there, but she humored Felicia as much as possible in hopes that her kindness would help her daughter overcome her speech impediment. When Rupert spoke excitedly about the Speak Up Center, some of the words were lost in his throat or nose—Ariel wasn't sure which—but she clearly understood the message and decided to send Felicia there.

So now—finally, you're probably thinking—we get to how Felicia Marie Winstock happened to meet Daniel Alldon at the Speak Up Center in South Carolina and why she spoke to him of Jesus washing her feet.

Once a week at the center, Dr. Melinda Floyd-Hendricks held a recital of sorts in which her clients read or recited or otherwise presented their progress to friends and family invited to the gathering. It was a round robin sort of arrangement. Visitors would move from table to table as Dr. Floyd-Hendricks directed so that they ultimately heard all of the clients. Daniel came because of a tongueless in-law there. When he first moved to Felicia's table, she felt the tingle immediately, the strongest tingle, she was quite sure, she had ever experienced. She meant to be bold and direct with him and tell him that he quite captivated her. Instead, she spoke of being kidnapped in France. He seemed, too, to be quite captivated by her and did not want to move to the next table.

She eagerly anticipated his visit the following week, and sure enough, he appeared. She meant to tell him that his eyes were like the ocean but instead told of her terrible misfortune at sea during her honeymoon cruise. She meant to tell him how much she enjoyed their last visit but instead spoke of gluing noodles into the Last Supper for an art project in junior high. The tingling was so strong that for the first time in her life she thought she might actually want a man—this man—to do the nasty things to her that her mother had spoken of so many years before.

On Daniel's third and—unbeknownst to Felicia—last visit, she tingled so intensely that her eyes did that googly thing so that she could not quite see him clearly, but she could certainly feel his presence with every pore of her body. She told him, she thought, how she felt and what she wanted him to do to her. But, alas, what she actually told him was about Jesus washing her feet and the less well-known story of his washing the rest of her body as well. Before leaving, he begged her not to be insane, which she took to mean she should not go crazy in his absence because he would return. Yes, she knew he felt what she felt and that he would return and take her away and do things to her that she had only read about but that she was ready, now, to have done to her.

Dr. Melinda Floyd-Hendricks patted her back and asked how the session had gone. Felicia turned to face her and said, "He was married, you know, and so was I when I first met him. But I was vacationing in Yalta alone, except for the company of my sweet little dog. I never imagined the passion I would come to feel for Gurov nor the passion he would shower on me." She smiled, quite proud of herself for being brave enough to confess to the good doctor the illicit but beautiful relationship she had established with Daniel.

Saved
Elizabeth Cox

When Josie Wire walked down to the front of the tent at a revival meeting, her friend Alice was with her. The words of the preacher had stirred their hearts, and for weeks afterward they spoke of nothing but being missionaries in Africa. Alice would be a medical missionary, Josie a regular one. Both girls were twelve, though Josie would turn thirteen in June.

"My dad thinks we'll change our minds later on," Alice told Josie. "He says just wait till we get interested in boys."

But Alice was already interested in boys, and Josie dreamed of them at night. "I can't imagine changing our minds, can you?" said Josie. "I mean, I have seen pictures of Africa. I've wanted to go there even before I knew about God."

"I'm just saying what he told me," said Alice.

Alice's father was a neurologist who lived in a big house where Josie loved to spend the night. On Saturday mornings Alice and Josie sat at a table in the dining room with sun pouring through the long windows. A Spanish woman named Rosa served them eggs and bacon and hot cinnamon rolls. She said, "¿Por favor?" if she didn't understand something.

Josie liked to try to talk to the Spanish woman. She liked to imitate her accent, and flounce around the kitchen copying Rosa. Rosa wore skirts that made her look like a flamenco dancer. She told Josie that she had grown up in Barcelona. Once Josie had walked into the kitchen and seen Alice's father standing next to Rosa with his hand on her shoulder. Rosa was barefoot, her head down, and she looked beautiful. Alice told Josie that Rosa kept some magic beads in a box by the sink.

"And whenever Rosa prays," said Alice, "she rolls those beads around in her hands."

223

After that, Josie stole one of her mother's worst necklaces, and when she prayed she held the necklace, rubbing each bead hard. Josie's family did not have servants, had never had them. Her own father taught history at a private school, and her mother, until recently, had worked as a clerk in a downtown store. Mrs. Wire had stopped working a few months before, and money was now tight.

Alice lived in a posh neighborhood, though it was situated not far from a housing project. The girls enjoyed walking into the poor section to give dollar bills to children or beggars. Their parents did not know they were doing this. Each Saturday since they had dedicated their lives, the girls gave away their weekly allowance to poor people.

"We've got to stop giving all our money away," said Alice. "We don't even have enough to go to the movies anymore."

"But I don't mind staying home, if it's for a good cause," said Josie. She felt that her dedication was stronger than Alice's, and wanted Alice to feel the way she did. "There are so many people who need us."

"Like who?"

"Like that lady we gave money to today, and others who hang out in bars. People like that."

"We can't do anything for those people," said Alice.

"Maybe we can." Josie began to thumb through the phone book looking for the number of a bar called the Wagon Wheel. Each time she thought of its name, her blood grew excited. The bar was located not far from where Josie lived, so she passed it going to school, or to town. She grew silent trying to look inside, trying to see what was going on. On this Saturday night she suggested to Alice that they find the number and make a call to someone at that bar.

"What would we say?" asked Alice, putting her own finger on the words in the phone book. For the first time she looked excited about Josie's idea.

"We could just talk. Whoever answers, we'll just ask them about their life. It'll be good."

Since the idea was Josie's, she had to make the call. A man with a gruff voice answered.

"Yeah. Who is it?" The man was used to getting calls from wives checking up on a husband.

Josie couldn't speak.

"Hello?" said the voice.

"Uh, excuse me," Josie finally said. "To who am I speaking?" She tried to make her voice sound gravelly and older.

"Who the hell is this?" the man asked.

Josie tried to hand the phone to Alice, but Alice wouldn't take it. "My name is Josie." She was almost shouting. "And I'm calling to see if you are a saved person or not."

"Is this a joke?" the man asked.

"You have to answer if you are saved." There, she said it. Josie could hear the tinkle of glasses and wild music in the background.

"No," he said. "I'm not." He expected a punch line.

"Do you want to be?" she asked.

"What does it mean?" the man asked prudently.

"It means everything," said Josie, and smiled at Alice. It was working. She and Alice grew excited at the idea of their first prospect. "You won't have to worry about anything, like if you're going to heaven. Stuff like that."

"I'm not ready to die anyway," the man said.

"I mean when it's time, then you will go to be with the angels instead of to—you know."

"What do I have to do?" The man sounded mollified.

"You have to love Jesus," said Josie.

"Okay," the man said quickly.

"Really?"

"Yeah." The man hung up.

Josie dialed the number again.

"Yeah?" said the voice.

"Listen," said Josie. "That was mean. I just wanted to ask you about something and you hung up on me."

"We musta been cut off," said the man. "How old are you?"

"I'm fifteen," lied Josie, excited that the man who was not saved, and probably drunk, was asking her about herself. She did look fifteen. She had breasts and a deep curve at the waist; her hips moved out like little hills. She and Alice had both developed figures that were catching the eyes of boys, and men. Alice had even begun to go to the drugstore with Boog Barnett, who was the handsomest boy in the eighth grade. Boog said words like *piss* and *damn*. Sometimes Alice repeated the words. She let him put his arm around her waist and buy her Coke floats. Since her interest in Boog had accelerated around the same time as their being saved, they had talked almost as much about Boog as they had about being missionaries.

"I bet you're pretty," said the man. "I bet you look like some of the students I used to have in my classroom. What's your name?"

Josie told him her name, and said she had a friend named Alice. She and Alice shivered with the thrill of talking to a strange man on the phone at ten o'clock at night. They had not expected anyone to be friendly. "What's yours?"

"Samuel Beckett," said the man.

"That's nice. That's a nice name," said Josie, mouthing the name to Alice. "I think I've heard of you."

"I don't see how."

"What do you do?" Josie asked.

"I used to be a teacher but got fired."

Josie grew silent.

"I probably taught little girls like you. You don't sound so little, though." He spoke his words as though he were proffering a gift.

"What do I sound like?" she asked.

"Like a young woman. I'm wondering what you look like, though. What kind of hair do you have?"

"What do you mean?"

"I mean is it long or short, and what color is it? I'm just trying to picture what you look like."

"It's brown," said Josie. "It's kind of curly."

"Well," said the man. He was waiting to hear more.

"I thought we were talking about whether or not you were saved."

"I said I wasn't."

"But don't you want to be?"

"Depends."

"Depends on what?"

"On who's saying it. I have to hear something like that from somebody I can trust. I have to be sure the person's telling me the truth. Are you telling me the truth?"

"Oh, yes. My friend Alice will tell you too. She'll tell you the same thing. We work together."

"I don't care about any Alice," said Samuel Beckett. "I want to hear about you."

Josie tried not to look as pleased as she felt. Over the last couple of weeks, Alice had spent more and more time with boys, and Josie had been left alone in her quest to be faithful. She thought Alice was being drawn away from God, and Alice kept saying that you could like a boy and still like God. Josie didn't see how.

"I bet he's old," said Alice when they hung up. "I bet he's old and decrepit."

"He didn't sound it," said Josie. "He sounded real nice."

"How nice can he be, him being in a bar?" Alice folded back the bed and fluffed the pillows. Each of them had two large pillows on their bed. At Josie's home each person only had one pillow. It occurred to Josie that the reason Boog Barnett was asking Alice out was because Alice was rich. Alice said it was time for bed and they should say their prayers now.

"Do you think God likes jokes?" Josie asked.

"I don't know," said Alice. "Why?"

"Sometimes when I pray, I tell him a joke. I think he likes for me to. I bet not many people do that." Alice said she was tired. But they talked for a while about what their life in the Congo would be like, until there came a long silence when Josie asked Alice a question about native rituals. Alice didn't answer.

"You asleep?" Josie asked, and the lack of an answer made her feel alone. Josie prayed silently for the man in the bar. Then she prayed to be sexy like the woman from Barcelona. She also prayed for her mother, who seemed to be crying all the time now.

* * *

Over the last year, whenever Josie came home she would find her mother in the kitchen with her head on her arms, crying. So one night, Josie asked her brother if their parents were going to get a divorce. The next day Mr. Wire reassured Josie that she need not worry about divorce.

"Did James tell you I asked about that?" said Josie.

"Yes," said Mr. Wire, "and I wanted you to know that your mother's sadness is about you. She worries about you, and the operation that's coming up."

A few years ago Josie had been diagnosed with aortal stenosis, and would need an operation on her heart. The operation was scheduled for August. The doctor had explained how the procedure would be performed; but he had waited for Josie to be older, stronger. Josie thought about what the doctor told her, but she hadn't worried until she saw her mother's sadness. Every night she prayed that her mother would stop crying.

On the next Friday night Josie and Alice called the Wagon Wheel again to see if the same man would answer. He didn't, and the harsh voice who spoke to Josie hung up on her. She called back, remembering the persistence of the disciples, and asked for Samuel Beckett. She tried to make her voice sound older by lowering it. She heard the gruff-voiced man call out the name "Sam Beckett?" and a long pause. When he returned to the phone he said, "Nobody here by that name," then, "Wait a minute. Here he is."

"Hello?"

"Samuel Beckett?"

"Yeah."

"It's Josie."

"Well, I recognize your voice. Pretty Josie." His voice slurred against itself. "Pretty baby." He sort of sang her name. "I sure think you oughta le' me see ya."

"Why?" asked Josie. She didn't want Alice to know what he had said, but she had blushed and Alice was saying, "What? What did he say?"

"He wants to meet me," Josie mouthed. Alice sucked in her breath.

"I think if I meet you I'm more likely to see whether I wanna be safed. You could tell me what's like, and maybe I'll be confinced."

He did not sound like someone who had ever been a teacher. "Well," said Josie. "I wouldn't be able to come there. I'd get in trouble if I did."

"We could meet in the park," he said. "Would you meet with me in the park? You know how the benches have numbers on them?"

"Yes."

"You could come to Bench 23."

"I would bring Alice with me," Josie said, but Alice was shaking her head no. "I mean, if I come, I would bring Alice."

"Sure," he slurred. "Alice is a pretty baby too." He hung up, and Alice and Josie argued about whether or not to go to Bench 23 during the coming week.

"He didn't say when we should go. Does he think we're just gonna go and wait every day?" Alice said.

"I don't know."

Alice and Josie went to Bench 23 on Monday afternoon, but no one was there. Alice was relieved. They waited almost twenty minutes.

"We probably ought to get home," Alice said. "My mom will be worried."

They called the Wagon Wheel again the next weekend; but this time on Sunday night, and Samuel Beckett answered the phone. His voice was clear, not slurry.

"Hello?" Samuel Beckett said.

"I waited for you at the bench," said Josie. "I waited on Monday and you didn't come."

"I'm sorry about that," said Beckett. "I'm afraid I was drunk. But I'll meet you this Tuesday afternoon," he said. "That's my day off. Did you know that I got a part-time job as bartender? I think you're bringing me good luck."

"I am?"

"I might turn into a believer yet." She could tell by his voice that he was smiling, happy.

"Really?"

"I'm busy now and have to go, but you meet me on Tuesday at two o'clock."

"I don't get out of school till three-thirty."

"Four o'clock, then."

"Is it still Bench 23?" Josie asked.

"Yeah," Sam said.

"I'm not going with you this time," said Alice. "I have cheerleading practice."

Another thing that was coming between Alice and Josie was the fact that Alice had been selected as next year's cheerleader. She was cheerleader, plus she had Boog Barnett. Josie had only one boy interested in her—a guy who was good in math class. Fred Jacks had body odor and his hair was long and unruly. Every time she looked at him she wondered if someday in the future he might look good. She had seen pictures of Cary Grant when he was young, and thought how unappealing he was. She wondered if Fred Jacks could turn out better than she imagined.

On Tuesday morning Josie wore a red sweater and a navy-blue skirt to school.

"You're getting so dressed up today," her mother said. Her mother's crying had lessened and she was becoming even cheerful, but sometimes the cheerfulness felt forced. "What's the occasion?"

229

"Just felt like it," said Josie. Her mother smiled.

"That Freddy Jacks is just as smart as he can be," said her mother.

The first half of the day dragged; but after lunch, English class and social studies went by quickly. By 3:30 p.m. Josie was leaving the school, walking toward the park. Alice was not with her.

She saw Samuel Beckett sitting on Bench 23. He was tall, even sitting down he looked tall. He was thin and wore old pants and a clean shirt. His hair was combed, and Josie guessed his age to be about forty, though she couldn't tell for sure. She hoped she looked older than her thirteen years, and imagined she would have to admit that she had lied about her age.

"Well you certainly look older than fifteen," Mr. Beckett said upon seeing her. "If you are Josie, I would have said you were sixteen or seventeen, at least."

"Thank you." Josie sat on the bench where he had scooted over to create a space for her.

"I brought my Bible and some religious tracts." She handed him the tracts, but her hands were shaking. "You can keep those."

He slipped the papers into his shirt pocket and thanked her, but kept his eyes focused on Josie's purse, which hung from her shoulder. His eyes were bright blue and his face thin. He did not have a beard, as she had imagined, but was clean-shaven. Josie had expected him to look scruffier. He was actually handsome. He had a low, calm voice. He sounded like a teacher now. His words were not slurred, though the whites of his eyes looked bloodshot and watery, as if he had been crying for a long time.

"So what do you want to tell me?" He was going to let her begin. He was going to listen to whatever she had to say.

"I don't know what to say," Josie began. Then she thought. "When I got saved in April, I had to walk up to the front of the tent at a Billy Graham meeting. I walked all the way."

"Did that scare you?" he asked.

"A little bit, but afterwards I felt so different. Happy, you know? I want to make everybody else feel that same way."

"I'm not sure you can do that," Mr. Beckett said. He laughed and touched her arm, the arm that held her purse, and Josie jumped. She pulled away from him.

He took a strand of her hair and pushed it behind her ear. Josie's heart leapt at his touch. What awakened in her made her body collapse inside and she grew sweaty. Her breasts felt at attention.

"Now, what do I have to do?" he asked. "There's no tent, no long walk."

"Well," said Josie. "You have to want it yourself. If you don't want it, it won't work." Her voice was unsteady, and her hands shaky. She felt she was doing the Lord's work, and that this was how hard it was going to be. She thought about what it would feel like if this man kissed her. She pursed her lips as she had seen women do in the movies. She felt older, sexy. She felt wild, and held tightly to her Bible.

"Maybe you don't want to be saved," she offered. "Some people just aren't interested. I have a brother named James, and he doesn't care a thing about it." Josie put the Bible on Sam Beckett's legs, and he looked down at it as though she had dropped a stone in his lap.

"Why not?" he asked her.

"James likes being bad. He thinks that if he's saved he can't be bad anymore."

"That's probably not true," said Mr. Beckett.

"I don't know," she said, "I don't think you can want to be bad."

"Sometimes you can't help it, though," he said. "I mean the wanting."

His words were so exciting that Josie felt trembly. His eyes grew bright looking at her, and she thought she saw his mood change. He gave her back the Bible.

"Come with me," he said, and offered his hand to lead her away. Josie followed him into a section of the park that led to a stream. She tried to walk the way she imagined Rosa would walk. She tried to pretend that she was Rosa. When they were in the trees, Sam looked around, then he put his hands on Josie's shoulders and turned her toward him.

He leaned to kiss her forehead. For the first time Josie could smell him. He did not smell like her brother, or her father. He smelled the way she imagined Africa would smell. He had the odor of fur and ground. She loved his smell.

Josie did not try to squirm away but stood very still and let Mr. Beckett run his hand down to the small of her back, over her bottom. She let him touch her breasts and thought that this might be the only man who would ever touch her. If she had her operation, and if something went wrong, then this might be her only chance for love. She let him roam

231

around her body at will. Then he moved her toward the ground until he was almost on top of her. He looked at her for a long moment, and Josie couldn't tell what he was thinking. He looked sad. She could feel a stiffness in his groin that Alice had told her about. Alice had laughed when she told how Boog Barnett had gotten stiff at the drugstore.

Sam Beckett was kissing Josie's forehead and cheeks, but he had not yet kissed her mouth. Josie had never been kissed on the mouth, except when she was seven, and that boy had moved away. She didn't count that as a kiss, and wanted her mouth to be kissed now. She thought if she could be kissed that maybe her operation might be put off again, until after Thanksgiving, after Christmas. But when she turned her mouth toward him, Mr. Beckett stopped abruptly.

He moved to get up. "You are very young," he said.

"¿Por favor?" said Josie. She wondered if he had realized that she was not yet fifteen.

"You know, Josie." Beckett spoke, confused, but taking charge of himself. "You shouldn't be so willing to trust people."

"I don't trust people," she said.

"Anyway." He brushed some dirt off his arms. "I'm thinking that maybe you brought me good luck."

"Why?"

"Because I got a job after I talked with you."

"I thought you said you were a teacher," Josie questioned.

"I was. But I lost that job, and when I was out of work I just drank more than ever. I lost everything."

Josie kept wondering if he might take her money. She had ten dollars in her purse, and she thought he might take it all. "Are you poor?" she asked.

Mr. Beckett said nothing.

"Maybe you could get back your job," said Josie. "I mean, I bet you were good." She was trying to think of a way to bring back the fervor of his previous attention, but he already seemed through with her. She didn't know what had gone wrong.

"I really was a good teacher," he said.

She could see him tear up.

"Mr. Beckett," she said, and opened her hand to him like offering a small bird. His hands were large and warm. He didn't seem old at all, and for once in her life Josie felt richer than Alice. "I have a secret," she told him.

Josie decided to tell him something she had not even told Alice, though Alice would have to know sooner or later. "You want to know what it is?"

"I guess so." Sam Beckett was smiling, but his smile seemed impatient now. He wanted to leave. "I don't have long," he said.

Josie could not believe she would tell this man what she was about to say. She licked her lips. "Four years ago the doctors found a hole in my heart, and on August tenth, they're going to operate. So when I have the operation, they don't know if I'll come through it or not, so that's partly why I decided to be saved. Because if I'm saved, then maybe God will let me live, you know? And then I can go to Africa, which is my main dream. Do you know there are animals there that people don't even know what they are?" She paused to take a breath. "And if I do not come through, then I figure since I'm already saved I'll go to heaven and look down on everybody, watch what people do. Maybe I can watch you, what you do. Maybe you will look through a window one day and see me there."

Her story jangled this man, visibly made him jump, and he looked at Josie Wire for a long time without speaking. He looked at her as if he were not seeing anything, but instead was seeing someone he used to know.

"How did they know about the hole in your heart?" he asked.

"I would get so tired, and blue in the face," Josie said. "My face turned blue, and my lips." She looked at Mr. Beckett. She wanted him to kiss her again. She wanted him to kiss her on the lips.

"I have a secret too," Sam said. He would give this girl the truth. "My name is not Beckett. It's Hunnicut. Bob Hunnicut. I was just teasing you when I said Beckett." He covered her hand with his.

Josie didn't think that was much of a secret, and said so. "That's more like a lie," she said.

He lifted the Bible from the ground and held it.

"I think I might like to look at this book," he told her. "I might like to read it myself."

"You would?" Josie could hardly help from asking. "Does this mean you might hope to be saved?"

"I think it does," he said slowly, and held out his hand. Josie shook it, pumping Bob Hunnicut's arm hard.

"I can't believe it!" she said. "Wait'll I tell Alice."

Josie began again. "Listen, my daddy's a teacher," she said. "He teaches at Webb School. Maybe you could get a job teaching there."

"Well," said Beckett-Hunnicut, "I think I better take care of that matter myself." He stood and the length of him amazed Josie.

"You got to have faith," said Josie, and she stood up facing him. "I have faith. I am going to go to Africa someday, and see everything. Have you ever been over there?"

"No," he said.

"Listen," said Josie. "Would you kiss me? I mean, before you leave?"

Bob Hunnicut leaned over and meant to kiss Josie's forehead, but Josie at that moment turned her mouth to his mouth; and her first thought, after he kissed her, was that kissing was overrated, that it didn't feel like anything. He walked away.

As she went toward the edge of the park, Josie couldn't decide whether or not to give him all her money; but as she opened her purse, he was gone. She did decide, though, to keep the secret about her defective heart awhile longer. Alice did not need to know yet. If Alice knew the truth, they could not plan to go to Africa. Josie Wire loved dreaming about Africa. She kept that dream inside her. She would love the smell of it there. She already knew what it would be like.

The Great Derangement
Jerry Bradley

My diploma says *Doctor of Philosophy*. A real philosopher might learn to live without the job he's been trained to have, but I can't see myself doing that. My mother told me that what you do determines who you are, but she also told me that where you are determines who you are. Who's to know?

Late spring really is nice here. It's not too hot. The winds of March and April begin to subside, and the flowers stand like ponies with their faces in the breeze. Also the students are gone.

I reported grades this morning. Because I did, I won't check my email for several days. Most of my students passed—not that they should have—but no matter the grade, some always ask for more. They tell sad tales. John Prine said, "If heartaches were commercials, we'd all be on TV." They definitely want to be on TV, to be the stars of their own life.

When you are an economic geographer, you make it a point to know something about places, especially about the one where you live. People expect me to know where everything is—and what it's worth. I wasn't born here, but I've been here twenty years already. I haven't calculated that cost. Some people tell me that you have to know where you've been to understand where you're going. I don't know whether to believe them or my mother.

On the first night after our last final, Sid Haycock and I always eat at the Pig. He's my department head, but we've gotten to be pretty good friends. The department used to be bigger, ten or so; now there's just two of us. We shouldn't really be a department anymore, but Sid has been here longer than I have and has a lot of pull. In fact, he'll probably ride out being chairman until he retires. They wouldn't think of closing the department before he goes.

The students at Carson City CC aren't very good at geography. They won't read and can't write, but they really don't want any help either. What they want is charity. I suspect they don't do well in their other courses either. Winnemucca's 196 miles from here, but they couldn't find it if you gave them a map, spotted them both n's and c's in its spelling, and put them on the on-ramp of 80 East. Most haven't ventured much beyond western Nevada. They know little about the world, so geography is hard. They haven't even found the Pig; but aside from their late-semester whining, they don't cause much trouble.

After the sun sets here, the nights cool quickly. I like to drive slowly with the windows down. Even on the backstreets you can savor the smells of the place: the cigar shops, the gustatory aroma of grilled onions and meat, the faint hint of sage. A fragrance like the kiss of a departing lover hangs in the air.

The food at the Pig is good, so you'd expect it to be busier than it is. You've seen places like this—two-story jobs, former warehouses that got refashioned by overly optimistic investors. But some places are a tomb. They're doomed from the start. The Pig-n-Chews is like that. It's always been doomed; it just doesn't know it yet. It's just behind the Nugget, so the location isn't bad, but it still can't attract anyone. No tourists, no poker players, no lobbyists.

I ask my students about places in the news, but the wars of the world are far away and are fought for the most part in unpronounceable places, just like those of old civilizations that have fallen to ruin.

Sid knows all the moves. He put geography in the core, and no one tried to stop him. Because of that we have a steady stream of *customers*—as the old provost called them. Though the dropout rate is high, frequently over forty percent, "the dumb turds," Sid says, will just have to take the courses again. "Money in the bank," he crows. "Money in the bank."

When I was coming up, none of the public colleges in Texas gave degrees in geography. Even in the Dallas colleges where I'd worked, it held little appeal. It was a "soft" subject, one intended for athletes and the otherwise ineducable—like photography, culinary arts, and religion—more avocation than education. I could have stayed there and been a nomad, migrating from campus to campus each semester; but the prospect of a tenure-track job was alluring, even if it was a long way away. Life teaches that, if you find something irresistible, you may have to go far from home to get it.

On top of the Pig, there is a winking neon swine. Inside, the waitresses wink too sometimes. They wear red blouses and bright lipstick, and they flirt with the customers. You can see the sign for blocks, the eye slowly opening and closing; but no matter how much you believe the signs, some places are still losers.

Tahoe isn't far from here. My students like to spend weekends there. They talk about hiking and biking the Flume Trail Loop. Many work part-time and seem content to toil in the hotels, casinos, bistros, and tourist traps as they work their way toward the middle of something, something that is likely illusory.

Sid and I met at the Pig. It's where we first broke bread. It's where we interviewed, though he was the one with the job. No committees, no formal HR questions—just two guys sizing up one another over platters of home cooking and unlimited dessert.

When I was fresh out of graduate school, I had answers and a lot of debt. There were no jobs for economic geographers, though the world's economy, like now, needed explaining. No one wants a man with debts to explain the world. I was trying to sell something no one wanted to buy.

At the end of the semester, Sid is always full of stories. He's seen everyone's files. He knows who's on his way out, even if he won't admit it.

I give it credit. This place has stories. It was named for Fremont's famous scout, but he was a little rough on the Indians and isn't spoken of kindly. The Bliss mansion was built with square nails. It was the first

237

home piped for gas lighting, once the largest in Nevada. And the Ferris House is where the fellow who invented the amusement park ride grew up.

When I got here, no one met me at the airport. Janice, the department secretary, instructed me to take a cab to the Pig where Sid would see me at 7 p.m. It was easy enough to find. It wasn't much of a test for a geographer. It wasn't hard for him to recognize me either since he knew everyone else in the place. We shook hands and sat. Sid held my resume and letter of application in front of him. He cautioned me not to fill up at the salad bar. "Jell-O and lettuce are for chumps. Stick with the 'cue and the sausage. The ham'll make you see God."

It took Carson City a century to grow as large as it once was, back in the days of the gold and silver strikes and the Comstock mines. Then for a quarter-century, it was home to the mint. The mint is closed, the Indians are gone, and the mines have played out. Everyone still wonders where the money went.

We talked while we ate. "We need someone to teach political and economic, physical, world capitals, maybe cartography every other year. Are you that man?"

"I'd like to believe I am," I said.

Jesus once made a public appearance in candle wax dripping from a church pulpit in Wiltshere, England. In Polvadera, New Mexico, he was seen in peeling paint on a shed door. A woman spotted him in a Walmart receipt in Anderson, South Carolina. Kudzu grew into the shape of the crucifixion on a telephone pole in North Carolina. In Australia a tomato left too long in an office refrigerator bore his resemblance. In Blue Springs, Missouri, he emerged from crayons that had been melted for a science class project.

"There'll be summers too if you want them. Maybe even if you don't."

"That's okay." I didn't tell him about all the loans, but he knew how many places I'd been an adjunct.

238

The governor wanted an Internet university. He called it Nevada On-line Master of Arts. He was trying to establish his education bona fides. He wanted to be "ahead of the curve." (But even my students know that the whole planet curves. How do you stay ahead of that?) He thought a presidential candidate might look to the West for a running mate. It was not, he said, a political move.

"Ambres," he said, vocalizing the "s" in mispronouncing my name. "Is that French?"

"Actually Cajun . . . so it is sort of French. My family's from southeast Texas and Louisiana. They're mostly gone now."

When the railroad left town, it took much of Carson City with it. Now the Virginia and Truckee, once "the crookedest railroad in the world," is nothing but a tourist ride to Virginia City. You board it from a sham depot outside of town.

"It's pronounced *hambre*—like the Spanish word for hungry—but Cliff will do."

"If you're a hungry man, you're in the right place. How old are you, hungry man Cliff?"

"Thirty-eight," I hesitated. I knew he wasn't supposed to ask.

The waitress's pink name tag was shaped like a pig. Its eye blinked on and off just like the sign outside.

Nevada is the seventh largest state in land area but is sparsely populated. On-line education is cheaper than gas. The governor said students wouldn't have to drive. He called himself an environmentalist.

"I'll speak to Pagnozzi about this," Sid said. "I can tell you where it all went wrong. They named the streets after attorneys. Then they turned the hotel into a prison. Why should prisoners live in a spa when you live in a shithole on the east side?"

I wonder, if Jesus is everywhere, where does that leave you?

"Are you a thirsty man too, Cliff? Let's have a little snort of

239

something. Bring me the usual, Cherrie, and get Mr. Ambres whatever he wants . . . just not one of those girlie drinks."

Cajun is the corruption of an ancient Greek word meaning "idyllic place." Since all sacred places are now pretty much ruins, the Cajuns knew something about corruption from the very start. In 1710 they refused to sign an oath of allegiance to the British. Their deportation became known as the Great Upheaval: Le Grand Dérangement.

I ordered a rusty nail, a double. I wasn't sure what was in it, but it was the manliest drink I could think of.

"You think she's pretty?" Sid asked. "You ought to see a gal I know in Reno!"

In graduate school we were told not to drink alcohol during interviews. I broke that rule. Go without full-time work, and you'll drink too. You'll drink plenty.

"You're not a fisherman, are you, Cliff?"
"No, not really. Used to as a kid with my granddad, but I guess I could learn."
"Don't bother. I hate fish," Sid said. "And I hate fishermen."
I imagined a coffin lid closing on my chances and Sid Haycock holding a hammer, but the only thing in his hand was a large pork rib.

Cherrie brought the drinks and patted Sid's broad shoulder. He beamed. "You have kids, Cliff?"
"No."
"How about bad habits? You won't make me sorry if I hire you, will you?"
"I hope not."
"Well, I've learned to live with both."

That Pagnozzi knows how to repay a favor. "The woman's a Vesuvius!" he bragged. "There's no telling how many men have died just from her heat."

Sid said that fishermen lack ambition. "At least fish move—though not always fast enough. That's why they're on every menu in town—but I don't want to see them here, and I don't want fishermen in my department. I want someone who moves. A mover, got it? Maybe not a shaker, but at least a mover."

Sid paused, took another bite of rib, and then lowered it to his plate. Eyeing the potato salad, he gestured with his fork. "How about a higher power? You believe in one?"

"Well, I was married once—so I guess I do."

"I understand. Florence thinks she runs me. She sure tries." Sid mused for a moment as if thinking of a place far off instead of right in town. "Those boys over there beneath the capitol dome think so too. They're just like our students, need to learn a lesson or two. What kind of fool wants to butt into our business?"

When he mentioned her name, Sid raised his upper lip as if he had smelled something bad. The knot of his tie rode up over his Adam's apple. He swallowed hard. "Caldera Fidelli isn't just a Reno whore. She's worked in Vegas too," he said.

Sid waved to Cherrie and made a signing motion for the check. He paid with a school credit card and tossed ten scratchoffs on the table. "If you hit it big, I'm running off with you," he teased. He stood and hugged her mightily. She kissed him on the cheek.

Some people don't want the world to change. A city, even a country ages, but it isn't allowed to show it. Sid and I both have gray hair but try to hide it. This country hasn't gone to the dogs; dogs would eat scraps and be happy of it. It's gone to the kids.

"Cliff, do you want to screw around in Texas or head west?" The blotch from Cherrie's kiss was visible on his cheek like the mark of sin. "You'll do. You'll be fine. Just do your work. See you in August. Here's twenty for the cab. You're at the Holiday Inn."

That was a long time ago. Over the years some of our colleagues took jobs on other campuses; one or two made it to retirement; some quit teaching altogether. He and I plugged on. It got so that no one would challenge him. He was, as he reminded us, the only chair the department

241

had ever had.

"How's Florence?" I asked.
"You know those ugly pills she's taking? They're working."

A man's vision is often held hostage by his appetite. Some people see Jesus in a tortilla, but you don't question it when he appears to you in something as substantial as a scorched slice of ham.

Sid said we were conspirators, although I was not always sure in what kind of enterprise. He could be shady, he could be menacing, but you could also find good reasons to trust him. He didn't have to put his finger in the air to know which way the wind was blowing. He could smell a deal when everyone else just smelled shit.

Three weeks later I received my reimbursement check for the flight and a note from Janice with my class schedule. I bought a condo, a small one, a four-roomer.

Beausoleil scalped two soldiers and four British settlers. There were two hundred on the *Santo Domingo* when it sailed it to the Lesser Antilles. How bad does a place have to be to leave it for Louisiana? *We will die from want*, he wrote, *if we do not receive succor.*

I suspect Cherrie would be about forty today. She was replaced by Naomi, Monica, two Lindas. We knew them all.

Every politician makes his career on the misfortune of others. Pagnozzi could have been governor, but he couldn't abide losing power. Every bridge and schoolhouse depended upon his approval. To him a state contract was like chicken: there was always enough to put a little meat on everyone's plate.

"Look," I said. "If you do this, you're doing what the casinos do—playing against the odds. The problem is that the line is always changing. Just because suckers bet doesn't mean you have to make a sucker bet. You're sixty-five. I've crunched the numbers. Only 83% of us make it that far."

When the legislature took over the county government in '69, it got control of the college too. And when it pushed education reform, Sid proposed a course in "Climate and Myth." They swallowed it like cobbler.

"I'm beating the system," he said, "because millions of people are already dead. I've already drawn the long straw, see? But it is getting shorter. The kid who parasailed off Heavenly Mountain? Gone. Didn't make thirty."

The governor turned over NOMA to a fraternity brother, Russ Birkofer, who billed the state. Some of the expenses were legitimate he said: lobsters and junkets to Silicon Valley. By the time the legislature caught on, he'd sold the company. The governor was ashes.

"I tell you what. When that woman kisses me, my toes curl. Too bad you'll never feel anything like that." That's the way Sid was. He might defend you to the death, but you'd be bleeding from how he'd carved you up along the way.

Andrew Pagnozzi advised the legislature to merge the state's two troubled campuses. A few teachers lost jobs, but the legislature applauded. CCCC and Nevada On-line Master of Arts became, believe it or not, Carson-NOMA College. Isn't it funny how often politics seems like a bad joke? It really does. They said no students were harmed.

There are risks in having sex with a woman like Caldera Fidelli, even if you do live through it.

"My odds of being alive at seventy-five aren't good. Each year will be worth less, especially if I'm not around to enjoy it. Eventually we all die. You, me—maybe not Florence." Sid knew that, even if he saw his eighties, Florence would likely still be around them with him. The nineties? Forget about it. "Would you want to face your future certain that your wife would be there too?"

He told me the department was mine now. He said he knew when to walk away. He'd send a card when they got settled. I wondered if I'd hear from him again. If I didn't hear from him, I figured I'd at least hear about him.

243

When I saw the face in the ham slice, I wasn't sure it was Him. It didn't taste like Him. I'd had holy communion before and knew the Lord didn't have much flavor. Still, it didn't seem right to put what remained of Him in a to-go box—and what would I do with Him then? So I just whittled away, eating my way in from the margins as I went. When Linda2 asked me how my meal was, I told her it had been a real revelation.

I heard from Sid. His postcard read: *When I bathe her in flowers, I know where God lives.* It was signed *XOXOX*. He said I'd know what the triple X's meant. To be sure, he'd drawn nipples on the two O's.

Starlings
Jill McCorkle

At ten in the morning the temperature has already hit a hundred degrees and the weather station says it will keep rising. Mary squints out at the thermometer. The glare from the tin roof of her porch is making everything in the yard wavy. The big oak tree that was already big when she was just a little girl trying to climb up its rough trunk quivers limply overhead. She remembers squashing her face into the bark as she grabbed the branches and pulled herself up. But that was back when the only thing beyond her yard was a couple of houses down the road and the flat tobacco fields, the strip of woods that kept that old snake-infested river shady and cool. That was back before the interstate plowed through town, taking away the fields and the woods and bringing with it all kinds of businesses and crime.

Now she is seventy-six and it is the hottest summer that she can recall, every summer of her life spent here in this very house, though now everything is overgrown and changed. Now the downtown area has spread in every direction and she lives on the corner of what is considered an old black neighborhood. Now her road is paved and the area is overrun with college students who want to live within walking distance of the campus, where Mary spent the last good years of her life working. She swept and mopped and cleaned up somebody else's garbage, somebody that knows better or ought to, given what their folks pay for them to sit and spraddle their long legs out, toes of dirty sneakers marking up the walls. Retirement. Hah.

She has worked every day of her grown life. She has worked in dry cleaning, breathing steam and chemicals, feeling the folds of her lungs starching and stiffening. She has kept other people's babies, changed their dirty diapers and whispered love words when the young mama is out somewhere in a business suit, trying to look like she might be somebody.

They say, "Oh Mary, how we love her." They say, "She is like family." This is what they want to believe to be true. Sometimes she wants their lousy wish to be true as well, but then there'll come a moment of reckoning that sends the skin of her neck up in little points. A rabbit running across her grave. She don't want to be somebody's charity. Don't you go doing your good deeding on me.

But now she wishes she'd let that young college boy from next door help her get that air conditioner out of its huge carton by her front door. He said, "I can put it in the window for you," and his thin white hands trembled when he spoke, like he might be scared of an old wrinkled-up black woman. Like maybe he'd never carried on a conversation with a black woman. Maybe he was taught at an early age to fear darkness. Like she might say, 'boo' and he'd up and run for the hills like that salesman done the day he come calling where she was setting with some children and he gets a scared look when she glares at him like she might up and slit his puny white throat, with those little children standing there in the doorway in diapers all wide-eyed.

Lord, yes, that's how a child is meant to run. Naked as a jaybird. Squat by a tree or down by the creek. Sprawl your limbs out in a warm patch of grass or over a hardwood floor that's cool. The coolest spot in the house is always right down on the floor, where the cool air seeps up from the dark underneath part of the house. She loved playing down there as a girl. She loved the feel of the cool black dirt and she saw it all from down there. Her mother and the other women who lived down that dusty road being picked up on summer mornings, their white dresses pressed perfect like they might be high-paid nurses heading off to the hospital. But then her mother came home late afternoon smelling like somebody else's little girl while her own little girl had spent the afternoon with the children from nearby who ran wild without any grown-ups telling them what to do. The teenage girl who smoked cigarettes, her stomach already swole up with a baby. The big brother who was known to pin a girl down and rub hisself up against her belly, only giving in to her begging and crying if she lifted up her shirt. Mary had done that, turned her face into the cool black dirt while the whole neighborhood watched, while he called her Tiny Tit and pinched her there. She counted in her head all the while picturing her mother walking the clean padded hallways of a big brick house, the little girl's room with a closet full of Sunday dresses and ruffly blouses that nobody was going to push up off her thin frightened chest.

"I hate that girl you keep," she told her mother that night and on many others before bed, her mama too tired to even tell a bedtime story. "I hate her with her old white face. I hate her for thinking you love her!" And then she wanted to ask, 'Do you love her? Do you?' But her mother just frowned and let out a tired heavy breath. What could she say if she did love that girl and what difference did it make if she didn't?

And Mary hates that skinny witch on The Weather Channel right now, too, with her flashy red jacket like she might be Miss Patooty. They all the time is wearing bright red and bright blue, strutting their feathers and saying, 'Look at me, look at me, I'm over here in the television set.' Look at the sky and tell the weather. Lord. She gets it better than most of them on the average day. You ain't got to go to school or wear a suit that costs the same as an automobile to be able to lick your finger and hold it in the air. You ain't got to live in a mansion with a Jacuzzi like all these folks have to be able to see how fast the clouds is moving or to take note of the sunset. People have thrown out common sense and trucked in a bunch of horse mess to make themselves feel great big and important.

* * *

The oak is quivering, quivering in the heat, the very movement putting her in mind of the old man who once a year stood at the front of the church and played his violin. That sound made people cry; it was a sad sound. People said he knew it all by ear—that he couldn't read words or music; he just played what his heart felt like playing. It was a lonely sound like that sad bird she hears every morning, calling and calling, hopeless of an answer. Now as she watches the branches in that bright light, she feels the same sadness. Beneath the tree is a ring of jonquils her mother planted, the Lord only knows how long ago, and every year they come up, weak green shoots, no blooms. They haven't bloomed in over twenty years.

Once when she was a child, she stared up at the sky on a bright hot day. She searched the uppermost branches of that same old oak tree for a bird she heard calling. A sad sound. She waited and waited. She passed out from the brightness, the whole world growing dark and grainylike, the sounds in the air buzzing like something she could see, something she could reach out and touch. Her father scooped her up then and carried her to the shade of the back porch where her mama was running some sheets through a wringer. She never told them that she had forgotten to breathe while standing there, that the heat and brightness made her feel like a candle melting down into a shapeless puddle.

* * *

"Let me help you," that white boy said. "I know you live alone here and I don't think you can get the air conditioner in the window by yourself. Please, let me do something for you?"

She had read stories of young men muscling their way into old women's houses to rummage their purses and then rape them to death. It was in the paper all the time. Poor old woman comes out of the Harris Teeter and gets kidnaped, and what did they want? Her car. Her food. Surely she'd have given them that if there was no other way. She'd've said, 'Take it, children, take the money and the car keys and just leave me here in the parking lot and I won't even call the policeman until you are way out of town.' But it seemed that killing was a part of the plan. They wanted to kill is all. Many of them do.

"I can manage," she told that boy and watched him amble back over to where he lived with a herd of wild ones of all sizes and shapes and colors. The kids from the university had been coming and going in and out of that old eyesore of a house for over twenty years, strewing their beer cans and talking the same stuff; the only thing that changed was their hairdos and outfits. That boy looked kind of hurt when he turned to go back into that zoo of a house, but she couldn't worry on that. Would she have let a black one in? She had to think it through. But no, she thought, she absolutely would not. This had nothing to do with color. It had to do with being alone in the world.

* * *

"You are prejudiced, Mary," her coworker Bennie used to tell her when they took their breaks from cleaning up the campus buildings. "You are bad prejudiced, girl."

"Maybe. Maybe I am," she said. "Or maybe I'm just jealous of their clean easy worlds!"

"They don't all have clean easy worlds."

"In a town like this one they do."

"So do a lot of the black folks."

Those times there with Bennie were the best part of her life. Those were the times when all the anger that churned her insides just up and flew away. It made her want to sing. It made her want to crack jokes and laugh great big. She liked to tell jokes that were kind of dirty just to see Bennie get nervous and have to stare down at his feet while he chuckled. "You're something else, Mary," he said and she knew deep down that he meant that; she knew deep down that he felt something stirring. It was like the world was humming then, the great big oak trees there on campus filled with starlings, their wings shiny black in the light. People talked of these birds as a problem, the racket they made, the filth they dropped, the way they clustered together in one big mass and then took to the sky all at once: a screeching black cloud that drowned out everything else on the face of the earth. "Pests," people cried, like they was one of the Bible plagues, but Mary liked when they gave her that loud second to catch her breath and turn her attention off of Bennie and what was a hopeless calling. She liked changing the subject after the racket like about how she had ordered herself a radio with a built-in cassette player that could also just play sounds. Like you could have yourself a thunderstorm or the ocean or birds at sunrise just by throwing a switch.

* * *

One day she will get everything organized. She likes the catalogs. That is her favorite thing, to sit and choose pretty things and then pick up the phone and call, put on a fancy-sounding voice. It is like being a kid with the Sears and Roebuck's only she's old and she has worked hard enough to save. She owns her house and she gets her pension. Her daddy paid off half the house and then she finished all by herself. Didn't need a man even though there was many who offered. You think I want to spend my life feeding your fat behind and all those children you've planted in other women's patches over the years? Come here to this garden to rest till the end of your days? Think again, you. Think again, old dog.

* * *

The only man she'd've ever had was Bennie, and as is true with everything good in life, he was spoken for, and his wife was the salt of the earth. Still sometimes when she closed her eyes after long days at the university she pictured herself laying there with Bennie. She'd rub her face up on that Egyptian cotton pillowcase she was so fond of and think of him. This was a pillowcase anybody would be proud to have; it comes from a place that has made bed linens a specialty of sorts. Her sheets are just like those she used to spend hours ironing in a big house on Main Street where she worked a little as a young woman. She loved to iron those fine linens. It was the finest cotton she'd ever run her fingers over. Buttery smooth. When she closes her eyes at night ain't a soul on earth, not the president and whoever, and not Prince Charles and Camelia, or whatever the harlot calls herself, sleeping on a better piece of fabric.

* * *

There are boxes to unpack and when she pulls out the new things, it will give her a burst of energy and she will be able to get busy. It will be like Christmas morning right in the thick of a hot-as-Hades July. She'll put on the sound of a tropical rain forest, and she'll hang herself some new curtains, white priscillas with some beautiful hummingbird tieback holders. Pottery Barn and Crate and Barrel and Ross-Simons and Bloomingdale's. She fancies that they see her name come up on the computer screen and they comment what a good customer she is. What exquisite taste. She laughs. If they could see her now. Skinny black woman standing in the kitchen in nothing but underwear, nothing but a pair of size medium cotton drawers from Dillards, her breasts hanging and swinging to and fro like a Watusi. She imagines stepping out on her porch this way next time a white greasy-faced thing comes selling something. She'll put an old chicken bone up in her hair and she'll shoo him off with some mumbo jumbo, leaving him to think she'd cast a spell like she once done somebody at the dry-cleaning store.

That man was hateful like she'd never seen, talking to that skinny little white girl at the counter like she might've been a dog. Mary stepped forward and held out her hands and begun to twitch like she was picking up some kind of wave or something. "What is wrong with you, woman?" he asked, and Mary just shook her head. "Oh, I ain't the one with the problem I fear!" And she told him—much to the shock of everybody there waiting in line—that she had picked up on his sex problems and she sure was sorry. He acted like she was crazy as a bat but still he pushed her.

250

What did she mean by that? She didn't answer, just went on about her business; but as he was leaving, she went over and whispered in his old waxy ear, "Your lovin' days is over, sir. Your equipment is likely to just ride around in your drawers like a little dead varmint for the rest of your days!" She was asked to leave soon after, but that was fine enough. The other workers looked up to her. She was a legend. Besides, her lungs needed a break from all the chemicals and heat.

* * *

And it is so hot. Too hot to breathe. The hottest summer in a long while. By noon it is a hundred and five, and the woman on the television set says it ain't over yet. Mary has pulled all of the heavy yellowed shades to block the sun and feels her way around the boxes and piles of newspapers. She makes her way over to the crate with the air conditioner and sits on top of it. Order from Sears. Why didn't she let them install it? Was she ashamed for folks to see the unopened boxes? The trash that needed to be hauled out? The recycling? Or was she scared of him, scared of what he might do to her if she didn't tip him enough cash? Now she can't remember. She hears that stray cat meowing and scratching on her door. Her feet are swollen or she might ask it in. But the last time she did that it was a spooked cat and left a bloody stripe down her arm. It is odd how dark it is in here. Beyond the shade there are kids blowing their horns and riding their bikes. They are buzzing and screaming.

* * *

She raises the blind. Bees in the clover. A distant knocking. A woodpecker? That boy again? She does not trust such young men. There was once one that let her know she was an animal herself if she had to be. He acted like he wanted her for herself, but that wasn't what he wanted at all. What he wanted didn't even need a face or a brain. She could have killed him so easy. She said, "Don't make me kill you." She had a tiny little crochet hook she grabbed from her bedside table—one for making lace—and it was pointed right at his ear. She said, "Don't make me kill you because I will." She said, "I will puncture your brain. Or maybe I'll let you live and go on to prison because old butt-buggering bubba might need hisself a date to the prison prom." She could have killed him, could have

251

beaten the everlovin' life from him. A few things like that happen in life and you stop trusting even when you want to so bad.

By 1 p.m. the sun is beating full down, pressing the cracked ceilings closer and closer to her face. The old oscillating fan lifts the pages of the catalogs at her feet and she can't keep her eyes open at all. She struggles to stay awake; the next radio show is a gardening show and they have lots of tips that she will need in another week or so when she is feeling better. She has bought herself some half barrels and several big bags of good rich potting soil and a couple of bags of moo doo and great big red geraniums. The porch will be beautiful then and when the heat breaks, she'll put on that frock she ordered from Bloomingdale's, a frock that nobody would ever expect her to wear—bright green jungle print with loud-colored animals turned every which way—and she'll set there in the swing with some iced tea in that pretty crystal goblet from the Ross-Simons set and she will open all her Harry and David goodies, maybe break out the Godiva chocolates she ordered several weeks ago and that caviar she was aching to try out even though she suspected that it was probably going to be a lot like when she got herself lox and bagels. Orange fish on a piece of tough bread. What was the Jews thinking, she wondered. "You can have it. Buy yourself some mouthwash, too," she told that old man in the fish market. She said, "What has happened to you, man? This ain't no fish market. Smoked fish and orange fish and ole slimy mess. Where's the catfish? Where's the flounder? Where's the cornbread crumbs to roll it in before you fry it?" He laughed. He wanted to say that's a black thing, a colored thing, a Negro thing, an African American, Afro-American, Kwanzaa-celebrating thing. Kwanzaa is what the white folks latch onto in a town such as this so they can act like they're teaching their children something. Teach them collards. Teach them don't cross the street and hold tight to your purse when you see a black man.

That bird with the sad sound is high in the oak, and now Mary knows she has to go and see it for real. She makes her way, naked and dark, heavy bare feet wedged into satin slippers, the perfect end of the busy day for the woman of the nineties. She stares one step ahead, the brown painted floor. Who painted it last? Her daddy? That man that tried to take up with her that time? Don't trip. Don't fall. Dark floorboards she used to walk as a child, arms held to the sides and balanced. She was on a plank high above the Pee Dee River. Below her were alligators and above her were snakes swinging from the limbs. And watching her was everybody in the whole town—man and woman and black and white. All the children in her school held their breath as she crossed, her own breath held. 'You can do it, Mary,' they say, 'You can do it.' In her mind she is always being a hero.

* * *

Her daddy said, "Mary, what are you doing?" and he yanked her through the kitchen doorway, her white cotton socks stained brown from the paint. "Didn't I tell you not to walk on that floor? Didn't I tell you?" And his grip on her arm hurt and she shut her eyes and waited for a slap to sting her bare leg. Fly swatter, switch—ligustrum limb stripped of its leaves, a whistle through the air, a slap, a sting, pulling the skin up into a thin welt. She never got a whipping in her life that made her want to be a better person. It was the opposite. It made her want to be a bad person. It made her want to beat them right back. Bennie hisself thought that children who were beaten on would grow up to do the same to theirs unless they got hold of a book or two or talked to a person who might teach them different.

"Bennie, you act like a white man," she told him. "Like one of these teachers packed with brains."

"I act like a man is all," he said, and she was thinking, I wish you did, honey. I wish you did 'cause if you acted like most men, like the men I know, then I'd've had you by now. I'd've had you at least once.

* * *

She wanted him. He was the one she wanted. But he was too good for her. The floorboards are straight and narrow, and it's hard not to tip to the side. She made herself a promise never to strike a child. Never to hit a loved one. But beyond that any fool is fair game. She ain't one to go hunting, but you muscle your way into her life with some bad intentions and she will kill you. She says, "I can kill you. I will. I will kill you if I have to."

She'd done just that before when an old bloodthirsty bulldog belonging to some no-good down the street come into her yard like something from the wild and went after a little puppy belonging to those students next door. That dog walked right up and grabbed that puppy by the throat, broke its little neck, shook it like a dust rag, and that young boy was off on the steps wringing his hands and sobbing. And without thinking Mary got herself an axe and went after it. By then the animal had tore open the little one's belly and was lapping right into it like it might be a bowl of milk, and she brought that axe down before the mongrel could think. And yes, it looked at her. And its eyes looked frightened. Its eyes seemed to say, 'I can't help that I was raised this way. Raised to be angry and mean,' but that didn't stop Mary. And when a full day and night passed and nobody came looking for it, she wrapped its body in some old bath towels and called up the department of sanitation. The boy from next door came back later to say that there was nothing the doctor could do for his puppy. He stood outside her locked screen door, hands in his pockets as he shifted from side to side. "Thank you," he said. "I hope I can help you some time."

* * *

Oh that sad sad bird. Her daddy should hear it. He should have to hear it. And her mother. The boy from next door, his little bloody puppy wrapped in his nice leather jacket. He should hear it. She could let him help with the air conditioner. He is a grateful boy. He means well. And Bennie, God rest him. She opens the shade, but now the bird has moved. It's flown to the rooftop, then up past the hot glint of tin, rising and circling, higher and higher. She cups her hands up to the glass and watches, waits, holding her breath. She holds her breath, the pulse in her temple keeping beat with the kitchen clock that has hung there over the doorway since she was just a child watching the hands turn closer and closer to when her mother would get home. A mother should tend to her own home first. She stretches out on the cool floorboards to wait, pulling deep breaths in and out, in and out. She closes her eyes to the bright glint of the tin roof as she pictures the bird there, circling and swooping. When she can get up, when she is not feeling so tired, she will set up that air conditioner and she will unpack all of her beautiful things. And who would ever believe she had grown up to own such beautiful things? But for now she just needs to rest and wait, to tune her ear to that bird far far away, its wings spread as it lifts and circles the hot tin roof of her porch, circling and calling until others swarm in, filling the sky with darkness.

So Much Carrion in the Night
Laura Rebecca Payne

I think I may say now, that I liv'd indeed like a Queen; or if you will have me confess, that my Condition had still the Reproach of a Whore, I may say, I was sure, the Queen of Whores; for no Woman was ever more valued.
—Daniel Defoe, <u>Roxana</u>

September 28, 1922

Dear Diary,
    My old teacher, Miss Fairchild, gave me a book to read—with a very knowing look. She says she is happy I have come home, despite neither Mama or Daddy being here at present. I told her that I suspected Mama would be coming home from the whore-tent city she is living at over west toward Borger. That was when Miss Fairchild sucked in her breath and started rummaging in a chest behind her desk until she found this book, <u>Roxana,</u> by Daniel Defoe. Her hand shook slightly, and she seemed nervous—or shifty—I cannot ever tell with women. She says to read it, to understand the plight of the fallen woman so I will stay in school and be a valuable member of the female race.
    I have read it, Diary, and I am unclear as to Miss Fairchild's understanding of the plot. I agree that Roxana had some ups and downs, but that was from her society not wanting her to live independently as a woman, not because she chooses and succeeds in the only profession that would give her opportunity to become rich, happy, and fulfilled (which she does, Diary). I wish to go have tea again with Miss Fairchild and point this out, but I am afraid this might get me expelled from Vernon High School, which would not please me.
    So I will try to live the way Miss Fairchild suggests and finish a

degree, become her idea of a value (as if being loved and admired for my beauty—which even my teacher admits I possess—is not a value). We shall see: Perhaps this might prove my route to a fine city life.

Yours,

C—

or, Roxana for today!

P.S. I did leave Miss Fairchild's room wanting a chest of books, perhaps one for you, Diary, and the sisters of volumes I plan to write. Even the dreaded Roxana found time to fill her volumes of thoughts on many subjects, not the least of which is beauty—and love.

Chippy lies on the ground, some paces down from her house, on her back, under the fading blue sky, light and sad in its waning hour before evening. It is the time for vultures, early fall. The birds are migrating south—Chippy has heard they fly all the way to Brazil, to Rio, even, and she watches them slowly circle above, higher than the clouds. They seem to float in the atmosphere, barely moving—black, majestic wings dipping, precarious yet powerful.

The small group, perhaps five birds, builds to dozens. Chippy knows they are scouting giant junipers to the north of the house—wind breaks. All Chippy's childhood, Mama has hated the trees. "Vultures portend bad omens, the Bible says it, I am certain," Mama complains heartily, loudly, as she does about everything. "Can't stand the smell, no how," Mama yells up through the huge, swaying limbs, while beating two mesquite branches together until, en masse, the dozens of raptors which have settled for the night into the huge junipers take flight, one elemental wave—only to resettle on creaking and swaying limbs as soon as Mama throws down mesquite branches to scratch dust before returning herself to settle again heavily on the porch step.

Hundreds of the birds stop off for the night each spring and fall, coming and going, to Mama's great regret. But Chippy likes them, their mystery, their flight.

* * *

Once, when she is a girl, she finds a single vulture lying inert in the back beyond the barn. Chippy creeps up to look at it, never considering

256

that vultures could or would drop to the ground; they seem immortal in the clouds so far above. And the home-site is a stop-over, not a place to land long. As she approaches the bird, Chippy pauses, struck by the red of its beak, the brown of its feathers—not black as they appear in the sky.

I will bury it, Chippy thinks; but when she returns with a shovel and scoops under what she assumes to be a corpse to lift it, the vulture opens its eyes, blinking blindly in the sunset, almost appearing frightened. Chippy swiftly backs away from the bird, herself frightened. Later that night, the vultures descend as always in the trees, weighting down the branches until Chippy wonders that the junipers do not snap with the heft of so many. Chippy cannot shake the feeling that the dying vulture will become carrion to its own kind as she lies on her pallet that night listening for the sound of swooping birds, for mortal struggle. The wind-play scratches a constant song in West Texas so consistently that Chippy periodically starts at sounds, runs out into the night air, claps loudly, yells, "Heeyaww, heeyaww," and watches satisfied as the birds rise, again en masse, flap their giant, sluggish wings before settling again into the trees.

Hours into this routine, Mama finally bellows, "Get into your bed before I come out and chop down them trees myself—with you under them."

In the waning hours of night, Chippy lies listening, intent and helpless, for sounds of the dying vulture, but she hears nothing over the wind blowing branches on the tin roof. Nonetheless, the next morning, Chippy rises early and rushes to the barn to find no trace of the bird—neither of bloody remains nor even a disturbance in the dust where the bird lay half-dead.

* * *

And now years later, Chippy herself plays the injured bird, lying inert, still, in sandy-clay dirt, staring up at the sky and its building circle of returning vultures, flying slow and deliberate. They continue high a bit to the north in the distance. The numbers will grow as their mysterious messaging assures the masses of the existence of junipers. Chippy wonders if she lies completely still will they come to the ground to greet her as so much carrion. But she doubts it—just as they communicate the existence of trees, she must communicate the existence of a beating heart.

Chippy has been home for a day, lying in wait of vultures for

257

perhaps only hours, but she is determined not to count hours or days—or even minutes and seconds—until she decides what to do. Being back at the home-site is not in Chippy's plans—she'd have thought she would be to Ft. Worth by now—but Jimbo Jones turned his Model A north to Woodward, Oklahoma earlier in the morning, leaving Chippy to think on the fact that she has always known he would do so, leave her here, return north to his scratchy farm. Chippy has felt it from the beginning of the tenuous relationship built on his lust for her young body and her unswerving desire to make it a lifetime of hours east to the city she dreams her father forever flees to escape the drudgery of life on the home-site, with Mama and—she must admit it—Chippy.

Lying in the dirt, feeling blue sky seep into her eyes, Chippy also knows firmly that Jimbo Jones has fled in his car so rapidly she can still taste the dust his wheels churned up in the dirt yard because of Chippy's impatience at the charade that he loves her enough to save what he believes to be an untried innocent girl. Chippy has learned from Jimbo Jones that she abhors subterfuge and has shown him, out of sheer impatience with the stupidity of men, that growing up the daughter of an oil camp whore leaves no innocents within the thin walls of a canvas tent village hastily constructed in the Texas Panhandle.

* * *

The night previous to Jimbo Jones's fleeing north, abandoning her, Chippy almost agrees to lie down with Jimbo, give him a taste of what taking her to the city will produce. Now, looking back, after all of the cajoling for him to take her away from Borger and her mother's whore tent, escape with her east to Ft. Worth so she might find her daddy—or at least find some good times in Cowtown, times Daddy has whispered about on countless nights to the beats of settling vultures—and later in the summer with its westerly breeze blowing sand even across starscapes, which remain always elusive and too high, Chippy knows Jimbo plans instead to settle on a scabby, scratch of a farm in the Panhandle of Oklahoma. "Oklahoma will make you honest, girlie," Jimbo Jones says, apparently believing he is hauling a virgin to the red light district. Somehow, this is more a sin than hauling her to a lean-to shack with an intent of enslaving her there for the same favors she would kindly bestow him on a feather mattress in a fancy hotel. The firm belief in the temerity and veracity of her perspective spurs Chippy's determination that Jimbo Jones drive her to Ft. Worth. He will either change his mind or go to his farm alone, Chippy considers. Either way, she imagines herself in Ft. Worth to make her way. This is what matters.

Chippy cannot for the life of her think how Jimbo Jones comes to this conclusion: that she is an innocent or that she would wish to be a farm wife in Oklahoma—her, the daughter of the top whore in Borger's whore-tent city. But there you have it—who is the innocent, she thinks low in her thoughts, waiting for Jimbo Jones to buy supplies for their car trip. Chippy takes his delusion as the best opportunity to lead Jimbo Jones east by allowing him his fantasy.

"Mama's life makes me nervous, Jimbo," Chippy whispers.

"I know. My own mama can make it right, honey-baby, teach you what you need to know to make us a good life. Be a wife to me, a mama to our little ones," he slurs into her ears, hands roaming across her backside.

The scene replays itself over and over, sometimes moments after he has stood in line and then paid Chippy's mama a dollar for her own favors—Chippy at times even in the tent, tucked into her corner pallet. Jimbo Jones watches Chippy while moving rhythmically and stiffly over Mama, lust awash in his watery eyes until he squeezes them shut. Chippy stares back unblinking until the moment he shuts his eyes, then she rolls to face the canvas wall of the tent, further to contemplate Ft. Worth.

"I need to find Daddy so you can ask his permission to take me away. I promised him when we were separated . . . when Daddy had to leave to ride broncos in Cowtown to make money so I would not have to follow Mama to the whore-tents much longer. I promised to find him if I found my happiness." Chippy gazes deeply into Jimbo Jones's eyes, his light green, vacant; hers piercing, cold grey-blue, and calculating. Jimbo Jones has failed to offer to drive her east of his own initiative so she forces his hand. The story clinches the decision to travel east, but Chippy knows it is borrowed time; she will not jump out of the Texas Panhandle only to land in the Oklahoma Panhandle, much less allow Jimbo Jones's mama to hold her down as a farm wife.

Yet, Chippy's own power dissipates as they drive across the Palo Duro breaks and Jimbo Jones continues a constant babbling about their domestic future: "Been meaning to build a lean-to onto the back of the farmhouse. Mama will want us living with her, I imagine. Gets lonely up there, what with me and the boys running off to call the herd and then drive it to Oklahoma City for sales. Mama says women got no business in cities. We won't tell her about this little trip—make it a honeymoon, won't we?" Jimbo Jones rattles constantly in this vein, as Chippy watches the eastern horizon, perking up only near the Canadian River when trees spring up tall and thick—as she has heard they stand in the east, near the Trinity River.

When she fails to answer, appears not even to listen, Jimbo Jones also becomes impatient. "I ain't thinking on taking you on no joy ride, girlie," he finally slurs after a second beer and countless swigs off a bottle of gin he stashes under his feet on the floorboard of the car. "We either gets hitched or you can walk to Ft. Worth. I ain't taken you out of that tent, quit easy wildcatting money, to treat a dollar whore's girl to see the lights. I got a ranch and family waiting, needing me and my wages. Don't need to be wasting it none on pleasure trips to Ft. Worth."

After miles of diatribes, Jimbo finally pulls into a cottonwood stand and cuts the car, grabs a blanket from the second seat, and staggers off toward the river. "Come on now—I'm hungry. Think about what I said: We can turn right around back to Borger and your Mama if that is what you want."

So it is a bit later that Chippy finds herself walking deliberately toward the blanket and Jimbo Jones, telling him calmly to take his boots off. She strips herself of her clothes at the car, carefully laying them across the seat's edge. She strides up to him, cotton shift, rolled white stockings, scuff-heeled shoes. Her black hair is pinned up, and she stands over him, unpins the red-wooden stick holding it in place. The stick is a present from Chippy's daddy, a cactus flower, bright yellow and green, a delicately painted ball on its end. He bought it after a rodeo in El Paso, he claims, from a beautiful street vendor whose hair reminded him of his daughter's. Chippy imagines this to be a lie, figures he stole it from a whore. But she is used to top whores and thinks the stick pretty. She has worn it since she was ten.

Standing above Jimbo Jones, stick in hand, Chippy's eyes shine against the moon, but Jimbo Jones will see only the glint of hatred and impatience at his dreams of familial Oklahoma farmlands and of Chippy as a wife—plans that have run crosswise to Chippy's. But he looks beyond Chippy's eyes to some image of her nakedness, her functioning as his possession.

"My daddy taught me to ride when I was nothing but a girl, and my cousin Corley taught me to lie back and enjoy a swim in rocky springs. Which way you like it, Jimbo?" Chippy almost whispers, her voice low and husky. She stands firm before him as he lies on the blanket, mute. Chippy intuits her boldness might queer the deal, but she has been forced forward by instinctive frustration.

The cottonwood leaves brush dryly above, their trunks creak and pop against the movements. The river laps, smelling slightly of sulfur, and Chippy breathes in a moment, savoring the solitude of skin and breeze and water and trees.

Jimbo Jones says nothing for ten beats while she stands before him, enjoying the cool breeze brushing her skin, breasts reacting to the coolness. With one hand, Chippy feather-touches fingers against her stomach and up toward her hair and feels frustration begin to dissipate. Chippy knows she must turn back to the car, perhaps cry a bit for Jimbo Jones, continue—even heighten—the charade, but Jimbo Jones reaches out for her hips and, forcing her onto him, pulls her legs to straddle him. "Ride me," he growls, fierce and firm in the moment.

Just before walking from the car, before even beckoning to Jimbo Jones to remove his boots, Chippy calls to the wind in which she imagines her father to be waiting, listening for her: "I feel like taking a ride," and, a day later in the dirt, west of Vernon, stuck again on the home-site land, Chippy will think back on the moment as particular to her fate.

But fate will be later, after Jimbo Jones pulls Chippy onto him. Chippy sees his look of unchecked lust and knows in the instant that she must shock him out of it or he will have achieved his desire and she will never achieve hers. She realizes the folly of her impatience and the strength of Jimbo Jones's body—hers is tall but thin, no match for the strength of a man who builds rigs, drives cattle. The reality that he could and might actually force her to Oklahoma—the probability of this fact—wakes up Chippy's senses. Chippy allows her body to go limp and forces tears to form and puddle in her eyes. The slide of coldness ever-present in her eyes, her expression, becomes masked by the sheen of tears, and Jimbo Jones stiffens a moment, pausing as tears hit his face below where he holds Chippy tight and close, bruising her hips with his fingers grasping bone and skin.

"Oh, honey-baby," he suddenly blubbers, "You ain't all tough—that was just playing. You trying to act like your mama and all them other whores you been growing up around. See, Jimbo's here to make you right.

We'll get married—and I won't do nothing with you before that minute."

He lets go of Chippy, allows her to slide from atop his hips, her hands free to wipe at tears, curl a moment in a ball of solitude as he wraps the blanket around her, picks her up, and carries her back to the car.

* * *

I should have stayed wrapped in the blanket, Chippy thinks later, lying still in the dust-clay dirt of the home-site, still gazing at vultures. The trumpet vines grow wild on the home-site outside of Vernon. Chippy often thinks they should have named the town Trumpet. The beauty of the flowers in June makes up for the choking invasiveness of roots that dig deep, produce suckers all across the ground—yards and yards away from the parent vine. Like mesquites, they suck all the water, keeping it for themselves, preventing other flowers or even trees from taking root, from thriving. But their yellow and orange flowers are vibrant and strong, lasting until winter when death takes flowers, as its own haunting memory, leaving bare barbed wires of grey twisting wood.

Tiny sharp sucker shoots trouble Chippy's back, buttocks, and thighs as she remains lying, prone and stretched, still, thinking she wished for the blanket. I should have gone to sleep in that blanket in the car—stayed that way until we got to Ft. Worth. I had him for a time, Chippy ponders. But in the car after her performance by the river, she feels too empowered by her trick over Jimbo Jones, whom she begins to regard as a buffoon, a slower wit, to continue to plot. So when Jimbo Jones hands her his bottle from beneath his feet and says, "Come on, honey-baby, take a nip of gin. It'll make you feel better," Chippy sniffles loudly, if uncertainly, for him, throws back her head, and gulps without a cough.

It is not too long, as the Model A, its top still down, picks up speed in the flat road which rises up from the breaks of the Palo Duro, up even from the Canadian River, then stretches interminably eastward across plains all the way to Arkansas, until Chippy's tongue loosens with half a bottle of gin and she giggles and flirts, a hand laid flippantly over Jimbo Jones's shoulders. "Oh, Jimbo, I am going to show you what city life will be. I hear Ft. Worth has night life and speakeasies, and bootleggers, and whorehouses—real ones, not like those tents in Borger, not like Mama's. I want red lipstick and a silk dress. Oh, and a platinum handbag. Can you buy me slippers with buckles? I hear they are the rage in all the magazines, I hear—and I will look fine in silk stockings—not these old cotton ones," Chippy slurs into his ear, lifting a leg to the dash, plucking at the rolled-down, white-cotton stocking. And because Chippy feels good, she slides over cool leather to press her body closer to him, rub her lips across his salty neck, taste him lightly with her tongue and whisper into his ear, "Buy me nice things, you hear, Jimbo? You do, and I will show you how I ride."

It is because Chippy takes a further swig or two from the gin and because she feels so good that she fails to notice Jimbo Jones's body stiffen as he accelerates the Model A. She lets fall her head onto his shoulder and later into his lap and there finally sleeps. When he awakens her hours later to ask her if they can stop over at the family home-site still a few hours and a lifetime west of Ft. Worth, he assures Chippy, "The stop will be for only a bit, girlie. Freshen, stretch my legs." It is then likely because she feels tired and kind of queer that Chippy fails to note the curtness in his tone as she agrees this to be a sage thought and gives him the directions down the dirt path that crosses cotton fields then pastureland toward the giant juniper trees forever marking the home-site against the horizon. Chippy's daddy claims always the junipers guide him home from running after rodeos. "Your daddy might be waiting for us there—no need for the city then," Jimbo Jones almost whispers into the wind, flying past the Model A.

It is not until he stops the car and gets out from behind the wheel, himself still drinking deeply from a second bottle of gin that finally and too late Chippy realizes his anger. He moves around to her side in what she will remember as three strides, opens the door, and drags her by her wrists into the dirt. The blanket also drags a moment behind her, having caught on her legs, then falls discarded into the dust beside the Model A. At first, Chippy is too stunned to react and allows herself to be pulled along, legs scratching, splayed, along the rough ground. But the shock of the ground's friction causes her to instinctively struggle to right herself, grab a footing. Jimbo Jones yanks her arms hard and Chippy fears a long moment that her arm has been knocked out of its socket; but he continues dragging her, yanking her up to fling her legs out each time she begins to gain some footing. He gets her toward the house and there in a patch of grass Jimbo Jones thrusts Chippy to the ground, this time pinning her under him by sitting on her hips.

Chippy feels her spine flatten into dead native grass as Jimbo Jones takes both wrists into his left hand above her head. His face leans into hers. She smells the soured gin of hatred on his breath as he spits into her face. "You are a whore after all, like I figured you might prove." He fumbles with the buttons of his trousers before ripping off the light cotton tack pants Chippy wears, shoving up the shift. Later, she will wonder why she failed to redress herself when she got back to the car earlier, while still under the stand of cottonwoods, off the Canadian River. Fancy whores in Cowtown would never ride in a Model A with the top down in nothing but a cotton shift and some tack pants, Chippy berates herself for years after.

Chippy does not go limp to stop him, anger and shame will not permit it, and the coldness that comes over her countenance shields her face and steels Jimbo Jones's attitude as he holds her down firm and hard—and moves even harder into her, against her. Chippy becomes a stone finally, focusing not on his angry grunts and soured breathing inches from her face but on the early morning sky. She allows the blue to take her in for just a moment as only Jimbo Jones's noises begin to be real and she ceases to feel the constantly increasing movements of his body inside of hers, his hands holding her wrists, her backbone, in an attempt to bring her body to life for his.

Chippy begins to think over and over, do not let him scar your face, do not let him scar your face, over and over to the thrusts of his body. Chippy fixates on this mantra to get her through. She sees too many whores with scarred faces and bodies—women she imagines to have been lovely at one time only to lose it at the hands of men like Jimbo Jones. Chippy turns her face from the sky, tastes dirt from the ground, feels it in her eyes, breathes it into her lungs and continues, do not let him scar your face. Chippy passes through Jimbo Jones's heft upon her, floats high toward Ft. Worth.

After Jimbo Jones finishes, he lies still on top of Chippy, still pinning her down with dead weight. Chippy listens to his breathing slow until Jimbo Jones begins to snore, becoming heavier in his sleep. Chippy tries to take one deep breath and cannot. She fears she will suffocate under his weight, and this is the last thing she thinks before herself passing out.

* * *

264

Chippy is unsure how long she is out; but she wakes to the sun shining bright and warm on her face, despite the fall weather, making the space behind her closed eyelids a sickening greenish-yellow, forcing her eyes to open. For a moment, she does not quite know where she is but knows somehow it is late afternoon. Chippy contemplates the swaying tops of the juniper trees high against the sky. The creaking of their limbs soothes Chippy as she feels the memory of the previous day and night creep back into her consciousness and remembers these are her junipers. The home-site.

"Jimbo," Chippy whispers at first, then louder, "Jimbo Jones—you there?"

Only the juniper limbs answer. This proves no surprise to Chippy, and she attempts to sit up, survey the damage to her body by stretching gingerly against the ground. She winces quickly as each muscle contracts against her movements. Chippy sees her bag, and even a tiny red something—as small as a trumpet flower—discarded beside it. Chippy blinks and squints in hopes it is her hair stick—that, in his shame and anger, Jimbo Jones will crave no remembrance of Chippy. Turning her head slightly, Chippy gazes at the ground to the north, shielding her eyes against the sun. Ruts from Jimbo Jones's tires cross the plane where, in her childhood memory from years before, the vulture disappears with no trace, coming and going, leaving Chippy to sigh and wonder, to lie back again, give in to her fate, remain inert, still—wait to be carried off by her own kind in the night, as so much carrion.

Hard Times
Ron Rash

Jacob stood in the barn mouth and watched Edna leave the hen-house. Her lips were pressed tight, which meant more eggs had been taken. He looked up at the ridgetop and guessed 8 a.m. In Boone it'd be full morning now, but here light was still splotchy and dew damped his brogans. This cove's so damn dark a man about has to break light with a crowbar, his daddy used to say.

Edna nodded at the egg pail in her hand.

"Nothing under the bantam," Edna said. "That's four days in a row."

"Maybe that old rooster ain't sweet on her no more," Jacob said. He waited for her to smile. When they'd first started sparking years ago, Edna's smile had been what most entranced him. Her whole face would glow, as if the upward turn of her lips spread a wave of light from mouth to forehead.

"Go ahead and make a joke," she said, "but little cash money as we got it makes a difference. Maybe the difference of whether you have a nickel to waste on a newspaper."

"There's many folks worse off," Jacob said. "Just look up the cove and you'll see the truth of that."

"We can end up like Hartley yet," Edna replied. She looked past Jacob to where the road ended and the skid trail left by the logging company began. "It's probably his mangy hound that's stealing our eggs. That dog's got the look of a egg-sucker. It's always skulking around here."

"You don't know that. I still think a dog would leave some egg on the straw. I've never seen one that didn't."

"What else would take just a few eggs at a time? You said your ownself a fox or weasel would have killed the chickens."

"I'll go look," Jacob said, knowing Edna would fret over the lost eggs all day. He knew if every hen laid three eggs a night for the next month, it

267

wouldn't matter. She'd still perceive a debit that would never be made up. Jacob tried to be generous, remembered that Edna hadn't always been this way. Not until the bank had taken the truck and most of the livestock. They hadn't lost everything the way others had, but they'd lost enough. Edna always seemed fearful when she heard a vehicle coming up the dirt road, as if the banker and sheriff were coming to take the rest.

Edna carried the eggs to the springhouse as Jacob crossed the yard and entered the concrete henhouse. The smell of manure thickened the air. Though the rooster was already outside, the hens clucked dimly in their nesting boxes. Jacob lifted the bantam and set it on the floor. The nesting box's straw had no shell crumbs, no albumen or yellow yolk slobber.

He knew it could be a two-legged varmint; but hard as times were, Jacob had never known anyone in Goshen Cove to steal, especially Hartley, the poorest of them all. Besides, who would take only two or three eggs when there were two dozen more to be had? The bantam's eggs at that, which were smaller than the ones under the Rhode Island Reds and leghorns. From the barn, Jacob heard the Guernsey lowing insistently. He knew she already waited beside the milk stool.

As Jacob came out of the henhouse he saw the Hartleys coming down the skid trail. They made the two-mile trek to Boone twice a week, each, even the child, burdened down with galax leaves. Jacob watched as they stepped onto the road, puffs of gray dust rising around their bare feet. Hartley carried four burlap pokes stuffed with galax. His wife carried two and the child one. With their ragged clothes hanging loose on bony frames, they looked like scarecrows en route to another cornfield, their possessions in tow. The hound trailed them, gaunt as the people it followed. The galax leaves were the closest thing to a crop Hartley could muster, for his land was all rock and slant. You couldn't grow a toenail on Hartley's land, Bascombe Lindsey had once said. That hadn't been a problem as long as the sawmill was running; but when it shut down, the Hartleys had only one old swaybacked milk cow to sustain them, that and the galax, which earned a few nickels of barter at Mast's General Store. Jacob knew from the Sunday newspapers he bought that times were rough everywhere. Rich folks in New York had lost all their money and jumped out of buildings. Men rode boxcars town to town begging for work. But it was hard to believe any of them had less than Hartley and his family.

When Hartley saw Jacob, he nodded but did not slow his pace. They were neither friends nor enemies, neighbors only in the sense that Jacob and Edna were the closest folks down the cove, though *closest* meant a half mile. Hartley had come up from Swain County eight years ago to work at the sawmill. The child had been a baby then, the wife seemingly decades younger than the cronish woman who walked beside the daughter. They would have passed without further acknowledgment except Edna came out on the porch.

"That hound of yours," she said to Hartley, "is it a egg-sucker?" Maybe she wasn't trying to be accusatory, but the words sounded so.

Hartley stopped in the road and turned toward the porch. Another man would have set the pokes down, but Hartley did not. He held them as if calculating their heft. "What's the why of you asking that?" The words were spoken in a tone that was neither angry nor defensive. It struck Jacob that even the man's voice had been worn down to a bare-boned flatness.

"Something's got in our henhouse and stole some," Edna said. "Just the eggs, so it ain't a fox nor weasel."

"So you reckon my dog."

Edna did not speak, and Hartley set the pokes down. He pulled a barlow knife from his tattered overalls. He softly called the hound and it sidled up to him. Hartley got down on one knee, closed his left hand on the scruff of the dog's neck as he settled the blade against its throat. The daughter and wife stood perfectly still, their faces blank as bread dough.

"I don't think it's your dog that's stealing the eggs," Jacob said.

"But you don't know for sure. It could be," Hartley said, the hound raising its head as Hartley's index finger rubbed the base of its skull.

Before Jacob could reply, the blade whisked across the hound's windpipe. The dog didn't cry out or snarl. It merely sagged in Hartley's grip. Blood darkened the road.

"You'll know for sure now," Hartley said as he stood up. He lifted the dog by the scruff of the neck, walked over to the other side of the road and laid it in the weeds. "I'll get it on the way back this evening," he said, and picked up the pokes. Hartley began walking and his wife and daughter followed.

"Why'd you have to say something to him?" Jacob asked when the family had disappeared down the road. He stared at the place in the weeds where flies and yellow jackets began to gather.

"How'd I know he'd do such a thing?" Edna asked.

269

"You know how proud a man he is."

Jacob let those words linger. In January when two feet of snow had shut nearly everyone in, Jacob had gone up the skid trail on horseback, a salted pork shoulder strapped to the saddle. "We could be needing that meat soon enough ourselves," Edna had said, but he'd gone anyway. When Jacob got to the cabin, he'd found the family at the plank table eating. The wooden bowls before them held a thick liquid lumped with a few crumbs of fatback. The milk pail hanging over the fire was filled with the same gray-colored gruel. Jacob had set the pork shoulder on the table. The meat had a deep wood-smoke odor, and the woman and child swallowed every few seconds to conceal their salivating. "I ain't got no money to buy it," Hartley said. "So I'd appreciate you taking your meat and leaving." Jacob had left, but after closing the cabin door he'd laid the pork on the front stoop. The next morning Jacob had found the meat on his own doorstep.

Jacob gazed past Hartley's dog, across the road to the acre of corn where he'd work till suppertime. He hadn't hoed a single row yet but already felt tired all the way to his bones.

"I didn't want that dog killed," Edna said. "That wasn't my intending."

"Like it wasn't your intending for Joel and Mary to leave and never darken our door again," Jacob replied. "But it happened, didn't it?"

He turned and walked to the woodshed to get his hoe.

* * *

The next morning the dog was gone from the roadside and more eggs were missing. It was Saturday, so Jacob rode the horse down to Boone, not just to get his newspaper but to talk to the older farmers who gathered at Mast's General Store. As he rode he remembered the morning six years ago when Joel dropped his bowl of oatmeal on the floor. Careless, but twelve-year-olds did careless things. It was part of being a child. Edna made the boy eat the oatmeal off the floor with his spoon. "Don't do it," Mary had told her younger brother; but he had, whimpering the whole time. Mary, who was sixteen, eloped two weeks later. "I'll never come back, not even to visit," a note left on the kitchen table said. Mary had been true to her word.

As Jacob rode into Boone, he saw the truck the savings and loan had repossessed from him parked by the courthouse. It was a vehicle made for hauling crops to town, bringing back salt blocks and fertilizer and barbed wire, but he'd figured no farmer could have afforded to buy it at auction. Maybe a store owner or county employee, he supposed, someone who still used a billfold instead of a change purse like the one he now took a nickel from after tying his horse to the hitching post. Jacob entered the store. He nodded at the older men, then laid his coin on the counter. Erwin Mast handed him last Sunday's *Raleigh News*.

"Don't reckon there's any letters?" Jacob asked.

"No, nothing this week," Erwin said, though he could have added, "or the last month or last year." Joel was in the navy stationed somewhere in the Pacific. Mary lived with her husband and her own child on a farm in Haywood County, sixty miles away, but it could have been California for all the contact Jacob and Edna had with her.

Jacob lingered by the counter. When the old men paused in their conversation, he told them about the eggs.

"And you're sure it ain't a dog?" Sterling Watts asked.

"Yes. There wasn't a bit of splatter or shell on the straw."

"Rats will eat a egg," Erwin offered from behind the counter.

"There'd still be something left, though," Bascombe Lindsey said.

"They's but one thing it can be," Sterling Watts said with finality.

"What's that?" Jacob asked.

"A big yaller rat snake. They'll swallow two or three eggs whole and leave not a dribble of egg."

"I've heard such myself," Bascombe agreed. "Never seen it but heard of it."

"Well, one got in my henhouse," Sterling said. "And it took me near a month to figure out how to catch the damn thing."

"How did you?" Jacob asked.

"Went fishing," Sterling said.

* * *

That night Jacob hoed in his cornfield till dark. He ate his supper, then went to the woodshed and found a fishhook. He tied three yards of line to it and went to the henhouse. The bantam had one egg under her. Jacob took the egg and made as small a hole as possible with the barb. He slowly worked the whole hook into the egg, then tied the line to a nail head behind the nesting box. Three yards, Watson had said. That way the snake would swallow the whole egg before a tight line set the hook.

"I ain't about to go out there come morning and deal with no snake," Edna said when he told her what he'd done. She sat in the ladderback rocking chair, her legs draped by a quilt. He'd made the chair for her to sit in when she'd been pregnant with Joel. The wood was cherry, not the most practical for furniture, but he'd wanted it to be pretty.

"I'll deal with it," Jacob said.

For a few moments he watched her sew, the fine blue thread repairing the binding of the Bear's Claw quilt. Edna had worked since dawn, but she couldn't stop even now. Jacob sat down at the kitchen table and spread out the newspaper. On the front page Roosevelt said things were getting better, but the rest of the news argued otherwise. Strikers had been shot at a cotton mill. Men whose crime was hiding in boxcars to search for work had been beaten with clubs by lawmen and hired railroad goons.

"What you claimed this morning about me running off Joel and Mary," Edna said, her needle not pausing as she spoke, "that was a spiteful thing to say. Those kids never went hungry a day in their lives. Their clothes was patched and they had shoes and coats."

He knew he should let it go, but the image of Hartley's knife opening the hound's throat had snared in his mind.

"You could have been easier on them."

"The world's a hard place," Edna replied. "There was need for them to know that."

"They'd have learned soon enough on their own," Jacob said.

"They needed to be prepared, and I prepared them. They ain't in a hobo camp or barefoot like Hartley and his clan. If they can't be grateful for that, there's nothing I can do about it now."

"There's going to be better times," Jacob said. "This depression can't last forever, but the way you treated them will."

"It's lasted nine years," Edna said. "And I see no sign of it letting up. The price we're getting for corn and cabbage is the same. We're still living on half of what we did before."

She turned back to the quilt's worn binding and no other words were spoken between them. After a while Edna put down her sewing and went to bed. Jacob soon followed. Edna tensed as he settled his body beside hers.

"I don't want us to argue," Jacob said, and laid his hand on her shoulder. She flinched from his touch, moved farther away.

"You think I've got no feelings," Edna said, her face turned so she spoke at the wall. "Stingy and mean-hearted. But maybe if I hadn't been, we'd not have anything left."

Despite his weariness, Jacob had trouble going to sleep. When he finally did, he dreamed of men hanging onto boxcars while other men beat them with sticks. Those beaten wore muddy brogans and overalls, and he knew they weren't laid-off mill workers or coal miners but farmers like himself.

Jacob woke in the dark. The window was open and before he could fall back asleep, he heard something from inside the henhouse. He pulled on his overalls and boots, then went out on the porch and lit a lantern. The sky was thick with stars and a wet moon lightened the ground, but the windowless henhouse was pitch dark. It had crossed his mind that if a yellow rat snake could eat an egg, a copperhead or satinback could as well, and he wanted to see where he stepped. He went to the woodshed and got a hoe for the killing.

Jacob crossed the foot log and stepped up to the entrance. He held the lantern out and checked the nesting box. The bantam was in it, but no eggs lay under her. It took him a few moments to find the fishing line, leading toward the back corner like a single strand of a spider's web. He readied the hoe in his hand and took a step inside. He held the lamp before him and saw Hartley's daughter huddled in the corner, the line disappearing into her closed mouth.

She did not try to speak as he knelt before her. Jacob set the hoe and lantern down and took out his pocketknife, then cut the line inches above where it disappeared between her lips. For a few moments he did nothing else.

"Let me see," he said, and though she did not open her mouth, she did not resist as his fingers did so. He found the hook's barb sunk deep in her cheek and was relieved. He'd feared it would be in her tongue or, much worse, deep in her throat.

"We got to get that hook out," Jacob told her, but still she said nothing. Her eyes did not widen in fear and he wondered if maybe she was in shock. The barb was too deep to wiggle free. He'd have to push it the rest of the way through.

"This is going to hurt, but just for a second," he said, and let his index finger and thumb grip the hook where it began to curve. He worked deeper into the skin, his thumb and finger slickened by blood and saliva. The child whimpered. Finally the barb broke through. He wiggled the shank out, the line coming last like thread completing a stitch.

"It's out now," he told her.

For a few moments Jacob did not get up. He thought about what to do next. He could carry her back to Hartley's shack and explain what happened, but he remembered the dog. He looked at her cheek and there was no tear, only a tiny hole that bled little more than a briar scratch would. He studied the hook for signs of rust. There didn't seem to be, so at least he didn't have to worry about the girl getting lockjaw. But it could still get infected.

"Stay here," Jacob said and went to the woodshed. He found the bottle of turpentine and returned. He took his handkerchief and soaked it, then opened the child's mouth and dabbed the wound, and did the same outside to the cheek.

"Okay," Jacob said. He reached out his hands and placed them under her armpits. She was so light it was like lifting a rag doll. The child stood before him now, and for the first time he saw that her right hand held something. He picked up the lantern and saw it was an egg and that it was unbroken. Jacob nodded at the egg.

"You don't ever take them home, do you?" he asked. "You eat them here, right?"

The child nodded.

"Go ahead and eat it then," Jacob said, "but you can't come back anymore. If you do, your daddy will know about it. You understand?"

"Yes," she whispered, the first word she'd spoken.

"Eat it, then."

The girl raised the egg to her lips. A thin line of blood trickled down her chin as she opened her mouth. The shell crackled as her teeth bit down.

"Go home now," he said when she'd swallowed the last bit of shell. "And don't come back. I'm going to put another hook in them eggs and this time there won't be no line on it. You'll swallow that hook and it'll tear your guts up."

Jacob watched her walk up the skid trail until the dark enveloped her, then sat on the stump that served as a chopping block. He blew out the lantern and waited, though for what he could not say. After a while the moon and stars faded. In the east, darkness lightened to the color of indigo glass. The first outlines of the corn stalks and their leaves were visible now, reaching up from the ground like shabbily dressed arms.

Jacob picked up the lantern and turpentine and went to the shed, then on to the house. Edna was getting dressed as he came into the bedroom. Her back was to him.

"It was a snake," he said.

Edna paused in her dressing and turned. Her hair was down and her face not yet hardened to face the day's demands and he glimpsed the younger, softer woman she'd been twenty years ago when they'd married.

"You kill it?" she asked.

"Yes."

Her lips tightened.

"I hope you didn't just throw it out by the henhouse. I don't want to smell that thing rotting when I'm gathering eggs."

"I threw it across the road."

He got in the bed. Edna's form and warmth lingered on the feather mattress.

"I'll get up in a few minutes," he told her.

Jacob closed his eyes but did not sleep. Instead, he imagined towns where hungry men hung on boxcars looking for work that couldn't be found, shacks where families lived who didn't even have one swaybacked milk cow. He imagined cities where blood stained the sidewalks beneath buildings tall as ridges. He tried to imagine a place worse than where he was.

Rev. Richards's Confession
James Hoggard

There is one point I need to get to you, one thing I need to tell you in terms of background, and that is: I don't usually read fiction; but my brother does, and I remember him telling me as he handed me a book, "Here, and when you're finished, give it back." He sounded almost rude, but that didn't surprise me.

Fact, what really surprised me is that the story he marked for me to read turned out to be maybe the truest tale I've ever heard—and I still feel that way, though there continue to be things in it I don't understand. The story even took me to some places where Jesus went. And I don't mean geographical sites. I'm talking about portions of the mind and heart, and I wasn't counting on that, certainly not in a piece of fiction set here in our own country instead of far away and long ago. And because the characters were so poor and odd, it's likely a lot of people would assume they didn't amount to much, certainly not enough to give good advice.

Although they were living through the Great Depression, I saw pretty quickly they had a lot to do with things like our own situations. And some of the several people in the story were so bad off they were getting close to having nothing to eat.

So as I was getting ready to say, Exle and his wife Eula Fae in the story were good Christian folks, but they had come on hard times and were getting ready to be truly hungry. And Exle's pale blue eyes, forlorn looking as they were, and the way his back humped a bit, too, made him look like a ghost. You could tell he might drop down sick any day. But this next was likely as important: There didn't seem to be anyone around who'd heard or seen Exle's tractor fired up in nobody knew when. And not only that, somebody or some creature was getting all the eggs their hens were laying. I have to emphasize, too, that their minister hadn't seen Exle or Eula Fae at church either, not in a long time. Fact, you'd have thought, with their worsening situation, the church would be where they all would be, where we would be come a Sunday. But that wasn't true, no more than it is now. Look at how few of us are here today, troubled as all of us are.

Fact, I got to thinking how many people—here and all over—were and are chronically absent from church. I was also getting the idea that ever'body's kids had fallen away. Most of them had moved off elsewhere and must've gone into bad straits themselves. From what I kept picking up, the children didn't seem to want to get involved in helping their relations, their parents and others who were having hard times. They didn't talk, they didn't visit, and they didn't write, sometimes not even on big holidays.

I couldn't quit thinking about all this, and about Exle and Eula Fae's place in it, but not just because of all the snake stories Exle was telling. Fact, to my hearing, he got obsessed with snakes, ever' bit as much as some Pentecostal holiness types a few roads away, here near our own place.

And what Exle was saying in his snake stories was awful—foretellings of disaster. It got so, he said, he wouldn't enter the henhouse at night anymore, or go anywhere else that tended toward dark, and the result of the horror the country was living in, then and now too, played into his notion of disaster, which placed rattlesnakes and copperheads in henhouses and homes, even though they hadn't gone in there to suck and steal eggs. Vipers, Exle said, weren't partial to eggs—or homes either, though I never figured how he knew that. But the snakes were in there and that was the point, though nobody, it seemed, knew what the point meant. Fact, Exle never had liked to go anywhere at night, which seemed to corrupt his point about things. I began thinking, too, that all this was connected with a lot of my own flock staying away from church, as if they were trimming away points of painful concern. But I don't condemn them for it, I really don't. Fact, I have to say this: Even the land had been blown away, just flatter'n I don't know what. But the people were tough, scorcht as their place was—and this one, too. One time, for example, an outsider came—all this in the story—and commented on the land's flatness to some old lady in the area, and the old lady said, "I know. That's what I like about it. They ain't anything to interrupt the scenery."

At the church over near Tutwiler's Gap, however, the people appeared to be doing fine, though they were likely short on vittles themselves, even though the story didn't say so. Their good fortune, though, and big crowds at Sunday church didn't come from their own enterprise but from the preacher there bringing out snakes with some degree of regularity and jumping around with a choke hold on them, as if he had the St. Vitus Dance or a knot in his shorts, and the folks there were too dumb to know that all they were being faithful to was a pitiful level of show business. And I have to say, too, we have our own Tutwiler's Gap close by—and what I think that means is that snakes can mean a lot of different things. That's why there's a call to rejoice in folks here when we get the news that a serpent's more than nicked a preacher somewhere, like at that place in the story near what's called Tutwiler's Gap, which actually might refer to some preacher's teeth as much as anything else. And I'll confess that when I was reading the piece, the joy in my heart stirred when news came that a fang had gone deep in an arm or neck and pumped out poison into that hypocritical, ignernt flesh. I say that not because I'm a bitter man or a better man than anyone else, I'm not. I just don't like preachers—or anyone else—pretending to be holy when all they're doing is pressing flesh and passing gas.

I understand, too, that what that story had in mind was not just observations about Exle and his wife, but all of us. So what I began to see was I hadn't realized fiction stories could do all this, though I should have, the Bible itself being full of stories when you think about it. So Exle and his wife were markers, signposts to point out our own bad habits. And thinking about that now, let's draw closer to the story, the one my brother gave me to read but wouldn't tell me what it was about or why he thought I ought to read it. But I had no choice. It was as if all this was fore-ordained. I couldn't stop reading because I couldn't quit thinking about Exle and his wife and how no one was talking or visiting or writing each other. No one was keeping up—that's what I mean: No one was keeping up, not keeping up at all.

Still, faithful as an angel, Exle's wife kept checking on the chickens. Fact, she went to check on them daily, but to no avail. And she had no help. Exle had given up checking on them a long time back. He told his wife, too, she was wasting her time trying to find something that wasn't there. That sound familiar? You ever been there yourself—where you're just mumble-mouthing back, like all you here?

"Amen."

I can't hear you. Speak louder, flock.

"Amen!"

Good. Then I saw how Exle's wife persisted and flat out told her husband she was going to keep on doing what she was bound to do. "And I don't care what it costs," she said, "I'm going to be faithful to my responsibilities, so just hush."

But he wouldn't budge. He said it could be anything swallerin' the eggs: certain kinds of snakes. There was even one called a chicken snake, and he had seen one of those himself, the sucker about eight feet long with a dark red back and a kind of creamy, silver-colored diamond design all down the top of that long red body. Then again Exle said it could be a skunk or a fox or some kind of wandering human thief. Likely, though, he told her, it's not a rattler or a copperhead; but if they are in there—which they might well be—just mark my word: It's not because of the eggs, it's because in their mind something needs to get fanged. That's why, Exle told his wife, he quit going in the henhouse at night. And his wife started trembling, so he touched her, touched her right in the middle of her back to relieve her of her grief; but all she did was stiffen and switch herself away from him as she told him, "Don't you dare touch me like that. I know what your sham of tenderness is trying to aim for, and it's not going to happen—not tonight it's not."

So in all sorts of ways these people were in hard times, and with nobody trying to help anybody either, ever' one making it harder on each other than it had been.

You ever done that?

Say it! Say it louder!

You're not speaking up.

"Amen!"

Good. That's why that flock—and our flock, too—was staying away from church. They were tangled up with their own troubles, and that means guilt. We've all had that wretched sense of failure. And I don't condemn them or you either for staying away. Fact, Jesus won't let me condemn anyone—or at least he doesn't want me to. Fact, he doesn't really get upset when I'm inclined to nick and needle folks. And I'm glad for that point of generosity, I'm grateful for the blessing.

Now if I've indicated the people in the story are different from us, I was wrong. Sure, they used to be part of a shoutin' church—and so did we—and that's fine. I even imagine there'll come a time when they—the poison-handlers—start staying away from services, too, in spite of all the entertainment those serpent deals give. And think about this: all the pleasure you'd have being in church the day the snake nailed the preacher. Enough to make you never want to miss a service. Am I right?

"Amen!"

Good. I heard you that time.

So I think we all understand what our enemies, our competitors, are doing that we aren't. And they're not all that different from us, and it's our duty to acknowledge that. Like the rest of us, they're suffering several points of depression at once: hopelessness, poverty, being suckered in by false witnesses, and there's no let-up in sight. All of us might be going down in ruin, but I have some special grief. I confess I do. My preaching and my public prayer life are not getting through, so much sometimes I think I ought to give up, but I'm not—not yet—and I'll even face the fact that those who show up at Sunday church sometimes probably ought to have stayed home. I say that because those who do come are mostly sick—coughing and wheezing and hacking up little but being loud about it, so nobody can hear what I'm saying—or whoever's preaching, not that what I'm saying makes any difference about the state of your flesh or mine. We're all in a freefall toward ruin.

I feel for my sheep, and so does God, but they're sick and they're dying and they're in despair—except for those inbreeding idiots over near Tutwiler's Gap. So in my church, in our church, we'll have no snakes, and soon all of us will have likely eaten our last egg. But we'll bring no snakes into our midst. After all, being a Christian—or more accurately, becoming Christian—does not demand that we be squealing idiots.

I've been tried myself, just as my sheep have. I've been in the deep valleys, those valleys that turn death into deep shadows, and four years ago, as most all of you know, I found myself down in the pit when I lost my wife, when she passed. I thought I never would rise out of my despair, and I'm not sure I have. But I also know some of you were—and still are—down in that pit with me. And I call each one of you a comfort because when I was down, you put your arms around me. I'm also talking about Exle and Eula Fae who you don't really know yet. They're still living in a story. They're like people who are struggling, like people who haven't been with us for weeks, maybe months. Are they dead? No. They're struggling, but their eggs keep disappearing, and no one knows what's causing that: one more staple gone, one more source of income lost.

But after reading about them, Exle and Eula Fae, and the despair they were fighting, I realized I knew their struggles, and if anyone says all their despair means is that they're separated from God and are wretched sinners not worth agonizing over, I'll rise up out of my own pit, and take up a bat, and smite the thighs and foreheads of anyone condemning them.

"Amen!"

And now I'll take us to the end of the story, the continuing trial of our brothers and sisters, for one day on their walk to and from town, Exle met his neighbor Murray Chism, and passing a few moments of idleness—Chism with his wife and dog and daughter Janie there—Exle said to Murray he sometimes wondered if it was possible that his dog—Murray's—got out now and then and ate those just-laid eggs that had been disappearing. Murray said that didn't happen—his dog never gets out or goes loose—and Exle said he appreciated that because it showed Christian goodness, even though Exle said he still worried about the dog, not that he blamed the beast, mind you. Fact, he said he'd never really blame the dog because liking eggs might just be his nature.

A day or so later Exle met the Chisms again, and again they talked about this and that till Murray said it's a rotten, unearned shame when your neighbors think wrong of you. And keeping his eyes on Exle, Murray reached in his pants pocket and pulled out his big Case knife, then levering it open, he turned his eyes on his dog, as if to say something, then yanking the dog's head against his leg, he slid the blade through the side part of the animal's neck. No yelp at all came into hearing. The dog just collapsed, the strength in his legs disappearing as the blood pulsed out. Then Murray and his wife and their daughter walked away, Murray saying, "We'll be back to get him this evening when we're finished with town and heading back home."

Exle was staring straight ahead, shocked. He didn't know what to say.

Several days later Exle took a notion that he had to find out what had been happening to the eggs. It was a job he had to finish. That's what I'm telling you. You understand? He had a job he needed to finish. And I do, too.

Then that same evening, around twilight, because a distance had risen between Exle and Eula Fae, Exle he got up and left the house, saying he was going to check on the chickens.

Several days later, he again felt an odd sense of mission that took him back to the henhouse. But this time he found an egg—just one—beneath a laying hen. The spell, he thought, had been broken. But that didn't satisfy him. It wasn't enough to find a single egg. He had to find the thief, and he realized there was only one way to do it.

So he took out his pocket knife and worked a small hole through one end of the egg, then he sucked out the yolk and the white and spat that out. He then reached in his shirt pocket and pulled out a substantial length of white thread that he had secreted there. Then he reached up and pulled a fishhook off a low-set beam. Others were there with it. He pushed the lip-moistened thread's end through the eyelet of the hook and tied it tight.

Taking several deep breaths to calm himself, he tried to relax but found himself fighting to keep his hands steady as he curled the hook carefully through the tiny hole he had drilled in the eggshell. Now all he had to do was to set the shell carefully where the hen had been, and he did that.

Still later that evening, after Eula Fae had turned the radio off, Exle went back to the henhouse; but the eggshell was gone, and he started shaking, he was so nervous. The thief had to be in there with him, but what was it? Then glancing down at the thread, he saw it moving. Then he heard something he couldn't identify, and that frightened him even more.

Slowly he went toward the corner where the thread led, where he thought the sound had originated. Needing light, he struck a match, and cowering before him was Janie Chism, her eyes full of fright and her hand over her mouth. As much for self-support as for kindness, he squeezed her free hand to try to let her know he meant her no harm. But thinking that made him feel like a coward and a hypocrite. He was the one who had caused her disaster. He was the snake.

As slowly now, and as gently as possible, he worked his finger inside her mouth then asked her to open up wider—"Just a bit more," he said. He struck another match to see how deeply the hook had lodged. "Thank heavens," he muttered, "she didn't swallow it," but he still kept shaking. The hook had snagged in her cheek, but too deeply for him to pull it free from inside her mouth. He struck another match, and this time he saw the girl was trying to stay still but couldn't. And it frightened him to know he would have to work the hook out himself. He didn't dare take her to a doctor, or to anyone else, not after what he had done. So all this would have to stay a secret, but that was impossible because of the wound. He would have to dig and twist a hole through her cheek, and he would have to do that by feel, the light was so bad.

When he told the girl what he had to do, she started crying again, but he didn't know what to do about it.

What he needed was a constant light, but he didn't have one. Then he found himself reaching up on a shelf and pulling down the kerosene lantern he and Eula Fae kept out there. But when he lit it, all he could see was Janie Chism begging him with her eyes not to hurt her for stealing his eggs. This lantern he was holding was useless. There was no way to stop its light from flickering and blurring his vision. Then a sound came out of her mouth that sounded as if she was trying to say *please*.

"Don't worry," he told her. "Those eggs aren't important. You're going to be fine. Just try to ride the pain on out."

Closing her eyes, she started convulsing; but he caught her and managed to steady her as he grabbed a box and set her down on it; but that messed up his light even more.

Somehow, though, he finally succeeded. He worked the hook all the way through her cheek and then out, the bloody white thread passing through her face now like a blessing.

But this next is what really turned me on my head. Old Exle never told his wife what he had done, though, of course, like all the others, she found out. Fact, he lied to her. He told her there had been one of those chicken snakes in the coop, but he had killed it with a shovel then buried it so it wouldn't stink up their place.

There for a moment you'd have thought he was expecting to be honored for what he had done. But his sense of good fortune didn't last. He was now being plagued by the fact that he now understood deeply there could be no secret. The moment her parents—or anyone—saw her, they would know what had happened. Everyone else would know, too, and the law would know.

There would be no place for him to hide what he had done.

Fact, what I'm saying here is what the story says when it stops: There is no escape, and there will be no hiding. Our sins will be revealed, yours and mine. Especially mine. But maybe we all feel that way. And I don't want to say this; but I have to, because, my brothers and sisters—there are only a few of you left—and I've been thinking I really ought to leave my ministry. I've been such a failure—the flock, the charge I'm to tend to, dwindling. Even the numbers of the shoutin' and dancin' snake folk are beginning to dwindle, too. There's shriveling everywhere.

But telling me the truth, bringing the truth to me in its own odd way, that story my brother lent me might be bringing me home. And confused as I am, I know, too, I can't up and leave. I can't just turn around and renounce my calling, failure that I am. For as long as a couple or three of us are gathered, God will be among us. And though it's not happening now, maybe someday a light will shine on us. But till it does, we'll keep on singing, we'll try to keep singing, weak-voiced and off-note as we're sure to be.

So now as we prepare for the benediction, let us turn to the last page of our hymnal where, pasted in place, we have "The Church in the Valley of the Wildwood, the Church in the Valley of the Dale." And as we sing, let us pay attention to the words and try, my brothers and sisters, try to let those words bring us on home.

Contributors

Texas Writers

Jerry Bradley is Professor of English at Lamar University. He is the author of five books including *The Movement: British Poets of the 1950s; The Importance of Elsewhere*; and *Simple Versions of Disaster*, which was commended by the *Dictionary of Literary Biography*. A member of the Texas Institute of Letters, Bradley is the author of more than one hundred fifty published stories and poems and has published more than thirty critical articles and eighty reviews; he has received more than forty grants in support of his literary activities, including grants from the National Endowment for the Arts, the Witter Bynner Poetry Foundation, and the New Mexico Arts Division. His work has appeared in many literary magazines including *New England Review, American Literary Review, Modern Poetry Studies, Poetry Magazine,* and *Southern Humanities Review*. He was the featured poet in the February, 2011, issue of *Red River Review*. Bradley is currently poetry editor of *Concho River Review*; he founded and edited for sixteen years *New Mexico Humanities Review*. Website: www.jerrybradley.net.

Oscar Casares was born and raised in the border town of Brownsville, Texas. He is the author of two books, a collection of stories and a novel, which have earned him fellowships from the National Endowment for the Arts, the Copernicus Society of America, and the Texas Institute of Letters. His collection of stories, *Brownsville*, was selected by the American Library Association as a Notable Book of 2004 and earned critical praise from such publications as *The New York Times, Washington Post, San Francisco Chronicle,* and *Entertainment Weekly*. His first novel,

Amigoland, received a "starred review" from *Publishers Weekly* and was selected by the 2010 Mayor's Book Club in Austin for that year's citywide reading campaign. Since 2003, his essays have appeared in *The New York Times, Texas Monthly,* and on "All Things Considered" for National Public Radio. A graduate of the Iowa Writers' Workshop, he now teaches creative writing at the University of Texas and directs the New Writers Project, a Master of Fine Arts Program in English. He lives in Austin with his wife and two young children. Website: http://www.oscarcasares.com/.

Terry Dalrymple's books are *Fishing for Trouble,* a novel for middle readers, and the collection *Salvation and Other Stories;* he recently edited *Texas Soundtrack: Texas Stories Inspired by Texas Songs.* He is the founding editor of the literary journal *Concho River Review,* and his short stories and essays have appeared in a variety of journals and magazines. A member of the Texas Institute of Letters, he currently teaches English at Angelo State University. Website: http://www.angelo.edu/dept/english_modern_languages/faculty/dalrymple_terry.php.

Robert Flynn, professor emeritus at Trinity University and a native of Chillicothe, Texas, is the author of thirteen books: ten novels, two story collections, and a collection of essays. His dramatic adaptation of Faulkner's *As I Lay Dying* was the United States entry at the Theater of Nations in Paris in 1964 and won a Special Jury Award. He is also the author of a two-part documentary, *A Cowboy Legacy,* shown on ABC-TV. Flynn's work has received awards from the Texas Institute of Letters, the National Cowboy Hall of Fame, the Texas Literary Festival, and the Western Writers of America. A member of the Texas Institute of Letters, he received its Distinguished Achievement Award in 1998. Website: http://www.robert-flynn.net/.

James Hoggard is the author of more than twenty books, including six collections of translations, five of them of collections of poems by Oscar Hahn; he has published six collections of his own poems, as well as two collections of stories, two novels, and a volume of nonfiction. The winner of numerous awards, including an NEA Creative Writing Fellowship and the Soeurette Diehl Fraser Award for Literary Translation, he was named Poet Laureate of Texas for 2000; he has served as President of the Texas

Institute of Letters, of which he was recently named a Fellow. He currently serves as Perkins-Prothro Distinguished Professor of English at Midwestern State University in Wichita Falls, Texas.

Stephen Graham Jones, a native of West Texas, is a major figure in contemporary Native American literature, especially in its more experimental forms. He is a prolific writer, the author to date of over a dozen novels and a hundred and thirty short stories. Among his most notable titles are *The Fast Red Road, A Plainsong*, which follows the half-blood Pidgin on his quixotic quest to find the stolen body of his father; *All the Beautiful Sinners*, which traces Blackfoot lawman Jim Doe's hunt for a serial killer; and *Ledfeather*, which recounts how teenager Doby Saxon discovers a link to the past that informs the present. Jones currently teaches in the MFA program at the University of Colorado Boulder. Website: www.demontheory.net.

Dave Kuhne is recently retired as Associate Director of the William L. Adams Center for Writing at Texas Christian University, where, since, 2000, he edited *descant*, TCU's literary journal. Kuhne is the author of *The Road to Roma* and *African Settings in Contemporary American Novels*, and principal editor of *descant: Fifty Years*. He currently directs the Angelina River Press.

Laura Rebecca Payne is Associate Professor of Creative Writing at Sul Ross State University, the University of the Big Bend. Her fiction, poems, and essays have appeared in fine journals such as *Night Train, Iconoclast,* and *Iron Horse Literary Review*, and been anthologized in *New Stories from the South* and *CrossRoads*.

Clay Reynolds, native Texan novelist, essayist, scholar, and literary critic, is the author of nearly 1,000 publications ranging from scholarly studies to short fiction and poems, essays, critical reviews and a more than a dozen published volumes. A Professor of Arts and Humanities at the University of Texas at Dallas, he is Director of Creative Writing. His published books include the novels *The Vigil, Agatite, Franklin's Crossing, Players, Monuments, The Tentmaker, Ars Poetica,* and *Threading the Needle*; a collection of essays, *Of Snakes and Sex and Playing in the*

Rain; and a collection of short fiction, *Sandhill County Lines*. His nonfiction books, authored and edited, include *Stage Left: The Development of the American Social Drama, Taking Stock: A Larry McMurtry Casebook, A Hundred Years of Heroes: A Centennial History of the Southwestern Exposition and Livestock Show, Twenty Questions: Answers for the Inquiring Writer, The Plays of Jack London*, and *Hero of a Hundred Fights: The Western Dime Novels of Ned Buntline*. His novels, short fiction, and essays have won numerous awards and he is the recipient of a Spur Award for Short Fiction from the Western Writers of America; he is also a National Endowment for the Arts Fellow and is a member of the Texas Institute of Letters. Reynolds lives in Lowry Crossing, a community near McKinney, Texas, with his wife Judy.

Jim Sanderson has published two collections of short stories: *Semi-Private Rooms*, winner of the 1992 Kenneth Patchen Award, and *Faded Love*, finalist for 2010 Texas Institute of Letters' Jesse Jones Award; an essay collection: *A West Texas Soapbox*; four novels: *El Camino del Rio*, winner of the Frank Waters Award, *Safe Delivery*, finalist for Writers' League of Texas Violet Crown Award, *La Mordida, Nevin's History: A Novel of Texas*, and *Dolph's Team*; and a composition textbook written specifically for Lamar University, *Ways of Writing: A Writer's Way*. An as yet untitled novel set in Beaumont, Texas is forthcoming from TCU press in 2014. In addition, he has published over sixty short stories, essays, and scholarly articles. Sanderson currently serves as Chair of the English Department at Lamar University. Website: http://sites.google.com/site/jim2sanderson/home.

Jan Seale is the author of eight volumes of poetry, the latest being *Jan Seale: New and Selected Poems*, published by TCU Press. She has also authored two books of short fiction (*Airlift* and *Appearances*), three volumes of nonfiction, and nine children's books. Her work is published nationally in such venues as *The Yale Review, Texas Monthly*, and *Newsday*. She is the recipient of a National Endowment for the Arts Fellowship in Creative Writing and seven PEN/NEA Syndicated Fiction Awards, and two of her stories have been broadcast on National Public Radio. She is the 2012 Texas Poet Laureate. Seale teaches memoir and creative writing workshops both in the Rio Grande Valley of Texas, where she lives, and nationally for writing groups and learning centers. A resident of the Rio Grande Valley in deep South Texas all of her adult life, she spent summers in the Panhandle as a child, where it seems she unwittingly absorbed some of the unique culture of that region.

Betty Wiesepape's latest book is *Winifred Sanford: The Life and Times of a Texas Writer*. Her other book is *Lone Star Chapters*. She has published numerous articles on Texas literary history; and her short stories, book reviews, and creative nonfiction essays have appeared in many journals and anthologies. One story, "Let's Hear It for the Red Shoes" is the title story in an anthology entitled *Let's Hear It: Stories by Texas Women Writers* and was selected for presentation at the 2005 Arts & Letters Live, Texas Bound Series and the 2006 Texas Book Festival. She teaches creative writing and literature at the University of Texas at Dallas.

Carolina Writers

Elise Blackwell is the author of four novels: *Hunger, The Unnatural History of Cypress Parish, Grub*, and *An Unfinished Score*. Her work has been translated into several languages, and her books have been named to numerous "best of the year" lists, including the *Los Angeles Times* and *Kirkus*. Her short stories and cultural criticism have appeared in *Witness, Global City Review*, and elsewhere. Originally from southern Louisiana, Blackwell now directs the MFA program at the University of South Carolina in Columbia. Website: http://eliseblackwell.com.

Elizabeth Cox has published four novels—*Familiar Ground, The Ragged Way People Fall Out of Love, Night Talk*, and *The Slow Moon*—and a collection of short stories entitled *Bargains in the Real World*. A book of poems is scheduled to come out in the fall of 2013. Her novel *Night Talk* won the Lillian Smith Award given by the Southern Regional Council; her stories have been cited for excellence in both *Best American Short Stories* and Pushcart Press; she received the Robert Penn Warren Award for Fiction from the Fellowship of Southern Writers in 2011. Cox taught at Duke University and Wofford College. Website: www.elizabethcox.net.

Phillip Gardner is a three-time South Carolina Fiction Project winner and a Piccolo Spoleto Fiction Open winner. His stories have appeared in the *North American Review, New Delta Review, LIT, Interim, The Chattahoochee Review,* and others. He is the author of two short story collections: *Somebody Wants Somebody Dead* and *Someone to Crawl Back To.* His third collection, *Available Light,* is forthcoming from Bitingduck Press in 2014. He currently lives in Darlington, South Carolina and teaches at Francis Marion University. Website: http://www.phillipjgardner.com/.

Marianne Gingher has written plays, short stories (*Teen Angel and Other Stories of Wayward Love*), a novel (*Bobby Rex's Greatest Hits*), and two memoirs; she has also edited a grammar book and a flash fiction anthology. Her fiction and essays have appeared in numerous periodicals, including *The Southern Review, The Oxford American,* and *North American Review.* From 1997 to 2002, Gingher was director of the creative writing program at UNC Chapel Hill where she now holds the title of Bowman and Gordon Gray Distinguished Term Professor. Website: http://englishcomplit.unc.edu/people/gingherm.

Cecile Goding's stories, poems, and essays have appeared in a number of publications, including *The Iowa Review, Fourth Genre: Explorations in Nonfiction,* and *Inheritance: Selections from the SC Fiction Project.* She won the Theodore Roethke and Richard Hugo Prizes from *Poetry Northwest,* a fellowship from the South Carolina Academy of Authors, and a Bread Loaf Scholarship. A native of Florence, South Carolina, Goding now teaches at Mount Mercy University and the Iowa Summer Writing Festival.

Randall Kenan is the author of a novel (*A Visitation of Spirits*), a collection of stories (*Let the Dead Bury Their Dead*), and two works of nonfiction. He edited and wrote the introduction for *The Cross of Redemption: The Uncollected Writings of James Baldwin.* Among his awards are a Guggenheim Fellowship, the North Carolina Award, and the American Academy of Arts and Letters' Rome Prize. He holds the rank of Associate Professor of English and Comparative Literature at UNC Chapel Hill. Website: www.randallkenan.com.

Bret Lott is the bestselling author of thirteen books, most notably the novel *Jewel*, selected by Oprah Winfrey for her on-air book club and subsequently made into a major motion picture. His latest publication is the novel *Dead Low Tide*. Since 1986 he has taught at the College of Charleston except for a brief period from 2004 to 2007 when he held the position of editor of *The Southern Review* at Louisiana State University. His honors include serving as a Fulbright Senior American Scholar and a member of the National Council on the Arts. He and his wife, Melanie, live in Hanahan, South Carolina. Website: http://english.cofc.edu/about/faculty-staff-listing/lott-bret.php.

Jill McCorkle, a native of Lumberton, North Carolina, is the author of four short story collections and six novels, including *Life After Life*. Five of these works have been named *New York Times* Notable Books. She is also the recipient of the Dos Passos Prize for Excellence in Literature and the North Carolina Award for Literature. Her work has appeared in numerous periodicals including *The Atlantic, Ploughshares, American Scholar*, and *Best American Short Stories*. Her story "Intervention" was included in the *Norton Anthology of Short Fiction*. McCorkle has taught at UNC Chapel Hill, Harvard, Brandeis, and the Bennington Writing Program. She currently teaches at North Carolina State University. Website: www.jillmccorkle.com.

Michael Parker is the author of five novels and two collections of short stories; a new novel, *Five Thousand Dollar Car*, is forthcoming from Algonquin Books in 2014. He is the recipient of three lifetime achievement awards: The North Carolina Award for Literature, the R. Hunt Parker Award for the Arts, and the Hobson Award for Arts and Letters. A professor in the MFA program at UNC Greensboro, Parker divides his time between Greensboro, NC and Austin, Texas. Website: www.michaelparker.com.

Ron Rash is the author of four poetry collections, five novels (*One Foot in Eden, Saints at the River, The World Made Straight, Serena*, and *The Cove*), and five books of short stories, including his latest publication *Nothing Gold Can Stay*. Twice a Pen/Faulkner finalist, he won the 2010 Frank O'Connor International Short Story Award for his collection

Burning Bright. He teaches at Western Carolina University. Rash was inducted into the South Carolina Academy of Authors in 2010. Website: www.rusoffagency.com.

George Singleton has published two novels (*Novel* and *Workshirts for Madmen*), one book of nonfiction, and five short story collections (*These People Are Us, The Half Mammals of Dixie, Why Dogs Chase Cars, Drowning in Gruel,* and *Stray Decorum*). His short stories and essays have appeared in *The Atlantic Monthly, Harper's, New Stories from the South* (ten times), and elsewhere. He received a Guggenheim fellowship in 2009 and the Hillsdale Award in Fiction from the Fellowship of Southern Writers in 2011. Singleton currently holds the John C. Cobb Chair in the Humanities at Wofford College. He was inducted into the South Carolina Academy of Authors in 2010. Website: www.gwsingleton@charter.net.

Deno Trakas writes poetry, fiction, and nonfiction; his work has been published in magazines such as *The Oxford American* and six anthologies, including the award-winning *New Southern Harmonies*. He is the recipient of five South Carolina Fiction Project Prizes and a South Carolina Individual Artist Grant. Trakas lives in Spartanburg, South Carolina; he is the Hoy Professor of American Literature at Wofford College. Website: http://sites.wofford.edu/trakasdp/.

Cover Artist

Eric Beverly, an Austin, Texas-based painter and musical artist, lets nature, intuition and his life experiences and travels guide his brush and call his tunes. He comes by his creative pursuits naturally as the son of an artist father and pianist mother. The environments of his youth emerge in the lines and patterns of his paintings. One sees the flow and roll of water on Galveston Bay. Similarly the swirls and swoops of seagulls and hill country hawks imbue fluidity to his brushstrokes. His technique is largely self-taught and instinctive. After completing his studies at the University of Texas at Austin, where he earned his Bachelor of Arts in French, Eric settled in Texas's capital city where he paints, writes, records his songs, and performs with his band The Sunday Best in Austin's storied nightclubs. Rather than follow the lead of any inspirations and influences, Beverly instead absorbs them. His Texas roots at the juncture where the Deep South and the Southwest meet find expression in a folk art and primitivist cast to many of his canvases. His visits to France and passion for French culture bring what many see as Impressionist and Fauvist elements to the works he paints. Travels in South America also inject a sense of magical realism to his composition and inform his vivid sense of color. Beverly likes to explore intersections, transitions, and vibrations as he paints. He eschews working within any specific style or school for an approach that offers him a broad proverbial "Tex-tiso" palette of Scottish, Irish, Cajun, German, French, and Latino plus various American elements that he mixes and matches as the vision for each canvas calls. His musical pursuits inform his paintings with both harmony and counterpoint. He does adhere to the long painterly tradition in his feel for the human and especially female form and the all-but-infinite variations found in the faces of people. One sees that in his *A Shared Voice* cover painting that captures the essence of a variety of visages in bold and basic strokes. Eric's paintings have also appeared on book covers for *Dixie Fish* by Andrew Geyer and *Tiger, Tiger* by Jerry Craven. Website: www.ericbeverly.com.

Editors

Tom Mack joined the faculty of the University of South Carolina Aiken in 1976. Since that time, he has established an enviable "record of teaching excellence as well as outstanding performance in research and public service" for which the USC Board of Trustees awarded him the prestigious Carolina Trustee Professorship in 2008. He currently holds the G. L. Toole Chair in English. Over the years, Dr. Mack has written over 100 articles and chapters about American literature and American cultural history. Furthermore, since 1990, he has contributed a weekly column in *The Aiken Standard* on a wide range of topics in the humanities. He is also the founding editor of *The Oswald Review*, the first international refereed journal of undergraduate research in the discipline of English; all articles published in TOR are available in digitalized form on library databases hosted by EBSCO Publishing. Tom Mack's other book titles include *Circling the Savannah: Cultural Landmarks of the Central Savannah River Area*, *Hidden History of Aiken County*, and *The South*

Carolina Encyclopedia Guide to South Carolina Writers. Dr. Mack is currently Chair of the Board of Governors of the South Carolina Academy of Authors, the organization responsible for managing the state's literary hall of fame.

Andrew Geyer's latest novel is *Dixie Fish*. His other books are *Siren Songs from the Heart of Austin,* a story cycle; *Meeting the Dead,* a novel; and *Whispers in Dust and Bone,* a story cycle that won the silver medal for short fiction in the *Foreword Magazine* Book of the Year Awards and a Spur Award from the Western Writers of America. His award-winning short stories have appeared in dozens of journals and anthologies, and have been nominated for the Pushcart Prize. In addition to writing and publishing fiction, he has served in various editorial capacities for several literary magazines including *Iron Horse Literary Review, Journal of the American Studies Association of Texas,* and *Concho River Review.* A native Texan and a member of the Texas Institute of Letters, Geyer currently serves as Associate Professor of English at the University of South Carolina Aiken where he holds the Bridgestone/Firestone Chair.

For Further Thought

1. Consider any pair of tales in the collection. Of the six unifying strategies discussed in the introduction—setting, repeated and developed characters, plot or chronological order, themes or ideas, myth, imagery, and point of view—which is the most important for the pair you have selected? Which other connections are present?
2. Do you believe, as the editors assert, that humor is part of the traditional Southern mindset? Do any of the stories in this volume strike a particularly resonant chord in this regard?
3. At first blush, some stories in this volume may not appear to be especially "Southern." What do you think? Which ones require more careful consideration in this regard?
4. The editors of this volume have delineated a number of cultural links between the Texas tales and the Carolina tales. Can you think of any not covered in the introduction?
5. Many readers are often drawn to a work of fiction because of identification with a particular character. What character in which tale or pair of tales did you find most compelling and why?
6. If you could sit down with any of the authors of the stories in this volume for a thirty-minute conversation, which author would you choose, and what questions would you ask the writer?
7. If you were asked to write a fictional response to any of the tales in the anthology, which would you choose, and why? Which of the unifying strategies would you focus on?
8. If you could change anything in any of the tales, which tale would you choose and what would you change?
9. Besides character, the tales in this anthology are linked by a variety of literary devices. Some are obvious; some are more subtle. Which paired tales posed the most challenge for you? Why?
10. The editors argue that the stories in this collection form a story cycle of sorts. How can a case be made for that assertion?

CPSIA information can be obtained at www.ICGtesting.com
Printed in the USA
LVOW10s1302270713

344946LV00004B/14/P